No More Yesterdays

JESSICA MARLOWE

LYRIC
PRESS

NO MORE
yesterdays

JESSICA MARLOWE

First Edition

ISBN 978-1-949262-03-2 (paperback)

Editing by Kelly Hartigan (XterraWeb) editing.xterraweb.com

Cover Design by Eight Little Pages

Interior Design by Lyric Press

Published by Lyric Press. For questions or comments, please contact info.lyricpress@gmail.com.

Visit Jessica at jessicamarloweauthor.com

❊ Created with Vellum

To my family and friends. Without their unending support and feedback, including calming me down during the occasional freak-out over all the stuff I had left to do, this book wouldn't have been possible.

I love you all.

Dear Reader,

Thank you from the bottom of my heart for giving my novel a chance to entertain you. Your time is valuable, and I cannot express how much it means to me that you're using some of it reading Jack and Emily's story. I hope you enjoy reading it as much as I did writing it.

If you find any errors, I would be very grateful if you could contact me. Not only have I read my novel a bazillion times during drafting and editing, but it was also professionally edited and proofread. However, errors are inevitable, and I would like to make any necessary corrections. Please email me at jessica@jessicamarloweauthor.com with "Corrections" in the subject line.

Thank you.

Jessica

Pets for Patriots

Pets for Patriots is a 501(c)(3) nonprofit organization. Their mission (taken from their website) is to find loving homes for the most overlooked sheltered animals: adult, special needs, and long-term homeless pets and large breed dogs. After qualifying, veterans are able to adopt program available dogs and cats from a shelter partner and receive reduced rate veterinary care at a veterinary partner.

If you would like to help this amazing charity, please visit their website for more information: petsforpatriots.org/10-ways-to-give/

Attention: Exlcusive Offer

Want more? Sign up to my VIP reader group to get access to prologues, epilogues, cut and extended scenes, cover reveals, and insider updates exclusively for my subscribers.

Chapter One

Months of planning the perfect meeting while the band was in New York for a week were not to be thwarted by some stupid groupie whore after all. Jack looked so sad last night when he left the Garden it nearly broke my heart, but now that she's gone, Jackie's vulnerable. This may have been fortuitous after all. He'll be happy to see a friendly face, and I'll comfort him. He's always the one to take care of everyone else, but finally, he'll be with someone who gives him exactly what he needs.

The Phoenix has risen from the ashes, and he'll see I'm not a weak, pathetic creature he needs to save.

Chapter Two

S unday morning, Jack was startled awake by his alarm, and he was alone. Terror gripped him, and he shot up. *Shit.* Em was still asleep but had moved to the far side of the bed. *Fuck.* He hated that; he wanted to wake up with her in his arms. Since he'd have plenty of lonely nights ahead of him, when they were together, he needed her next to him. The band would be leaving Thursday for Hartford, and he had no idea when he'd see her again.

Yesterday had been hard, but it all turned out in the end. Last night, Em had come to his room at The Yorkshire Hotel, and she'd agreed to give them a fair chance, and he had no doubt she would. He needed to remember she was afraid, and no matter how strong she was, she was fragile right now. She still had to work out what happened with the fucker, but Jack felt more secure in their future. Em was his. And today, she'd agreed to meet his family.

It was early, but his dad always got up at five, so Jack picked up his phone and dialed his dad's cell.

"Jack, you're still coming, aren't you?"

"Good morning to you, too." Jack glanced at his girl. "Absolutely."

His dad sighed in relief. "Great, what's up, son?"

What's that about? "I'm seeing someone, and I'd like to bring her today. Okay?"

Jack heard his father rub his hand over his face. He always did that when he was trying to break bad news.

"If we say no, are you still coming?"

What? Jack hadn't expected this. As far as he was concerned, asking had been a formality, but apparently, Em had been right. "Of course. I thought it'd be nice to have all the people I love in one place at the same time."

His dad sighed.

Jack's head dropped. "Look, it's okay—"

"Your mother's sleeping. Let me discuss it with her when she gets up, and I'll call you back."

"Okay." Jack paused. "Dad, everything okay?" Maybe there was a family crisis, and they didn't want any outsiders. Although, Em could probably help. She was great at that.

"No, we're all well. It's just this is last minute. We didn't know you were seeing anyone new. She is new, isn't she? You're not back with Christie, are you?"

Jack thought they'd loved Christie. "No. It's over with Christie. Her name's Emily, and she's a writer." *Shit.* He probably shouldn't have told him that. Em wanted to remain anonymous. He'd fix it later if it came up.

"Okay." Will sighed. "I'll call you back after I talk to Mom. Love you, son."

"Love you too, Dad." Jack turned up the ringer on his phone, placed it on the nightstand, and shifted closer to Em so he could spoon her. *Bliss.*

Jack woke at eight with Em in his arms. Much better. His hand cupped her breast, and his hard-on nestled between her cheeks. He rubbed his groin against her, and she moaned softly as her hips rocked into him. He kissed her shoulder, and she sighed.

"Mmm, that for me?" Her voice was still raspy with sleep.

"Sure is. Fuck me." Jack rolled onto his back, grabbed a rubber, and rolled it on.

"The only thing I like better than late-night dirty talk is early-morning dirty talk." Em settled herself over him and slid down.

Her warmth surrounded him. *Fuck, that feels good.* He wished he was bare. It drove him wild that she wanted sex as much as he did. He had a very healthy sex drive, but his past girlfriends hadn't always matched up to him in that area. Especially when they were passed out drunk or high as fuck on drugs. *Fuck.* Why was he thinking of Christie? Probably because his dad had brought her up.

He pushed all thoughts aside as Em leaned forward and kissed him while she continued riding his cock. He fondled her breasts and broke the kiss so he could take her nipple in his mouth. "Baby, your tits are fucking perfect." She smiled and contracted her inner muscles around him. Fuck, that did it. "Oh fuck, baby."

Her hands stroked his pecs as she rose and fucked him harder. God, she was perfect. He came hard and was so lost in his orgasm he hadn't realized until she collapsed on him that she'd come. If she hadn't, he'd have eaten her pussy until she did. He still might.

Emily nuzzled his neck and kissed his shoulder. He didn't want to move, but he needed to use the bathroom. "I gotta get up."

Em rolled off him and snuggled under the covers with a satisfied grin.

When he returned, she was on her back with her legs spread wide. Nothing turned him on more than a woman who wasn't shy about telling him what she wanted. He crawled up the bed and kissed his way up her inner thighs, careful not to linger near her scars. She was sensitive about it, but he hoped, in time, that she'd let him touch and kiss her freely. They were part of her, and he loved her completely. He dipped his tongue in. "Mmm." He was almost ready himself, but this was for Em, so he focused on her pussy, loving her sweet, musky taste.

Em groaned. "Oh, yes. I love that."

He knew she did.

Rush's "The Trees" sounded from the nightstand. "Shit. That's my dad." He'd hoped it wasn't bad news. Grabbing the phone, he connected the call. "Hey, Dad."

"Jack, we'd love to have your new girlfriend join us for dinner."

That sounded more like his dad. "Great. What time?" Em gestured to him. "Hold on."

"I have to go home first. I need clothes."

"Right. Dad, is one o'clock okay?"

"That's what I was going to say. See you then."

"Can't wait, bye."

She pulled the sheet up to cover her beautiful naked body, but he wanted to finish what he started, so he whipped them off her.

"Jack, we don't have time for this. We have to eat, shower, get to my place, change, and then get to your parents' house. I don't want to be late."

Damn. She was right. He licked his lips to get the last bit of her essence. "Okay, rain check. You'll need to pack clothes for here."

"Why?"

"Aren't you staying this week?"

Emily scooted off the bed. "I have to go to work." She walked into the bathroom and closed the door.

Jack stared at the paneled door. They needed to talk. He'd expected her to spend the next four days with him at the hotel.

Since Emily should've been on her honeymoon for the next three weeks, he'd assumed she was off. He wanted her to stay with him and not just time after she got off work. He needed more. They'd be apart enough because he was on tour. *Too much.* But most of all, Jack needed to stop pressuring her, like he had last night, to get her to agree to come to see his folks today. For the life of him, he just couldn't stop himself, and he didn't understand why.

After breakfast and an argument with Jeff over spending the day with Em without security, they left the hotel in the rental that Jack had ordered. Em's apartment in Oakdale, New Jersey, was thirty minutes west of Manhattan, and they arrived at eleven thirty. He parked in back and they walked hand in hand to her door.

Once inside, Em turned to him. "I'll only be a few minutes." She walked down the hallway and disappeared into the bedroom. He followed, waiting in the doorway, until she turned to see him.

"What?"

Jack walked in and sat on the bed. "I want you to spend the week with me."

Her brows drew together. "I thought that was the plan."

"I'd assumed that you were off all week."

Em sat next to him and took his hand. "You want me spend the week at your hotel?"

"Yeah."

She stood and paced, and he could see the wheels turning. "I canceled my vacation time."

"But you were off Thursday and Friday."

"Yeah, because my bosses told me not to come in until I got my shit together." Emily smiled. "They were nice about it, but I'd been screwing up everything. I'm usually reliable, but after I sent copy for approval to our client's competitor by mistake, who's also our client, which cost us both accounts, I really thought they'd fire me."

Jack stood and hugged her. "Hey, you went through something terrible. I'm sure they understand."

She rested her head on his shoulder. "They do. They've been good to me." Jack felt her smile. "I started as the receptionist, and they gave me the opportunity to move into copywriting."

"I'm sure you earned the opportunity."

"I didn't have a degree to back it up, but they didn't care about that. A lot of places would've."

"Can you take a few days off?"

Emily pulled out of his embrace. "That's what I'm trying to figure out. We have two new clients coming in this week, and I could probably miss those appointments, but the established client asked for me specifically, so there's no way I can miss that one."

He'd thought she was concocting an elaborate excuse to not be with him. His chest swelled with pride that one of their clients respected her work so much that he wanted Em on his next campaign.

"I have to call my bosses and see what works for them." She walked into the living room to make the call.

Her bedroom wasn't overly feminine, but there were touches here and there. The bedspread was purple with gold trim. *Oh fuck.* That fucker slept in this room with her, in that bed. Under that bedspread. Jack shook his head to dispel the images.

"You okay?" Emily asked.

Jack stared at the bed. "You need a new mattress." No way was he making love to her in that bed after—

"It's only three weeks old. I got rid of the sheets and bedspread too. They made me sick."

He was such a prick. He should be worried about her not himself.

Emily smiled. "I had a hard time hauling the mattress out, but the box spring was easier."

"Why didn't you ask for help?"

Emily looked down. "I was humiliated, Jack. I didn't even tell Nicki until Monday. Besides, Vince lives in California, and I couldn't wait for Eddie to drive up. It exited the apartment shortly after they did."

Vince and Eddie were Emily's friends who helped her survive the aftermath of the accident, and Jack remembered what Nicki had told him about how Em had thrown he fucker out. He was proud of her, and he couldn't help but grin.

"Nicki told you, didn't she?"

"Yeah. Naked, huh?"

"They were lucky they got out in one piece." Emily took out an overnight bag and packed. "I have to be in the office Thursday by one and Friday. Damn."

"What's wrong?"

"I never called Vince."

"Call him now. I'll call my dad and tell him we're running a little late."

"I hope Vince isn't at the airport." At Jack's puzzled expression, she added, "He threatened to get on a plane if I didn't call him this weekend."

Jack liked Vince already and couldn't wait to meet him. "Take your time." Jack went to the living room to give her privacy. He was on the phone with Buzz when Em walked in. Unfortunately, Buzz had a bad night but had just left a NA meeting. Since Buzz was going to visit his family later, they might see him because their families were neighbors.

"Ready?" she asked.

That bag didn't look full, but he was used to traveling with Christie. "Uh, one more thing."

Emily raised her brows.

"I'd like to read your books, but I don't know your pen name." Emily's shocked expression surprised him until he remembered that the fucker hadn't been interested in her writing career. *Asshole.*

"Paperback or e-book?"

"Paperback."

Smiling, Emily turned and went into her office. She returned with a canvas bag. "Here."

Jack opened the bag and pulled out the first book. *In A Heartbeat* by Emma Ryan. The cover featured a bare-chested man and a woman in a skimpy bikini. They were kissing, and his hand rested close to her breast. Her arms were around him, her hands disappearing below his waist. Jack swallowed hard and looked up at her. "I meant so I could buy them."

"The four on the bottom are the most recent ones, the others are all out of print, so don't lose them, okay? They're my only copies." Em smirked at him. He knew she understood his reaction and was enjoying his discomfiture. He'd like nothing more than to bend her over the kitchen table and fuck —shit, they had to leave. "Nice cover."

"People do judge a book by its cover." Emily headed down the stairs.

Jack adjusted himself and followed.

EMILY STARED OUT THE SUV WINDOW AS JACK drove north on the Garden State Parkway. The thirty-five miles to his parent's house in Pine Hill, New York went by in a blur. The only indication that they'd crossed into New York was the welcome sign. This section of New Jersey and New York were so similar. The neighborhoods nestled among tree-lined streets were such a stark contrast to the skyscrapers of

Manhattan. Emily was glad she and Sully had decided to look for a house after the wedding. One less memory. Unlike Sully, Jack wanted to read her books.

When the SUV hit a pothole, Emily jolted awake. She stretched and smiled as she glanced at Jack. Then she remembered where they were going, and a groan escaped.

"What's wrong?"

Emily shrugged.

"Hey, talk to me."

"I'm nervous."

Jack pulled the SUV over and cut the engine. He tilted her chin so she'd meet his eyes. "Tell me."

"It's been a long time since I did the meet the family thing, and usually, we'd have been dating for several months." Emily sighed. "Sully's parents are...reserved. They're not openly affectionate to each other or Sully. Certainly not to me. I don't know what to expect with your family."

Jack grinned. "Total opposite, very emotional. My dad will probably hug you."

Her family had been like that, but she didn't want to reminisce.

"My dad's a plumber, and my mom teaches high school English. My sister, Trish, is getting her PhD in psychology, and my brother, Jimmy, is doing an internship for his fifth year toward his bachelor's in architecture. I have tons of aunts and uncles and about a million cousins."

Emily had no family except her grandparents. The only time she'd heard from them in ten years was the response card from her wedding invitation with the box checked for regrets. No explanation, letter, or phone call. She'd known they wouldn't come, but it'd still hurt.

"Hey." Jack kissed her tenderly. "I don't want you to be upset. We don't have to go." Jack looked down.

"It's not that. Your family sounds wonderful."

"They are. My folks are cool, and they'll love you. Trish is nosy, probably why she's interested in psychology. Jimmy's a good kid, but..."

"What?"

"I don't know, he doesn't seem to like me very much. One day, we were buddies and having a good time, and almost overnight, he couldn't stand to be in the same room with me. And if he does talk to me, it's always something nasty. I don't know what his problem is."

Emily thought she might. She'd had a similar reaction to Riley moving out. "We'd better get going." She hoped their being late didn't mess with his mom's dinner plans. Emily wanted them to like her. She didn't have to think why; Sully's parents hadn't liked her very much.

As Jack pulled back into traffic, Emily used her mantra to calm down. She radiated peace, love, and goodwill to all.

Jack exited the New York State Thruway. The village had an old-world charm about it. As they turned down the main street that ran though Pine Hill, a large clock in the center median read 12:57. The sun glinted off the windows of the store fronts. A few more turns and Jack pulled into the driveway of a white bi-level house with dark blue shutters and trim. A large red van with McBride Plumbing and Heating in white lettering across the side was parked next to the garage.

The front door opened, and Jack's dad jogged out, his arms spread wide before Jack was out of the truck.

Jack hugged his dad. "Dad, you look great."

Emily walked around the truck and stood next to Jack.

"Oh shit, sorry, baby. I should've gotten the door for you."

"No rock star language in this house, young man."

Emily bit back a chuckle. She liked Jack's dad already.

"Sorry, Dad. This is Emily. Em, William McBride."

"Emily, a pleasure to meet you. Please call me Will."

Nearly as tall as Jack, Will was more muscular, but he had

the same friendly smile and blue eyes. His dark brown hair was shorter than his son's. "Thank you for inviting me." She extended her hand, but Will pulled her into a bear hug. Out of the corner of her eye, she saw Jack grinning.

Will released her and turned as the front door opened again.

"James Marcus McBride, now!" Jack's mom yelled as she wiped her hands on a towel that rested on her shoulder. When she saw Jack, all aggravation left her face, replaced by love and a brilliant smile. "Jack." She sprinted into Jack's open arms. He lifted her and swung her around.

He kissed her cheek. "Mom, you look beautiful, as always."

"You look thin, Jack. I know touring is grueling, but you have to take care of yourself." Her worried expression warmed Emily's heart. "You're not eating enough."

"I eat plenty. Just ask Em, she doesn't know where I put it." He stepped back and placed his arm around Emily's waist. "Mom, this is Emily. Em, my mom, Margaret McBride, but you can call her Maggie."

Something flashed in the jade-green depths of Margaret McBride's eyes. Wariness maybe. Her light-brown hair was cut in a neat bob. Emily extended her hand. "Mrs. McBride, nice to meet you."

Jack shot her an odd look.

Margaret McBride accepted her hand. Another flash, this time aimed at Jack. "Please call me Maggie." Her lips curved in a smile that didn't reach her eyes.

"Thank you for inviting me." They all knew Jack strong-armed them into her being here. Emily had no doubt they were reluctant to say no to him.

"Let's go inside." Will took his wife's hand.

Jack took her hand, swinging their arms slightly as they followed behind his parents. As they walked up the lawn,

Emily was sure of three things. Will wanted to like her, Mrs. McBride didn't, and there was no rock star bullshit allowed in the McBride household.

A handsome young man, about Jack's height with a leaner build, same eyes, and lighter hair greeted them in the kitchen. Greeted wasn't right. When he heard them enter, he looked up from the sandwich he was eating at the counter and nodded in their direction. "Hey."

Mrs. McBride walked to her son, opened a cabinet, and handed him a plate. "If you have to eat standing up, at least use a plate."

"Don't need one." Jimmy pointed to the sink.

Will smacked the back of Jimmy's head. "Use a plate. And chew with your mouth closed. We have company."

"Right, Prince Jack has a new girlfriend." He turned from the sink as he wiped his hand on his pants. "'Sup?"

Will smacked his head again, and Mrs. McBride turned away in disgust.

Master of conversation. Emily assumed he was addressing her. "Hi, I'm Emily. Jack tells me you're getting a degree in architecture? Where are you going?"

Surprise flashed across his face. "NYIT." He looked down. "I'm Jimmy, very nice to meet you." He tilted his chin at Jack. "She's pretty."

That was all the invitation Jack needed. He grabbed his brother and hugged him. "Good to see you too, Squeak." Jack lifted Jimmy off his feet then dropped him.

Jimmy smiled. Will smiled. Damn, now she knew where Jack got that charming lopsided grin.

Will stepped between his sons and put his arms around them. "Magpie, how long until dinner?"

"Trish and Brad should be here in half an hour, so about an hour." She smiled at her family.

"Come and see the GTO. Jimmy and I have been making progress," Will said.

Jack hesitated.

Emily smiled at him. "It's okay, go do guy stuff." *Shit.* The last thing she wanted was to be alone with Mrs. Doesn't Like Her, but Jack looked so happy she'd suck it up. He'd owe her. Her dirty mind supplied a picture, and she was certain he'd be happy to pay the price.

Jack grabbed her, dipped her, and kissed her passionately. When he finally let her up, she grabbed his shoulders for support. Then she remembered they weren't alone. *What the fuck is wrong with you?* She narrowed her eyes at him. Emily could tell from the look on Mrs. McBride's face she knew. *Fuck.*

Jack grinned. "Thanks."

The clacking of the screen door was the last sound she heard. She'd never realized it before, but silence had a weight, and about a thousand pounds of it was bearing down on her. Mrs. McBride busied herself with slowly washing the dishes. *This isn't good.* Emily cleared her throat, not sure the woman realized she was still standing there. Mrs. McBride didn't turn. *Okay.*

Emily forced a smile and walked to the sink. "Can I help?" Emily looked around for a towel to dry.

"I've got this." She placed another dish on the drying rack. "You can make the salad."

"I'm great at salads." Emily wished she'd stayed home.

"Everything's washed and in the refrigerator." Mrs. McBride sighed.

Emily opened the refrigerator and grabbed the lettuce, tomatoes, cucumbers, carrots, radishes, and onions.

"Cutting board is on the table." Mrs. McBride handed her a knife and a large bowl.

"Thanks." Emily broke up the lettuce into bite-sized

pieces. Her leg ached; she must've fucked Jack too hard this morning. *Don't think about sex around Jack's mother.*

A thousand pounds turned into a million. Emily continued cutting and chopping vegetables while Mrs. McBride checked the roast, turned the potatoes, stirred a sauce, put a kettle on to boil, and did pretty much anything else so she didn't have to talk to or look at Emily.

"How long have you been seeing my son?"

Oh, God. Emily put the knife down. Mrs. McBride stood opposite her. She lifted her head to meet the woman's cold green eyes. "Thursday night."

Shock ripped across her face. Her lips tightened. The high-pitched whistle from the kettle broke the silence. Mrs. McBride turned off the stove and poured the water into a cup.

Emily braced herself. She wouldn't lie.

Mrs. McBride turned to her, meeting her eyes. "You're sleeping with my son."

It wasn't a question, so she didn't answer. Emily wished she'd stop calling Jack her son. It made her feel like she was robbing the cradle. Which was stupid because Jack was a grown man, and Emily was pretty sure he was older than her, but she should know how old he was. Wherein lay the problem. They should know more about each other than what got the other off. She couldn't stop the blush from creeping up her cheeks. *Damn fair skin.* Emily picked up the knife and resumed chopping. Better than throwing.

"He's in love with you."

Emily's head snapped up. "Yes." Kudos to Mrs. McBride; she knew her son well.

"You're not in love with him." It was an accusation. In one sentence, she'd gone from disgusted to indignant.

"No."

"Why not?" Maggie huffed. "He's a wonderful young man."

"We just met."

"That hasn't stopped him." Her eyes narrowed, and her lips were tight.

Emily set the knife down on the table and stood. "My life is...complicated."

"Everyone's life is complicated."

Emily growled in frustration. Now she knew where Jack got his tenacity from. And his complete lack of caring if it was any of his damn business. *Fuck.* "Until three weeks ago, I was engaged."

"Mom, what the fuck?" Jack asked.

Emily jumped at the sound of his voice. She hadn't heard the screen door open. Jack glared at his mom, and Will and Jimmy stared at her open-mouthed. *Just. Fucking. Great.*

Will smacked Jack upside the head.

Behind Jack's mother stood Jack's sister and her boyfriend. Great, two more strangers to witness her utter humiliation. The crush of emotion sent tears to her eyes. Emily needed to get out of here. She was sweating, and her face burned, but she absolutely refused to cry in front of Jack's family. She couldn't have written this any worse. "I need some air." She walked toward the kitchen door, and Will and Jimmy stepped out of her path.

Jack grabbed her arm. "Em, don't."

She looked up at him, and Jack flinched. "I need a few minutes."

"I'll come—"

"No." He looked hurt, but she couldn't, wouldn't, recount that awful conversation to him. She had no idea how much they'd overheard.

Jack nodded curtly and strode into the living room. Before she reached the door, he stopped her. "Take your phone."

She gave him a weak smile, took the phone, and muttered, "Thanks." She opened the screen door and escaped.

Jack took a few deep breaths to try to calm down. He'd assured Em his family would love her. She was amazing, so how could they not love her? But he walked in to find his mother grilling her. Em looked humiliated, and Jack could only imagine what transpired before they interrupted. Despite his best effort, his anger bubbled over. "Mom, what the hell?"

"Don't use that tone with your mother, Jack." Will stood next to his wife.

No one spoke, and no one moved. Even Trish looked shocked but said nothing. He didn't need to be analyzed right now, but he did need to calm down. Jack loved his mom, and he was sure she meant well, but he didn't understand. She'd always been sweet to his girlfriends. She'd loved Christie; his whole family had, and they'd welcomed her with open arms and hearts.

Jack took a calming breath. "Mom, I need you to explain what happened."

"Jack, you just met this girl. You're moving too fast, and I don't want you to get hurt again."

Neither did he. When he'd been home at Christmas, he'd

been hurting, but he'd thought he'd done a better job of covering it. He'd offered to pay Christie's airfare so she could visit her parents, but she'd refused, saying she didn't want his charity. It wasn't charity; Jack worried about her and didn't want her to be alone on Christmas.

When Christie had called him, obviously stoned out of her mind, she'd passed out while they were fighting. At the time, he'd been terrified she'd OD'd again. He couldn't get a hold of Amber from across the hall as she'd gone home for Christmas. He'd had no choice but to get on a plane.

Later, Elliot had pointed out Jack did have a choice. He should've called the police to check on her, but that hadn't occurred to him because he was so used to cleaning up her messes. Elliot was convinced Christie had manipulated him, going so far as to suggest she hadn't passed out, but Jack hadn't wanted to believe it. He sighed. "I appreciate your concern, but why not talk to me about it privately? Why ambush her?"

"When you called this morning asking to bring someone, it came out of nowhere. We didn't know you were dating someone new, and you've never brought a girl home you just met."

Jack got a sick feeling in the pit of his stomach. He hadn't thought this through. No wonder Em had looked embarrassed. His mom knew. This was his fault, and he'd fix it. Trouble was, he didn't know how.

"Son, your mother and I are concerned about you. You were distraught at Christmas, then you bring this girl we knew nothing about. What are we supposed to think?"

"Maybe that I'm an adult and know what I'm doing?"

"Do you?" Will asked.

Jack's head shot up. He saw their concern. There were a lot of conversations he and Em needed to have, ideally before he left in four days. "We met Thursday night. I'm crazy about her. She's in a bad place right now, her ex cheated on her." His mom's shocked expression told him Em had left that detail out. *Of course, she did.* "We have a lot to work out, but she's an amazing woman, and..." Jack looked down. He'd never been so unsure of what the future held, but he knew he wanted it, needed it, to be with Emily. "We're still figuring things out." When he looked up, he saw the love and support he'd always had, and they were alone. "I'm leaving Thursday, and I don't know when I'll see her again. See, things are slowing down already."

"She seems nice," Will said. "Maybe a little...standoffish?"

Jack laughed. "Not at all. She considers her circumstances before rushing in. Gets that from her dad."

"How so?" Maggie asked.

"Marine." Jack stood, took out his phone, and dialed Em.

She picked up on the second ring. "Hi."

"Where are you?" She had enough time. If he gave her too much, after what happened with his mom, she might change her mind about giving them a chance.

"Not sure. I'm in front of a yellow house with a white concrete retaining wall on Maple."

"Be there in a few minutes." He disconnected the call and turned to his folks. "Mom, I'm sorry."

His mom smiled her forgiveness.

"And thanks for today. It means a lot." He hugged her and left in search of his girl.

A few minutes later, he walked up behind her. She was sitting on the Parkers' retaining wall looking for him. He wolf-whistled to alert her.

Her head snapped around, and she smiled. "Hey."

Smiling was a good sign. The knot in his stomach untied. He plopped down next to her and smiled. "You okay?"

She shrugged. "Not the day you expected, huh?"

He shook his head. "But you did, didn't you?"

"I didn't think we'd all be singing 'Kumbaya' by the end of the day, but I didn't expect to be grilled either." Emily smiled weakly. "She's concerned about you, Jack. I can't fault her for that. Frankly I'm concerned for you, too. Her delivery sucked though."

"Yeah."

"Everything okay with you two?"

"Yeah. This is my fault."

Emily quirked a brow.

"I didn't think this through. I was selfish. You were right when you said I'm spoiled."

Emily moved closer so their thighs touched. "With all the screaming fans and people telling you how great you are, telling you what they think you want to hear, it'd be hard not to get a little spoiled."

Jack put his arm around her. "I hope you'll never do that."

"Count on it."

He would.

EMILY HAD CALLED NICKI AFTER SHE LEFT THE house. Nicki had understood how Emily felt, which made her feel better because she'd been concerned she'd overreacted. Nicki assured her she hadn't, and had it been her, the drama could only have been described as epic.

She thought about calling Eddie but didn't know how long Jack would give her. She was amazed she'd actually made it out of the house alone. He wanted her to lean on him, but Emily wasn't like that. She'd taken care of herself for over six years now, and she enjoyed her independence. It was one of the things Sully loved most about her. Or so he'd said. "This is a nice neighborhood." All the houses were well maintained and the yards all loved. It reminded her of the neighborhood she'd grown up in in New Jersey.

"Yeah, it's a great place to raise a family. Want a tour?"

She nodded.

As they stood, his phone rang. "Hi. Okay. The tour will have to wait, dinner in ten minutes."

Emily took his hand. "Lead the way."

They walked hand in hand back to Jack's parents' house. When they turned the corner, the quick burst of a car horn had them turning.

Buzz slowed and yelled, "Hey, guys."

They both waved. Jack told her Buzz was going to visit his family today, but she'd been so wrapped up in her own drama she'd totally forgotten. Buzz and Jack had been friends since they were four, when his family had moved in next door to the McBrides. It was still early in his sobriety, but he was working the program, and the band supported him fully. Stone Highway was a family.

By the time they got back to the house, Trish and Mrs. McBride were ready to bring the food in, so Emily washed her hands, grabbed the salad and dressing, and followed them.

The rectangular oak dining table seated eight. When they'd finished laying out all the food, Jack pulled her chair out, and he sat to her left, next to his dad, who was at the head of the table. Trish and Brad sat opposite them, Jimmy next to Brad and his mom sat at the other head of the table. She didn't want to be petty, but she was glad there was an empty chair between them.

They said grace. Mrs. McBride had prepared a feast: roast beef, corn on the cob, roasted potatoes, and salad. There was plenty of wine, but Emily declined when Jack offered. She needed to keep a clear head to navigate through dinner as she didn't want to embarrass him any further.

They weren't the kind of family who ate in silence—like

the Sullivans—therefore, she knew the silence was due to her. No one knew what to say, so it was up to her to start a conversation. Her parents wouldn't expect any less of her. "This room is bigger than I would've thought."

Everyone seemed to visibly relax, except Jimmy; he kept staring at her. Jack patted her thigh beneath the table.

Will smiled. "Maggie and I have large families, so as soon as we were able to afford it, we had this room extended. Thanksgiving and Christmas are crazy here. Even with the four leaves in, we're packed in tight, so enjoy the elbow room while you have it."

Emily didn't think she'd be getting any invitations to the McBride family holidays any time soon.

After that, conversation picked up. Trish was gearing up for finals and announced she'd be returning to the outpatient center at St. Peter's Hospital for the summer.

"Emily, Jack tells me your dad's a Marine. Does he have plans to join the private sector?" Will asked.

Emily froze. Her water glass hovered in midair. She hadn't seen that coming. Not in a million years. Her heart hammered in her chest, and bile rose in her throat.

Jack leaned over and whispered, "I'm sorry, baby. I didn't think."

Everyone stared. Blood pounded in her ears, and she was sure everyone could hear it. She stood, still holding the glass. "Excuse me, I'm sorry, I need a minute." She put the glass down with too much force. She turned to Jack. "Bathroom."

"Down the hall to the left."

Emily forced her legs to carry her forward. When she reached the bathroom, she made sure not to close the door too hard. She flicked the light switch, sat on the toilet lid, and put her head between her knees. She refused to ask if this day could get any worse because history had taught her as soon as she asked it did.

She took a few deep breaths, and the wave of nausea passed. She'd returned her phone to her purse, which was a good thing; otherwise, she'd be tempted to call a cab and get away from here as fast as possible. No way she was ever getting invited back. His mother was probably telling Jack he could do better than a broken drama queen. Maybe she could just stay in here forever. But Jack would never let her. The last thing she needed was him coming to check on her. That move had to be in the *Drama Queen Handbook*. Make a scene, leave, wait for boyfriend to rescue you. Emily didn't need rescuing.

Her dad's voice echoed in her head. "My little warrior, you can do this. You can do anything you set your mind to." With a deep exhale and a quick glance to the heavens, Emily splashed her face with cold water and dabbed it dry. With a deep breath, she soldiered on.

When she returned to the dining room, conversation had resumed. She resisted the urge to stop and listen before she entered as eavesdropping usually didn't end well. Jack stood and tucked her chair in. "I apologize for causing another scene."

Jimmy snorted. "Ha! That wasn't a scene. Jack's ex was a drama queen. She was the queen of scenes." He laughed at his own rude joke.

"Jimmy, enough," Will said. He sent his son a "watch it or else" look.

"Will, to answer your question, before he died, my father and his best friend operated a private security firm, and they'd planned on branching out into home security." Emily swallowed hard.

For the second time today, a weighted silence hung over the room because of her. Maybe this would convince Jack to cut his losses.

Jack took her hand under the table and squeezed it only

once. She longed for two more squeezes, but he didn't know the hand thing. "I'm so sorry, baby," he whispered.

"I'm sorry, too. I had no idea." Will shot Jack a look.

If Emily ever wanted another invitation, she had to fix this. "Please, it's okay."

Everyone relaxed.

"How did it happen?" Trish asked.

Everyone tensed.

"Trish, butt out," Jack said.

She'd rather not talk about it ever, but that was her problem. People were curious, and Jack had warned her his sister was nosy. Trish got that from him. "It's okay." Emily took a deep breath. "We were driving down the shore on vacation." She swallowed hard. "Hit head-on by a drunk driver." She focused on Jack's hand holding hers, helping her. "I woke up in the hospital a week later. They didn't."

Everyone gasped. Jimmy's eyes filled with compassion. He was a good kid. Emily got the distinct impression that Jack made a slashing gesture across his neck.

"That's awful. I'm so sorry for your loss," Maggie said. She looked across the table at her husband.

"Dinner's getting cold. Let's eat," Will said. "Everything's delicious, Magpie, as always." Love shone in his eyes.

Emily picked up her fork and forced herself to finish her dinner. Jack continued to hold her hand, which she appreciated. After a few minutes, the easy conversation returned, and the rest of the meal passed without incident.

Was it really only yesterday that she'd promised Jack to give them a chance? As if they didn't have enough issues, Jack's mom hated her. People had a hard time letting go of first impressions, and she'd made a stellar one; an emotional wreck with a tragic past, who they'd never see as anything but pitiful and broken. A *terrible* choice for Jack.

Chapter Four

E mily had been quiet on the ride back to The Yorkshire. And even though, it was after midnight, Jack couldn't sleep because Emily was on the far edge of the bed. After they'd made love, Jack had dozed off, but he woke when she moved away. Soon after, she'd stopped fidgeting and her breathing steadied. He hated that she moved away from him. He wasn't even close enough when he was inside her, but she had a rough day.

Her expression when his dad asked about her father scared him. Jack thought that'd send her over the edge, but she just took a few minutes to compose herself and made a quick explanation, and the rest of the day had been wonderful. Jack suspected Trish would get engaged soon. He liked Brad, and he treated Trish well. He had a way of getting her out of therapy mode, reminding her gently that not everyone wanted her help.

Emily stirred in her sleep. She made small sounds, rolled onto her back, then bolted up, and looked around.

He laid his hand on her shoulder. "You okay?"

"Bad dream. I gotta pee."

He watched as she walked into the bathroom and shut him out. He hated the sound of the click when the door closed. Just when he couldn't stand another minute, she came out. She'd been in there for eighteen minutes.

Emily grabbed his T-shirt and slipped it over her head. "We need to talk."

Jack sat up and turned on the bedside lamp. They did, but he hoped it was about the challenges they faced and not that she couldn't do this.

Emily paced at the foot of the bed. "I'm feeling overwhelmed. You told your parents we were going to look at apartments this week, but that was news to me. And we should go over your tour schedule. I have to start my next book, at least get an outline to Meg. My bosses understood needing more time off, but I need to have my shit together when I go back on Thursday."

On the outside, Jack chuckled. On the inside, his whole body unclenched. "Is that all?" He'd known she had a lot on her mind.

"No, but that's enough for now, don't you think?"

He patted the bed next to him, and she obliged, snuggling into his side. "Did you see the look on my mom's face when I told her I was moving back to New York?"

"Yes, she was thrilled until you told them *we'd* be looking at apartments, then the thrill was gone."

Jack hadn't noticed because Emily's body had tensed so much he'd thought she'd snap in two. "You knew I was going to move home."

"Yeah, but I didn't know you'd contacted a real estate agency and set up an appointment for this afternoon to discuss it."

She was cute when she was frustrated with him. "I called on Saturday, on the way into the city from your place. But I forgot after—Anyway, if today's no good for you, I'll reschedule."

Emily sat up and faced him. "Don't you think you should've told me about it first? You made it sound like we'd be moving in together. We're not."

"Not right away but eventually. Besides, I'll be on tour until the end of next year, so we have plenty of time to discuss it. But you'll be spending time there, and I want you to like it. I thought we'd find a place big enough so you could have an office."

Emily sighed and smiled. "That's very sweet of you."

He'd taken her by surprise, and he liked it. But she had a point. If he wanted her to open up to him, he needed to stop making assumptions. He'd move in with her today, hell, he'd bought her a ring which was locked up tight in the room safe. Jack kept reminding himself they'd only met three days ago. "You're right, I should've talked to you about it, certainly before mentioning it to my parents. I'm sorry. After I work out with Buzz in the morning, I'll have Viv get me a copy of our itinerary. We can go over when I'll be able to fly home and when you can come see me."

Emily's face paled. Right, he was assuming again. It was too soon for her to spend her weekends flying to see him, or maybe she was worried about the money. "Of course, only when you're ready to, and I'll pay for your flights." Jack was pleased with himself until he realized she looked like she was going to be sick. "Baby, you okay?"

Emily didn't move. He wasn't even sure she was breathing. Her eyes were closed, but a tear escaped. Jack pulled her to him. "I'm sorry, I thought you wanted to talk about my schedule. It's too soon."

More tears rolled down her cheeks, and she took a shuddering breath and tried to move away from him, but he didn't let go. He couldn't stand it if she shut him out again tonight. "Hey, tell me what's wrong." When she shook her head, anger bubbled over. "You can't keep running to the bathroom every time something upsets you. I need you to talk to me."

Emily pulled out of his arms and rolled off the bed. She grabbed a few tissues and sat.

Jack tensed but didn't move.

She stood and paced for a minute before sitting next to him. "I can't fly."

Jack's heart dropped. She wouldn't meet his gaze and looked ashamed.

She took a deep breath. "We were flying to New Jersey from Reno. My dad had retired from the military, and we were moving from Bridgeport Marine Corps Base in California. I'd been on an airplane before, and I'd never had a problem. We hit some turbulence, which was no big deal. I'd look at my dad, and he'd wink at me, letting me know we'd be okay. Anyway, halfway through the flight, one engine failed, but I was still okay. Planes are designed to fly if one engine fails, but when a second failed, we dropped." Emily swallowed hard. "When I looked at my dad, I knew he was scared. I'd never seen him fear anything, and that scared me more than the loss of altitude. I thought we were gonna die. Riley held my hand so tightly I thought he'd break it." She blew out a breath. "The engine came back on, and the plane made an emergency landing, but I haven't been able to get on a plane since."

"How old were you?"

"Eleven."

Shit. "Baby, it's not a problem. I'll do all the flying." It sucked he wouldn't get to see her every weekend, but he'd deal as long as she didn't end them.

Emily stood and glared at him. "It's a huge deal, Jack. You travel enough, and I can't even help. You should run. A million other girls would be a better—"

Jack jumped up and stood in front of her. "First off, if I had two million to choose from, you'd still be my only choice. Second, if you're looking for the door, it's through there." He swung his arm toward the bedroom door.

Emily took a step back from him.

He hadn't meant to scare her, but he wouldn't take this anymore. "I thought we agreed you'd stop trying to make my decisions for me." Jack's muscles tightened. "I don't want you to go. I'm in love with you, but this won't work if you keep threatening to leave." His stomach clenched. Jack sat on the bed and waited for her to grab her bag and run from him.

Emily hugged him to her. "Sorry, didn't mean it that way. I told you I didn't come here to bail on you again." She kissed the top of his head.

When he looked up at her, sincerity shone in her eyes. Now he was confused and pissed at himself for blowing up at her. "Explain it to me."

She placed her hands on the side of his face. "It's been three days, and you've already been exposed to all my...crazy. Normally, this stuff comes out slowly."

He pulled Em onto his lap. "You're not crazy."

"I wish I didn't have so much baggage."

Jack kissed her lips. "You're perfect the way you are." His hand slid down from her side and touched her right thigh, where her scar began. "I don't care about this." He gently stroked over her battered skin. Em tensed, so he withdrew his hand. "I don't care that you can't fly. It's a hiccup. We'll work around it."

Em slumped against him.

"Let's get some sleep." Jack stood with her in his arms, turned, and laid her on the bed. Em moved to the center, and he moved in next to her. She turned on her side and snuggled into him.

EMILY LAY IN JACK'S ARMS, ABSORBING HIS WARMTH. The nightmares started again after her breakup with Sully, and they were getting worse. This one left her cold. Their screams as the truck rolled still echoed in her head. When the nightmares began, the therapist had suggested she turn on the faucet. Water had a calming effect and helped her focus on something besides the screams. *Shit.* She should call Eddie tomorrow. He always made her feel better.

Jack called her fear of flying a hiccup, like it was just another hurdle they'd face together. He traveled for a living, and he'd have to do a lot more of it if their relationship would stand a chance.

"You still awake?" Jack's sleepy baritone interrupted her thoughts.

"Yeah. I thought you were asleep."

"Nope. Just enjoying the blissful feeling of you in my arms."

Jack tightened his arm around her, so Emily snuggled closer. "Better?"

"Mmm-hmm. Much."

"I can't sleep."

"What's on your mind, baby?" Jack adjusted the pillow but didn't turn on the light.

"Is there anything I can do for you?" Emily asked.

"What'd you have in mind?"

Jack's playful tone told her what he had in mind, and she could practically hear him waggle his brows. Not that she didn't want to, but it wasn't what she meant. The long, trying day had taken its toll on her verbal skills. "You're going out of your way to accommodate me, the flying thing, taking things slower than you'd like. I was wondering if there was something I could do to make you happier."

"You mean that?"

"Yes." When he didn't answer, she lifted her head. "Tell me."

"Why didn't you bring more clothes? You don't have enough for four days."

Emily hadn't missed the look he'd given her half-empty bag, and she'd been surprised when he hadn't said anything. She wasn't comfortable staying here, and she'd agreed but only went halfway. *Damn.* "I'm sorry. I should've brought more stuff with me, I guess I was hedging my bets."

"Why?"

"I'm not comfortable staying here. It's like we're living together."

"So how many days do you feel comfortable with?"

"Honestly, none. But we'll be apart a lot, and I wanted to see you this week, but I didn't know what your plans were, you know, band-business-wise. We were in a hurry to get to your parents' house, so I didn't have time to think it through."

Emily felt his chest rise and fall in steady breaths. She didn't think he was angry, but he didn't say anything either. Men got quiet when they got angry.

"We could both do better with communication. We'll have to if this is going to work. I should've said something when we were at your place. I know I keep saying we'll slow down, but I don't seem to be able to accomplish that." Jack hugged her closer. "I'll get you your own room here, that way we can see each other without you being uncomfortable."

Emily smiled. He was so sweet. "I don't need my own room. I'll sleep on the couch."

He sat up "The hell—"

"Kidding, Jack." Emily sighed. "How about I make a quick run home on Tuesday to get more stuff?"

He relaxed back. "I'd love that."

Emily kissed his chest. "What else?"

"More of that, please."

"We spend too much time screwing and not enough talking." She couldn't believe she just said that.

"Okay, talk now, screw later." Jack flipped on the light. "I hate it when you shut me out. I want to know when something's wrong."

Fuck. Emily sat up. Sully had hated that too, but he'd gotten used to it. "Sometimes, I need a few minutes. I'm used to dealing with everything by myself and—"

"You're not alone anymore. I'm here, and in case you haven't figured it out, I need to help."

Emily swallowed hard. Over the past weeks since her breakup, she'd spent a lot of time going over their relationship and realized that there'd been signs that things hadn't been so fairy-tale perfect as she'd thought. She also knew that she hadn't listened to her gut most of those times. Emily had been so anxious to move away from her past that she'd glossed over things that hadn't felt right to her so she could keep moving forward.

In the early days, Sully had been just like Jack was now, always pushing her to share her feelings. Emily was used to fending for herself, and she'd never go back to that helpless, trapped girl she'd become after the accident, and the sooner Jack realized that, the better. He was a good guy, but she couldn't afford to make the same mistakes. She wouldn't.

Waves of anger and fear washed through her, so she took a deep breath. Anger at Sully and fear that Jack was no different.

"Hey, what's going on with you?" Jack caressed her cheek with his thumb. "Em?"

Emily closed her eyes and tried to calm down. It'd be easy to unload her anger on to Jack, but that wouldn't fix anything. Tears pricked, so she kept her eyes closed. Those didn't belong to Jack, but she didn't want to explain what she was feeling.

She needed to work through her feelings regarding Sully without Jack's input.

"Talk to me."

"Why do you have to know everything?" Her voice cracked. "Can't you just allow me the time I need to—"

"You're pushing me away. Em, we've got three days before I leave. We have to be open with each other."

This was crazy. *How could I have thought this would work?* "I have been open with you, more so than any other relationship I've had, but it's never enough. You said you'd give me time and space, but you never do. Can't you trust that things will work out without you having to *fix* them? What happened to make you so...needy?"

Jack looked as if she'd slapped him. Maybe she had. She hadn't wanted her anger at Sully to spill on to Jack, but it just did. It needed to be said, but she shouldn't have said it like that. Some of her anger drained away.

Jack slumped back against the pillows. "You're right, I do keep saying it, and I don't know why I keep pushing." He ran his hand over his face. "I could tell you it's because we're not going to have much time together, which is true, but it's not just that."

Emily scooted closer. "What then?"

"I don't know, fear."

"Of what?"

Jack shook his head and shrugged. When he reached out for her, she snuggled into his side. "I'll work on giving you space if you'll work on not hiding in the bathroom."

"I'm not." Maybe she was. Sully had said that to her during a fight but never brought it up again. "Okay." Her stomach turned. It wouldn't be easy, but she'd promised, and she'd damn well do it. "Anything else?"

"That's enough for now, don't you think?"

"Definitely." *How can we already have so many issues?*

Jack turned off the light and settled back down. She lay on her back because her leg throbbed but took his hand because she didn't want him to think she was mad at him.

On Monday, Emily woke before dawn. Jack was next to her, and she was still on her back. She moved around in her sleep, so it was unusual for her to wake up in the same position. She was horny, so she snuggled into Jack's side, caressing his chest while kissing a path up his neck to his lips. Jack moaned. She whispered in his ear, "I want you."

"Mmm, go for it baby."

Grabbing a condom from the nightstand, Emily made quick work of protecting them. She straddled him, and they both moaned as she sank onto his cock. *So good.*

Still sleepy, she rode him, enjoying the sweet friction. Emily loved sleepy early-morning sex. She reached behind her and cupped his balls, gently rolling them in her hand.

"Em...so good."

She knew he loved it when she paid attention to his balls. Emily leaned forward to kiss him, his mouth opening, inviting her in. Jack palmed her breasts and tweaked her nipples, which sent her over the edge. She moaned as she came, and Jack followed with a low grunt. She lay atop him, but she mustn't fall asleep yet because she had to take care of him first. Sleep tugged, so she forced herself to sit up and climb off, which had Jack lazily grabbing for her.

"Stay."

"Just let me take care of this." She slipped the condom off, tied it, and used a tissue to clean him up. Emily wrapped the condom in tissues and chucked it in the trash can. She snuggled next to Jack who was already asleep. Emily closed her eyes and drifted off.

The next time Emily woke, bright sunlight flooded the room, and Jack stared at her with a goofy grin. "What?"

"You made love to me this morning."

"Yeah." She tried to roll to her side, but he stopped her. Emily had to pee, and she needed coffee. "Was that okay?"

Jack rolled his eyes at her. "Yeah. It was amazing."

"Sleepy early-morning sex usually is. Low effort, orgasm, sleep." Her smile faded. "I need to use the bathroom."

Jack held firm. "What just happened? One second you were smiling, and the next you shut me out."

"I have to pee." She didn't want to talk about Sully.

He released her. "Okay, pee then talk."

"Can't you let it go?" *He's never going to let anything go.* She walked to the bathroom and closed the door. *I'm entitled to some privacy.*

When she opened the door, Jack sat on the bottom of the bed. He'd pulled on a pair of sweatpants. When he looked up, she knew he hadn't let it go. *Shit.* She slipped into the complimentary bathrobe. "Jack, I'm still working things out from my breakup. Normally, I wouldn't have an audience for that, and I don't want to talk about every little thing."

He seemed to consider that for a moment. "Okay, but that didn't seem like a little thing. Your whole body tensed, and you looked hurt."

She hadn't realized she'd tensed. "It wasn't about you or us."

"It was about *him*, wasn't it? The fucker didn't like sleepy morning sex?"

Emily nodded but wouldn't discuss her previous sex life.

Jack stood. "Why?"

Never a break. She'd understood how Sully had felt, and she didn't feel right exposing him to other people that way, especially Jack. It was hard enough dealing with the never-ending resentment that popped up every time she remembered all the concessions she'd made. Why hadn't she seen all the cracks that were now so very obvious?

Emily glared up at him. He was so close she had to tilt her

head back to meet his eyes. "It's none of your business." She hated feeling like she had to protect that bastard.

Jack sat and pulled her between his knees. "I think it is my business." Emily tried to pull away. "Hear me out. Four days ago, even from the stage, I could see something awful had happened to you. Even when you smiled, you looked sad. The fucker destroyed your self-esteem. I don't want to make the same mistakes."

"You couldn't." Jack loved sleepy early-morning sex on a Monday. But he didn't have to get up at five. "I hate this." She pulled from his embrace and paced. "It's really hard to move forward with you when my past keeps interrupting."

"I know, baby." He grabbed her hand and pulled her back into his arms. "I respect that you don't want to reveal personal details even though he doesn't deserve your discretion. It makes me love you more."

She was glad he hadn't used the word loyalty because she felt none toward Sully. It simply wasn't the right thing to do. "How am I supposed to get over this if we keep talking about it?"

"The only reason I want to talk about it is because you got upset, and I don't like that. Can you understand?"

She nodded and walked over to the window. They'd both need to make changes. Jack had to ease off, and she had to let him in. She'd pushed forward after the accident by compartmentalizing her life because it was the only way she'd known how, but now, Jack was threatening that. And if she couldn't let him in, she'd lose him. Just like she'd lost Sully.

Jack jumped up. "I got...something I gotta do." He quickly dressed and left.

Chapter Five

E mily looked shocked when he'd taken off so abruptly, but Jack needed to get out before he said something stupid. The clawing need he felt was only getting worse, and Em needed time and patience. He had to get his emotions under control, or he'd lose her, but it was near impossible when she was so close. The engagement ring he'd bought was in the room safe, and he constantly looked to their future: a home together, marriage, kids. Jack wanted it all.

He'd need to give her an explanation, but he didn't know what to say.

Jack went to the gym to work off his bad mood. Em had insisted he continue his routine with Buzz because she didn't want to come between them. By the time Buzz joined him, Jack felt better.

"Jack!" Buzz stopped walking on the treadmill next to his.

Jack's attention snapped back to him. "What?"

Buzz tried to hide his smile. "Looks like you had a nice day."

Jack wiped his brow with his shirt. "Sorry." His own smile

spread wide. He jumped off and walked over to the bench and grabbed a towel.

"Don't apologize for being happy." Buzz rubbed his head with a towel, leaving his thick brown hair sticking up. He slid his hands into his gloves and adjusted the Velcro straps. "So, how'd yesterday go?"

Jack groaned. "We had a good time, but my mom was acting weird."

"How so?"

"She grilled Em about our relationship, and she was kinda cold toward her."

"That doesn't sound like your mom."

"Right?" His dad had been weird over the phone, too.

Buzz worked the bag while Jack held. His mind wandered back to Em. What guy turned down sex ever? Em was beautiful, sexy, and creative, not to mention she wanted sex as often as he did. Most guys complained that their girls or wives didn't give it up enough. Jack wondered how long he'd be able to keep up with her.

Jack couldn't stop thinking about what Em had said about him being needy because she was right. That was how he was behaving at least. He'd never fallen so totally headfirst in love in a matter of hours like he'd done with Em, but he hadn't been totally honest with her. Some of his fear was related to how fast he'd fallen for her because the intensity of his feelings had his head spinning. Jack also knew that the fucker would be back, and even though Em insisted she wouldn't take him back, their relationship was so crazy it just might be enough for her to consider giving the fucker a second chance. He'd loved to have stopped there, but Jack always tried to be honest with himself. Something else had him coming off the rails, but he didn't know what. What he did know was that if he didn't stop pushing her, he'd be the reason their relationship derailed.

When Buzz kicked the bag, Jack wasn't ready, and he lost his balance and landed hard on the mat. Buzz stepped around the bag and hauled Jack to his feet. With a goofy smile and his brown eyes shining, he said, "Where's your head today?"

"Up his ass," Elliot said as he strode past them, stopping at the free weights. His black hair and T-shirt were soaked in sweat from his run. He also wore a smile wider than Jack had seen in a long time.

Jack and Buzz grinned at each other. Elliot had called Siobhan, and it'd obviously gone well. He was so wrapped up in his own life he'd forgotten. "How's Siobhan?" Jack slipped his hands into his gloves.

Elliot faced him. His dark eyes were lit from within, and he smiled. "We talked Friday and half the night Saturday. Then I went by the house yesterday, and we had dinner and talked some more."

He'd seen that look in Elliot's eyes several times and always because of Siobhan. The first time had been when Jack told Elliot that he and Siobhan had broken up. Jack had known how his friend had felt about her. Elliot had been having a tough time after his folks split up, and he'd been moodier than usual, but whenever Siobhan was around, Elliot smiled. A lot. Jack and Siobhan knew they were better off as friends, so he encouraged her to ask Elliot out.

The second time had been when Elliot told Jack she'd agreed to marry him. And again, when he, Buzz, and Curt stood as best men at their wedding. And when he'd told Jack that, after two years of trying, Siobhan was finally pregnant.

It was Jack's turn on the bag. He forced himself to focus so he wouldn't break his hand.

Thirty minutes later, he entered his hotel room to see lunch waiting for him, and Em was on the couch typing away on her laptop. She stopped typing and cocked her head to the side.

"I'm sorry about before. I just didn't want to say anything stupid."

She quirked a brow, and her lips curled into a small smirk. "Okay."

"Do I have time for a quick shower?"

"Yeah. Food just got here."

Jack stripped, showered, and was back in ten minutes. When lunch was over, it was time for that talk about touring. He'd run into Viv in the hallway, and she'd given him a printout with their schedule.

Em pulled out a pen and a calendar from her bag, and they sat on the couch and planned when they'd be able to see each other. Jack would fly to her whenever he had a break of two days. The first one wouldn't be for almost three weeks after their last day together. The next two times, he'd only have to wait a week to see her. He had a week off over Father's Day weekend, but he'd promised to spend a few days home, since he'd only be able to spend Sunday home for Mother's Day. After that week, it'd be over a month before he'd see her again, so they stopped planning there because Jack didn't want to think about what a month without her would be like, and he didn't want her to feel bad because she wouldn't be able to fly to see him.

He would've loved to have nailed her down to spend that week with him, but it was too soon. Em already looked shocked at the reality they faced. She sat back and rubbed her temples. His head ached but not nearly as badly as his heart did at how little time they'd have.

But right now, they had three days left. They had a gig tonight and an acoustic gig at the local rock station tomorrow in the afternoon. Since they had Tuesday night off, maybe they could all go to dinner. Having dinner with friends was normal.

Em picked up her laptop.

Shit. He'd promised her she'd have time to write. If she was on a roll, he wouldn't interfere with that. He glanced at the calendar where she'd marked down his schedule. Emily had made little hearts on the days they'd see each other. Jack liked that.

"You'll be in Albany on Saturday. It's only four hours by bus. What time will you be arriving?"

Heat expanded throughout his body. "You'd be willing to do that?"

"Jack, you're going to be flying around on tour, and then when you have two days off, you're going to fly more just to see me. It's the least I can do." She smiled but then looked down.

Jack took her laptop and placed it on the coffee table, and then he hauled her onto his lap and kissed her. Relief flooded his mind. He hadn't wanted to give the negative thoughts a foothold, so he'd pushed them aside, but now he let them go. She wanted to see him. She wouldn't end it on Thursday when he left for Hartford. Before they'd sat down, he didn't know where they were scheduled next. He always focused on where he was because every one of their audiences deserved their full effort and attention. It was hard to do that when you were preoccupied with what came next. "I love you."

Em crawled off his lap.

"What's wrong?" But Jack knew. Em didn't want him to tell her how he felt. How could he not? When they were together, it felt like his heart would burst through his chest. If that's what she needed—

She touched his arm. "I'm not comfortable with your public displays of affection. Yesterday, at your parents' when you kissed me in front of your family, I didn't like that, and neither did your mother."

Blood rushed through his veins, and his body tensed.

"When we're alone, you can be as affectionate as you want, but around other people, could you tone it down?"

Relief flooded Jack's body. They had a lot to learn about each other, and time and his career worked against them. He leaned over and kissed her lips. "I can do that." It wouldn't be easy. Her smile had him pulling back. "What?"

"How far off the cliff did you get?"

Jack looked down. "Almost didn't make it back."

She kissed him, her tongue dipping as her hands explored. "It's okay, baby," she said between kisses.

He cupped her breasts and deepened the kiss. The room phone rang. Without breaking the kiss, he fumbled for the phone. "Hello?"

"Mr. McBride, this is Aaron from the front desk. Barbara Callow is here to see you."

"Who?"

"She's from Wickham Realty"

Shit. The real estate agency he'd called. Jack groaned. "Send her up." Jack's head dropped back. Em was on his lap, he had a raging hard-on, and she looked thoroughly kissed. Damn. "The real estate agent is on her way up."

Em climbed off his lap, tugged her shirt down, smoothed her hair, and wiped her lips with the back of her hand. "We'll continue this later." Her sassy grin inflamed him further.

She drove him mad. He stood and adjusted himself. Looking at her didn't help, so he closed his eyes so his dick would calm down. Her evil chuckle told him Em knew what he was doing. She'd pay for that. Later. "If you'd rather not come, I understand."

"I thought we agreed to put off coming until later?"

Jack's dick hardened. "You're evil." Even her smirk aroused him.

He walked to the window. "I know it's too soon for you."

He tried to keep his voice level. Too soon be damned; he wanted her to go, damn it.

Her arms circled around him, and she rested her cheek against his back. "I got a lot done this morning. I'd be happy to go with you." He felt her smile.

Jack turned, but before he could kiss her, a knock sounded on the door. Dropping a kiss on her head, he answered the door, surprised to see Nicki and Curt, kissing.

Curt broke away from Nicki's lips. "What took you so long?"

Nicki chuckled. "They were busy getting busy."

Em stood next to him. "Curt, nice to see you." She hugged Nicki. "You look happy."

"I am. Wonderfully, ecstatically, rapturously, ardently happy."

"Nic, what's the first rule of writing?"

"Lose the adverbs, pick a stronger verb." She sighed. "That doesn't apply to real life. Nobody talks like that."

"What're you guys doing today?" Curt asked. "We're going sightseeing. Wanna come?"

Jack looked at Em, who bit her lip and looked away, but Jack didn't bother to hide his smile. "You both live here. Haven't you seen it all?"

"Not together." They answered in unison, smiled at each other, and kissed again.

Jack smiled. Curt was toast.

A young woman, stylishly dressed, stood behind Curt and Nicki and cleared her throat. "I'm looking for Jack McBride."

Curt and Nicki stepped aside.

"That's me. Ms. Callow, a pleasure to meet you."

She looked shocked. "Please call me Barbara. I'm sorry to be late. The traffic in this city is crazy."

Nicki eyed the woman suspiciously and then glanced at Em with a look he didn't understand.

"Ms. Callow is a real estate agent, she's showing Jack some apartments today," Emily said. "He's moving back to New York."

Curt high-fived him. "Dude, awesome. Nobody tells me anything," Curt said. "So that's a no on sightseeing?"

"Just made the decision on Thursday, then I...forgot." Jack looked at Em. "You guys have fun." They were cute together. At least sightseeing didn't cost a lot.

Em and Nicki hugged again, and she and Curt left.

"Please, have a seat." He gestured to the couch. "Can I get you anything?"

"No, thank you."

"Don't worry about getting here late. We weren't ready either."

Her mouth hung open slightly. "You're really Jack McBride."

"I can prove it." He pulled out his wallet.

"I'm sorry, it's just that when the call came in, I didn't make the connection." Composing herself, Barbara took out a pad and pen. "Tell me what you're looking for."

"Two bedrooms, three baths, large kitchen. We need two rooms that can be converted into offices. Preferably renovated, but for the right place I'd tackle the renos."

"Anywhere in particular?"

"Definitely West Side." He winked at Em. At her puzzled expression he said, "Closer to Jersey."

They spent the next hour taking virtual apartment tours on Barbara's tablet. None of the places were quite right, but he wasn't in a rush. They'd hammered out more details of what he wanted, and he was confident he'd find a place in no time. Their first place together, and Jack couldn't wait.

I smile as Jackie walks off the elevator. Our moment, the one I've been waiting for, is finally here. I stand and check my reflection one last time to make sure I look perfect. Before I even take a single step to him, my heart thuds and blood pounds in my ears.

What the ever-loving fuck is that groupie whore doing back here? The lobby of The Yorkshire is crowded and noisy, but all sound and movement fade. Every beat of my heart echoes in my ears; the volume is deafening. My nails dig into my palms and draw blood. My body is locked so tight every muscle makes itself known. I feel like I might shatter.

As his arm curls possessively around her waist, I feel like a dagger has been thrust into my heart. Nooooo!

He's walking toward the door, and out they go to the New York streets.

My mind is spinning. I spent months giving Jack time to forget, but now it appears that was a mistake. I love him, and I won't lose him to some stupid groupie whore.

This thought finally unlocks my legs, and I follow them out. I don't remember putting my sunglasses on or using my scarf to cover my straight blonde hair. Just as I step on to the sidewalk, Jack helps her into a cab. Jackie shouldn't be going out without his security. He could get hurt. Luck is on my side as another cab pulls up to the curb. I instruct the stupid driver to follow. There's an extra fifty if he doesn't lose him.

Jack's cab pulls up at Central Park. Taking the groupie whore to the park? How sweet. I pay the driver and get out a few blocks ahead.

When the black SUV pulls up a block from where a crowd has formed around Jack, it seems he's not out without security after all. That fucking jarhead is useless, always watching but never seeing. I can be a wallflower when necessary. Still, Jackie's so famous we'll need security for the rest of our lives.

When the last of his fans leaves with a smile, Jack takes the whore's hand, and my stomach turns. When his rich, full laugh rings out at something she says, a bead of sweat rolls down the side of my face, and I swipe it away. This one could be trouble. Nothing I can't handle, but still. We are meant to be.

Ha! The little whore walks funny. Jack deserves someone perfect like him. He deserves me. My next love letter is set to be delivered. He loves the chase, so I hope I haven't made it too obvious.

Boys will be boys, as my mother used to say. Have fun now, Jackie.

AFTER THEIR WALK IN THE PARK, EMILY TOOK HER time freshening up before they left for the gig Monday night. She and Nicki would get to watch from the side of the stage. Emily was excited at the prospect of seeing how the band and their crew prepared for a gig. Until then, she needed a few minutes to herself. Since Jack had returned from working out with Buzz, Emily hadn't been able to get a minute to herself. After Barbara left, they'd gone to Central Park. It was good to get outside. The winter had been bitterly cold, so even at fifty degrees, it felt warm.

Even though she'd done yoga this morning, her leg ached. One yoga session couldn't make up for the almost month she'd missed after she'd caught Sully cheating. Jack had noticed, so they'd stopped several times so she could rest. Emily hated that, after nearly ten years, it still affected her. She'd never be able to forget; the scars wouldn't let her.

Again, Emily had gotten that creepy feeling of being watched. She'd thought she'd seen Jeff, but the sun had been in her eyes, so she couldn't be sure. He was supposed to be the band's security, but it seemed he spent most of his time around Jack.

They'd been stopped several times by fans wanting pictures and autographs. Jack happily obliged. As long as she wasn't in the pictures, she was okay with it. Emily still felt funny about the picture Ariana had taken of them at Casa Amici that now served as the lock screen picture on Jack's phone. She didn't have a picture of him. Maybe he'd let her take a few naughty shots. He'd wanted to take them of her, so why not?

That reminded her of Jack on his knees, going down on her, in front of the mirror Friday morning. He was a great fuck. She couldn't get her mind out of the gutter, so when they'd gotten back to the hotel, she'd pounced on him. The door was barely closed before she had Jack's pants down and his cock in her mouth. He'd loved it, and so had she. He'd reciprocated threefold.

Jack strode into the bathroom. "You almost ready? Jeff wants us in five minutes."

Jack looked sexy as hell in dark wash jeans, black T-shirt, and black boots. "That shirt looks familiar." Emily couldn't hide her smile. It was the one she'd worn the first time she'd gone down on him.

"It's my new favorite." His blue eyes sparkled with lust. She wore the burgundy sweater he'd bought her with a pair of black skinny jeans. And the outrageously expensive underwear. Emily reminded herself that was for later, and she smiled as she walked past him.

Jack pulled her into his arms and kissed her hard on the lips, their tongues tangling. "You look lovely." His breath came in short bursts.

Emily caught her reflection. Her eyes were glazed with lust, her nipples were hard, and her panties wet. Damn the effect he had on her. She gazed at his groin, and the bulge behind his zipper had her smirking as satisfaction washed through her.

Jack's phone blared out with Alice in Chains' "Rooster." His blue eyes darkened to sapphire. "Stop enticing me." He connected the call. "We're on our way."

"So now would be a bad time to describe what I'm wearing under my clothes?"

"That's just mean." He pulled her in for a kiss before she could protest.

They held hands on the way to the elevator. Her mind wandered back to the park and that sense of being watched. Maybe it was because everyone stared at Jack: men, women, children, baby animals. He had a magnetism unlike she'd ever experienced before. Sully was charming, but Jack was ten levels above that.

"You look deep in thought."

"Am I a groupie?"

Jack burst out laughing. "No. Why would you think that?"

"Well, you're a musician, groupies sleep with musicians, I'm sleeping with you..."

Jack pulled her into his arms. "You're my girlfriend."

"Yeah, now, but not that first night. Was I a groupie then?"

"No. I wanted to date you, so you were already considered girlfriend material. Groupies sleep with many musicians, sometimes in the same band, sometimes whoever is available. We've never been into that scene."

"Well, you're the only musician I've ever slept with."

"See, not a groupie."

"But you've slept with fans?"

Jack hesitated. "Yeah, I guess. I've never actually picked a girl out of the audience before, mostly just girls after a gig, at an after-party or bar. They know who I am, and a lot of the time they say they like our music."

Backstage at Madison Square Garden bustled with activity

even though it was only five in the afternoon. Jack stopped to talk to members of their crew, just as he'd done on Thursday, and he introduced her to them.

Emily noticed Bernie, one of the female members of the crew, giving Jack appreciative glances after he moved on. She didn't blame her; he was handsome and nice, a hard combination to resist. But she had the decency to keep it subtle. Looking was fine, but it was touching that would piss Emily off.

They passed several tables of food. A few crew members milled there, filling their plates. As they walked to the side of the stage, Jack put his arm around her. "Holden, Beth, Val, this is Emily. You'll be seeing a lot of her."

Beth and Val were sisters, but there was no resemblance. Beth was tall, blonde, and thin while Val was shorter with brown hair and voluptuous. They were both very attractive, but neither flirted with him. They joked with him, and he with them, but nothing untoward. She noticed Nicki paying attention to the women Curt talked to. They'd compare notes later.

Curt pulled Nicki in for a long kiss, dipping her low. Some of the crew hooted and shouted, "Get a room." When Curt righted her, Nicki's cheeks were flushed.

Emily had never seen Nicki blush before.

A petite blonde with a tablet and a tall blond man walked over to them. "Guys, we need to discuss the VIPs."

"Hey, man." Jack shook his hand. "Emily, this is Brian Vale, our tour manager, and his assistant, Aviva Smith. We couldn't survive without them."

Aviva extended her hand. "Nice to meet you. Call me Viv." Her smile was warm and friendly.

"Nice to meet you both."

Nicki walked over as Curt joined the guys to talk with

Brian. Her smile was epic, and her eyes glowed. "Isn't this great? I had no idea so much work went into a tour."

Emily smiled. A lot of their friendship was based on the fact that they were both writers, and they loved learning and observing people. She never knew where she'd find inspiration for a character or setting.

The glow left Nicki's eyes as she stood in front of Emily. They were almost eye to eye since Nicki wore a pair of her stilts. "You okay?"

Emily looked at Jack and nodded.

"Hey, it's me, you don't have to pretend." Nicki stepped closer. "After everything that's happened, it's okay to be confused." Nicki's light brown eyes shone with understanding.

Emily didn't want to have this conversation here. These were Jack's people, and she didn't want to air her troubles or her reservations in their earshot.

Nicki hugged her. "We'll talk later."

The crew finished testing the lights, and a voice came over the PA. "Soundcheck."

Jack and Curt walked over. Holden handed Jack his guitar. "You don't mind, do you?" Jack asked.

He'd told her he had a surprise for her during the encore tonight, something the band needed to work on during soundcheck. "Of course not." Emily kissed Jack quickly. She didn't want the attention from the crew that Nicki and Curt had gotten.

Viv stood next to Holden. They stole glances at each other when they thought no one was paying attention.

When Viv turned toward Emily, her lips curved into a small smile. "Ladies, if you'll follow me." Viv led them through the backstage area to a hallway. It was the same route they'd taken with Jack on Thursday. "There are drinks in the dressing room. I understand you'll be eating with us, so as soon as soundcheck is over, I'll come get you."

"You seem like a tight bunch," Nicki said.

Viv smiled fondly. "Yeah, the guys in the band are great. I've been with Brian for almost three years, and we're more like a family than employer and employee." She leaned in. "I've heard horror stories about some bands, but the guys have always been great to us. The crew has been with them for years, they're totally loyal." Viv opened the door, and Nicki and Emily walked in. Viv handed Nicki a piece of paper. "That's my cell. Call if you need anything, anything at all." She smiled and closed the door as she left.

Nicki turned to her. "Okay, spill."

Emily sat on the couch she'd shared with Jack last Thursday. The room looked the same but so much had changed. She was over the hump of her wedding day that wasn't. Since she'd caught Sully, she'd dreaded it more and more as the day approached. She couldn't have imagined, even in her wildest writer's imagination, that she'd meet a rock star, sleep with him, and now be his girlfriend. Emily was torn from her thoughts by Nicki gently rapping her knuckles on Emily's forehead.

"Hey, out here, please." Nicki's voice held concern. "Get out of your head and talk to me. I know you haven't been talking to Vince and Eddie, as you implied you were."

"I implied no such thing. I'm not responsible for your false inferences."

"Don't use semantics with me. Need I remind you I had a 3.9 GPA in English?" Nicki's smile faded. "Come on, Emi, you need to talk about how you're feeling."

Emily stood and grabbed two bottles of water off the table, handing one to Nicki. "We've done nothing but talk about feelings for almost a month."

Nicki opened her bottle and took a sip. "No, we haven't.

We've talked about what he did, conjectured as to why, but you haven't talked about what's going on inside your head." She looked down at the bottle and peeled a corner of the label away. "You know that leads you down a bad road."

Emily flopped on the couch. Nicki was right. Emily had spent years in therapy while recovering from her accident and again after she'd dropped out of college. It was too easy to keep it all inside her head, where she was safe. She'd conquered that flaw until she'd caught Sully cheating. She hadn't even realized that she'd withdrawn into herself to such a degree until Nicki pointed it out.

"How do you know I haven't been talking to Eddie and Vince?"

Nicki shook her head. "Because I've been talking to them. You had us going, too. Implying to me—" Nicki raised her hand to silence Emily's argument. "Letting us assume that you were opening up to the others." Nicki furrowed her brow. "Look, I know most of the time my love life is a hot mess, but that doesn't mean I can't help you."

"It's not that." Emily's eyes teared up.

Nicki scooted closer. "Then what?"

Emily swallowed her tears. She wouldn't let Sully break her. "I trusted him. Totally. I never thought he was a cheater." That still blindsided her, and none of her willful oblivion accounted for that behavior.

Nicki pulled her into a hug. "None of us did. Hell, even Meg, with her complete and utter distrust of all things male, thought Sully was one of the good ones."

It turned Emily's stomach that her friends had been discussing her behind her back. But what choice had she given them? She'd shut down emotionally. Still was. She couldn't face the pain all at once as it threatened to swallow her whole. She'd never considered herself a weak person, but she felt beaten down. Her parents would be so ashamed of her.

Nicki hugged her tighter. "No, sweetie, they wouldn't be."

Emily pulled from Nicki's embrace. She hadn't realized she'd said that out loud. Emily took a deep breath and exhaled slowly. It was time to share what was haunting her inside her head. "How can I trust anything I feel ever again?"

The dressing room door burst open, and Jack, Curt, Buzz, and Elliot strode in laughing.

Emily turned away and wiped the tears that streamed down her cheeks, but it was too late. Jack was on his knees next to her.

"Baby, what's wrong."

"Nothing."

"Em—"

"Jack," Nicki said. "Just girl talk. We needed to catch up."

Jack pulled back and searched Emily's face. He looked at Nicki and then back at her. "Girl talk?"

"Yeah." Emily smiled.

He stood and pulled her to her feet. "Okay. Dinner?"

Emily nodded, turned to Nicki, and mouthed "Thank you."

Chapter Six

Girl talk. Jack wasn't buying it. Emily had been quiet all through dinner, and Nicki stayed close to her, but by the time they took the stage, Em seemed to have recovered. She and Nicki were at side stage cheering them on. Every time he glanced over, Emily smiled at him. He could get used to this. She looked like she was having a good time.

Tonight had gone smoothly with none of the guitar problems Curt had been having on and off since the tour started, and Jack was glad. He didn't want to have to explain it to Emily.

Jack exited the stage, handed Holden his guitar, and walked to Emily, picking her up and spinning her around while he kissed her. "How'd we do?"

Emily's smile glowed. "You guys were great. I recognized all the songs this time."

Jack cocked his head to the side.

Emily looked down. "I downloaded all your songs when I got home Friday, I fell asleep listening to them."

She'd told him that Nicki was the fan. He was honored that she wanted to listen to their catalogue. He set her on her feet and cupped her face in his hands. He leaned down and kissed her, pouring all the love he felt into it. She'd given him copies of her books, but he hadn't had a chance to read them yet. He'd make time. "Baby..."

Her eyes shone up at him with lust, for sure, but something else, too. *Love?*

"Enough, you two," Elliot said. He stood next to them, smirking. He rubbed his unruly black hair with a towel. "Encore time." He clapped Jack on the shoulder.

Jack's heart leaped in his chest. Suddenly, he wasn't so sure they should do "With You" as part of the encore. It still needed work, but he'd played that song for Em. She knew what it meant, and she was a private person. Jack swallowed hard and rested his forehead against hers. "I'll be back."

As Holden handed him his Martin, Elliot said, "Man, if you're having second thoughts..."

Curt and Buzz nodded in agreement. "Yeah, we don't have to do it," Buzz said.

Jack looked at his brothers. They knew each other so well. "Thanks. How about 'Empty Shapes?' It's been awhile."

Curt cocked his head to the side. "What about 'Letting You Go?' The single and video drop Friday."

Jack winced. He was sorry, now more than ever, they'd agreed for that song to be the third single. They'd shot the video in the beginning of April. As soon as they'd finished, he'd flown to L.A. because Christie's friend Amber had called him, concerned that Christie hadn't been answering her phone or door.

"Fuck, Jack, I'm sorry..." Curt said.

"No, it's fine. We've been putting it off long enough."

Buzz craned his neck around Jack. "What about Emily? Should we really be doing a song about your ex while she's here?"

Jack looked over to where Em and Nicki were deep in

conversation. Nicki had been here on Saturday when they'd done "With You" as part of the encore, and he'd told Em he had a surprise for her, but he hadn't thought this through.

Elliot clapped Jack on the back. "'Empty Shapes' it is."

Buzz and Curt nodded in agreement. "It's better anyway," Curt said. "We don't need to change guitars."

"What're you gonna tell Emily?" Buzz asked.

"I haven't a fucking clue."

The band returned to the stage and killed the three-song encore. He glanced over and saw Nicki's confused expression, so he winked at her. She nodded and looked relieved.

After the encore, the band cleaned up before doing the VIP meet and greet. Emily and Nicki waited in the dressing room. One of the fans was particularly handsy, and Jack had Jeff escort the young lady away. Most of their female fans were respectful, but every so often, one took liberties they weren't entitled to. Nicki had been one of the worst, but she was with Curt now and never gave Jack another glance.

On the way to the dressing room, he pulled Buzz aside. "How you doing?" Jack felt bad he hadn't been spending as much time with Buzz since Em had come into his life.

Buzz smiled. "I'm okay. I haven't spent much time in the city"—Buzz shuffled his feet as he looked down—"a lot of memories."

I'm such an asshole. "You wanna hang?"

Buzz looked back at him. "Man, stop it, okay. It's not your job to babysit me. You and Emily have two days left. I really like her, and it's good to see you happy. Listen, if you want to skip working out—"

"Not a chance." Jack smirked. "Em insisted. She doesn't want me to stop working out, says I have to maintain my body just the way it is."

Buzz's grateful smile was all Jack needed. He'd never have blown Buzz off, and he was glad that Em understood.

It was well after midnight by the time they got back to their room. Jack showered while Emily brushed her teeth and washed up. When he strolled into the bedroom, naked and ready, she was sound asleep. He looked down at his dick, like a divining rod pointing at Emily's sleeping body. "Looks like we'll have to wait."

He crawled into bed, turned off the light, and spooned his girl.

In the middle of the night, he awoke to feel Emily's lips close around his cock. He'd been having a sex dream. Emily had been stroking his cock and eyeing his erection with a wild hunger that made him throb. But now, he suspected that Emily had been providing external stimulation.

He was on his back, the covers tossed aside. Moonlight poured in through the windows, and a wide beam of it was across his groin. He watched as his engorged cock disappeared into her mouth, only to reappear a few moments later. She cupped his balls, gently rolling them, and her other hand wrapped around the base of his cock. Every so often, her hand would follow her mouth up the length of his shaft, and her tongue moved back and forth on the underside. She held his cock in place while her tongue circled the head. He felt a bead of cum form and watched as she eagerly lapped it up with her tongue.

She loved sucking his cock as much as he loved eating her pussy. His dick jerked in response to the image in his head of him eating her pussy while he plundered her with three fingers. His balls tightened, and he felt tingling at the base of his spine. "So close." When he was fully in her mouth, she hummed, and he came hard.

She moaned as she swallowed, licking him carefully from base to tip, cleaning every last drop off. She sat up with a satisfied grin. She crawled up his body and straddled his torso, leaning down to kiss his lips.

He opened his mouth, enjoying the taste of himself on her tongue. Several minutes passed as Jack sank into the joy of making out with his girl. Her lips were soft, and she nibbled him with her teeth. "Give me five minutes, and I'm going to fuck you into tomorrow."

Her hand traveled down his chest and grasped his semi-hard cock. "A, it is tomorrow." She paused to kiss him, biting his bottom lip. "And B, I don't think you need five minutes."

He held her face in place so he could kiss her while she continued to gently stroke his cock back to hard. "What you do to me..."

Catching her off guard, he flipped their positions, sheathed himself, and thrust into her so hard her breath caught. "Too much?"

She chuckled. "You know I like it rough."

He fucked her hard, pumping into her with such force her head knocked against the headboard. He quickly adjusted them and then resumed slamming into her. He dipped his head and took her nipple into his mouth. She arched her back, giving him better access. She moaned his name, and he felt her tighten around him. Her convulsions pushed him over the edge, and he came.

He rolled off and lay on his back. He needed to take care of the condom, but he couldn't move. His heart pounded against his rib cage, and he struggled to get enough air in his lungs. Emily rolled onto her side, her breathing as erratic as his.

"That was fucking incredible, Jack."

She lay in his arms with her head resting on his shoulder. Fuck the rubber. Even though his body was sated, Jack's mind darted around with the uncertainty of their relationship. He loved her, but Em wasn't in love with him. Not yet, anyway.

ON TUESDAY, EMILY WOKE AS THE SUN BARELY crept over the horizon. She crawled out of bed, trying not to wake Jack. He groaned in his sleep and turned onto his side. She slipped on his T-shirt, grabbed her laptop, and went into the living room. It was chilly, so she turned the gas fireplace on and sat cross-legged on the couch.

"Hey, why didn't you wake me?" Jack said, running his hand through his hair as he walked naked into the living room.

Startled, Emily looked up. Morning sun cascaded through the seam of the curtains. She looked at the time on her computer. It was after eight. She saved her work, put her laptop on the coffee table, stood, and stretched. Her leg ached from being in one position too long. She needed to do yoga and get her butt back in the gym to resume strength training. Jack gabbed her around the waist and hauled her to him. His lips crashed onto hers.

"Mmm," she moaned against his lips. "Good morning to you, too."

Jack glanced at her laptop. "Did you get a lot done?"

Emily nodded and rested her cheek on Jack's chest. Her eyes stung from staring at the screen too long. She usually took a break every thirty minutes or so, to keep her leg loose and rest her eyes, but she'd been sitting at the computer for over three hours.

She felt Jack's stomach rumble, which her stomach answered with a rumble of its own. And she needed coffee.

Still holding her, Jack picked up the room phone and ordered breakfast.

Thirty minutes later, they sat at the table, enjoying pancakes, scrambled eggs, and sausage. Emily smiled to herself, remembering their first breakfast together.

"Wicked smiles will get you in trouble, young lady." From the lustful gleam in his sparkling blue eyes, she knew he was remembering their first breakfast, too.

She looked at Jack over her orange juice glass and batted her lashes at him. "I have no idea what you are referring to," she said in a prim tone.

Jack stood. He'd pulled on a pair of sweatpants but no shirt. Emily wanted to lick him everywhere. Jack's phone bleated from the bedroom. Jack glanced at the clock on the mantel. "Shit. Buzz."

Jack walked to her and pulled her up against him. "Rain check?" He waggled his brows up and down.

Emily pouted. "Okay." Jack was being a good friend to Buzz, and Emily would never want to come between them.

"I need this." He grabbed the hem of the T-shirt and whipped it over her head and pulled it on. Emily stood there naked, gaping at him.

Jack grinned, grabbed his phone, and dialed Buzz back. "On my way." He smirked at her as he opened the door only far enough so he could slip out.

Emily picked up a pillow off the couch and threw it at the closed door. She smiled as she went into the bedroom and quickly dressed in yoga pants and a T-shirt. She unrolled her yoga mat in the living room and sat. Stretching both legs out in front of her, she inhaled deeply and bent forward, wrapping her hands around her feet. Her left leg was fine, but the muscles in her right leg didn't want to cooperate. She closed her eyes and tried to relax the muscles in her thigh.

When she heard footsteps outside the door, Emily sat up. Jack had only been gone a few minutes. "What'd you forget?" she said. When the door didn't open, she realized Jack must've forgotten his key card. "Coming." Emily stood and opened the door, but no one was there.

She looked out into the hallway and didn't see anyone, but there was a faint whiff of perfume. A housekeeping cart was parked in front of the room three doors down. The hair on the back of her neck stood up.

The chambermaid came out of the room with an armful of sheets. When she saw Emily, she asked, "Miss, do you need something?"

"Were you outside room thirty-seven twenty-one a minute ago?"

"No, I've been in here for ten minutes. Is everything okay?"

Emily nodded. Her new novel had a suspense element, so her imagination must be running amok. Maybe one of their neighbors stopped to check their phone. "Thank you." Emily suppressed a shudder and went back into her room.

Chapter Seven

Jack strummed his guitar as he watched Emily work. She was jotting down notes for her new book because she had a dream last night that sparked an idea. He felt more connected to her than ever because that happened to him, too. They'd won their first Grammy for "Empty Shapes," a song he'd written in the middle of the night after waking from a dream. Em had such laser focus while working that he felt like she didn't know he was in the room.

Christie used to say that all he cared about was his music. It wasn't true; he'd loved her. But she'd grown to resent the amount of time he spent in his studio. Jack loved music, and she'd accused him of loving it more than her, which he'd dismissed because it was stupid. But watching Em work now, locked in her own world, maybe he understood what she'd meant.

He knew when he was working on a new song that he had tunnel vision. And yeah, he spent seventy-five percent of his life on the road, but Christie knew that going into it, and he'd spent plenty of hours running lines with her. It only started to be an issue after they'd moved to California. Jack was beginning to think that had been the beginning of the end.

Christie was an amazing actress, but it took a lot of hard work to get ahead in any creative industry. She'd told him the night they'd met that her dream was to move to L.A., get discovered, and be a famous actress. She'd been so young, barely twenty-one, and naive. She'd also been sweet and caring, and Jack had been attracted to those qualities as much as he'd been to her physical beauty.

Maybe she'd really thought she'd be one of the lucky ones to be an overnight success. Jack doubted that overnight success was even a thing, but it made for a good headline.

Jack's text alert sounded. Jeff's typical text: *Garage 5*

He closed his notebook and set his acoustic in the stand. "Gotta go."

Em wrapped her arms around him. Tilting her head up, she kissed him hard. Damn. Not that he didn't love it when she kissed him like that, but he had to leave. And now he wanted to stay; he wanted her. "Baby, I have to go," he groaned.

She immediately stepped back but had a wicked gleam in her eye. She wanted him to stay, too. His heart stuttered. He forced his legs to walk him to the door. His hand rested on the doorknob. *Why's this so hard?*

"Jack."

He looked over his shoulder. "Yeah?"

"When you get back... I'm going to need you to fuck me." She turned and sauntered into the bedroom.

He quickly turned the knob, opened the door, stepped in the hall, and closed the door. He took two steps in the wrong direction and leaned up against the wall. "Where have you been all my life?" When his text alert went off again, he knew he was late. He was never late. He took a deep breath, pushed off the wall, and started in the wrong direction again. *Shit.* He turned and ran to the elevator.

On the ride down, he checked the text. Jeff again: *?!*

He laughed as the elevator doors opened. He hustled over to the SUV waiting to take them to the radio station. As soon as he closed the door, the SUV lurched forward.

The guys had knowing smiles on their faces and looked at each other but not at him. Even Curt had beat him. "Sorry."

"For being happy?" Elliot asked.

Jack grinned. "Em's amazing."

"Is she coming with us?" Curt asked.

Jack's heart sank. He wished. He refused to ask her because he knew it was too soon, and she had a job.

Elliot smacked Curt upside the head, dislodging a chunk of his blond hair from his signature ponytail. "What the fuck is wrong with you?"

"What?" Curt said, fixing his hair. "Oh shit, sorry, man."

Jack sighed. "It's okay. Nicki seems great."

Curt beamed, and his blue eyes sparkled. "She is. I'm...I think I'm falling in love with her."

Jack was truly happy for his friend. When Curt's ex-fiancée had ended their engagement, he'd been heartbroken. Curt had a gentleness about him that Jack never wanted to see crushed.

"That's cool, man," Elliot said.

"Yeah," Buzz said, looking out the window.

"Buzz, maybe it's time you got back out there," Curt said.

Buzz looked at them and shook his head. "Not ready."

Since they'd been on tour, to Jack's knowledge, Buzz hadn't indulged. He was introverted, and alcohol had always helped him loosen up enough to be more social. He had it under control until he'd met Sally, who didn't drink but loved pot. After Buzz fucked up his knee skiing, pain killers entered the mix, and it went downhill from there.

When Sally had overdosed, Buzz had gotten her to the hospital just in time, thank God. She'd been in a coma for four days; the worst four days of his life he'd said. When she woke, she'd blamed Buzz because she'd found his stash and had a party. Jack never understood how that had been Buzz's fault. She went into rehab and broke up with him when she'd gotten out. Turned out she'd met a guy in rehab, which was a huge no-no. There was a reason they told recovering addicts not to dive into any new relationships.

Buzz kept falling until his parents had surprised him at his apartment last summer. He was unconscious on the kitchen floor. Poor Aunt Mel had thought he was dead. Uncle Garth had called 911, and they'd rushed him to the hospital. Turned out he'd slipped on spilled water and hit his head. He had a mild concussion, but he hadn't OD'd.

Buzz went into rehab and had been sober ever since. Two hundred and twenty-one days. Jack was so fucking proud of him. He tried to play it down, but Jack could always tell when he was struggling. Like yesterday morning. They'd worked out longer than usual. Jack was glad to help.

When they got to the radio station, the crew had their guitars and Buzz's Càjon box drum ready to go. They played ten songs, a mix from all their albums. They took questions in between songs from the audience, and they loved it. Playing huge venues was great, but they lost a certain intimacy that they all enjoyed when they played to a smaller crowd.

After the gig, they went upstairs for the interview with the afternoon DJs, Brandon and Bobbi. Brandon was cool, and he asked a lot about the inspiration for the songs on their new album, since they'd played their third single "Letting You Go."

"Wow, that's a great song," Brandon said.

"Thanks." Contrary to popular belief, every song he wrote wasn't about him. But this one was.

"How's Christie?" Bobbi asked.

Fuck. Bobbi had been eyeballing Jack since they'd gotten here. From her tone, Jack knew she was a fan of Christie's. Jack's instincts told him to cut the interview short, but he decided it was better to not make a scene.

He looked at Elliot, Buzz, and Curt. "Honestly, I don't know. We don't keep in touch, but I hope she's doing well." Jack meant that. Unfortunately, there was nothing more he could do to help her. If she decided to get help, he'd promised to pay for it. That would be money well spent.

"Isn't it true that you kicked her out of your house? Forced her to move into some dumpy apartment in a bad neighborhood?"

Jack swore silently. "We're done here." He stood, and his brothers stood with him. Jeff opened the door, and they walked out. Brick, Polson, and Miller waited outside. Brick took point with Jeff, and Polson and Miller followed behind them. Jack ignored the shocked expressions of Brandon, his producer, and the staff that watched them leave. *Fuck it.* Let them call him a spoiled rock star. Dex could deal with the fall out. That was what they paid him for.

He kept it together until they were safely inside the SUV. "Fuck! Brandon was cool, but what was up with that…"

"I believe the word you're looking for is bitch," Elliot said.

"Personally, I'd have gone with cunt. That was a fucking ambush," Curt said.

Jack agreed with all of it.

"Last time we go there," Buzz said.

Since Jack was the frontman, he got the most attention and the least privacy. He'd grown into acceptance of it slowly. He was happy for any attention they got as a band, but some people wanted dirt. They'd never get it from him. He'd never said, and would never say, a bad word about Christie. But that bitch Bobbi ambushed him. He knew, that like Christie, some people blamed him for her problems.

He couldn't wait to see Em. Then he remembered her parting words and smiled.

As they rolled up to the elevators in the garage, Jeff said, "Dinner reservations at seven. Meet here at six forty." He looked at Jack in the rearview mirror. "That's ninety minutes for you timing impaired, not ninety-one." Jeff almost smiled.

Jack acknowledged with a nod and jumped out as soon as the SUV stopped. Curt was right behind him. Elliot and Buzz whistled and yelled, "What's the rush?" Juvenile laughter echoed through the garage.

At the elevators, Jack and Curt turned to them and flipped them off, and Jack used the finger to punch the up button. Curt got out on thirty-five, and Jack pushed the button for thirty-seven ten times before the doors closed. His dick hardened more with each passing floor. At this rate, by the time he opened the door to his room, his dick would be inside before he was.

♪ ·•·•· ♫

EMILY FINISHED HER SURPRISE PROJECT FOR JACK, AN idea sparked by something Nicki said while they were in the salon. She wrapped it up with some ribbon she'd gotten from the hotel's boutique. She wished she could see Jack's face when he opened it.

She heard the doorknob and turned as Jack raced in and slammed the door. He crossed the room to her, and then she was in his arms, their lips crashing together.

"I fucking missed you, baby," he said in a strained whisper.

It had been a little mean to taunt him before he'd left, but he looked like he'd forgiven her. She ached for him, and a slow burn had started in her that only Jack could extinguish.

She tugged at Jack's belt, popped the button, lowered the zipper, and thrust her hand in. His dick was rock hard, and a bead of fluid had formed at the tip. She stroked him as he whipped off his shirt and stripped out of his jeans. He undressed her as best he could, with her hand occupied, until she was forced to release him so he could get her shirt off.

He stepped back, his dick pulsed, and he gulped. "Oh, Em..."

This was new—white lace and satin bra with matching thong. She'd burned all her lingerie, anything she'd worn for Sully. Just having it in her closet made her sick. Nicki had supplied the fireplace and the wine. She'd gotten so drunk that night she'd had a headache for two days.

His eyes glazed over, and his lips parted slightly, but he didn't speak or touch her. He just stared. She felt like the sexiest woman on the planet. He watched as she brought a finger up to her lips, but she didn't take it in her mouth. Instead, she slowly turned. When he saw the back view, he grunted. When she faced him, she toyed with her nipples, plucking at them gently. Still, he made no move to touch her. Maybe she'd broken him? "Baby, you okay?"

He seemed to snap out of his daze, and his jaw clenched. "Say it," he said through tight lips.

She could ask what, but she knew. "Jack, please fuck me now."

He reached into the acrylic phallus—Elliot's idea of a joke —pulled out a condom, tore it open, and rolled it on. Jack lifted her and rested her back up against the wall. *Their wall.* Moving the thong aside, he thrust mercilessly inside her until he filled her completely. He paused for a moment, forcing her to meet his eyes, before he pulled out and pounded back in. Over and over.

She clenched her internal muscles, increasing the pleasure for both of them. Jack eased off, taking her lips in a deep kiss. His tongue thrust into her mouth as his cock thrust into her pussy.

He rested his forehead against hers, not letting up. "You're so fucking wet, baby. I wish I could fuck you and eat you at the same time."

She giggled, and Jack gave her a warning look. She occupied her mouth by licking the salty skin of his jaw. Her arms tightened around his neck as he resumed his unrelenting assault. He nipped behind her ear and down her neck until he reached her shoulder, gently biting. She exploded around him, screaming out as her body convulsed.

"Fuck yeah," he said as he came.

Jack rested for a moment before carrying her into the bedroom and laying her on the bed. He disposed of the condom and then lay next to her, pulling her halfway onto his chest with his arms closing around her.

Emily enjoyed the sound of Jack's heartbeat: strong, steady, and solid. Just like him.

"What evil thought did that brain of yours concoct?"

She chuckled. "Not evil. Just that to fuck me and eat me at the same time would probably require a very advanced yoga posture. If you invented that, you'd be a multi-millionaire." When he didn't say anything, she looked up at him. "What?"

"I am."

Oh. She stretched up so she could kiss him. "I don't care about your money." She rested her head back on his chest. "I guess paying for your siblings' education won't be a burden for you. I'm surprised your parents agreed to that."

"They didn't at first."

"Jimmy and Trish don't know?"

"When my folks finally agreed that it was silly for them to bear the burden when I could easily help out, they insisted Jimmy and Trish couldn't know about it. They took out loans over what my parents had saved. Mom and Dad want them to appreciate their education. They're less likely to take it for granted if they don't know that I'll be paying off their loans."

"You never appreciate things that are given to you as much as the ones you've had to earn."

"Their point exactly."

Emily shifted off him and onto her back.

Jack turned on his side. "What they don't know is that I'm going to pay off their house, and I've opened a retirement account for them, but they can't touch it until their sixty-five."

"You wouldn't want them to blow their retirement money on fancy clothes and extravagant vacations."

"Exactly." He grinned at her. "I'm buying my dad a fully loaded SUV for Christmas. They only have one car that my mom uses since he has the van for work. Whenever they go out, they use her car, but I know my dad would love a truck." Jack placed his pointer finger over his lips.

That made Emily laugh. "So sweet." She took his finger between her lips and sucked it.

Jack moaned.

Round two.

A SINGLE KNOCK ON THE BATHROOM DOOR startled Emily out of her reverie.

"Babe, you almost ready?" Jack asked.

They were having dinner with Curt, Nicki, Buzz, Elliot, and Siobhan. She'd taken more time than necessary changing and washing up. Emily redid her makeup and fixed her hair. "Another two minutes." Emily would've rather stayed in, but Jack had been so excited when Elliot called and told him Siobhan was coming to dinner with them, she'd gone with it. She liked seeing Jack happy.

When she opened the door, her breath caught. Jack wore a black silk, fitted button-down shirt, black jeans, his favorite boots and was freshly shaven and just gorgeous. His blue eyes sparkled, and his dark brown hair was combed neatly. She wore a black beaded knit shirt with gray leggings and black patent leather flats.

"You look lovely." Jack pulled her into his arms.

She blocked his kiss with her hand. "Don't start. I don't want to look well-fucked when we meet your friends for dinner." Nicki had sex-dar, and what Nicki knew, everyone would know. Emily didn't need to make it easy for her.

"Well-fucked?" Jack grinned. "I like that."

"Me too." She darted away as Jack lunged toward her. "Stop that."

Jack caught her and just as their lips touched, Jack's phone rang with "Welcome Home," Elliot's ringtone, and they groaned. Jack answered and said, "On our way."

The elevator doors opened in the garage and they walked to a van where Jeff waited. A black SUV waited behind the van. Jeff opened the door as they approached.

Nicki, Curt, and Buzz sat in the first row and Elliot and Siobhan in the second. Emily sat next to the window, and Jack sat next to her.

Elliot turned to face her. "Emily, this is my wife, Siobhan." His grin was epic.

Emily leaned forward and shook her hand. "Nice to meet you."

"Elliot's told me so much about you." Siobhan's smile was as wide as her husband's.

The van moved so they were forced to sit back in their seats.

They arrived at the restaurant within twenty minutes and were immediately seated in a private room. Rock star treatment didn't suck.

While they looked over their menus, Emily watched Elliot with his wife. His black curls were tamed, he'd shaved, and his dark eyes sparkled. When he smiled, he looked years younger than he had when they'd met. He was good-looking before, but now he was downright handsome. Siobhan was drop-dead gorgeous with long red hair, green eyes, and pale skin with a dusting of freckles. Love shone in her eyes for Elliot, and they held hands, nuzzling each other and sharing private jokes. It was the cutest damn thing Emily had ever seen.

The waiter came, and they placed their orders. Bottles of wine were delivered, but Emily passed; she wanted to support Buzz. She never drank in front of Vince even though he was okay with it, but Emily knew Vince appreciated it.

She turned her attention to Nicki and Curt. She'd never seen her so toned down. Nicki had a great body which was usually on display. Her makeup was subtle, and her long, blonde hair was pulled in a high ponytail. Nicki wore a pale yellow sweater with black leggings and a modest heel. Emily suspected it was because with her five-inch heels she'd be as tall as Curt. Men had a thing about height. She chuckled to herself. And length. And width. Jack had all three.

She hadn't spent much time with Curt, but he looked like a man in love. His dark blond hair was pulled back into a low ponytail, and his eyes never left Nicki. He didn't have the same air about him as the jerks Nicki usually gravitated to. He was sweet. She'd seen Nicki "in love" a least a dozen times over the years, but this was different.

Curt stood and tapped his fork on his water glass. "I have an announcement."

Oh God, no. Her grip tightened on Jack's hand. His tightened back.

"Nicki has agreed to come on tour with me."

Emily and Jack shared a shocked glance. They'd both thought the same thing, and that hadn't been it.

Elliot and Buzz clapped, and Nicki smiled.

"Nicki, nice to have you join us," Jack said. Something in the tone of his voice struck Emily as jealousy.

Emily was relieved, but still. They just met. Emily shook her head. Well, she couldn't use that argument anymore, could she? She was living in Jack's hotel room. Emily smiled and raised her glass. Nicki looked happy, but then she always did right up until the romance crashed and burned. Hopefully, this time would be different.

It was still early when they got back to the hotel, but Emily was tired. Her mind ached, and she wanted some time alone to think. Nicki suggested the girls have a drink in the bar so they could get to know each other since the guys were going to work on a song.

They sat at a small table at the far end of the bar. Nicki ordered a margarita, Siobhan ordered a pinot grigio, and Emily ordered a glass of merlot. The server returned with their drinks, and Nicki paid.

"Thank you for inviting me out," Siobhan said. "The girlfriends don't usually include me."

"Why not?" Nicki asked.

"We're homebodies, and we've been married for six years. When Elliot's home, we like to stay in."

"Plus, you have a lot of sex to catch up on." Nicki winked.

"Nic, really, you just met the girl, can't you ease into your...youness?" Emily asked.

Siobhan laughed. "It's okay, I have a younger sister just like Nicki."

"Oh crap, you mean there are two of them?"

Nicki stuck her tongue out. She was behaving; if Siobhan wasn't here, she'd have used another gesture. "You think I'm making a mistake, don't you?"

Emily smiled. "I'm not really in a position to judge you, sweetie. I want you to be happy."

"Being with Curt makes me happy, happier than I've ever

been. I know we just met, but it's different this time." Nicki held up her hand. "I know, I say that every time, but this time, it really is different."

"I know."

A wicked smile curved Nicki's lips. "You shoulda seen the look on your face when Curt made our announcement."

Emily narrowed her eyes. "You knew what I'd think. You could've given me a heads-up."

"This was more fun." Nicki took a sip of her drink. "Come on, Emi. Do you really think I'd marry Curt after knowing him less than a week?"

That's exactly what Emily had thought. "It's a very *you* thing to do." And since Jack had thought the same thing, apparently, it would also be a very Curt thing to do. Emily was glad she'd been wrong.

"Elliot tells me you're both writers. What do you write?" Siobhan asked.

Emily was glad to move away from this topic before Nicki brought up her and Jack. She didn't feel comfortable discussing it in front of Siobhan. Especially since his feelings were obvious. "He didn't elaborate?"

Siobhan blushed. "I don't know the terminology."

"My stories are romantic and sweet and always have a happy ending." Nicki's smile turned wicked. "Emi writes porn, sometimes with a side of suspense."

With mock effrontery, Emily said, "My stories always have happy endings, too." She couldn't help the wicked grin. "Sometimes in the beginning and middle as well."

Siobhan gasped and Nicki laughed.

"I'm not the only one who needs to ease into her 'youness,' Emi."

"Sorry," Emily said to Siobhan.

"Don't be, I'm not shocked really. Elliot told me you were funny and frank. They all appreciate honesty, especially Jack.

Elliot opts out of all the bullshit, as he calls it, but it has to be done, and Jack's great at it."

"Yeah, he is." Emily admired his ability to promote the band. Having a pen name to keep her privacy made all aspects of publishing more challenging.

Siobhan touched her hand. "I wanted to thank you. We" —she paused and smiled at the word—"still have things to work out, but we're talking again, thanks to you. I loved your idea about traveling with the band. I've always wanted to travel, but Elliot travels so much that when he gets a break he'd rather stay home." Siobhan looked down. "I miss him so much when he's on tour. It's hard being left behind."

Emily swallowed the lump in her throat. She refused to look past Thursday when the band moved on to Hartford.

"I love traveling, and I love meeting my fans..." Nicki commandeered the bulk of the conversation, which Emily was grateful for. A melancholy settled in her chest. Not only would her new boyfriend be leaving in two days, but now her best friend would go with them. Emily remembered the young, impulsive girl she'd lost in the accident. She definitely would've gone along for that ride.

An uneasy feeling shuddered through her. Their relationship was so new, and Jack met beautiful women every day. Emily shook her head to clear those thoughts away; Jack wasn't Sully. But then she'd never thought he was the cheating type either.

Chapter Eight

Jack wanted to spend the rest of the night with Em, but he also wanted to work on the song he'd written for her with the guys. They'd worked on it during soundcheck, but they all felt there was more magic to distill from it, so they'd keep at it.

Curt, Buzz, and Elliot got off at the thirty-fifth floor to get their instruments. Jack's room had been on the same floor, but the room had a leak, so he'd been moved to a floor where Jeff could be close by.

As he approached his room, Jack saw the corner of a white envelope peeking out from under the door. *Please, no.* Jack's body tensed, and his pulse hammered through his veins. *This cannot be happening, not now, not with Em here.*

"What'd you lock yourself out?" Elliot asked, as he, Buzz, and Curt walked up. Elliot's laughter died. "Motherfucker."

"Shit," Buzz said.

Curt walked over to the door and squatted. "Fuck."

"Don't touch it." Jack called Jeff. "I hope the girls have a good long drink." The last thing Jack wanted was to have to explain this to Em. She'd freak out and dump him for sure.

Jeff rounded the corner. "I'm here." He walked over and knelt. "Did you touch it?"

"No."

Jeff swore a string of curses. He made a quick call, and within a few minutes, Miller, Polson, and Brick jogged down the hallway.

"Brick, search the room." At Jack's puzzled expression, Jeff added, "We're not taking any chances."

Jack used his key card, and Brick opened the door and went in.

"Let's take this into my room," Jeff said.

Jack's head pounded. It had been over a month since he'd received a letter, and he'd hoped this shit was finished. As he paced the room, his mind raced. He had to protect Emily. If anything happened to her...

Jeff arranged with hotel security to see the footage from the thirty-seventh floor.

Brick walked in holding the envelope in his gloved hand. "Room's clear."

Jeff laid out a newspaper on the bed, and Brick placed the unopened envelope on it face up. No doubt, it was from the stalker. Jack's name in magazine cut-out letters and hearts was glued to the front. Jeff donned gloves and turned it over. The flap was sealed with a cutout of female lips painted red and pursed in a kiss. He used a small pair of scissors to cut the flap above the lips, careful not to disturb the stalker's work. He checked the interior, then slid the letter out, and unfolded it.

Elliot handed Jack a glass with amber liquid in it. "Drink."

Jack placed the glass on the table. He didn't want a drink; he wanted to kill someone. If Em was in danger because of him—

"You don't want her to see you like this, buddy. You look like you're about to explode. Emily's smart." Elliot picked up the glass and handed it to him again.

Fuck! Elliot was right. Jack downed the drink and wanted to smash the glass against the wall but didn't. He needed to calm down. Jeff held out the letter, but Jack didn't want to see it; the cut-out letters were creepy. "Just read it."

Jackie,

Have you missed me? I dream of you every night. Last night, you fucked me hard in the ass. I came twice. I know just how you like it. I can't wait to feel your cock inside me. You're the best lover I've ever had.

I will give you everything you need. Soon.

SWAK

This disturbed him more than the last one where the psycho described in nauseating detail all the ways she got off thinking about him. He fucking hated being called Jackie. Whoever this was obviously didn't know him. The liquor burned in his stomach.

Jeff's face was grim. "With Curt's girlfriend traveling with us, I'd like to add another body to the detail." Jeff looked pointedly at Jack. "No more going out without security."

Jeff was right, and he wouldn't do anything to put Em in danger, but what about after they left on Thursday? He wanted someone on her, but she'd never agree to that. How would he even explain it? "What about Siobhan? Is she coming?"

"We're only talking, we still have a lot to work through, but I want her protected. I don't care what it costs. I'm not taking any chances."

Jeff nodded. "I'll take care of it. I know a local guy. I assume this is covert?"

"Yeah, I don't want her to worry."

"Curt, you haven't said anything about this to Nicki, have you? She can't keep a secret for shit," Jack said.

"Come on, man, you know me better than that. I'm glad she's coming, I don't need to worry about her—shit, Jack. Sorry."

"No one says anything to Emily." Jack paced the room. *Fuck.*

Jeff cleared his throat. "She may already know something's up."

"How so?"

"When you were out Friday, and again yesterday, I'm pretty sure she saw me. Has she said anything to you?"

"No." Jack rubbed the back of his neck. "Fuck."

"What?" Jeff asked.

"I got the impression on Friday that she... I don't know. She's a writer, but she may have seen something. She was looking around, and I chalked it up to her taking in her surroundings, but now, I'm not so sure."

Jeff addressed Brick. "They don't go anywhere alone. If they have to shit, I want someone close enough to hand them toilet paper."

Before Jack could protest, Jeff turned to him. "Don't. This is serious. Whoever is doing this is smart and crazy. That's a bad combination. I'd hoped they would've made a mistake long before now."

"Like what?" Buzz asked.

"None of the letters have held any clues, no fingerprints, no DNA, generic paper and envelope. That magazine cut-out letters crap is low tech, untraceable. But whoever it is will make a mistake, and they'll get caught."

"Before or after she makes Jack her love toy?" Buzz asked with no hint of a joke.

He was in real danger. Until now, all the letters had been mailed, but the psycho hand-delivered this one. Now they were all in danger because of him. "What about our families? Should we tell them? Get them protection, too?"

"Let's not panic. Is there anyone you didn't include on the first list? At this point, we have to consider everyone."

Jack shook his head. He hadn't taken this as seriously as he should have. The first list had included a couple of ex-girlfriends who'd been clingy and some fan mail that Dex had kept.

"Jack?" Jeff barked.

Jack shrugged.

Jeff handed him a notepad and pen. "Everyone." He cleared his throat. When Jack made eye contact, he said, "Including the redhead from Quivers."

He glanced at his bandmates. Elliot's normal response to tense situations was to make a sarcastic crack, but he just looked dazed. Curt and Buzz stared at the floor, and Jack felt like the biggest asshole on the planet. He'd put them all in jeopardy because he hadn't taken this seriously.

The silence drew on as he spent several minutes making a new list. He knew the stalker wasn't Tabs; she'd never do this. They'd known each other for ten years and had had a casual hookup arrangement, which suited them both. He wrote her name down anyway. Jack listed all his ex-girlfriends, including Sandra and Erica, as well as the other women he'd hooked up with on a regular basis. There had been a lot of one-nighters, but he couldn't make that list because he didn't keep track.

Jack was glad he'd told Em about Tabitha. If it turned out to be Tabs—*No.* It wasn't her. It couldn't be.

He included Sasha, who used to work for Dex. Luckily, Christie had been visiting her parents when Sasha had broken into their apartment, stripped naked, and crawled into their bed. Jack had come in at three in the morning from the airport, and he'd been so exhausted he'd dropped his bags at the front door and dragged himself to the bedroom. He hadn't even taken his clothes off, just collapsed on the bed.

He'd woken several hours later to a soft whispering in his ear. "I want to fuck you, Jackie."

His sleep-clouded brain snapped awake. Christie only called him Jackie when she was pissed at him because she knew he hated it. He'd rolled out of bed so fast he landed on his ass, and a naked Sasha was on him before he could get up. He pushed her off and scrambled out of the bedroom, pulling the door closed with his weight while he phoned the police.

She'd fixated on him because, whenever they were in Dex's office, Jack was always nice to her. She was a lonely, lost soul. But he'd never said or done anything to give her the impression that they had a relationship. After the initial shock had worn off, Jack had felt sorry for her. Dex convinced him to not be stupid, so he'd pressed charges, and she'd ended up in a psychiatric hospital. As far as he knew, she was still there. Jack handed the list to Jeff.

"Brick and I will look over the security footage. Hopefully we can get some clue as to who's behind this. In the meantime, I hate to say it, but the less you go out, the better, especially if you want to keep this from your ladies."

"Fuck!" Jack vaulted to his feet. "They're alone in the bar right now." He ran to the door with Elliot and Curt on his heels.

"No, they aren't," Jeff said. "I sent Miller and Polson."

Jeff was worth double what he paid him. And why the fuck hadn't he thought of that? Emily would've. Shit. "There's something else."

Jeff's eyes narrowed. "What?"

"I don't know if it means anything, but Em's dad owned a private security firm."

A slow smile crossed Jeff's face, and he nodded a few times. "Fucking Marines are the best. No way he didn't—never mind. You sure you don't want to tell her?"

"I'm sure."

"She's gonna be pissed when she finds out. And make no mistake about it, she will find out," Jeff said with pride.

Jack wouldn't be surprised if she already had.

Jeff's cell vibrated at the same time The Temptations' "My Girl" blared from Curt's phone. "It's Nicki," he said. "They're on their way up. What do we do?"

"Shit, we're supposed to be working on the new song," Buzz said.

"Get over there and act like you were," Jeff said.

The four of them rushed over to Jack's room. Jack grabbed his notebook and guitar. Elliot sat next to him, and Curt and Buzz sat across from him. He opened the notebook, ripped out a few sheets, and balled them up, tossing them on the table.

"What're you doing?" Elliot asked.

"It has to look like we've been working. Em doesn't miss a thing." Jack needed to calm down. It was hard to breath past the lump in his throat.

"Whoa." Curt's eyes widened. "When you said giant cock, Jack, you weren't kidding."

Elliot turned and laughed. "Shit, I forgot all about that." He could barely speak through his laughter. "That was full when it got here."

Jack just shrugged and joined in the laughter, remembering Emily's reaction to it. By the time the girls entered, Jack felt less stressed.

Nicki went straight to the phallus and grabbed a handful of condoms. "Our room doesn't have one of these."

Siobhan sat on Elliot's lap and swatted his arm. "Why?"

Elliot's brilliant smile lit up his face. "Funsies." He kissed her tenderly on the lips, and Siobhan melted into him.

Curt yelled, "Get a room." He hoisted Nicki over his shoulder, grabbed his guitar, and left. Nicki's squeals of delight echoed down the hallway.

"I'm beat," Buzz said. "Goodnight."

"We should go too. I have to drive you home." Elliot pulled Siobhan close, his arm draped possessively around her shoulders. A panicked expression flitted across his face.

Siobhan yawned and nestled her head against Elliot's side. "It's late for me."

"Why don't you sleep over?" Jack suggested. "Black-hole can take the couch."

"That's a great idea," Elliot said.

Siobhan pouted. "I have work in the morning."

"I know you love your job, but maybe you could take the next few days off. We need to spend time together," Elliot pleaded.

Siobhan smiled up at him, her hand caressing his cheek. "I love you more, E."

"Aw, hear that Black, she loves you more."

Elliot responded with a single digit, and Siobhan just shook her head.

As soon as they were alone, he pulled Em into his arms. She looked tired and sad. He knew this stalker shit would blow up in his face at some point, but he just couldn't bring himself to tell her about it. Her mind was overloaded, and this would just add to her worries. Maybe tip her over the edge of giving up on them.

Yesterday, they couldn't even walk in the park without being interrupted. He'd never thought of meeting his fans as an interruption before, but he'd resented it. He'd wanted to show her that they could have a normal life together.

Headlining a tour of this size was new to them. Many of the venues were fifteen to twenty thousand people. They'd played festivals with fifty thousand or more attendees, but they weren't all Stone Highway fans, at least not before the gig. They had several up-and-coming bands as openers. He was grateful, but it had been a huge leap and a little nerve-racking to have that responsibility. He hoped he lived up to everyone's expectations.

And he was recognized more than ever. Their fans were great though. He'd sign autographs and take pictures, and they'd leave happy. It happened more and more, and he hadn't thought twice about it until Em came into his life. He'd promised her they'd have normal time, but now he wondered if he had that to give her. He knew at that moment he wanted her in his life no matter what. He'd give it all up for her. For the first time, he understood what Elliot had been going through all these years.

She yawned against his chest. "You're exhausted. Let's go to bed."

Em smiled up at him, went on her tiptoes, and kissed him. "Sounds good to me."

They walked into the bedroom, and Em grabbed a clean shirt of his from the drawer, went into the bathroom, and closed the door.

He sat on the bed, his head dropping into his hands. Would she ever trust him enough to share what was going on with her? He'd said he'd work on giving her space, and he'd meant it, but something was up, and he needed to know what it was. He hoped she hadn't put the pieces together of this stalker bullshit.

THE FULL REALITY OF WHAT SHE'D SIGNED UP FOR hit Emily hard. Jack would be on the road for nearly twenty months. Dinner at his parents' house, while awkward, was normal. The walk in the park had been nice even though, six different times, fans had come up to them. And dinner tonight had been normal—if having armed bodyguards could be construed as normal. She needed to accept this was how things would be.

As the tears streamed down her cheeks, she grabbed a towel so she could sob into it. She'd promised Jack she'd stop shutting him out, yet here she was. *Enough.* She washed her face and brushed her teeth, and when she opened the door, Jack sat on the bed.

"I'm sorry," she said.

He opened his arms and she walked in.

EMILY WOKE UP HOT AND SWEATING. THE LIGHT WAS off, and Jack was next to her, his arm slung over her like dead weight. She felt nauseated. Turning onto her back, she kicked the covers off. Jack's body heat smothered her. If she could get his arm off her without waking him, she could move to the edge. She inched away, waited, and then inched again.

"Where you going?"

She slumped back against the mattress. "I'm hot. I need some space to cool off."

"You mean away from me?" The mattress dipped as he sat up.

"Don't say it like that. I get hot and stiff in my sleep. If I can't move freely, I wake up and can't fall back to sleep. No big deal."

"It's a big deal to me." Jack moved closer until his erection poked her in the back. "I get hot and stiff because of you."

"Not all guys like to cuddle, Jack." Sully hadn't been a cuddler.

"I need it." He rolled away, and the bed shifted when he stood.

"You don't have to leave."

"I'm not."

The window creaked loudly in protest as it slid up. "Scoot over." He crawled into bed next to her and drew the covers up over their naked bodies.

"It'll get cold in here."

"Perfect for cuddling." Jack pulled her to him, spooning her as his hand cupped her breast. "It's been my experience that guys do like to cuddle."

"And you'd know this how?"

"Take Elliot for instance. He's a huge cuddler."

"Really?"

"Yes. He's a caring and sensitive guy on the inside, but he doesn't trust people, so he hides that part of himself."

"Can I ask you a personal question?"

"Anything."

"You never fooled around with Siobhan?"

"A little. I got to second base. She was very shy, and I guess it brought out my protective instincts." Jack yawned. "I saw the way Elliott looked at her. He was awkward around girls, and he'd gotten even more quiet after his folks split."

"Elliott doesn't mind that you got to second base with his wife?"

"She wasn't his wife at the time, and it's more conducive to a long, healthy life never to remind a guy that you've been in the ballpark with his wife, let alone on any bases."

"You're a wise man, Jack McBride." She couldn't get comfortable. "There's so much going on inside my head."

He snuggled closer. "Tell me."

"Some of it's really stupid, but it feels so important."

"Stupid how?"

"Sully's very handsome. Women gawked at him, then looked at me like he could do better."

"Em, you're the most beautiful woman I've ever laid eyes on."

"I know you feel that way, and he used to say it too, and I believed him, but—"

Jack tensed.

She turned to face him. "Baby," she caressed his cheek with her fingertips. "You're better looking, taller, more muscled, great ass, hair's longer, sexy tattoos, you're a musician, which is a get laid free card, and your dick's bigger." She emphasized the last three words by grasping him.

A slow smile crossed his face. "Go on."

"I know it's stupid, but after I caught him, I was hysterical, and I vowed to never date a really hot guy again."

Jack kissed her forehead. "Guys stare at you, too. There won't be other women. You know that, right?"

Did she? "Yes. But—"

"Em—"

"Let me finish. With you, the difference is even greater. I'm not glamorous, and rock stars usually date models or actresses."

"Been there, done that."

"Yeah."

His head settled on the pillow with hers. "Then what's the problem?"

"Even being in a mini-spotlight makes me so uncomfortable. Being stared at and picked apart, like they know about my scars." Emily swallowed hard. She hated that she was so self-conscious, but they were still so ugly and thick.

"I don't care about your scars. I only see beauty when I look at you."

Emily moaned.

"What?"

"No wonder women gawk at you. Sexy outside with a beautiful core, and your ability to use words like that..."

"Tell me."

"Makes me tingle with desire."

Jack rolled her on her back. "I have just what you need."

Their lips met and hands stroked and caressed. He kissed down her neck to the hollow at the base of her throat. His tongue dipped in as his hand caressed her breast. "Mmm, good." When he took her nipple into his mouth, she arched off the bed. "Oh." She'd never been so physically in tune so fast with a guy. Now if only her head and heart would catch up.

He dipped his tongue into her belly button, which made her giggle. Over her belly, down her right hip, to her thigh. He'd gotten halfway before she realized what he was doing. She hadn't meant to tense up. Jack switched to her other leg and kissed, licked, and caressed his way back to her lips. He grabbed a condom and protected them. Jack rubbed his cock between her thighs, coating himself and pleasuring her.

As he entered her, he whispered, "I love you."

Something deep inside melted. He loved her gently, deeply, until they were both covered in a fine sheen of perspiration. The last thought she had before she tumbled into ecstasy was that she was happy she'd met him.

Long after Jack fell asleep, Emily lay awake. Jack held her so tightly she could hardly breathe. She needed some space, so she lifted Jack's heavy arm and moved away.

But she was still unable to stop the anxious thoughts whirling about in her head. Tomorrow would be their last full day together, and then the real test would start. She wanted this relationship to work, but she had no idea how to make that happen.

I wish I could've seen Jackie's face when he read my love letter. He loves dirty talk. Even though that groupie whore's still in his room, I know he's just having fun with her. His last hurrah before we're together.

I've spent months planning my life around his tour so we could meet in New York. That whore cheated me out of my Sleepless in Seattle moment, but I'm adaptable, always have been. I'll just have to do some rewrites is all. I know Jack better than he knows himself, but I'll do some research on the groupie, if she's still around after the band leaves for Hartford on Thursday. She doesn't look the type to be a groupie, yet here she is, which proves you can never tell.

I still want a memorable beginning to our new life together. I tap the calendar app on my phone and pull up my schedule and compare it to Jack's. Fuck! I can maybe get away at the end of June while Jack's in Chicago.

Yes, I can use the excuse I'm going to visit my family. He'll never question that.

One thing that won't need to be rewritten is the ending.

Jack and I will be together.

Chapter Nine

J ack woke Wednesday feeling great. They'd had amazing sleepy early-morning sex. He'd woken first and gone down on Em, making her come twice before he eased inside her, loving her until they'd both come and easily fallen back to sleep. She was still nestled into his side.

He'd only gotten up once last night to switch sides with her because she'd needed to move. He didn't care; he'd do it ten times if that's what it took to feel her next to him all night.

"Babe, I'm leaving for the gym," he whispered. She'd made him promise to wake her before he left. She wanted to get her writing in so they could spend the rest of the day together. Their last full day. For now.

"I'm up," she said.

Except she wasn't. She'd fallen right back to sleep. Jack whipped the covers back. She was curled on her side, and at the sight of her luscious, naked body, he groaned. Jack wanted to blow off working out. Buzz would understand.

"Go," she said, as she rolled onto her back. "Buzz is waiting."

Jack nodded. She was great. He dropped a quick kiss on

her lips before using super-human strength to walk out of the bedroom. "See ya later, baby."

After their workout, Jack and Buzz rode the elevator up together. "Rooster" sounded from Jack's phone, and he pulled it out and connected the call. "What's up?"

"We need to discuss the new security measures."

"When?"

"ASAP."

"Hold on. Jeff wants to go over the new security. Em will think we're still working out. Is now okay for you?"

Buzz nodded.

"We'll be right there."

"You sure keeping this from her is a good idea?" Buzz asked.

"She hates that I'm famous. I don't want to give her any reason to break it off. Things still aren't settled between us."

Buzz sighed. "Not everyone falls in love as fast as you do, bro. It hasn't even been a week."

"I know that, but I'll feel a lot better when she..." Jack looked down. He was still pushing her, and his feelings were growing even stronger.

Buzz clapped him on the shoulder. "She just needs time. It'll happen."

"You sound sure?"

"I have never seen two people more perfectly suited than you guys. As long as you give her time and don't fuck it up, it'll happen."

"When?" Jack whispered.

Elliot and Curt were there when Jack and Buzz entered Jeff's room. Jeff had several files laid out on the table where he conferred with Brick.

Jack wanted to discuss getting someone to keep an eye on Em, but he'd wait to do that until everyone left.

"Security camera caught a nondescript individual exit the

north stairs, walk down the hallway, and slip the envelope under Jack's door, then leave the same way."

"What do you mean, nondescript? Was it a man or a woman?" Jack asked.

"Couldn't tell. Individual was about five foot eight, baggy black sweatpants, oversized black hoodie with the hood up, baseball cap, sunglasses. Nondescript."

Jack paced the room. "Motherfucker." He walked to the window and looked out but saw nothing. "I pay you good money—" He looked at Jeff. "Sorry, man. I really thought this was just some bullshit. I guess it's getting to me." He sat on the couch, dropping his head in his hands. "Go on."

"Elliot, I've arranged a meeting with Matias Clark. Since this involves your wife, I thought you'd like to meet him."

"Yes, thanks." Elliot's voice wavered.

"I've got two more guys coming in, Elijah Vargas and Wes Fletcher. Vargas will meet us in Harford. Fletcher is on his way from the airport now."

There was a knock on the room door. Brick strode to the door, checking the peephole. He turned to Jeff. "It's Emily and Nicki. What do you want me to do?"

Another knock.

Jack stood.

"Jack." Emily's voice pierced the door. "Tell Jeff to let us in."

"Shit." Jack nodded.

Brick opened the door. Emily and Nicki sauntered in with smug expressions.

"Look, Nic, they're having a party in our honor, but we weren't invited." Emily walked to Jack and kissed him. "I'm not stupid."

"I know."

"We'll talk about this later. Sitrep, please, Jeff."

"What exactly do you think you know?" Jeff asked, trying to hide a smile.

She raised a brow. "Fine. Here's what we know. Friday, when Jack and I were out, instead of coming with us, you followed us. Same thing Monday in the park. When we went out to dinner, there was extra security behind us. Curt told Nicki that someone's been screwing around with his equipment."

Emily paused to look at Nicki. "Have I missed anything?"

Nicki tapped her forefinger on her lips. "Let me see, extra security, sneaking around, equipment gremlin... Ah, yes. Last night in the bar, Miller and Polson walked in and tried not to look like they were watching us."

Emily snapped her fingers. "Right, I forgot about them. Thanks, sweetie."

"All easily explained. Routine security. The band is very popular, and we're here to protect them and their interests," Jeff said.

"Their interests? Hmm, that's a new word for it." Emily turned to Jeff. "Jack has a stalker."

Every guy that wasn't trained security looked down or away from Emily and Nicki.

"That's a leap, don't you think?" Jeff asked.

"No, I don't. Occam's Razor."

"Who's Occam and why do we care if he has a razor?" Curt asked.

"It's a theory by William Occam. The simplest explanation is usually the correct one," Nicki said. She put her arms around Curt and kissed him. "We know something is going on. I wanted to sex it out of you, but Emi prefers the more direct method." She made a face. "She never lets me have any fun."

"What makes you think it's Jack that has a stalker?" Jeff asked.

"His equipment wasn't screwed with. Whoever it is, probably a girl, is trying to make Jack look good by making Curt look bad."

Jeff nodded slowly. "Damn, I hadn't thought of that."

"So, sitrep?"

Jack was so proud of her. "Go on, we're busted."

Jeff gave a succinct explanation of everything that had happened since Jack received the first letter.

"Can I see the letters?" Emily asked.

Jeff looked at Jack, and he nodded. Jeff pulled out copies of the letters and handed them to Emily.

Nicki looked over Em's shoulder. "Ooh." Nicki shuddered.

Curt pulled Nicki to him.

"What do you make of this?" Jeff asked.

"Well, the creepy factor is a ten. But smart, no tech trail, no prints or DNA, can't match a printer. No postmark."

"The first ones were mailed, but the postmarks were all different. This is the first one that was hand-delivered," Jeff said.

"When did you get the first letter?"

Jack cleared his throat. "A week after Christie and I broke up."

Emily placed the letter on the table and turned to him. "Is she in town?"

Jack shrugged.

She turned to Jeff. "Has she been eliminated as a suspect?"

Jeff rubbed the back of his neck. "Yes."

"You don't seem so sure now."

Jeff sighed. "Brick, find out where she is."

Brick pulled out his phone and left to make a call.

This was a fucking nightmare. Jack felt the walls closing around him. He couldn't read Em's expression and it worried him. If this stalker cost him his chance with Emily—

"Person is patient," Emily said to no one in particular.

"Patient?" Jack asked.

"Yeah, cutting out these letters is labor intensive. They're all caps, so they'd have to plan out what they wanted to say first."

"Why?" Jeff asked.

"Because magazines only use this size on the first letter of an article. They'd need a bunch of magazines and have to search out the letters needed."

Jeff was obviously impressed. He made a quick note. "What else?"

Emily held the first and last one next to each other. "Nothing special about the paper or envelopes, but what about the scissors?"

"Scissors?" Jack asked.

"It's hard to tell from the copies, but in the first letter, the edges of the letters are sharp. This one, not so much."

Jeff looked at both letters. "I don't know, let me make a call." He walked into the bedroom.

Emily walked to him, and he opened his arms. "I never thought you were stupid." He was actually relieved that she knew; he hadn't liked keeping it from her. He was proud that she'd figured it out so quickly, but he was also scared.

Jeff returned. "They'll look into it. But they're not hopeful."

"I assume you vetted the crew?" Nicki asked.

"Handled it myself," Jeff said.

Emily made a face.

"What?" Jack asked.

She looked at Jeff, who gave her a slight nod, before answering. "Well, background checks are only part of the equation. If someone's never been in trouble with the law, doesn't mean they're innocent, just haven't been caught."

Buzz and Curt looked at each other. Elliot and Jack sat on the couch.

"Don't assume it's a woman, either." Emily paced the room.

"You said it was a woman," Buzz said.

"I said probably. Could be a man, could be a team. Anyone who could develop a sick obsession with another person would be a magnet to a similar person. Maybe she's in love with Jack, and her boyfriend wants to please her, so he stalks Jack to excite her."

Jack was fascinated with how her mind worked.

"Or, the man could be fixated on Jack, wanting to be him." Nicki joined Emily in pacing. "Imagining you somehow have the life he was meant to, getting extensive plastic surgery to look like you."

Emily nodded at Nicki's conjecture. At least Jack hoped it was conjecture.

"Why would anyone want to look like Jack-off here?" Elliot asked.

Emily and Nicki stopped pacing and looked at each other. "So he could dispose of Jack and replace him."

"Dispose of Jack?" Curt looked puzzled.

"Yeah, baby, you know, *cchhtttt.*" Nicki made a slashing gesture across her throat.

Curt dropped into the nearest chair. "What the fuck is going on here? We're musicians. This is so fucked up."

Nicki walked over and sat on Curt's lap. "I'm sorry, baby. We're only speculating."

Buzz still stood by the door. "Jeff, come on, this is just wild imagination stuff, right?"

"Until we can rule it out, anything's a possibility."

"Why didn't you tell us this was so serious?" Elliot sneered. "We thought it was some crazy broad who wants to make Jack her sex slave, not some psycho who might want Jack..."

"I made Jack aware of the possibilities."

Jeff had a few inches on him, but that didn't stop Elliot from getting in his face. "Why the fuck weren't we included? Jack's our brother, we had a right to know."

Jeff's lip twitched, but Elliot didn't back down.

"Because I told him not to."

Elliot's fury turned from Jeff. His faced reddened, and he balled his fists. "Why?" he asked through tight lips.

"Because I don't want you guys in the line of fire." Jack hadn't really thought this was so serious until now. Jeff had mentioned similar scenarios to the ones Em and Nicki had suggested, but Jeff had said the same thing—most likely one person, a woman, who had an unhealthy fixation on him.

"It was at my suggestion," Jeff interceded.

Elliot's full fury returned to Jeff. "Why? Because we're dumb musicians, who can't wipe our asses without help?"

"No." At Elliot's scoff, Jeff nodded. "Okay, yeah, in the beginning, before I knew you, yeah, I thought that. But once I got to know you, I've come to respect you as the responsible men you are."

Elliot's anger slowly faded. He slumped back on the couch. "You should've told us, Jack."

"Honestly, I hadn't taken this seriously. The scenarios Jeff laid out seemed more bad Hollywood movie than reality. I'm sorry."

They all shared a look, and then they were good. Guys were easy. Women, on the other hand...

"Since we're being all open now, Jeff, I assume you vetted *everyone*?" Emily asked.

Jeff nodded.

"What do you mean, everyone?" Buzz asked.

"Everyone. The crew, ex-girlfriends, your management

and their staff, anyone who ever sent a creepy fan letter, weird third cousins, you guys."

"Us? Why?" Elliot asked.

"To be thorough." Emily looked at Jeff expectantly then smiled at Elliot. "Well?"

"Yes."

Elliot dropped to his knees next to Jack and took Jack's hand. "My secret's out. Jack William McBride, will you marry me?"

Jack pushed Elliot away from him. "You're already married, Black."

"Siobhan's been my beard all these years, to hide my man-love for you."

Jack looked at Em, and her smirk said it all.

Curt and Buzz joined Elliot. "Hey, why do you get Jack? I've known him longer," Buzz said. "Jack, forget Elliot. I'm better looking and nicer. We belong together."

Curt took Jack's face between his hands. "I love you, Jack. Marry me."

Before Curt could kiss him, Jack shoved him away and walked to Emily. "Why?"

"You should've told me." She went up on tiptoes and kissed him. His bandmates, not ones to let a joke go, fell to the ground in agony.

"You know they're not gonna let this go anytime soon," Jack said.

Emily smirked. "I'm counting on it."

Agony turned to laughter. Elliot could hardly breathe, but he pointed at Emily. "Evil genius."

EMILY ENJOYED THE SHOW. THE GUYS WOULD BUST Jack's balls about this for a good long time, and it served him right. They were having a good time laughing their asses off. After the serious conversation, it was a way to blow off steam. Emily couldn't blame them. She'd hoped she was wrong, but when she brought it up to Nicki, and she'd told her about the equipment stuff, Emily had been worried.

Jeff was smart, efficient, and astute. Jack and the guys couldn't be in better hands. Still. "How many security guys do you have that know?"

"Three. I'm adding two more."

"Good." She didn't want to be alarmist, but she'd had that creepy feeling of being watched again yesterday, and she was pretty sure it wasn't because Jeff followed them.

"What is it?" Jeff asked. When she didn't answer, he added, "Nothing is silly. If you've seen something, we need to know about it."

"I didn't see anything. It's just that, when Jack and I were out, both days, I had the distinct feeling I was being watched. I'd assumed it was because people are always staring at Jack, but this felt different."

"How?" Jeff said.

"The hair on the back of my neck stood up, and I got a creepy feeling."

Jeff grabbed pen and paper. "When and where?"

"Friday when we left The Rock House, after I saw you"— Emily smiled—"while we were walking. Then again while I waited on line for water outside the jewelry store and outside the café where we had lunch. Yesterday in the park, when we were near Strawberry Fields."

"You saw me yesterday too, didn't you?" Jeff asked.

Emily shrugged. "Yeah."

Jeff's eyes narrowed. "Anything else?"

"I'm not sure." She'd thought someone was outside Jack's hotel room yesterday, but she'd chalked it up to another guest stopping to check their phone. "After Jack left yesterday to go workout, I thought I heard someone outside the door, that he'd forgotten his key card. When I opened the door, no one was there, but I smelled perfume."

"What time?" Jeff asked.

"Ten after nine."

Jeff called hotel security. "Son of a bitch."

Emily had a sick feeling in the pit of her stomach.

"System was down for routine maintenance from eight until noon."

Jack put his arm around her. "You think that was a first attempt to deliver yesterday's letter?"

"Could be." Jeff rubbed his beard stubble. "Jack told me your dad was in private security. Did he train you?"

Emily shook her head and smiled. "Ever since we were little, my dad played this game with us when we were out. He'd say he spotted something and give us one clue, and we had to figure out what it was."

"Did your mom play too?"

"Yeah, once you thought you knew what it was, you'd say 'got it' and wait for everyone else to catch up."

Jeff smiled. "You always got it first, didn't you?"

Emily considered that. "Not at first, Riley was four years older, so he'd been playing longer, but by the end, I left Riley and my mom in the dust. Sometimes, I'd hide things in the yard, you know, to test my dad. Got him a couple times."

"You lived on base?"

"Yeah, until my dad retired. When we were older, he'd have some of his Marine buddies, who worked for him, follow us to see who figured it out first."

"He was training you to be aware of your surroundings. Did an excellent job." Jeff shook his head as a small smile played on his lips.

Emily had always been proud of her dad, and it pleased her immensely that Jeff was impressed.

"Next time you get that feeling, I want to know immediately. Understood?"

Emily smiled at Jeff's authoritative tone. "Yes, sir."

"Good." Jeff smiled.

"Hey, Emi, now you and Jack have something else in common."

Emily turned to Nicki, giving her a warning look, but Nicki was looking at Jack.

"What's that?" Jack asked, standing behind Emily and wrapping her in his arms.

"Nic, ball gag, one word or two?"

Nicki narrowed her eyes at Emily. After a second, Nicki's confusion cleared away to understanding. "Two." She looked down.

Emily felt Jack tense. *Shit.*

"Nicki, what do we have in common?"

Nicki looked at her apologetically. "You both have stalkers."

Emily's chin dropped to her chest. *Fuck.* Jack's arms tightened around her, and Jeff stepped in front of her. Nicki returned to her kill list. "It's not like she's making it sound."

"Do you have a stalker?" Jeff asked. He tilted her chin up until she met his eyes.

"Not really." Damn Nicki and her ever-open mouth. She'd have to start carrying that ball gag. She'd get her a pink one.

Jack turned her to face him. "What the fuck does that mean?"

"He sent some letters and flowers and balloons."

"Is he in jail or dead?" Buzz asked.

"He's in a psych ward," Nicki said.

"No, he's not," Emily said.

"Since when?"

"About a year ago."

Jeff cleared his throat. "Details. Now."

Emily gave Nicki a death glare as she plopped on the couch. Everyone watched her expectantly, and they looked worried. She sighed. *Definitely need to buy a ball gag.* "It's really nothing like Jack's stalker. A fan got...obsessed and then a little...deluded. But he got help, and now he's monitored. He hasn't contacted me." Emily had never told Sully about it because they'd only been dating a short time, but Nicki had known.

Jack sat and hugged her. "You're so brave."

Emily laughed mirthlessly. She'd felt helpless and scared. "Yeah, so brave that I called Uncle Griff. He jumped on a plane from California, dealt with the police, and stayed for an entire week. Before he went home, he arranged for a buddy of his to keep an eye on me. I wasn't supposed to leave the house without him. I hated it."

"Uncle Griff?" Jack asked.

"My dad's best friend and business partner." For the first time in years, being the center of attention didn't make her wish she could disappear.

"Why didn't you tell me?" Nicki asked.

She looked genuinely hurt, which made Emily regret not telling her. "Because you thought he should get the chair for stalking me."

Nicki pulled away from Curt and stood in front of her. "You weren't worried enough."

"You were too worried, so we evened each other out."

"It doesn't work that way, and you know it," Nicki yelled. "I hired a private investigator to look into it. And you were constantly dodging your security detail."

Jack's head snapped up. "Why?"

"I can take care of myself. I never thought the guy was a real threat, just creepy." She turned to Nicki. "You hired a P.I.?"

Nicki softened. "I wasn't leaving my best friend flapping in the breeze. The sooner the guy got caught, the better."

Emily hugged Nicki. She was blessed to have her as a friend. Nicki was permanently removed from the kill list. Emily chuckled. "You finally kept a secret."

Nicki glanced around and then back at her and winked. "I think they're waiting for us to kiss."

"Okay." Emily leaned closer. At the last second, they said, "Pigs."

"Damn," Curt said.

Emily shook her head. *Men are so easy.* Jack wasn't amused. She went to him. "It was three years ago. I was never in danger."

"You couldn't have known that. You ditched your security. How could you?"

Emily scoffed. "Says the man who regularly ditches his security?"

"I don't ditch Jeff. Just wanted a normal outing with my girl. He followed us."

Her temper rose unexpectedly. "Yeah, that's normal."

"Enough, you two," Elliot said. "We have other business to discuss."

"Like?" Jack asked.

"Like no one says shit about this to Siobhan."

Everyone nodded in agreement.

Jeff stood. "I think that's it for now except to remind you this conversation doesn't leave the room."

"No one else knows about Jack's stalker?" Nicki asked.

"Just my team, Dex, the FBI, and now you two." He gave Nicki a pointed look.

"Contrary to popular belief, I can keep a secret," she said.

Just as they were leaving, Jack's cell rang. "It's Kevin." Jack walked to his door. "You guys want to hang around for a minute?"

They filed into Jack's room as he connected the call. "Hey, man, what's up?"

After a few minutes, he hung up and smiled. "Kevin was really impressed with Eric's proposal for revamping The Rock House. He still thinks it's risky, but since we all want to invest, he feels okay about it. You guys still interested?"

Nods of approval all around. Soon after, everyone left. Viv stopped by to pick up the items the band had signed for the ASPCA to auction off: two guitars, four tour jackets, a dozen shirts, and several sets of Buzz's drumsticks.

After Viv left, Jack paced the room. "Can we get it over with?"

"What?"

"The fight we're going to have about me not telling you about my...situation."

"No fight," Emily said.

Jack ran his hand through his hair. "So, you're not gonna scream at me and throw shit at my head?"

Emily furrowed her brow. "No."

Jack seemed to consider that. He resumed pacing. "Were you going to tell me about your stalker?"

"No."

"Just no?" Jack stopped short.

"It's no longer an issue."

"How can you say that? The guy's free."

"He's out but not free. His release was conditional on his continuing therapy, and he's not allowed to contact me or my publisher."

"Restraining order?"

"Yes."

"You're not concerned?"

"Not really. He's upheld the terms of his release."

She could tell he wanted to argue, but he managed to restrain himself.

"I'm going to take a shower." Jack stomped into the bedroom.

Emily sat on the couch. She was too upset to write. She hadn't thought about the stalker in quite a while. Jack was doing his best to give her some space. She got up and stripped on the way to the bathroom. When she walked in, Jack was already in the shower. She knocked on the shower door.

Jack opened the door and pulled her in.

"I'm sorry," she said. "It hadn't even occurred to me to tell you, but even if it had, I wouldn't have."

"Why?"

"It's not the kind of thing you bring up in the first week when you're dating someone."

Jack kissed her hard. "It feels like longer."

Emily didn't know what to say to that, so she said nothing.

Chapter Ten

Tonight was the band's last gig at the Garden, and Jack was both amped up and sad. Their last night together. He kept reminding himself that he'd be seeing Em Friday night. They decided she'd take the bus to Hartford instead of Albany so they could have two nights together. It was four hours either way, and she'd use that time to write, so she wouldn't feel guilty about the time they'd spend together. Since they'd be in Albany on Sunday, Jack planned on having lunch with Trish and Brad because Em was taking the two o'clock bus back to Oakdale. Jack felt more secure in their future. He was sure that they had one.

When they got to the Garden, the band went straight into their soundcheck. Siobhan sat with Emily and Nicki in the front row.

After the last song, Elliot jumped down and hauled Siobhan into his arms and kissed her. "How'd we do?"

When he finally let her up for air, she said, "Amazing as always." Her cheeks were flushed, and her eyes sparkled.

Siobhan had never looked lovelier, and Elliot practically floated on air when he walked.

"Guys, we need a minute to go over the details of the meet and greet," Brian said. Viv stood next to him with her tablet and a smile.

Emily wandered over to Holden. Jack could tell she asked him questions about his job because Holden, who was usually quiet, became animated and loud.

Wes, one of the new bodyguards that Jeff had hired, was dressed as a crew member, and milled around backstage. They hadn't told anyone they were bringing a new guy in, so hopefully the guitar gremlin would strike and be caught, and they could put an end to this stupid shit.

Brian stopped talking, and Jack realized he hadn't heard a word he said. "Shit, sorry, man. What?"

"When do you want to sign the merch for the meet and greet?" Brian asked.

All Jack wanted was to spend every second he could with Em, but he had a job to do. "After we eat." He walked over to Emily, who was now talking to the Pearlow sisters.

"Drums need to be tuned?" Emily asked Val.

"Sure do, and the heads have to be changed most days."

"How long does that take?" Emily asked.

"I get Buzz's kit from setup to ready to play in about ninety minutes," Val said.

Emily nodded and turned to Jack. "Wow, you weren't kidding when you told me you guys just show up. Did you know some of these guys get here at ten to start getting everything ready? And the light riggers start at six a.m.?"

The excitement in her eyes made Jack feel special. She cared. He knew it. "Yeah, baby, I do."

Emily blushed. "Of course."

He lifted her off her feet and kissed her. "Don't be embarrassed. I love that you're interested in this." *In my life.*

When Emily wrapped her arms around him, Jack had never felt more protected.

"Enough, you two," Elliot snarked. "The crew has to get back to work. I'm starving, let's get dinner." He bent and picked Siobhan up and carried her over to catering.

Emily's smile grew as she watched. "Another thing you weren't kidding about. Elliot's gooey center. He's like a different person."

Jack couldn't help himself. He kissed her with all the love he felt inside and only broke the kiss when Nicki whistled. He pulled back, expecting to see anger, but instead, Emily smiled at him.

EMILY SAT NEXT TO JACK AS THEY ATE DINNER. He had a small piece of chicken and some steamed veggies. Even though they were in the band's dressing room eating dinner, at Madison Square Garden, it felt normal. Friends having dinner before a concert was normal.

A single knock and the door opened. "We got him!" Jeff yelled. Relief washed through Emily. They caught Jack's stalker.

Everyone raced out the dressing room. Miller and Polson had one of the crew members by the arms. Emily had met him but couldn't remember his name. Then it dawned on her—guitar gremlin not the stalker. A lump formed in her throat. *Fuck.* When she saw the expression of disbelief and hurt on Jack's face, she forgot all about the stalker.

Curt walked over. "Jay, what the fuck, man? Why?"

Jay tried and failed to free himself. "Call them off, okay?"

"Not until you explain yourself," Curt growled. Jack, Elliot, and Buzz stood next to him.

Jay huffed. "When Milt left, you promised to hire my brother as your tech. He was crushed, and he's back to using."

Anger flooded Curt's face. "I have news for you. Bob was

high when he did the first gig with us. No way I was having that around here." Curt glanced sideways at Buzz.

"He was just nervous is all. He would've kept that shit out of Buzz's way. At least I'd have been able to keep an eye on him." Jay's face reddened.

Buzz stepped up. "Let him go."

Miller and Polson looked to Jeff.

"I said let him go," Buzz said through gritted teeth. "Jay, Bob's an addict. He needs help not more excuses. Believe me, he's making plenty for himself."

Jay's head dropped to his chest. "I don't know what else to do for him. He won't go into rehab."

Buzz nodded. "Until he's ready, there isn't anything you can do. He has to want it for himself."

"Would you...I mean...I know it's a lot to ask after what I've done, but would you talk to him?"

"Of course."

Jay took out his phone and dialed Bob, but it went straight to voicemail. No one expected it to go differently except Jay. Tears spilled down his cheeks.

"Listen, Jay, if Bob decides to get help, I'll pay for it," Curt said. "When I think about what could've happened to Buzz if he hadn't gotten the help he needed—"

Jay smiled at Curt. "I don't know what to say..."

Curt clapped him on the shoulder. "You don't have to say anything. One brother helping another."

Tears rolled down Emily's cheeks, and she took the tissue that Nicki offered. She was crying, too. As she glanced around, every crew member had either pained expressions or tears.

Brian cleared his throat. "What do you want to do about this?"

The guys formed a circle, and Jack shook his head. "Jay's always been such a solid worker and a great guy."

"Yeah, but after what he did, can we still trust him?" Elliot rubbed the back of his neck. "Buzz?"

"He's in a shitty situation. He took his anger out on Curt when he's really pissed at his brother. When my parents and Stephanie visited me in rehab for family day, it was the first time I'd really understood how angry they were at me for... everything. I had to accept that even though I'd never meant to hurt them I had. My sister's still mad, but it's getting better."

Curt wiped his eyes with the back of his hand. "I feel betrayed, you know? We're on the road with these guys for years, and I gotta know they have my back. But I get that he thought he could keep his brother clean if he was around. We all think stupid shit like that when we're scared for someone we love." The muscles in his jaw tightened and relaxed. "He didn't really do anything illegal, and nobody got hurt."

Elliot and Jack nodded.

"I say we give him another chance. If he fucks up again, he's gone," Buzz said.

"Agreed," Jack said. "Black?"

"Yeah." He looked at Brian.

"I'll handle it." Brian walked over to Jay who was still being guarded by security. He was visibly relieved that he still had a job. He waved in thanks and got back to work.

"Wow, I did not see that coming," Viv said. "Jay's been with the guys since their second tour."

Until she spoke, Emily hadn't realized that Viv stood next to her. "Obviously, no one did." Emily smiled at her. "Glad that's resolved."

Viv nodded and followed Brian as he went back to work ensuring the rest of the night would go smoothly.

After the gig, as they left the Garden for the last time, they stopped to watch Bernie beat Walt at arm wrestling.

"Sucker's bet," Jack whispered. "Bernie was a championship weight lifter."

It was their last night in New York, and Nicki and Curt wanted to go dancing. Emily didn't dance, and Jack wanted to be alone with her. Elliot wanted to spend the last night with his wife, and Buzz left to catch the end of a meeting. Nicki declared them all no fun and left with Curt to dance the night away.

They rode back to the hotel with Elliot and Siobhan. His hands never left her, and they smiled at each other like teenagers on a first date. They rode up in the elevator together, saying goodbye on the thirty-fifth floor. When they were alone, Jack pulled Emily into his arms and kissed her until their floor. The doors opened and closed twice before they got off.

The week had gone so fast, but it did feel like they'd been together for longer. This time last week, she'd been humiliated at work for being told to take time off, her wedding would've been two days away, and she'd been miserable. It seemed a lifetime ago. Emily didn't understand why she felt so sad at this being their last night together because she'd be meeting him in Hartford in two days. Even Jack couldn't expect her to have caught up to where he was, could he?

Chapter Eleven

As soon as they were inside their room, Jack took her into his arms and kissed her. He loved the way Em kissed him back, matching his passion, even surpassing it. He hadn't missed the look she gave the wall next to the six-foot penis, and Jack knew she wanted him to fuck her up against it like he had their first night, but he needed to make love to her.

Forcing himself to break the kiss, he took her hand and led her into the bedroom. He turned on the bedside lamp and pulled the covers down. Jack kissed the base of her throat and trailed kisses over to her shoulder, nipping her gently. His hands kept busy, caressing her warm, soft skin. By the time she stood before him naked, he ached with need. Emily's eyes glowed with desire. Her breaths came in short pants, and her body trembled.

Her smile turned wicked. "My turn." Emily wrapped her arms around his neck and pulled him down for a hot, wet kiss. When she pulled back, her skin had that lovely pink flush. Locking her gaze on his, she lifted his T-shirt, so Jack ducked to allow her to pull it over his head. Her hungry gaze ravaged his naked chest. His desire spiked.

Leaning in, she placed an open-mouthed kiss on his neck and then trailed her tongue down to his nipple. Every time her tight nipples grazed his bare chest, his dick throbbed. Emily knelt before him, and releasing the button and zipper on his jeans, she wasted no time in tugging them down. As soon as his dick was freed, she took him in her mouth, running her tongue along the underside.

"Damn, Em, that feels so good." He cupped the back of her head, stroking her hair. When he couldn't take another lick, he stepped back and helped her up. He shucked the rest of his clothes. Emily grabbed him by the hips and tugged him to her. Their lips crashed together, her warm mouth inviting him in.

Jack picked her up and laid her on the bed. "Lie back and put your feet up."

He couldn't take his eyes off her. She was spread open to him, already glistening, and he took a minute to enjoy the view. Jack stroked her calves and thighs, careful to avoid her scars. He didn't want her to feel anything but good tonight.

When Jack knelt before her, her moan of pleasure sent his blood racing. Inhaling deeply of her unique musky scent, Jack licked her clit before gently sucking it into his mouth. She was warm, wet, and swollen. When he licked her longways, Emily's back bowed off the bed. When he slid a finger inside her, her warmth surrounded him. Jack added a second finger, and her muscles contracted around them. "Oh." He sucked her clit into his mouth and brought Emily to her first orgasm of the night. The first of many.

Jack awoke around three to Emily stroking his chest. His brain and dick knew what that meant; she wanted sex. "Something I can do for you, baby?"

She leaned up and kissed him, her hand stroking his cock. "Yes. Can you guess what it is?" Her sleepy playful tone hardened him further.

"You want to talk about stock futures?"

She stroked him from base to tip. "No."

"The value of a diversified portfolio?"

This time when she reached the tip, her thumb circled, spreading his fluid around the head. "Nuh-uh"

"You want sleepy morning sex?"

"Bingo." She released him, reached over to her nightstand, and grabbed a condom. After protecting them, she straddled his hips, rubbing his cock between her wet lips. God, that drove him crazy. *Wish you'd do that bare.*

Emily stopped mid-stroke, shifted back, and rolled the condom off.

"What are you doing?"

"I think if we're careful, it'd be okay."

"What?"

"You wished you could rub your bare cock between my lips."

"I didn't realize I'd said that out loud."

"Not in so many words. It was more like so good, bare cock, pussy. Did I get it wrong?"

"No, but..."

"Let me drive, and we'll be okay."

Jack moaned and dropped his head back against the pillow. It was too good to refuse. "Okay."

She grabbed a condom from the nightstand and dropped it on the bed. Jack reached over and turned the light on; no way he was missing this. He adjusted the pillow behind his head to get a better view. Her pussy glistened. Soon he'd be glistening, too. Jack took a deep breath and reminded himself that he couldn't come like this. Someday, but not tonight.

Emily positioned him between her thighs, and the second she moved his cock between her wet lips, his head fell back against the pillow, and a long moan escaped his lips. "Fuck, yeah." She was so wet his dick glided between her folds.

"Aaaahhh," she moaned.

Emily cupped his balls in her hand, gently rubbing her thumb over the sensitive flesh. Jack's head spun. "Holy shit, that feels good."

She eased off.

"Don't stop."

"I'm not." Em shifted down, and cradling his balls, she rubbed her pussy over them.

His head shot off the pillow. "Holy fuck."

She continued to stroke his balls with her pussy, back and forth, driving him into madness.

Jack felt the familiar tingle in the base of his spine. "Sto—" Shit, it felt so good he couldn't even speak.

But she must've understood because she stopped. She walked backward on her knees, leaned over, and took him all the way in her mouth. She slowly released him, grabbed the fresh condom, and rolled it on. She moved into position, and with one final stroke between her thighs, he was inside her.

She moaned as she settled on him. Em leaned forward and kissed him, thrusting her tongue into his mouth. He cupped her breasts, their fullness filling his hands. On a groan, Em tore her mouth away from his. She braced her hands on his shoulders and rode him hard, her head falling back as her muscles tightened around him.

"Jaaack," she uttered as she climaxed.

Jack followed, coming so hard his vision blurred. She collapsed on his chest. He wanted to hold her, but his arms wouldn't move. Her breathing evened out quickly. Jack should take care of the condom, but he didn't. She felt too good.

His mind went over their first week together. Falling in love with her so fast and completely. Losing her. Winning her back. *Hopefully.* Jack was sure they'd made progress this week, but he wanted her to tell him she was in love with him even though he knew it was too soon. Tomorrow, the band would travel to Hartford, Connecticut, and he prayed that Em would follow through on her promise to visit him this weekend and not conclude that the craziness of his life was too much for her and end things. Ever the optimist, Jack pushed the fear away.

What he couldn't push away was the wildness of his emotions. Emily had come into his life and, like the roots of a tree, grown around every part of him. He wasn't complaining, but he would definitely fuck this up if he couldn't at least get some grip on his love for her. Which meant he needed to figure out why he was feeling so desperate and needy.

When he woke hours later, Em was tucked into his side and the condom was gone. They were scheduled to leave in four hours, and Emily would be going home. She had that meeting with a client who'd requested her. He felt a slight resentment toward the unknown client. If it hadn't been for him, Em might have traveled with them to Hartford instead of taking the bus tomorrow after work.

She was going to spend four and a half hours each way on a bus to see him. Warmth spread throughout his body. Em was making an effort, not leaving it all up to him, and Jack wasn't used to that.

Viv had dropped off Emily's tickets the night before because he'd insisted on paying. She'd fought him on it, but eventually, she'd seen reason.

Even though he'd see her tomorrow night, it wasn't good enough; he wanted her with him all the time.

Emily stirred in her sleep, making those small sounds that indicated she was waking up. She stretched and rolled onto her other side. Her leg was probably stiff, so he'd give her a few minutes to herself. His resolve lasted less than a minute when he realized she was crying. He stopped her when she sat up. "Don't, please." He wouldn't be able to stand it if she shut him out again.

Her shoulders rose and fell. "I need to cry."

"Come here."

Em lay on her side, and Jack cuddled up behind her, putting his arm around her and resting his head on her pillow. "Go ahead."

Her tense body relaxed as soft sobs escaped her lips. Jack didn't say anything, just allowed her the release she needed. When her tears subsided, he handed her a tissue. He'd hoped she'd confide in him, but she didn't speak. She also hadn't run, so he considered this a win. "Better?"

A small laugh escaped her lips. "Yeah." She turned onto her back. "You're the only guy who ever encouraged me to cry."

He kissed her lips. "It's a release. Everyone cries, there's nothing shameful in it. I don't like that you cry, but I much prefer this to you hiding in the bathroom."

"I thought guys hated crying because they're fixers."

Jack kissed her and smiled. "I'm still gonna fix what's wrong, but I'll never tell you not to cry." Her face was still damp from her tears. "You don't have to tell me." But he wished she would.

"I'm scared."

"Of?"

"I can't see my way with you; it's so far out of the realm of anything I've ever experienced. I don't know how we're going to be able to do this."

He knew she had doubts. Even if she hadn't just had her heart broken, their situation was unique. "We'll talk on the phone and Skype, but nothing will take the place of being together." He swallowed the lump in his throat. "We've planned out when we'll see each other for the next two months." Even though he'd been down this road before, it sounded paltry even to him. It certainly didn't resemble normal. "Anything else?"

"What happens later today?" Emily turned to face him.

"We'll say goodbye temporarily, and Jeff will drive you home."

"Shouldn't Jeff be with you?"

"I'll be fine. I'd take you home myself, but we have to leave at ten. No reason for you to rush out of here. Checkout isn't until noon."

"I'll leave when you do. I don't want to be here after you leave."

"Okay." That pleased him. "We'll say goodbye here for privacy. I know what I'm going to say."

"Say it now."

"Why?"

"The buildup is killing me."

Jack laughed. He should've guessed that. Something was always going on inside her head. He took her hand and placed it over his heart. "Emily Grace Prescott, I am in love with you. Head over heels, life-altering, can't be without you, love. My heart, soul, and body belong to you. If you were to roll up into a ball all the love I've ever felt, it'd be a marble next to a mountain. And I know that it's just going to keep growing, and it will have no end. Good thing the universe is expanding because it's going to need to."

"Wow. That was equal parts beautiful and scary."

Jack thought back to when Siobhan had yelled at Elliot to quit. Jack knew in that moment, if it ever came to that, he'd quit to be with Emily. "Whatever comes next, I want to be with you." He stroked his thumb over her lips. "Promise me you'll never tell me I have to give you up."

Emily furrowed her brow. "I don't understand."

"I know you don't, baby. It's still early, go back to sleep."

"You don't want to talk anymore?"

"I assumed you reached your threshold."

"I'm okay if you are."

Was he? It'd be easy to break the promise he made to himself not to beg her to give up her life here and be with him. He envied Curt having Nicki with him, and Elliot was optimistic Siobhan would join them soon.

"So..."

"What?" He could see the uncertainty in her eyes. "Ask me anything."

"It's not really my business."

"Ask away." Jack touched his lips to hers.

"Okay, was there any chance you'd have gotten back with Christie if you hadn't met me?"

"No."

"Zero?"

Jack turned on his back and Em snuggled into his side. "There was a tiny part of me that thought if she got sober maybe we could give it another try." Jack rubbed his hand over his eyes. "We were together over three years. I hadn't really moved on, but I knew the night we met that it was completely over for me."

He could feel her thinking. Maybe Jack shouldn't have admitted how he felt, but he believed in being honest.

Emily pushed up on her elbow and looked at him. "What did she do to support you?"

"Huh?"

"You moved to another state for her acting career. What did she do to help yours?"

He had no answer for that, so he shrugged. He'd been happy to help her; she was a good actress, and he'd been proud of her. She'd put in the effort but never seemed to get the return she deserved.

An unpleasant thought swirled in his head. That hot sex move Emily had used on him last night—he shook his head to get rid of the thought.

"Something wrong?"

What she'd done with a former lover was none of his business, so he lied. "No." Women had done a lot of things to him, but that was a new one.

"What happened to being honest with each other? Something's obviously bothering you."

Shit. "Fine. I know it's none of my business, but where did you learn that move?"

"Move?" Then she smiled. "Oh, that move. I didn't learn it. I just made it up. You were enjoying the other move so much I thought you'd like that, too."

"You've never done that before?"

"No, never even wrote about it."

Jack unclenched, but his relief was short-lived. He hated to bring the fucker up, but he felt compelled to warn her. "There's no easy way to say this, so I'm just gonna say it."

"I feel like we should cue the ominous music here."

Jack chuckled. "He's going to try to get you back."

Emily sighed. "A guy who does what he did can't possibly believe I'd take him back, which is an impossibility, or want to come back."

"And I'm telling you that he'll try to get you back."

"You can't know that."

Again, he placed her hand over his heart. "I do. Because if I did anything to fuck this up, I would spend the rest of my life trying to get you back. To be without you would be like asking me to live without air, and I would give up anything for you."

Her eyes glittered with emotion, but she didn't say anything.

They cuddled until the last possible second before Jack had to get ready to leave. They had a quick breakfast, and afterward, he had her up against the shower wall. Since Em had to go to work later, she took the time to blow dry her hair and apply some makeup. She looked beautiful to him either way.

They'd packed most of their stuff yesterday before leaving for soundcheck, so it didn't take long to pack the rest. Brick picked up Jack's suitcase, duffel bag, and guitar. He'd mastered traveling light on their first tour. The acrylic penis went to its new home in Curt's apartment in the Village. Apparently, Nicki liked it.

Jeff knocked when it was time to leave. The elevator whisked them to the garage—the fastest trip the fucking thing made all week.

He planned on understanding everything he could about Emily's life. Since Nicki would continue on with them, he'd enlist her help so he could be a good boyfriend to a writer. Which was just a warm-up to being her husband. *Husband.* Emily would be his wife. He'd never felt so sure about something. When they arrived in the garage, Jeff took her bag. Everyone was there except Elliot.

JACK'S LIPS CURLED INTO A DEVIOUS SMILE. "Elliot's late."

Emily looked at her watch. It was just ten. "Why's that funny?"

"He's never late. He always busts everyone's balls about being late, especially Curt. He won't live this down anytime soon."

"He's probably saying goodbye to his wife. Are you guys really going to bust on him for being late?"

Jack grinned. "Absolutely, and we'll enjoy it, too."

She swatted his arm. "That's not nice."

"Guys aren't nice."

Nicki came over and hugged her. Emily tried to stop the tears from forming in her eyes, but it was futile. Nicki was the perfect rock star girlfriend. She was glamorous, loved to travel, and wished her townhouse came with room service. When she pulled back, Nicki's brown eyes were filled with tears as well. Jack and Curt supplied tissues.

Emily had gotten to know Curt this week, and he was totally devoted to Nicki. He was sweet, and he loved taking care of her friend. But what really impressed her was how much Nicki had changed. She'd toned down her makeup because Curt had told her she was beautiful without it. Every guy she'd dated since Emily had known her had said the same thing, but this time, Nicki seemed to believe it. She hadn't needed her friend to tell her that she was in love with Curt because it showed in every move she made. Nicki was a born flirt, but she only had eyes for Curt. It didn't bother her that other women gawked at him or touched him. She called it an occupational hazard, and she could hardly blame them since she couldn't keep her hands off him either.

Emily wished she could be so casual about it. She knew she'd have to get used to the attention Jack got from other women. She wasn't worried about him, but it pissed her off that other women touched him so freely, much like Nicki had the night they met. Jack had agreed to keep their relationship quiet, but she suspected that her known existence wouldn't stop women from groping him.

Elliot arrived a few minutes later looking like a new man. His time with Siobhan had gone well, and Emily was happy for them. She hugged him, Buzz, and Curt goodbye. Everyone got in the SUV except Jack.

She knew what he wanted her to say and suddenly felt awkward. Anything she'd say would sound so silly compared to how he felt. When they kissed goodbye, she melted into him. She didn't have any words that could top that.

Jack pulled back and wiped a tear that trickled down her cheek with his thumb. He turned and got in the SUV, and Emily watched as it drove up to the exit.

Her throat closed, and her heart pounded in her ears. "She's never coming back," Emily whispered as the SUV turned out of the garage.

Jeff cleared his throat. "Ready?"

Emily used the wet tissue to dry her eyes. "Yeah." She walked around the front of the SUV and got into the passenger side.

Back to reality.

Emily glanced at Jeff as he drove. He had an economy of movement that reminded her of her dad. He never did anything that wasn't necessary. He focused on driving and was no more relaxed even though the band wasn't in his care. That reminded her of her dad, too. Every time he returned from deployment, he'd be hyper vigilant. It was an expected part of their transition when they returned home. His obligation to his men never ended as far as he'd been concerned. They had varying degrees of difficulty returning to non-deployed life. Her dad always knew which guys would need his help, whether they wanted it or not. Ryan Prescott was a Marine, but he didn't tolerate any macho bullshit. He leaned heavily on her mom when he came home, and later, when she and Riley were older, he leaned on them, too. He expected no less from those entrusted to his command.

It wasn't an uncommon thing for the phone to ring in the middle of the night. Her dad always answered the call. Her mom was just as strong, raising her and Riley and taking care of everything so he could focus on his missions. They complemented each other in every way. She'd always been so proud of her parents. They were the perfect couple.

Traffic eased after they crossed the George Washington Bridge into New Jersey. Emily cleared her throat. "So, what's his name?"

Jeff didn't look at her. "Who?"

She knew Jeff knew who, but she admired his loyalty to

Jack. "The guy three cars back in the navy sedan that Jack hired to watch over me."

Jeff slapped his hands on the wheel and smiled at the same time. "Damn, you're good. Fletcher did everything right, and you still saw him."

Emily laughed. "Actually, I didn't, but I suspected Jack would hire someone, and since he never brought it up, I was sure. I happened to look in the rearview mirror and saw a navy sedan." She turned and grinned at him. She wasn't sure Jeff had a sense of humor, but she decided to find out. "Rookie mistake."

Jeff burst out laughing.

Good, she'd never want to be on his bad side.

"You're a smartass," Jeff said with affection.

He used the Bluetooth to call Fletcher and bust his balls for being spotted. After he hung up, he glanced at her, taking his eyes off the road for the first time. "Can I ask you something?"

"Sure."

"What are your thoughts on this stalker bull—oney."

He was a gentleman, too. "Permission to speak freely?"

"Absolutely."

"The obvious choice is one of the women on the crew, but I talked to everyone and didn't get any weird vibes, and neither did Nicki. It has to be someone who's known him for a while. When Jack got the first letter last October, it wasn't common knowledge that they'd broken up yet."

"You think his breakup with Christie was a catalyst for this person?"

"Maybe she saw it as her chance. Or maybe she's lost touch with reality."

"Like your stalker?"

"Did Jack ask you to look into it?"

"Yes. I told him I wouldn't lie if you asked me."

"He wanted you to lie?" That didn't sound like Jack.

"No, I just told him I wouldn't, and he said he'd never ask me to. Anything you left out of the story?" Jeff asked.

"I left out some details, but nothing pertinent."

"What kind of details?"

"Like how he wrote intimate scenes in his emails, wanting to act them out with me."

Jeff's hands tightened on the steering wheel. His mouth opened then closed.

"I think the word you're looking for is ew."

Once they arrived at her apartment, Jeff carried her bags and waited while she unlocked her door. When she turned to take them from him, he grunted at her, so she led the way up the stairs. "Thanks, Jeff, I really appreciate it."

He put her bags down and looked around before walking into the dining room and then the kitchen.

She followed him into the kitchen. "Can I get you anything?"

"No."

"What are you doing?"

Jeff checked the window over the kitchen sink, then turned, and leaned up against the counter. "Only one entrance?"

Ah, recon. "Yes, I couldn't find an apartment with two, but it's second floor, and third in the back where the bedroom is because there are garages underneath."

Jeff nodded curtly and walked through the doorway back into the dining room. Emily leaned up against the hallway wall. "Did Jack ask you to survey the place?"

"No. This is for my peace of mind."

Emily was touched. Turned out, the hardened Marine had a soft gooey center. Just like her dad. "Would you like to see the rest of the place?"

"Yes."

Emily walked down the hall, stopping at the first door on the right. "This is my office." She stepped aside so he could enter. He opened one window and looked down then closed and locked it again. Across the hallway was the bathroom, and she flipped the switch. There wasn't a window, so Jeff nodded, and she walked to the end of the hallway and into the bedroom. There were two sets of double windows, one opposite the door and the other over the bed.

Jeff looked out the first set that overlooked the parking lot in back. "No fire escape?"

She pointed to the double windows behind the headboard of her bed.

"Not easy to get to." Jeff looked around and seemed to conclude what she had; the queen bed wouldn't fit anywhere else. "Poor design."

"Yeah, but if I have to get out, I'll just climb over the bed."

"Good."

He nodded, and they returned to the living room "This was a good choice, second floor apartment on the end. If you have to jump, throw out the couch cushions and anything else that could soften your landing."

She knew better than to salute, so she smiled and said, "Sir, yes, sir." Just like she used to say to her dad when she was being facetious.

Jeff smiled. "I was a gunnery sergeant." He turned, and she followed him down the stairs. "Lock the door behind me."

He was so much like her dad, and he was looking out for her. Marines did that. Her father had kept in touch with the families of his fallen men up until the day he died. "And, Gunny, take the babysitter with you."

Jeff turned and sighed. "He'll be pissed."

"I understand he's concerned, but he should've talked to me about it. Now he will."

Jeff gave his signature curt nod. "Will do."

When she shut the door, she looked out the peephole as she locked it. Jeff waited until he heard the click of the lock before leaving.

She went into her bedroom and changed into her work clothes. She was glad she'd gotten ready at the hotel. Her cell blared with "Riot" by Vince's band. It was the first song he'd written. She knew because he'd written it in rehab. "Hey, Vince. What's up?"

"Something you want to tell me?"

"No. Why?"

"Does Eddie know?"

"Know what?"

"That your dating Jack McBride."

A rush of heat flooded her system, and it was hard to take a breath. Luckily, Sully's favorite chair was nearby, so she sat. Anger boiled over. He'd had four weeks to pick up the rest of his shit. *What the hell was that about?*

"Hellooooo?" Vince said.

"What?" Emily barked into the phone, snapping her back to Vince. She took a few deep breaths.

"I asked if Eddie knew you were dating Jack McBride?"

How the hell did Vince know? *This is a disaster.* She'd never lied to Vince or Eddie, and as tempting as it was, she wouldn't start now. "No."

"Just no?" Vince asked.

"How do you know? It's supposed to be a secret."

"His picture is plastered all over *LA Today* with a headline proclaiming the Jack and Christie dynasty is over. Jack moves on."

They'd seen paparazzi the few times they'd gone out, but she always turned away. What had she gotten herself into?

"Unclench, Prescott, there's no clear picture of your face, McBride did a good job of obscuring you. I'm the only one who knows it's you."

"How's that possible?"

"Because I'm the only one with the math skills to pull it off."

"You suck at math."

"Normally, that's true, but even I can add one plus one."

"What's the other one?"

"You think I don't know what backstage sounds like?"

"Backstage?"

"When you called me Thursday about your friend who couldn't reach his sponsor, you were backstage. Buzz's voice sounded familiar, and after I saw the pictures in this morning's paper, one plus one."

"You know them?" She slumped back into the chair.

"We're not best friends, but we've crossed paths with them over the years, been at the same festivals. I see McBride around town every so often."

Shit, she should've thought of that.

"He's a good guy, Emi. Not into all the Hollywood bullshit, or rock star bullshit for that matter, down to earth."

Emily rubbed her temples. She did not need a headache today.

"Are you sure you're ready for this? It's not like you to jump into another relationship so quickly. Not to mention, he's about as famous as it gets."

"I'm not sure about anything."

"Better figure it out before he falls for you," Vince said.

"Too late." No one understood her better than Vince, Eddie, and Trina. They'd been there for the rebuild of her shattered life. Nicki was a close second.

"Does he know?"

"Most of it." Vince didn't say anything for so long she checked to see if they were still connected. "What?"

"That's not like you."

"Yeah, I have no explanation, except he asks a lot of questions, and I felt comfortable with him.

"Huh."

"What?"

"Nothing. When are you telling Eddie?"

"I have no plans to tell anyone right now. Nicki knows and now you." Emily laughed. "You want someone to commiserate with, is that it? Call Nicki, she's always good for a two-hour conversation."

"No shit, Eddie and I got stuck on more than one three-way with her this past month."

She let that three-way comment go. "Really, why?"

Vince sighed. "We were worried about you. You weren't talking, so we had to resort to subversive measures."

"Thanks." She'd promised herself she wouldn't do a search on Christie, but Emily broke down yesterday after Nicki told her she was stunning. And she was. Tall, blonde, flawless skin, no makeup needed, stunning. Even her hair in a messy ponytail looked impeccable. "You've met Jack's ex. Is she really that...perfect in person?"

"Emi, don't do this to yourself." Vince's tone softened.

"She is, isn't she?"

"She's an addict with an entitled attitude. *You* are perfect."

"You know that's not true." No one knew better than Vince and Eddie what her body had been through. The surgeries, the rehab, and the anger she felt over the hideous scars. She thought she'd come to accept them, but seeing Jack's beautifully unmarred, perfect skinned ex, with long legs that looked great in a miniskirt and sky-high heels, had proved unnerving. She'd never be able to wear anything like that again. She hated feeling this way, but she couldn't help it; no mantra was strong enough to counteract the ugly scars. They won.

"Does Jack feel that way?"

"No, but—"

"But nothing. I told you, he's a good guy. No guy that loves you cares about your scars. I don't."

"You sure they didn't matter to you?" She'd wanted Vince to be her first, but he'd said no.

Vince growled in frustration. "I turned you down because I refused to be a part of that fucked-up bucket list of yours."

Emily froze. "What bucket list?"

"Do you really want me to say it?"

Emily's face heated. "No. You searched my room?"

"I knew something was going on with you, and I was pretty sure what it was. Finding that list confirmed it."

They'd bonded over two things: they'd both been in a terrible car accident, and both had no family although Vince opted out of his because they were awful. "Did you tell anyone?"

"What am I stupid? If I'd told anyone, they'd have committed you. You needed out of that place not a state-sanctioned imprisoning."

Vince had always been smarter than her. He'd say street smart because of how he'd grown up. He'd known all these years and never said anything. A surge of anger rose, and she grabbed on to it because it was better than crying. "What guy turns down sex?"

"A guy that loves you."

"That makes no sense."

"Emi, do you forget how well I know you? Stop trying to pick a fight with me. I love you."

"Love you, too." But would she ever be able to say it to Jack?

Chapter Twelve

Emily arrived at her office thirty minutes before the meeting. The owners, Ben Bradford and Jerry Ross, greeted her as she walked in the front door. "You look lovely today, young lady," Ben said.

Ben looked sharp as always in a navy suit, white shirt, and blue-and-gray-striped tie. He and Jerry were the same height and build and had the same dark eyes and identical graying at the temples of their dark blond hair. Jerry still hadn't shaved his winter beard, and it was grayer than this time last year.

"What's up?" she asked.

"You were missed. Can't we just be happy to see you?" Jerry asked.

"Of course." In the five years she'd worked at Bradford and Ross, Emily had grown accustomed to their eccentricities. She loved their quirky sense of humor. Some of the employees thought they were nutters, but Emily knew better. They'd shared their story with her, and it explained a lot. They were devoted family men who saw their employees as an extension of their families. They treated everyone with respect. If one of their employees had a personal problem, they'd offer any assistance they could.

Cassidy, the receptionist, stepped from behind her desk and hugged Emily. "I'm so glad you're back. They've been nuttier than usual. You have a calming effect on the geezers."

Emily pulled back and looked Cassidy in the eyes. "They're not old enough to be geezers."

Cassidy was only twenty-two, and she thought everyone over forty was a geezer. Emily had been twenty-two when she'd started here, but she didn't think she'd ever been as young as Cassidy.

Ben and Jerry returned to their shared office. They each had a weird expression which she didn't have time to decipher. Her part of the presentation was completed before she left, but she went over it anyway. She'd been so crazed last week, and she wasn't as confident in it as she'd have liked.

As one of three copywriters in the office, Emily was part of the behind the scenes team that produced the marketing angle the client wanted. Ben and Jerry handled most of the presentations, and their sons handled the rest. Mr. Bennett had asked to meet the team when he'd first signed on with B & R and always requested Emily work on his campaigns.

The meeting went smoothly. Her copy had been well received with only a few changes requested. The deadline was Monday, but the ideas flowed, so she worked late to finish while they were still fresh in her mind. Her bosses were happy when she submitted the revisions to them by the end of the day. They never left their female employees alone in the office after hours. If they couldn't stay, one of their sons would.

They walked her to her car which wouldn't start. She called Triple A, and they returned to the office to wait with her.

"Can I get you gentleman some coffee?"

Ben stood at the bar that was enclosed in a large armoire.

"No, thanks. I'll never sleep. Jerry?"

He nodded, so Ben poured a second glass of The Balvenie Caribbean Cask fourteen-year-old scotch. "Emily, will you join us?"

"No thanks, I'll stick with water."

Ben grabbed a bottle of water from the mini fridge and waved her in. He handed his brother his glass and then sat on the corner of Jerry's desk. Jerry hated it when he did that, so Ben did it all the time.

"You poured yourself more, as always," Jerry noted.

"I'm older," Ben replied.

"Two days," Jerry said. "That barely counts."

Emily smiled. Ben would remind Jerry of that till the day they died.

"Counts enough," Ben said.

She sat in one of the two club chairs in the office.

"Did you enjoy your time off?" Jerry asked.

Emily nodded. "I'm sorry that—"

"My dear," Ben said. "You're like a daughter to us, stop apologizing."

"Does that mean I get a say in what home to put you two in?"

They burst out laughing. They'd always enjoyed her snarky sense of humor.

"I'd sooner trust you." Jerry leaned forward. "I think my daughter-in-law is trying to poison me, you know, to get the family fortune." He clutched his chest for effect.

"She adores you," Emily said.

"You don't know which one I'm referring to?"

Jerry had two sons and three daughters. "They both adore you, as you are well aware."

He smiled affectionately. "They are both exceptional young women, AJ and Doug are lucky young men. Still, it would make for an interesting story, don't you think?"

Ben and Jerry were two of the handful of people that knew Emily was a writer and the only two in the office. She'd told them when she'd asked to cut her hours down so she could focus more on writing. They were constantly coming up with story ideas for her. "I don't write murder mysteries."

Ben stood from his perch on the side of his brother's desk and sat in the large leather chair behind his own. "No, but one of your series is romantic suspense. Your next book could start as a whodunnit."

Emily swallowed hard and shook her head. She could never murder one of her characters; they were like family.

"It's a great niche to be in."

"How do you know that?" Emily asked.

"Research, young lady. It's part of what we do here."

Emily froze.

Jerry stood. "Ben, you're an idiot." He walked to the chair next to her, sat, and took her hand. "We did the research ourselves and cleared our browser history."

Emily relaxed back into her chair. "I'm sorry."

"Don't be. We're honored that you trusted us with your secret. We understand your reticence to be in the public eye, and I, for one, have never told another soul, not even Marjorie."

"Of course, you didn't tell Marjorie. Your wife can't keep a secret," Ben said.

They also knew about her accident. She was never really sure how they'd found out, but one day, they'd come out and asked her how her leg was and was there anything they could do.

Her cell rang. Damn, it was Jack. She'd forgotten to call him. "Excuse me." She walked into her office. "Hi. I'm sorry, I worked late and forgot to call you."

"You're still at work?"

Emily checked her watch. It was after seven. *Crap.* "Yeah, I finished a while ago." She was afraid he'd overreact if she told him about her car, but he'd said they needed to be honest with each other. "I tried to leave half an hour ago, but my car wouldn't start. I'm waiting for Triple A."

"You're alone in the office?"

Emily imagined Jack grabbing his jacket and running to save her. It was sweet, but she could take care of herself, and the sooner he learned that, the better. "No. The women in the office are never allowed to work late alone, so either my bosses or their sons stay until everyone's ready to leave. Company policy."

Jack gave a relieved chuckle. "Sounds like a good policy to me."

She'd always thought it was sweet—if a little old-fashioned —but she knew better than to argue with the brothers over company policy. The call waiting tone sounded. "Hold on. This might be Triple A." Emily switched over to the other call. "Hello?"

"Hi. Rick from Casablanca Towing. I'm outside."

"Great, be right out." She switched back to Jack. "Gotta go, truck's here. I'll call you when I get home."

"Okay, baby."

Emily grabbed her stuff. "Truck's here."

Her bosses waited while the tow truck driver gave her a jump start. The battery was completely dead, so he switched it out with a new one. As soon as the engine turned over, her headlights came on, which was weird because it'd been sunny all day. Rick figured she'd put them on by accident. She paid him, and when she pulled out of the parking lot, Ben and Jerry were right behind her.

By the time she got home, it was after eight, and she was starving. Emily changed into her pajamas and then called Jack. "Hi."

"Everything okay? What was wrong?" He sounded nervous and pissed.

"Yeah, battery died, the guy replaced it, no big deal."

"Any signs of tampering?"

Emily heaved a sigh. She hadn't pegged Jack as a worrier. "No, I left the lights on."

"Oh."

"What time do you go on?"

"Fifteen minutes. How'd your meeting go?"

She put Jack on speaker and opened a can of soup. "Great. Our client loved the copy, only needed a few tweaks, which I finished before I left. Ben and Jerry were happy with the revisions, so they're all set for Monday."

"Ben and Jerry?"

"My bosses."

Jack chuckled. "Your bosses are named Ben and Jerry?"

"Yes, but not that Ben and Jerry, so no free samples."

"They waited with you?"

"Yes. They worry about us like they would any member of their families. We had a nice chat."

"Did you tell them about me?"

"No."

Jack grunted. "Why not?"

"Because we agreed to keep this quiet." She tried to keep the frustration out of her voice but failed.

"You're not gonna tell any of your friends?" His voice lowered in volume, the way it did when he was pissed and trying to restrain himself.

Since she didn't want him to connect the dots to Vince the way he had to Jack, she'd decided he didn't need to know that one of her best friends knew. Emily wouldn't betray Vince's trust for anyone, not even Jack. "The more people that know, the more likely it'll get out. I thought you understood that." She wouldn't back down, and her body tensed.

Chapter Thirteen

Jack ground his teeth together. He couldn't help how he felt. "I thought we agreed to keep our relationship quiet from the press, not the people we care about. I feel like I'm your dirty little secret."

"That's bullshit, and you know it. If that were the case, I wouldn't have been seen in public with you at all."

"I don't want to fight. I miss you."

"I don't want to fight either."

He was pushing again. Fuck. "I had a great time this week."

"Me too."

And I'm head over heels in love with you. And being apart sucks, but you can't even say you miss me.

"Jack—"

"I'm sorry, baby. I said I'd give you all the time you needed. I'm not being fair. Gotta go. Love you."

After the gig, Jack went back to the hotel to sulk. He knew he was being unreasonable—expecting Em to fall in love with him so quickly after all she'd been through—but he couldn't help it. The entire day, he had trouble concentrating on anything but her. He'd begun her first book, *In A Heartbeat,* on the drive to Hartford, but he'd had to stop when he got to the first sex scene and imagined him and Em. It wouldn't do to be stuck in a vehicle with a hard-on and an audience.

He figured he had another two weeks before the fucker returned. He was having fun with little Miss Fake Tits now, but that was all it was. Jack had been there. There were girls you fucked and girls you married. Any girl who would do what she did was the former. Em was definitely the latter. As soon as the fucker realized his mistake, he'd try to win her back. He believed Em when she said she didn't want him back, but that wouldn't stop the fucker from trying.

What Em couldn't realize yet was that the longer they saw each other the harder their relationship would get. Being apart that much was bad for an established relationship, but for a new one, it almost always crashed and burned. She was so set on having a normal life. There was only so much normal he could guarantee her, and it wasn't much.

He stripped out of his clothes and opened his suitcase to grab his toothbrush and toothpaste. Inside the zippered compartment at the top, a piece of burgundy satin ribbon stuck out. That hadn't been there when he'd finished packing. He opened the zipper and pulled out a package of paper wrapped up in the ribbon.

His heart pounded in his chest. He placed the packet on the bed and slowly untied the ribbon.

Jack,
> *Something to help occupy your lonely nights.*
> *Em*

He flipped to the next page, and the title elicited a moan.

"Fuck"

There were six more. Each title made his dick harder until it moved with every thump of his heart. "My Slutty Professor," "Truth or Dare," "Skin," "Sex Therapy," "24 Hours: Dick Tock," and "Blown."

He lay back, fisted his cock, and jerked it like a teenaged boy. He closed his eyes, and naked pictures of Em flooded his brain. Her on her knees sucking his cock, the way she fondled her tits when she fucked him. Her bent over the arm of the couch as he fucked her from behind. The last image brought the release he desperately needed.

Fuck. That was just from the titles. Jack used some tissues to clean up and rested his head back on the pillow. It took several minutes for his pounding heart rate to return to normal. He grabbed the top story, entitled "Fuck," and turned the page.

Warning. Contains graphic sexual content and language. These are stories of pure lust. For your eyes only. Check reality at the door; it doesn't live here.

Em ;)

He turned the page, and even though he'd just come, his dick stirred in anticipation.

I walked into Cornell's on Fifth Avenue late. I'd been stuck in a three-hour meeting that would've lasted only thirty minutes if the CEO of Luthier Industries, John McCartney, didn't love the sound of his own voice so much.

I was supposed to meet my prospective client EV White an hour ago. I texted him I'd be late, but he never responded. I didn't know what he looked like. Fuck. The bar was packed with people dressed in business attire. It was New York City, for fuck's sake. People here still knew how to dress for work.

Then my heart stopped. I saw her standing there: long

dark hair, short burgundy dress, killer heels. Stunning. My pulse quickened, sending blood to my dick at an alarming rate. A round, high table near the bar opened up, and I raced to it for two reasons: to be closer to her, and I was afraid I'd pass out. I cast a surreptitious glance at my groin. My boner wasn't as noticeable as it could've been since my jet-black trousers offered some camouflage.

I should go to the men's room and rub one off, but I was afraid she'd be gone when I got back or, worse yet, with another guy. I couldn't say why I was so certain she'd leave with me, but I was. It was worth risking the embarrassment to keep looking at her. She was blowing off some asshole at the bar. Every guy in the place was checking her out. She was tall, big tits, full hips, and what I suspected was a spectacular ass. The minidress she wore ended mid-thigh, and her five-inch, black, fuck-me heels would allow us to have a conversation at eye level. And I can fuck her standing up.

I needed a drink, so I flagged down the nearest server and ordered a Hennigan's neat with a splash of water. My view of the burgundy goddess's profile was less than perfect. Her unrestrained laughter at something the bartender said captured the attention of everyone in the bar. Even the women were checking her out.

She turned, and our eyes locked. My pulse hammered through my veins. She was checking me out, so I turned to give her the full effect. My six-two body was in peak shape. She slowly scanned me head to toe, and when her eyes returned to mine, I knew she wanted me, too.

It wasn't the first time, and wouldn't be the last time, I got laid in the men's room of a bar, but somehow, I knew this would be memorable. I smiled my most charming smile—the one my college girlfriend told me made all her friends wet. Since I fucked most of the them, I knew that firsthand.

She smiled back, her eyes glittered, and her nipples were

knotted. That was all the encouragement I needed. The server put my drink on the table. I pulled out my wallet, but she stopped me.

"Compliments of the lady at the bar."

It wasn't the first time a woman had bought me a drink, but I was stoked that this chick made the first move. I was definitely going to fuck her. And soon. I tipped the server a twenty. The goddess sauntered over. If you'd asked me ten seconds ago if my dick could get any harder, I'd have said no. I'd have been wrong. I moved closer to the table, because no amount of jet-black fabric could hide my enormous erection.

"Hi," she purred.

"Hi. I'm—"

"Please, no names."

Holy fuck. Not only was she a walking wet dream, but every guy in this place had jerked it to the fantasy of a hot fuck with a nameless woman. If my dick got any harder, it might explode.

Normally, I took the lead, but she came to me, so I let her. I sipped my drink, almost wishing I'd ordered it on the rocks. I was picturing her ample "C" cups naked and in my hands. A bead of cum emerged from my dick. I pictured her full burgundy lips licking it off. I needed to abort this line of thinking, or I'd come standing here.

She smiled knowingly and licked her lips as she leaned in. "Let's go."

I threw back the rest of my drink and took her hand. She led me to the back of the bar, pulling me along with a strength I wouldn't have assigned her. She paused at the door to the ladies' room before pushing it open and peering in. She winked and tugged me in, locking the door behind us.

Our hands wasted no time. I cupped her tits, and she thrust her hand down my pants and grabbed my cock. Her lips tasted like gin and tonic.

She pulled back from the kiss. "I wanted to fuck you the minute I saw you."

Normally, I said that, but whatever. I knew we were on the same wavelength the second our eyes met. "I want to see your tits."

She pulled her hand out of my trousers, turned, and lifted her hair out of the way. I unzipped her, the dress fell to the floor, and she stepped out of it. I expected her to let it pool at her waist, but this was better. Her bra and thong were the same burgundy as her dress. Her ass was beyond spectacular. I couldn't wait to see the front, but I couldn't let an ass like that go unworshiped, so I dropped to my knees and cupped her ass cheeks in my hands, kneading the flesh. I kissed the top of her crack, and she moaned. The scent of her pussy filled my nostrils. My lips brushed her right cheek as my hand slipped between her parted legs; her cream coated her inner thighs. Foreplay was officially over.

I licked my fingers as I stood. She faced me, her hands deftly undoing my belt, the button, and zipper. Her dainty hand rubbed my dick through my underwear. It wasn't enough. Hooking my thumbs inside my pants, I shoved everything down. My dick burst out, and she knelt and devoured me. Still not enough, so I cupped her head as I fucked her mouth hard. If I kept this up, I was going to come, so I pulled out.

She sat back on her heels and looked up at me, licking her lips. "Your cock is huge. I was afraid it wouldn't fit." My cock responded with a jerk. Her nipples peeked out the top of the lace push-up bra. She knew I was staring, so she cupped her tits and pinched her nipples. Fuck, I loved a woman who touched herself. I stroked my cock. My nuts tightened. I'd like to come on her, but I really need to fuck her pussy. Unless... "There's a hotel a few blocks from here." I could definitely fuck her at least five times.

She stood. "Sorry. I have a flight out of JFK. I have to leave for the airport in thirty minutes."

Son of a bitch. My brain had conjured the five ways I'd fuck her. Standing, of course, wouldn't let those heels go to waste. She'd blow me. Bend her over and fuck her in the ass. She'd ride me, I love the view of a woman as she fucked me. Last, but certainly not least, I'd fuck that sweet, wet pussy from behind so I could bury my huge cock in her. I wasn't selfish, so I'd eat her pussy in between.

"Clock's ticking," she said, her voice echoing off the tiled walls.

I snapped back to reality, and she was naked except for the sky-high heels. "Your tits are fucking spectacular."

Her full lips formed a pout. "They're lonely." One of her manicured hands covered her tit, tweaking the nipple, while the other trailed down her flat stomach and between her lips. Her head dropped back as she pleasured herself. Fuck, I'd love to let her finish, but time was passing.

I kicked off my pants and underwear while unbuttoning my dress shirt. I would've ripped it off, but she was still playing with herself, so I thought she'd enjoy the show.

I'd like to get a picture, but as I stared, she looked at her wrist. She wasn't wearing a watch, but I got the idea.

I pushed her up against the wall and lifted her right leg, which she curved around my ass. My dick was in position, so I thrust. Her cream provided all the lubrication needed for my cock to slide deep. Her head was back against the wall, eyes closed, face locked in ecstasy. I stayed like that, enjoying her tight pussy around me. One hand scratched her long nails up and down my back while the other cupped my balls.

Gotta fuck her now. I lifted her slightly, and both long legs wrapped around my waist. I pounded into her, and with each thrust, she tightened her pussy around me, increasing the friction to almost unbearable levels. Her tits were in my face, so I sucked her hard nipple into my mouth and tugged on it with my teeth. Her head flailed from side to side.

Someone knocked on the door, but I didn't give a fuck. Neither did she. She was so lost in the moment I wasn't certain she even heard the pounding.

My balls felt like they were going to explode as she tightened even further, and her cream bathed my cock. I was going to come, so I fucked her harder. Our lips finally met as I exploded inside her. I kept thrusting, and she came again.

A satisfied smile crossed her lips as she lowered her legs. I made sure she could stand before I pulled out. My cock glistened with her cream. I took a piss in the stall while she cleaned up. We both dressed in silence. Words weren't necessary since we both got what we wanted.

Another knock on the door, and this time, someone said, "Evie, we gotta leave."

She smiled. "That's my driver."

"Wait. are you EV White?" Shit.

"It's Evie, not EV," she said with a smile and left.

Best business meeting ever.

Jack wasn't sure when he grabbed his cock and started stroking, but now he had to finish. It didn't take long. A few long strokes and he came hard. It was too late to call Em, so Jack went into the bathroom and cleaned up. Exhausted, he crawled into bed. He grabbed his phone off the nightstand and sent her a text: *You are the best girlfriend ever!*

As he typed out the word girlfriend, he said a silent prayer that she wouldn't bail on him tomorrow.

Chapter Fourteen

E mily smiled to herself as she waited in Grand Central Station for the bus to arrive. She'd woken on the couch at two in the morning, covered in sweat, a nightmare jarring her awake. The glass of wine sat untouched on the coffee table, and Nicki's manuscript was on the floor. She'd stood too quickly and lost her balance, hitting her knee on the edge of the table. She hadn't been able to sleep after that. She'd checked her phone and saw Jack's text. He'd found her surprise. She'd texted him back a single emoji: shit-eating grin smiley face.

It'd been too early to call him before she'd left for work. He'd called around ten, but she'd been busy and had to get off the phone. She had several clients to get copy done for, and since last week had been so bad, she was anxious to get the job done right. He had an interview during her lunch break, so they hadn't been able to talk then, and after work, she'd been in a rush to get into the city to catch the bus to Hartford. The band was doing soundcheck now, so she called Eddie.

"Hey, beautiful," Eddie said. "How ya doin'?"

"Better." It was too soon to tell him about Jack.

"You sound better. I'm glad your bosses forced you to take time off. It obviously helped. Have you been keeping up with yoga and strength training?"

"No. I blew everything off, but I'm doing yoga again, and I'll hit the gym next week."

"I can come up this weekend if you want a refresher. Crap. Hold on. Teddy, Michael, stop that right now."

Emily smiled. Her nephews were rambunctious on good days. From Eddie's voice, she could tell it wasn't one of those.

"Gotta go, beautiful, Teddy and Michael are using Nicholas as a canvas. Love you."

"Love you, too. Give my love to Sheryl."

When she'd been transferred to the rehab facility after months in the hospital, Eddie had been assigned as her physical therapist. Since she'd been a minor, and her grandparents had refused to take custody, her parents' best friends, Griffin and Ellen Boyer, had petitioned for and gained custody.

Eddie had come to her room to introduce himself and said he needed to see her leg. She'd burst into tears. Instead of leaving her there, he'd sat on the bed and held her. When one of the nurses walked in and told him his actions were inappropriate, he'd told her to fuck off.

Emily had developed a huge crush on him. Eddie had been twenty-nine with jet-black hair, blue eyes, and piercings and tattoos everywhere she could see. He wore black jeans and a gray scrub top and heavy black motorcycle boots. He rode a Harley and looked hot in his motorcycle jacket.

Despite his outward appearance, he had a way with kids. His popularity with his adolescent patients, she supposed, was why he'd been allowed to flout the standard uniform of scrubs and sneakers. She'd met Eddie and Vince on the same day. She hadn't realized it at the time, but it'd been one of the best days of her life. She wouldn't have survived without them.

Her bus was announced over the PA. She settled into her seat and spent the next four hours writing. The trip flew by, as time did whenever she wrote, so Emily hadn't noticed when the sun had dipped below the horizon and darkness fell. The bus pulled into the Hartford terminal at ten thirty-seven. As soon as she stepped off the bus, she saw Jeff.

"Shouldn't you be keeping an eye on Jack?" Their gig ended at ten thirty, but they had a meet and greet afterward, so she planned on taking a cab to his hotel and settling in.

"Did you really think he'd let you take a cab?"

"We'd agreed."

"Jack agreed because he didn't want you to argue, but he had no intention of letting you take a cab." Jeff's tone suggested she should've known that.

"He's in more danger than I am." If she wasn't so tired, she'd be pissed. He'd said he'd pay for all her travel, and apparently, that meant taking over. She'd set him straight tomorrow.

Jeff collected her bags, and within fifteen minutes, they reached the hotel. Viv waited in the lobby to let her know the meet and greet would last longer than expected. Due to a glitch on the website, double the slots had been booked, and since the band was donating all the money to the Hartford Youth Center, Emily couldn't complain. Not that she would've. Jack had respected her writing time, and this was his career.

She ordered room service and changed into the T-shirt and panties she'd purchased on her lunch hour shopping trip with her coworkers Terri and Cassidy. She hoped Jack liked it since she'd purchased several sets in different colors.

After Emily finished her sandwich, she lay on the couch, reading Nicki's manuscript.

"Hey, baby." Jack's soft voice roused her from sleep. He lifted her off the couch and carried her into the bedroom.

She snuggled her face into his chest. He smelled warm and spicy. "Mmm, you smell yummy. What time is it?"

Jack set her on the bed. She'd been chilly, so she'd put on the courtesy robe.

"Go to sleep. It's after midnight." Jack walked into the bathroom.

She'd forgotten to brush her teeth, so she forced herself to get out of bed.

They watched each other in the mirror. She managed to keep the toothpaste from spilling out. Jack stared at her in the mirror with the toothpaste running down his chin. She handed him a tissue. He let go of the toothbrush to grab it, so the brush hung loosely out of his mouth. She looked at herself in the mirror. The robe gapped at the neck, and her T-shirt peeked out. It was burgundy lace.

He spit and rinsed his mouth. "What do you have on under that robe?"

Her lips curled into a wicked grin. "Pajamas." The thong was also burgundy. Not the most comfortable pajamas, but from the look in Jack's eyes, she wouldn't be wearing them much longer.

"Pajamas?"

"T-shirt and matching panties. They were in the sleepwear section, so that's apparently what they are." She turned to Jack. He was aroused.

His hand grasped the end of the belt, and he tugged it free; the robe fell open, and he gulped.

The short-sleeved, all-lace T-shirt ended at her waist, and the waistband of the lace thong was several inches below that. She shrugged the robe off her shoulders. Jack scooped her up, set her on the counter, and kissed her. She stroked his cock as his hands fondled her breasts through the lace. Her nipples tightened, and she wrapped her legs around him, drawing him closer.

"I gotta fuck you now, baby." He carried her into the bedroom and deposited her on the bed. Emily rolled onto all fours as Jack rolled on the condom.

He groaned loudly when she wiggled her ass at him. He knelt on the bed, pulled the thong aside, and stroked his cock between her swollen lips. He gripped her hips and thrust in, settling her ass against his groin. She wiggled again and he tightened his grip. "Keep that up, and it'll be over before it starts." He pulled out and thrust back in.

"Jaaack."

"It drives me wild when you say my name like that." He pounded into her.

She reached down and stroked herself but had to stop when she lost her balance. He leaned forward and kissed up her back to her neck. Emily turned her head but couldn't quite reach his lips. Jack nibbled her earlobe and kissed below her ear, which drove her wild. "Oh yeah, that. I love that."

She tightened around him, and her orgasm broke as Jack returned to upright and fucked her hard.

Jack grunted his release. One last thrust, and he pulled out, and Emily collapsed onto her stomach. After a few seconds, Jack spooned her, and she snuggled closer and fell into the sweet, post-sex oblivion of sleep.

♪ ᵉ ᵗ ᵗ ○

EMILY WAS TRAPPED. SHE PUSHED WHATEVER IT WAS that held her, but it was too heavy. She screamed for help and kicked her legs in an attempt to break free. Pain shot through her right leg and radiated throughout her entire body. She heard the flames crackling; it was so hot, but then she was being pulled free, and she screamed again. She couldn't leave her family.

Emily shot up. The room was black and cold, but sweat

dripped down her face, her back, and between her breasts. The fear that gripped her constricted her throat, and she couldn't breathe. She struggled to get up but arms encircled her waist, and she was pulled against something hard.

"Breathe, baby." Jack's baritone soothed her. "It was just a bad dream."

Her throat loosened, and she gulped in air. Her head and leg throbbed. She had to keep her mouth open to suck in enough air.

Jack released her. "Lie back." The bed shifted as he stood. He went into the bathroom and ran the faucet. He returned a moment later with a wet towel that he used to wipe the sweat off her face and neck. "Lift your arms."

She did, and he removed her T-shirt and used the towel to cool her skin. Her heart pounded in her chest, slowly returning to normal. After he used the towel over her entire body, he tossed it away and pulled her back into his arms. She resisted, and Jack let her go. She wanted to get up and walk around, to remind herself that she could. Sometimes after the nightmares, her leg seemed to forget that it was healed. Emily scooted off the bed and held on to the edge for support.

The room was flooded in light. Jack watched her in silence as she made her way around the room, using the furniture to steady herself. After a minute, her leg's memory returned, and she took a few tentative steps. She stumbled but didn't fall. Jack darted out of bed and grabbed her around the waist. "I've got you baby, I won't let you fall."

Emily clung to him. *Fuck.* He was going to want to talk.

WATCHING EMILY HOLDING ON TO THE FURNITURE for support scared the shit out of him. When she stumbled, his heart stopped. Jack held her now. He knew she needed a minute, but he couldn't let go yet. Too soon, Em pulled out of his arms, walked into the bathroom, and closed the door, shutting him out.

He wanted to throw something. When would she trust him enough to open up? He needed to know what was going on. Jack listened at the door but couldn't hear anything. He hated that bathroom door. When he got his place in the city, he'd have all the bathroom doors removed so she couldn't shut him out. Fuck it, he'd have all the interior doors removed. That way she'd have to—What? Tell him everything that was going on inside her head? Yeah, that was what he wanted. He wanted to know everything. Every damn little stinking fucking thing.

Jack was losing it. From the time they'd parted yesterday, until he'd walked into the hotel room and seen her sleeping peacefully on the couch, he'd been miserable. He'd known his feelings for her already surpassed anything he'd ever felt, but it surprised him how empty he felt without her. Yesterday, as the SUV had pulled away, Jack had felt a pulling sensation in his chest, like a part of him, his heart, stayed with her.

Jack paced the room. What the fuck was he going to do? In all fairness, they'd only met eight days ago. *Only eight days.* He had to find a way to deal with this situation without losing his fucking mind. He sat on the edge of the bed, his head dropping into his hands.

When the bathroom door opened, his head snapped up. Em stood there, naked except for the thong. They needed to talk, but his dick didn't care about that. No woman had ever affected him like this. If anything, over the years, he'd realized the more women he'd slept with, the less of an effect it had on him. Sex was great, but the lack of emotional connection left him cold.

She pulled a T-shirt out of her overnight bag and put it on. It was the same one she'd worn a week ago when Jack went to her to beg her to give him a chance. Although, he hadn't done that much begging. When she'd opened the door, she'd been surprised it was him. But then a small smile flitted across her lips. She'd been happy to see him, even if she didn't want to be.

Em sat next to him. "I'm sorry about that."

"About what?"

"Waking you like that. That nightmare started last night, but I guess it wasn't finished."

That was what she thought he cared about? "How long has this been going on?"

"A month."

"Since..."

"Yeah."

Her eyes looked haunted. He wanted to pull her into his arms and never let go. "Was it about the accident?"

Emily nodded and padded to the window. "I don't want to talk about it."

He suppressed the primal urge to go to her, hold her, and tell her everything would be okay. He'd make it okay. He took a steadying breath. "Why?"

Emily faced him. "Because we just met."

"We're sleeping together." It hurt that she didn't trust him. Jack trusted her.

"Yeah, I still can't believe I slept with you that first night, not to mention spending a week in your hotel. It's so unlike me. I don't even recognize myself, butting into people's lives: Buzz, Elliot, Todd. What the hell's happening to me?" Emily hugged herself.

She looked lost. Okay, maybe it wasn't a trust issue so much as the fact that for the second time in ten years her life had been turned upside down. Then throw a new relationship into the mix, especially one as intense as theirs was. "You're feeling overwhelmed. It's understandable." Sitting there was the hardest thing he'd ever done. But she was talking, and if he moved, he was afraid she'd clam up.

"Ya think? I was overwhelmed before I met you. This relationship is already so big." Emily spread her arms wide. "Overwhelmed is an understatement. At the risk of using too many adverbs, I'm gigantically, immensely, enormously fucking overwhelmed."

He couldn't be apart from her for another second. "Baby, you're so brave. You rebuilt your life when you were so young. And you did an amazing job. Now, you have to do it again, but it's more of a remodel." When she relaxed into him, he felt a surge of love for her that he didn't think was possible. "Thank you for giving us a chance. I meant it when I said I've never felt this way before. It's overwhelming for me, too."

"Crap. One of us needs to have their feet firmly planted on the ground. I was hoping it'd be you." Emily yawned.

"It's late, let's get some sleep." When she resisted, he turned to her. "What?"

"I'm hot."

He waggled his brows up and down. "Yeah, you are."

She smiled. "Thank you, but not that kind of hot. Overheated hot."

"Get in." He opened the window. It was another cool night. He climbed into bed next to her and turned off the light. She was on her back, so they couldn't cuddle. But as soon as he settled next to her, she took his hand.

He glanced at the clock. It'd been at least twenty minutes, but she hadn't fallen asleep yet. "You okay."

"No."

Her answer surprised him. He'd expected her to say she was fine. At least she was being honest. "Still don't want to talk about it?"

"It won't help."

"It'd help me."

After a few seconds and a pained sigh, she said, "What do you want to know?"

He turned on his side. "Everything."

Em turned and faced him. "I'm not comfortable with that."

"Well, how about you tell me about your nightmare."

"I don't see the point in rehashing it."

"Okay, general stuff then. Are all of them about the accident?"

"Yes."

His relief at her answer shocked him. He was glad they weren't about the fucker. "Is this the first time you've had nightmares about it?"

"No. I had them for years after the accident, but over time, it was less often, and eventually, they stopped. Until last month."

Fuck. She hadn't had any that he was aware of since they'd been together. "Did you have them this week?"

Several seconds of silence passed. "Yes."

He tamped down on the anger that rose in his chest. They'd made progress this week. Little steps were better than none, but he needed more information. "Did something happen?"

"No. I'm tired. I couldn't fall back to sleep after the nightmare yesterday." Emily turned on her back. "These aren't like the nightmares I had before."

"How so?"

"They used to be more like flashes of images, at least that's how it felt when I woke up, and I was left with a bad feeling but couldn't really remember anything specific."

"And now?" He wanted to hold her, to love her, but he resisted.

She turned away from him. "These are very vivid, and after I wake up, I can't get them out of my head."

"Are you reliving the accident?"

She sighed. "I don't know. I have no memory of the accident."

Jack rolled onto his back. *Wow.* He wanted to know more but didn't want to upset her. She rolled over and into the side of his body, resting her head on his shoulder and her left leg across his legs. He loved when she did that.

"When I woke up in the hospital, I couldn't remember anything. The doctors told me I'd been in a car accident."

Jack tightened his arm around her.

"It was a horrible feeling, not knowing anything about myself. Even my name didn't sound familiar."

Jack's head spun, and his heart constricted in his chest. He wished he could take away all her pain.

She swallowed hard as he felt the first drops of tears on his skin. He bit his tongue to keep from asking her any questions or even encouraging her to go on. Elliot's voice echoed in his head, mocking him. *"See, buddy, this is what happens because you have to know everything."* He told Elliot's voice to shut the fuck up. But the bastard was right.

"The last thing I remembered was Riley coming home from college in May. I'd missed him so much. It was our last summer together before he'd move out for good, and I hated that so much. I didn't understand why he was in such a hurry to leave us."

Something popped in Jack's memory about Jimmy. The longer he'd been away from home, the worse their relationship had gotten. At first, Jimmy was always excited to see him when he visited, but after a few years, he'd stopped talking to him. Jack had chalked it up to moody teenage bullshit, but maybe it was something else. Their relationship was still strained, and Jack had no idea how to make it better. He didn't know why his brother hated him so much.

"Eventually, I remembered everything leading up to the

accident, even driving away from the house, but never any details of the accident itself. They told me it might never come back."

Jack handed her a tissue. "Do you think these are memories pushing their way to the surface?"

Emily sat up. "Why now?"

Jack felt her pain. "I don't know, baby." He wished he could offer her more comfort, or any, but he didn't know what to say. "You need to get some sleep." Em's head rested on his shoulder. He was relieved she didn't move away from him. He'd take that as progress. "Em?"

"Yeah?"

"Next time you have a nightmare when we aren't together, I want you to call me. Okay?"

Her body tensed. "I'll be waking you up."

"I won't be able to sleep at all if I'm worried about you. Please?"

"Okay."

Jack let out a breath.

"Jack?"

"What?"

"No bodyguard."

Jack sat up and turned on the light. "Em, be reasonable, I need to be sure you're safe."

Emily sat up and faced him. "Is it reasonable to have someone follow me around without talking to me about it first?"

Shit, she had him there. He hadn't asked because he'd known she'd say no. "I need to know that you're protected. If this stalker bullshit were to spill over on to you, I'd never forgive myself." The muscles in his jaw tightened.

Emily's eyes darkened, and her chest rose and fell. "Jack, I'm not going to be followed around by a bodyguard. That isn't normal."

His heart pounded in his chest and heat spread throughout his body. "Emily," he said through tight lips. "I need you safe."

"Jack," Emily said through equally tight lips, "I can take care of myself."

"But you shouldn't have to because of me." His pulse pounded in his ears. "I'm not convinced that what happened to your car yesterday wasn't connected."

Emily's smile leveled him. "Baby, listen, don't you think you're going off the edge here? I left my lights on, and my battery died. It happens."

Jack found it hard to stay angry. He didn't want to fight about this, and Em was right. Jeff was re-checking backgrounds, but nothing even hinted that the stalker was among them.

And Nicki was on tour with them. She was smart and diligent. She'd made friends with their crew, and she didn't think the stalker was one of them either. Jack felt bad that he'd judged her based on her appearance. "Okay, no bodyguard. But I need to know if anything happens even if you don't think it's related."

Emily's eyes narrowed briefly, but she nodded.

Jack sighed, turned off the light, and silently prayed this wasn't a mistake.

I THROW THE PHONE ON THE BED, AND IT BOUNCES to the floor. "Fuck! Why won't that stupid whore leave Jack be." Following him to Hartford, how pathetic. At least my week in New York wasn't wasted. I'm not the only one who's concerned about him.

That stupid whore lives in New Jersey, so now Jackie's only a few hours away. Soon his tour will take him farther and farther away, then she'll find a meal ticket closer to home.

Our meeting in New York would've been the perfect story to tell our children. After waiting all these months, I'd have played hard to get. Jackie would fly to spend every minute he could trying to convince me that we belong together.

"If loving you is wrong, I don't want to be right," he'd say. Then I'd say, "I knew the second I laid eyes on you that you were different."

He'd look into my soul with his deep blue eyes and realize that I've loved him forever. He'd take me in his arms, and just before our lips meet, he'd pause and say, "I was stupid for not seeing it all along. For not seeing you."

Our lips touch, gently at first. Then Jackie takes my mouth in a passionate assault. He picks me up and carries me into the bedroom, kicking the door closed behind us. Fade to black... End scene.

It's our time. And it'll be forever.

Chapter Fifteen

Their weekend flew by, and Emily walked into work
Monday morning feeling better than she had in a long
time. Due to his schedule, Jack wouldn't be able to fly to see
her for over two weeks. On the bus ride up Friday, that hadn't
seemed so bad, but she found herself losing focus on her work
wondering how they'd move forward like this.

She'd asked Jack not to call her while she was at work, but
they could text. He'd sent her a goofy selfie this morning when
he first woke up. His hair was all messed up, but that somehow
added to his gorgeousness. They'd argued over who looked
worse in the morning, and this was his proof. She texted back
that she'd taken a selfie, but the screen cracked, so she didn't
send it so his phone would be saved.

His next text contained a picture of him and Buzz in the
gym and a video—narrated by Elliot—of Buzz and Jack
boxing. According to Elliot, Jack was trying to impress her
with his half-naked body. Elliot then turned the phone to
himself and told her not to be jealous.

She liked Elliot. He was funny, and he smiled a lot now
that he and Siobhan were working things out. She liked Curt

and Buzz too. Nicki was happier than Emily had ever seen her. But she worried about Buzz. He seemed to be withdrawing into himself. She'd voiced her concerns to Jack, and he promised to be extra diligent in looking out for his friend.

Every time Ben or Jerry stopped by her office, they had grins on their faces. She'd expected them to tell her some good news, but they were just "checking in" as they called it.

She'd missed two calls over the weekend from a number she didn't recognize. Whoever it was hadn't left a message, so she'd forgotten about it until Tuesday during her lunch. She was in the office lounge eating when the mysterious number rang on her cell.

"Hello?" she said.

"Emily?"

"Edward." The only things Sully had in common with his father was his voice and his blond hair. The only distinction was Edward's voice carried an authoritative tone, where Sully's had a more playful quality.

"I know it's business hours, but do you have a moment? Gail and I have been wanting to talk to you. If now isn't convenient, maybe we could meet for dinner."

What the fuck? They'd never called her while she was dating Sully. She'd called them once, after Sully had finally introduced her to them, to see what he might like for his birthday. Gail had responded that she had no idea what her son wanted. It was the last time Emily made that mistake.

She absolutely did not want to have dinner with them, so she went into the empty conference room. She closed the door and paced. "Now's good." Better to get it over with than obsess over the possibilities especially since she couldn't enlist Nicki's help. *She's gone.*

There was a long pause. "Emily, Edward and I..." Gail hesitated. The double-team really freaked her out. Gail never had a problem voicing her opinions while she'd known her, and her hesitation now had Emily sitting in the nearest chair.

"What Gail is trying to say is how disappointed we are in Sean. His behavior toward you has been atrocious. The whole situation is mortifying. Cheating is so lowbrow."

Emily was glad she sat; otherwise, she would've collapsed.

"We were so very happy when Sean brought you home. You were like a breath of fresh air in our family," Gail said.

Emily leaned forward to rest her arms on the table, mostly to avoid falling out of her chair. *Holy shit.* "Thank you." She'd never pegged the Sullivans as liars, and if anything, they were brutally honest, usually when something didn't require complete honesty, let alone the brutal kind.

"As I'm sure you can imagine, the last month has been extremely humiliating for us," Gail said.

Humiliating for you? Emily bit her tongue. Her parents had taught her to be respectful even when people didn't deserve it.

Edward cleared his throat. "Even though you declined our extremely generous offer to pay for the entire wedding, since your family was unavailable to."

Ahh, that was the Sullivans she knew. Recriminations were their second-favorite pastime. This conversation had already lasted too long. Edward droned on, so she cut him off. "Is there something I can do for you?" Emily stood and paced in front of the windows.

Edward huffed loudly. He didn't appreciate being interrupted, but Emily no longer cared. "Yes. I understood from Sean that you had also declined his offer to pay because you didn't want a destination wedding. You shouldn't be too proud to accept help from people who are better off—"

"Edward, the point, please." She should've just hung up, but that wouldn't work with the Sullivans; they'd keep after her until they had their full say.

"You can allow us to repay your outlay for the wedding. Gail and I feel it's the least we can do."

She leaned against the windows, and the blinds protested loudly when they clattered into the glass.

A loud knock sounded on the adjoining door to Ben and Jerry's office. "Emily, are you okay?" Ben asked.

She wasn't; she was in shock. "Yeah." She moaned. Those codgers could be downright intrusive when they caught a scent.

"Emily, are you still there, dear?"

She hated it when Gail called her dear. She called the maid dear, too. Who even had a live-in maid these days? Bet Edward had a valet, too. "Yes, sorry, someone knocked on the door." What the hell was going on? "I don't..."

"Please don't let your infernal pride get in the way of our gesture. We are well aware of your circumstances."

That also sounded more like the Edward she knew, so the earth resumed its proper rotation. She wouldn't be surprised if they'd had her investigated. Shaking her head, Emily wished she could say they meant well, that they were looking out for Sully, but they looked out for what they cared for most. Their wealth. Apparently, they'd feared that Sully would marry a gold digger, who, after they died, would flit away their fortune on whatever it was gold diggers flitted away someone else's hard-earned inheritance on. "I'll think about it. I have to get back to work." She disconnected the call.

She was sure they expected an immediate answer, but she didn't care. Right now, she had to sneak back to her office to avoid the gruesome twosome. Emily opened the door to the conference room and groaned. Ben and Jerry stood there, tapping their feet.

Fuck me.

"Young lady, we'd like a word," Ben said, as Jerry ushered her into their office and closed the door. Ben turned to face her, relieved that she wasn't hurt. "What was that all about?"

"What was what all about?"

Ben snickered. Emily wouldn't open up easily; she never did. After the crash from the conference room, they'd listened at the door, but the damn wood was too thick. "We heard a loud crash. What was that?" Emily didn't fidget. She was a cool customer, probably got that from her father. He'd known a few Marines when he'd served in Vietnam. From what their friend had found out after they'd hired Emily, she was a lot like her father.

"Sorry, I leaned against the blinds. They're undamaged."

"We don't care about damage to any *thing*. We are concerned for you, young lady." Jerry sat on the corner of Ben's desk. Bastard was getting back at him for him doing that last Thursday. He loved his brother, but ever since they'd met, it was always tit for tat.

"I'm fine."

Short answers were her trademark when she didn't want to talk. Most women talked nonstop, and like most men, he'd learned to tune them out, but Emily was different. "You were peacefully eating lunch in the lounge when a phone call had you running into the conference room for privacy. What's going on."

Jerry sent him a look that said he was a dumbass.

"Since you realized why I went into the conference room, then you'll understand if I say it's a private matter."

I am a dumbass. Fuck. No chance of getting her to talk now. Ben hung his head in defeat. "Very well. We're done here. Take an extra fifteen minutes to finish your lunch."

Emily smiled. "Thank you, sir."

He loved that girl like one of his own, but only she could

get away with taunting her victory over him by calling him sir. At least she'd held her smirk until her back was turned, and Ben was sure Emily smirked.

As soon as the door to their office closed, Jerry said, "Nice going, Ben. You know you can't come at her head-on."

Ben gave his brother the finger. "And you know that she's not going to share until she's damned well ready to. It pisses me off. We could help her, but she's so damned stubborn."

"That's one of the things we love most about her. Nothing keeps her down. She's gets that stubborn Irish streak from her father." Jerry hoisted his ass off Ben's desk and sat behind his own.

"Her mother was half Irish too, so a double helping of stubborn. I'm glad she had it but sad she's had to use it so often."

"Yes, seventy-five percent Irish, one hundred percent stubborn." Jerry laughed. "Did you get in touch with that guy?"

Ben shuffled the papers on his desk. "What guy?"

"The guy about..."

"Oh, that guy." Ben smiled. "Unfortunately, he has standards, and tar and feathering isn't on the list of his services."

"What about maiming?" Jerry asked.

"That he could do."

"That bastard Sullivan has it coming. Can't even count on a background check anymore. People suck."

Ben sighed. "They sure do."

Chapter Sixteen

The guys had Friday night off, so Nicki and Curt spent the day sightseeing, while Jack, Buzz, and Elliot dealt with some radio interview. It had been Jack's idea for them to take full advantage of a day off together. Nicki liked Jack. He was in love with Emi, so that proved he had good taste, but she kept her eye on him though. He'd better keep it in his pants. The next person who hurt Emi would end up dead, and Nicki's conscience would be clear.

The three-hour drive to Gilford, New Hampshire from Springfield, Massachusetts was beautiful. Jeff had deemed it safer for the band to travel in a convoy of SUVs than a tour bus. Nicki didn't mind since hotels had room service and the tour buses didn't.

The crew left Thursday night after load out and had the full day off to rest. Most of the crew were from New York or California, but a ten-hour drive to see family for a few hours wasn't viable.

Sunday was Mother's Day, and she and Curt would be apart for the first time since they'd met. The guys were all going home for the day and then flying out Monday to meet the crew in Buffalo for their gig at the Key Bank Arena.

The hotel they were staying in wasn't as elegant as The Yorkshire had been, but she didn't care. Life on the road wasn't glamorous, but she loved being with Curt. They'd had an amazing time today, and shopping hadn't even been involved. They walked around Elacoya State Park, watched a crystal artist cut some Christmas ornaments, had a wine tasting at Star View Vineyard, followed by dinner at The Crow and Lion Tavern and Grille.

It was dark by the time they returned to the hotel. As they passed the hotel bar, she saw Jack sitting alone, so they went in to have a drink.

"Hey, man," Curt said as they sidled up to Jack.

Jack stared into his drink, which based on the condensation on the glass and the napkin, had once contained ice. It didn't look like he'd even taken a sip. At Curt's greeting, his head shot up. The sad look on his face reminded her of the time she'd run into Sully at a bar. She'd been on a date and saw him looking the same way Jack looked now. Lost. She knew better than to interfere, but that didn't stop her.

"Hey." Jack returned to staring.

Curt looked at her. She gave him a go on gesture as she sat on the barstool next to Jack. Curt quietly left the bar.

Jack glanced at her. "I'm not very good company tonight."

"I can help."

A humorless laugh tore from Jack's throat. "If only that were true."

The bartender came over and gave her a smile she was well acquainted with. He was definitely interested, but she wasn't, so she kept her smile small. The bar wasn't well stocked. "Bourbon neat."

Jack looked at her with raised brows.

"What?" she asked.

"I hadn't pegged you as a whiskey kinda girl."

The bartender placed her drink on the bar. "Thanks."

Before she even had her wallet out, Jack laid a twenty on the bar.

"Thank you." On top of all his obvious qualities, he was also a gentleman. Emi was a sucker for a gentleman. No wonder she'd broken so far out of her shell with Jack. Good looks, money, talent, and charm had never swayed Emi before from her traditional views on dating, only sleeping with a guy after a respectable amount of time. But she'd been in such a horrible place after what Sully had done Nicki had feared her friend might never recover. She owed it to Emi to interfere now. But only a little. She took a sip of her drink. *Gross.*

Jack hadn't so much as looked at another woman since she'd been on the road with them. Women did more than look at him, but he gently removed their straying hands as he'd done with her. Jack was a goner for Emi. "You need patience with Emi. She'll come around." Jack barely glanced at her, but she could tell she'd struck a nerve.

"I told her I'd give her all the time she needed."

"She told me." Nicki swirled the bourbon around in the glass. The amber liquid appeared deeper in the low light of the bar. "You think you're being patient, but you keep pushing her to talk. That won't work."

Jack glared at her. "We're a couple. We're supposed to talk."

"Of course, but not about everything all at once." She touched Jack's arm. "She's not like us, Jack. Emi has been on her own for a long time and has perfected self-sufficiency." Nicki waited for Jack to look at her before continuing. "I believe you're being patient for a man who's used to women falling at his feet." She held her hand up when he went to protest. "I know you're not a jerk, but women do fall at your feet. Non-rock star guys have to work harder to get a girl. That's all I'm saying."

Jack shrugged. "That's not my fault."

"I know. But you got used to a certain time frame with previous relationships, and if you use that to measure your relationship with Emi, you're setting yourself up for disappointment."

Jack turned his glass but didn't drink. "Go on."

"You need herculean patience."

"I don't know what that means."

"We are all spoiled compared to Emi. My family isn't perfect, but I love them. I spent years wishing my mother was different. She's not openly affectionate, but I know that she loves me even though she never supported what I wanted. She wanted me to want what she wanted for me. Like my grandmother had done to her. I resented it and was angry, so I pushed them away. Then I met Emi, and I was just grateful to have them."

Jack nodded.

"You're going to need the kind of patience Emi was forced to develop at seventeen, trapped in a hospital bed because she couldn't walk. The kind that pushes you not to give up when you have a setback during your rehab, when all you want to do is rush back to normal."

Jack took a sip of his drink. "I hadn't thought about it like that."

"Emi told me you asked to read her books. Have you?"

"I started one, but I wanted to enjoy every minute I could with her."

"Did she tell you how she picked her pen name?" Nicki knew Emily hadn't. She'd never told Nicki, but Nicki had figured it out.

"No." Jack looked miserable.

Nicki pushed her drink away. "You know why I call her Emi?"

Jack continued to stare at his drink. "It's her nickname."

"No. Because the one time, very early on in our friendship, I called her Em, she took my head off. Screamed at me never to call her that again."

Jack turned to her and sat up.

"Know what else? No one calls her Em." She let that sink in. "Not Vince, Eddie, or Trina, her oldest friends, not me, not her bosses, and most notably, not that fucker." She stood. "Except you, Jack. I've heard you call her Em at least a dozen times. I wonder what that means?"

Jack looked intrigued.

"I know you don't think she's being open with you, but you have to understand something."

"What?"

"In the two weeks you've known her, she's told you more personal stuff than she shared with Sully in six months. There's still a lot you don't know." As she walked past him, he turned on the barstool, and Nicki stopped in front of him. "Two things, Jack, the internet is an amazing source of information."

Jack nodded. "And the second thing?"

Nicki faced him. She was wearing sneakers, so even though he was sitting, she had to tilt her head back to meet his eyes. "If you hurt her, I'll cut your dick off with pinking shears." She smiled sweetly and left.

JACK RAN OUT OF THE BAR. WHEN THE ELEVATOR didn't open immediately, he took the stairs. He fired up his laptop, grabbed a bottle of water, and sat at the small table. His palms were sweating and his mouth dry. He felt like he was invading Em's privacy, but he needed answers. He opened the web browser and typed Emily's name into the search bar.

Dozens of results appeared. The first result announced her engagement to the fucker. He scanned down the page until he found what he was looking for. He hovered over the link. He knew he should wait until she told him, but Nicki had suggested this for a reason. She wanted him to figure something out without her having to betray Emily's trust. He stood and paced the small room. He was a fairly big guy, but the room seemed to have shrunk in size since he'd checked in. He needed fresh air but wanted to be alone, and he'd promised Jeff he wouldn't leave without protection. This sucked.

He'd read just a little. Jack took a deep breath, sat, and clicked the mouse. His eyes filled with tears as he read the headline.

Two Survivors Pulled from Burning Wreckage

Jack sat back. God, she was just a kid. He remembered what he'd been like at seventeen: carefree and unjaded. She'd lost that in a heartbeat. Then he remembered the title of the first book she'd written. *In a Heartbeat.* And how she'd described the accident to him on the cab ride to The Rock House. "In the blink of an eye, my family was dead." Jack grabbed his duffel bag and pulled out Em's books. He'd placed a Post-it on each book to remind him of the order. *Blink of an Eye* was her second book.

Jack's stomach turned over. He laid the books on the table in order. *Night & Day, Bring Me to Life, Dating 101, Surrender, Submission, Full Circle.* There was a definite progression. Jack took a deep breath and read.

Atlantic Herald
Monty Wall

Monday, August 7, 2006

In the early morning hours of August 6th, Ryan and Emma Prescott were killed when their SUV was hit head-on by a drunk driver. Their two children, Riley and Emily Prescott, were pulled from the burning vehicle by Glen and Roy Kincaid, brothers returning from a fishing trip, who'd stopped to assist.

The siblings were transported by air to Atlantic Valley Hospital. Marguerite Ogilvie, spokeswoman for the hospital, described their conditions as critical. No further details were given.

The driver of the other vehicle, Calista Horn, sustained a concussion, fractured ribs, and a broken wrist. She was arrested at the hospital and charged with two counts of vehicular homicide and DWI. She is the wife of Dirk Horn, Mayor of Woodrich Park in Gloucester County. Her three children were at home with their father when the accident occurred.

Jack was glad he hadn't drunk because he would've thrown up. The cold description made his skin crawl, and he broke out into a sweat. It wasn't the first accident he'd read about, not even the first of someone he knew. A couple of musicians they'd met early on in their touring career had been killed when one had fallen asleep at the wheel driving overnight to their next venue. That had been a shock. They were young and healthy, and drugs or alcohol hadn't been involved.

But he was in love with Em. Reading about her, delivered in such a cold way, sent a shudder thought him. His scalp tingled, and he had trouble breathing. He wanted to punch something. The hotel didn't have a gym, so he couldn't work off the intense anger flooding his system. *Fuck it.* He picked up his phone and tapped Jeff's number. It was almost eleven, but he didn't care.

Jeff answered on the second ring.

"I'm going for a run." Jack hung up and changed into shorts and a T-shirt. When he opened his door, Jeff waited dressed in sweatpants and a zippered jacket.

"Let's go," Jeff said.

Jack followed him down the hallway. He knew Jeff was armed, but he couldn't see the outline of his gun anywhere.

They ran in silence for the next hour until Jack burned off every ounce of rage. Returning to his room, he downed two bottles of water, wolfed down a protein bar, and showered. Unable to sleep, Jack grabbed his laptop and resumed his search.

He spent the next hour reading over a dozen articles about the accident, her parents' obituary, Riley's death, and Em's hospitalization. There was no mention of any other relatives. She was truly alone. Jack's heart ached at all she'd gone through.

Still not satisfied, he typed Calista Horn into the search bar, and a shitload of articles assaulted him. At first, he thought he typed her name wrong, but they were all about her, her husband, or the trial. Holy fuck, he'd never even considered that Em had to sit through a trial. The first few articles detailed her injuries, arrest, and bail hearing. The headline of the fourth screamed:

Calista Horn Wants to Be Tried

Atlantic Herald
  Monty Wall
  Tuesday October 10, 2006
  Calista Horn, responsible for the death of three people while driving intoxicated, has declined the plea offered by the

Atlantic County's District Attorney, Walter L. Herman. Ms.
Horn's attorney, William Davis, had no further comment.

He read four more articles, detailing the Horns' idyllic life.
Since her husband was a politician, there were no shortages of
publicity photos of their family or him and his wife at
fundraisers or charity events. Other than having killed three
people, the woman was a paragon of a wife, mother, and
daughter. No one had a bad thing to say about her.

He didn't want to like her; she'd killed Em's family and
had almost killed Em. He clicked page two, and his heart
stopped. *Oh Fuck.*

Husband Abused Me Daily

Atlantic Herald
   Monty Wall
   October 31, 2006
   In an exclusive interview, a tearful Calista Horn
recounted the years of spousal abuse she suffered at the hands
of her soon-to-be ex-husband, Mayor Dirk Horn.

Rage suffused his blood when any woman was abused, but
this seemed like she was making an excuse. Like getting in her
car and driving drunk wasn't her fault. He hadn't expected to
feel anything other than hatred for the woman who'd killed
Em's family and destroyed the life she'd had. But he did. Anger
battled with empathy, and empathy won. *Fuck.*

He skimmed the rest of the article. Mayor Dirk Horn was
a complete bastard. Verbal abuse had begun shortly after their
wedding and had slowly escalated to physical and
psychological abuse. Calista had feared for her children. Jack
hoped there was a ring in hell for a bastard like Horn.

As he read, a numbness spread throughout his body, and

his fingers and toes were cold. He took a few deep breaths trying to clear his head. His brain felt like someone with a jackhammer drilled into it. He wanted to throw his laptop across the room. A burning fury replaced the numbness. Jack jumped out of bed and dressed to go for a run. He couldn't stay here. Fuck Jeff; he'd go alone.

When his phone blared out "With You," Jack froze. *Shit.* If Em was calling him at two in the morning, she'd had a nightmare. "Hey, baby, you okay?" He tried to keep his voice even.

"No. Nightmare." He could hear the tears in her voice. "Sorry I woke you."

He felt like a kid caught with his hand in a cookie jar. Researching her like this was selfish. He should confess, but she was already upset about her nightmare, and he didn't want to add to it. "I'm glad you called. I wish I could be there with you."

She sniffled loudly into the phone. "Hold on."

Jack heard her blowing her nose and mumbling to herself. His anger drained away, and he slumped on the bed and waited.

"Hi."

"Hi." She hadn't said she wished he was there, and he reminded himself he needed to be patient.

"Is it okay if we don't talk about it? I know you want to know everything, but I can't."

"Of course." He adjusted the pillow and settled back against the headboard. "What would you like to talk about?"

"I looked up your venue for tomorrow. It's kind of small for you guys, isn't it?"

Jack smiled. It pleased him that she took an interest in what he did. She asked questions about their gigs and venues. "Some are even smaller. The Pavilion is in the middle. We've had a ton of requests from our fans to play in areas that don't have an arena, and we wanted to use this tour to try and hit places we've never played."

"Like New Hampshire?"

"Yeah. I kinda prefer the smaller to mid-size places. Don't get me wrong, playing an arena that holds twenty thousand plus people is mind boggling, but the smaller places have a different energy. I don't know how to describe it."

Emily chuckled. "Kind of like an orgy as compared to a one on one?"

Jack burst out laughing. "How do you figure that?"

"Well, an orgy, while fun if you're into that kind of thing, seems less personal than one on one."

He had to stop reading the stories she'd written for him and focus on her books. He hoped that wicked sense of humor of hers shone through. "That's it exactly. I'm grateful for our success, and playing to huge crowds has an unmatched energy, but I miss the smaller places we used to play." He loved that she could make him laugh. "So, do your books have orgies?"

"You don't know?"

"Well, I haven't gotten to them yet, because my incredibly beautiful and sexy girlfriend wrote me stories I can't seem to put down."

"So, a few stories for your spank bank, and it's my fault?"

"Yes, absolutely." He laughed at her fake huff of disgust. At least he hoped it was fake.

"I'm just kidding, Jack. Please unclench. You said you'd read my books, and I know you will."

Whew. "So, do they?"

"No, I don't do orgies or multiple partners, in my books or real life, so don't get any ideas there, rock star."

He laughed. She hadn't called him rock star in a long time. She used to say it to remind him they couldn't be together, but now it held a more playful tone. He liked it. "Never."

She stopped laughing. "You've never had a three-way?"

Shit. He didn't want to lie, but was she really asking? "Em..."

"Enough said, I shouldn't have asked. It's none of my business." She yawned into the phone. "I'm gonna try to go back to sleep."

"Okay, but call me if you have another one. Promise?"

"Promise. Thanks, Jack. This helped."

"Love you, baby." He quickly disconnected the call.

He woke Saturday morning still thinking about Em's accident. He'd promised himself he wouldn't do any more research, but something nagged at him, and he found himself scanning the web for more details. This time, he entered Emily's name and the word trial. The first result was a picture of Em being helped out of an SUV and into a wheelchair by a man and a woman. There was a house in the background, and whoever had taken the photo had to shoot around several gigantic men in full Marine dress uniforms. He clicked the link to the article.

> *Atlantic Herald*
> *Monty Wall*
> *Tuesday, February 5, 2007*
>
> *Emily Prescott, the lone survivor of the horrific crash that claimed the lives of her family on August 6th of last year, returned from the first day of the trial. Her guardians, First Lt. Griffin Boyer and his wife, Ellen, attended the trial, along with several other Marines. None of the parties would agree to an interview.*
>
> *Lt. Boyer was business partners with Miss Prescott's father, Captain Ryan Prescott. Lt. Boyer and his wife petitioned for custody after the accident.*
>
> *The Boyers' have placed several "No Trespassing - Violators Will Be Prosecuted" signs on their property. Two reporters were arrested Friday for rummaging through their*

trash located in the back of the residence. Several of their neighbors have put up similar signs.

It has been learned by this reporter that several former members under the command of Captain Prescott have donated their time to form a blockade in front of the Boyer residence. One such member, Lance Corporal Ron Gilles, was arrested for assaulting this reporter when asked for a comment. One was given but cannot be printed here.

Judge Garrison has issued a gag order on the trial.

Jack hurled the laptop across the room. It broke in two when it collided with the wall. *Motherfucking parasites.* No wonder she wanted a quiet life. If the first article was any indication, the trial had been a fucking circus. Why couldn't they have left her alone? Jack swallowed the bile that rose in his throat. He fully understood why she shied away from any spotlight.

Jack's cell rang. He thought about launching it to keep his destroyed laptop company, but it was Buzz. "What," he barked into the phone.

"Bad time?"

Jack took a deep breath and checked the time. He was late for their workout. "No, man, perfect timing. I got hung up. I'll be down in five." He disconnected the call, but it rang again as he dropped it on the bed. "What'd you forget?"

"Huh?" a woman's voice said.

Startled, Jack checked the number. Amber. Jack swore silently. If she was calling him, it could only mean one thing. "Sorry, thought you were someone else. What's up?"

"I'm sorry, Jack, I know you and Christie aren't together, but I don't know who else to call. I haven't seen her for weeks, and she's not answering her door. I'm worried about her."

Jack sat on the bed and scrunched his face up. "Amber, if you're worried, have the police do a wellness check." Elliot had been right. Jack couldn't keep running to her rescue even if every cell of his being wanted to.

"She's using again."

"Fuck." The one time she'd OD'd, he'd found her in time, and images of Christie's limp body flooded his mind. At the time, he'd thought she was dead. A sick feeling in the pit of his stomach threatened to overwhelm him. Jack swallowed back his fear. There wasn't anything he could do from here. If this was it... "Amber, I'm in New Hampshire, and I've got a gig tonight. I thought you guys had swapped keys?"

Amber sighed. "We did, but I told her she needed to get help, and we had a huge fight. She demanded her key back."

Jack's mind raced. He knew how Christie could get when confronted, and he didn't doubt she'd done just that. When she was high, whether from drugs or alcohol, she would say the vilest things. It was as if she were a different person. During her last rehab, the final therapy session they'd had together had quickly devolved into her screaming at him. Afterward, the therapist had tried to tell Jack that drugs and alcohol don't make a person do something they aren't capable of sober; it just lowers their inhibitions to a point where they don't care. He hadn't wanted to believe that because it would've meant that the woman he was in love with, the one he'd thought he'd marry and spend the rest of his life with, wasn't the person he'd thought she was. And that had broken his heart more than the nasty things she'd accused him of.

Christie needed to get help, but Jack knew from Buzz's addiction that it couldn't be forced on her. Christie had to want it, and she didn't. He'd promised himself and the guys that he wouldn't run to her aid again unless she agreed to get the help she so desperately needed. "Amber, there's nothing I can do. If you don't want to call the cops..."

Another long sigh. "I understand. It's just, she's my friend, and I'm scared for her. I'm afraid of what I'll find."

"Believe me, I understand." Jack was scared, too. He'd moved on with Emily, but he still worried about Christie, and he dreaded the day that phone call would come. His heart pounded in his chest, and his thoughts raced. If only he wasn't so far away. "It's probably not legal, but you could ask the building manager to check on her." He was a kindly older gentleman, and Jack didn't doubt that Amber could persuade him. "You know she'll be pissed."

"She already told me she hated me, so I don't think there's anything worse she could say."

Jack knew there were much worse things Christie could say when she was high and pissed. "I'm sorry I can't do more, but let me know, okay?"

"I understand. Bye."

He was terrified of what Amber would find, but at least if the building manager was with her... Who was he kidding? *I should be there.*

Jack placed the phone on the bed and forced himself to stand. Buzz had to be his priority. He couldn't help Christie, but he could help his friend. Today, they'd spar. Between the anger he felt over reading the articles on his new girlfriend and the never-ending shitstorm of issues with his ex-girlfriend, he couldn't wait to beat the shit out of the heavy bag.

After his workout, he checked his messages. Amber had called saying that Christie had just returned from visiting her parents after doing a commercial in New York the week before. Jack was relieved, but he knew it was only a matter of time if Christie refused to go to rehab.

He called his folks to confirm he'd be there tomorrow. His mom sounded excited, which made him happy. He hadn't seen them enough in the past year, which was his fault. With all the drama around Christie, he'd stayed away too long.

Then he called Em. She'd planned on writing early then

had a bunch of errands to take care of. He got her voicemail and felt insanely disappointed that he hadn't reached her.

She called back a few minutes later.

"Hey, baby, how are you?" He had an idea he wanted to talk to her about.

"I'm fine, but you sound like a kid on Christmas morning. What's up?"

"As you know, I'd planned to make a quick trip home for Mother's Day. How'd you like to come with me?" Jack could barely contain himself. They hadn't planned to see each other for another ten days, but a little bit of time shared with his family was better than nothing.

"Jack, you've had these plans with your mom for months. You can't just invite me last minute."

"My mom will understand." Jack's enthusiasm was greeted with dead silence. "What's wrong?"

"It's Mother's Day. Your mother expects to see you, not us. I'm not her favorite person in case you'd forgotten."

He had forgotten. "I'll call her so she's not surprised."

"No."

Jack paced the small room. "Why not?"

"Because it's not fair to put this on her. It's her day, the one day a year she can have you, your brother, and your sister all to herself. I would be intruding on that, and believe me, she'll resent me before she'd blame you."

Fuck. Jack knew she was right, but he wanted to see her. "But I'll be so close, there has to be something we can do." Jeff and Brick were driving them home after their gig since the earliest flights out of Manchester Airport weren't until almost eleven a.m. on Sunday. "We're driving, so what if I came by before I went home? We could spend a few hours together."

"Okay."

His heart somersaulted. "Really?"

"Of course."

He'd known she was amazing, but still, she surprised him. She could easily use her writing or fear of flying as an excuse to keep him at arm's length, but she didn't. "Great, I can't wait to see you." He hung up and called Jeff. They'd drop Jack off at Em's and then pick him up at eight. Jack decided that Jeff and Brick needed a bonus. He couldn't wait to see her.

Jack had called her when they left New Hampshire. Even though Emily planned on going to the cemetery to visit her mom later in the day, she wouldn't allow her melancholy to spoil Jack's mood. He traveled enough on tour, so she felt guilty about all the extra traveling he'd be doing because she couldn't get on an airplane.

Before she went to bed, she'd fixed her hair, put on the black lace T-shirt and thong, and left a key under the welcome mat so he could let himself in.

It felt like longer than a week since they'd been together, and even though they talked, Skyped, and texted every day, she was nervous about seeing him. She chalked it up to the unusual nature of their relationship. She'd get used to it, wouldn't she?

Jack texted her photos of highlights of his day, and she felt a little jealous that Nicki got to see him more often than she did. But he'd sent a really sweet one of Nicki and Curt that she used as her contact picture for Nicki. Emily missed her, too.

She was having the loveliest dream when she sensed someone in her room. She bolted upright to see Jack sitting on the bed taking off his boots.

"Hi," she said as she flicked on the lamp. No sense in missing the show. "Need any help." The covers had pooled at her waist, and the expression on Jack's face when he turned, warmed her all over.

She helped him off with the rest of his clothes, and they spent half an hour reacquainting themselves with each other. Gentle caresses and hot wet kisses stoked her desire for him until she thought she'd combust. Her heart thudded in her chest, and warmth pooled low in her belly. This wasn't sex; this was making love. When Jack finally entered her, tears pooled in the corners of her eyes, but Emily had no idea why. Afterward, she fell asleep in his arms, and an inner contentment she'd never experience before suffused her entire being.

She woke when Jack got up at seven. They made love and shared a shower and a bone-melting kiss goodbye. A look she didn't understand flashed in his eyes before he turned and strode down the walkway. With every step away from her, his heavy boots thudded on the concrete. Emily watched until she could no longer see the taillights before she went inside.

She pushed her unease away. They wouldn't see each other again for nine days. That was nothing compared to when her dad had deployed; he'd be gone for six months to a year at a time. But right now, nine days felt like an eternity.

Emily refused to feel like his booty call, but his odd look clawed at her. Her fear of flying made their difficult circumstances so much worse. He'd been the one to go the extra distance to see her today; otherwise, it would've been over two weeks until they'd be together. She swallowed the lump in her throat. Maybe Jack realized that Emily was too damaged and not worth the effort.

Chapter Seventeen

H e just left, but Jack missed Em like crazy. He almost asked her again to come with him, but he knew she was right about it not being fair to his mom. Jeff dropped him off at his folks' house at eight thirty. He forced himself to shake off his melancholy. His mom had supported him, and she deserved a happy, smiling son today. Jack opened the screen door into the kitchen. "Hey, Dad."

"Jack." Will stood and embraced him. "You're earlier than expected. Your mom's been looking forward to this all week."

He hugged his dad back. There was nothing quite as reassuring as his father's strong embrace. "It's good to be home." When he pulled back, he studied his dad's face. "You look tired. Everything okay?" His dad routinely worked long hours and frequently had his sleep interrupted by a plumbing emergency.

"Nothing for you to worry about, son."

"Dad, if it's a money thing, I can help."

Will sat and sipped his coffee. "Jack, you've done more than any child should."

His parents refused to accept his help. He'd been amazed

he'd finally gotten them to agree to let him pay for Trish's and Jimmy's education. "You work too hard."

"It's not work."

"What then?"

Jack's answer came when his brother stumbled through the kitchen door, obviously hungover and possibly still drunk. He'd slept in his clothes, and from the look on his dad's face, he hadn't called to say he'd be out all night.

When he saw Jack, Jimmy cringed. "Oh good, my two dads."

Will stood. Even though they were all about the same height, his dad's presence seemed larger than life. Jack had no doubt that his dad could kick both their asses. "Check your smart mouth at the door, James. You never called to say you wouldn't be home. You know the rules." It took a lot to piss off Will McBride, but when he got there, look out.

"Rules? You mean the ones that only apply to Trish and me? Prince Jack doesn't follow any rules."

"That's enough. I told your mother you came home last night, now get upstairs and shower, you reek of alcohol. We'll discuss this later."

Jimmy had the decency to look contrite. It was Mother's Day, after all, and Jack was here early so he and his siblings could make their mom breakfast in bed.

"Yeah, sorry. I forgot." He skulked out of the kitchen.

Jack knew better than to interfere now, but he'd have a private word with Jimmy later. Their parents didn't need this childish shit.

Jack poured himself some coffee, refilled his dad's mug, and sat. A few minutes later, Trish came downstairs, dressed in sweats and looking sleep deprived. She grunted a hello at him. Trish needed coffee first thing to function.

After half a cup, she was ready to offer him a hug. "I'm so happy you made it."

"What do you mean?"

Trish and their dad exchanged a look. "Never mind, the important thing is you're here. I've missed you."

Ten minutes later, Jimmy returned freshly showered, poured himself some juice, and downed it. "I'm ready."

He looked better than when he'd stumbled into the house, but Jack doubted his mother would be fooled. "The usual?"

Jimmy and Trish immediately starting chanting "Pancakes, pancakes, we want pancakes." Just like when they were little. They'd been making breakfast for their mom on Mother's Day since Jack was old enough to reach the counter.

"Pancakes it is." He'd do anything to see his siblings happy. Jimmy behaved less aggressively toward him, so he pushed aside the building animosity he'd been feeling so they could move forward.

Jack measured out the ingredients for the pancakes while Trish set up the tray, and Jimmy brewed a fresh pot of coffee. He enjoyed the way they all worked together so seamlessly. Their dad sat at the table, probably enjoying the silence.

With everything ready to go upstairs, Jack grabbed the gift bag and cards off the table, Jimmy carried the tray, and Trish followed as they went up to wake their mom.

"Happy Mother's Day," they yelled as they walked into the bedroom. Maggie was reading but tossed the book aside to hug them.

"Thank you. This looks delicious." She looked over their heads at Will.

Jack could see how much in love his parents were even after thirty-two years of marriage. He hoped to be that lucky. His heart flipped as he thought of Em; he wished she were here.

They chatted as their mom ate her breakfast. As soon as she finished, Jack handed her the cards and gift bag.

She looked at Jack. "You didn't need to buy me anything, Jack. Your being here is the best gift ever."

He ignored Jimmy's eye roll. "Where else would I be on Mother's Day?" More looks exchanged that he didn't understand.

His mom opened the cards and cried. She opened the box with the earrings that Em had helped him pick out, and his heart flipped again.

"Honey," Maggie said. "What's wrong?"

"Nothing. Do you like them?"

"Jack, they're beautiful. Perfect for every day." More tears welled in her eyes.

Jack leaned in and kissed her cheek. "Thanks for everything, Mom."

Will picked up the tray. "You kids get downstairs, eat, and get ready for church."

Jack went to his room and changed into a pair of navy Dockers and a white button-down shirt. He walked into the kitchen where Trish washed the pan from breakfast.

"How's school?" He poured himself a bowl of cereal.

"Ugh. I have four finals this week. Thank God for coffee. I can't wait until they're over. Then a week off before I start at the outpatient program at St. Peter's." She dried her hands, grabbed a bowl, and sat. "How's Emily?"

"She's great." He smiled so wide some milk spilled out the corners of his mouth. He wiped his mouth with a napkin.

Trish smiled. "You're in love with her."

"Yes." He threw her a warning glance.

Trish smiled, and they ate in silence.

Jack poured more coffee and answered a few emails. Jimmy slunk into the kitchen and grabbed a yogurt out of the fridge, standing at the counter to eat it. Trish ruffled his hair on her way out of the kitchen.

Jack put his phone down on the table. "How's school?"

"What do you care?" Jimmy didn't bother to look up from his yogurt.

"What the fuck's your problem?" Jack stood, cleared the bowls from the table, and put the cereal away.

"I don't have a problem." Jimmy dropped his spoon in the sink, tossed the yogurt container in the trash, and left.

Before Jack could follow, his folks walked in. "You look very handsome, Jack. Breakfast was delicious."

"Glad you enjoyed it."

"I'd have enjoyed anything. It's so nice to have the three of you together. I wish you could stay longer." Maggie looked down.

"I'll be here for four days in June."

Maggie raised her green eyes to his: joy and excitement sparkled there. "We're looking forward to it."

Jack wanted to ask if Emily could join him, but he hadn't broached the subject with her yet. He wasn't sure who to ask first, but he did know today wasn't the day to do it. Em was right about his mom, too. She hadn't asked about her, which wasn't a good sign. He'd gotten the impression from his dad that they'd expected him to bring her today, which he would've if Em had agreed.

Jack had done that several times over the years. He'd never even considered that whoever he was with would be unwelcome. He *was* spoiled and maybe a little bit of an asshole.

It was after one when they returned from church. Jack wanted to call Em, so he went to his room. He missed her like crazy and being so close and not being with her sucked. "Hey, baby, how are you?" It hadn't occurred to him earlier, but today must be hard for her. *I'm a selfish prick.*

"Are you having a nice time?"

He knew something was wrong. "Yeah. Trish, Jimmy, and

I made pancakes. She loved the earrings we picked out. How are you?"

"I'm okay."

Jack sat. *Bullshit.* He could tell she was upset. "Em, we agreed to be honest with each other. I can tell something's wrong. Please talk to me."

"I don't want to talk about it."

"If I was with you, I'd sit and hold you, and if you didn't want to talk, that'd be fine, but I'm here."

"It's Mother's Day, and I miss my family."

He flopped back on the bed, put the call on speakerphone, and set it next to him. "Where are you?"

"Cemetery."

Shit. He didn't know what to say. No wonder she hadn't even considered coming with him today. He'd made it all about him.

"It's okay, Jack."

"No, it isn't. I should be with you."

"No, baby, you're right where you belong. Today is a day to celebrate the living."

She had such compassion, and his heart expanded with the love he felt. "I don't understand why my mom is being so stubborn about you." Jack ran a hand through his hair. "If I explain it to her, I'm sure she'll understand. I'm coming to get you."

"No!"

"Em—"

"You can't do that to her. This is her day, and it was planned long before we met. You don't see her that often. It's not fair to foist me on her on Mother's Day.

"I love you. I love my mom and my family. Is it so wrong for me to want to be with all of you?"

"It's not wrong, but it's Mother's Day. She's shared you

with the world since you were nineteen. She deserves one day with you all to herself, doesn't she?"

Jack sighed as his anger dissipated. "Of course."

MAGGIE STOOD OUTSIDE JACK'S ROOM. SHE HADN'T meant to eavesdrop, but the door was slightly open, and Jack raised his voice. He was talking to that girl.

"Hey, what're you doing?" Will asked, hugging her from behind. "Isn't Jack a little old for you to be listening at the door?"

"Shush. He's on the phone with *that* girl. He wants to leave and bring her here." Maggie huffed. She loved her son, but his good nature was easily taken advantage of, and she hated that he let it happen. Ever since he was a toddler, he bore the weight of the world on his tiny shoulders.

Just like Will. It was why she'd fallen in love with him, but Jack also had her sensitive nature, which made for a bad combination in the hands of the wrong woman. Maggie shuddered as she thought of his last girlfriend. She'd been so wrong about Christie.

Will, always the supportive husband, stood with her listening in on their twenty-nine-year-old son's phone conversation. If he'd wanted total privacy, he should've shut the door. *Someone has to look out for Jack.*

"I love you. I love my mom and my family. Is it so wrong for me to want to be with all of you?"

"It's not wrong, but it's Mother's Day. She's shared you with the world since you were nineteen. She deserves one day with you all to herself, doesn't she?"

"Of course."

Tears formed in Maggie's eyes, and she turned in her husband's arms to bury her face on his shoulder. Will hugged her close. Jack's bed creaked, and they quickly went down the hall and into their room. Will shut the door quietly and joined her on the bed.

"Magpie, she seems really nice." Will pulled her into his arms. "This one's different."

"We thought that about the last one." Maggie wasn't convinced this Emily was any different than Christie or Sandra. She knew her son had more girlfriends, but they were the only ones he'd ever brought home.

"Jack could easily be on his way to pick her up now, but Emily stopped him." Will stroked her arm. "You know Jack can be very forceful in getting his way, but he listened to her when she made a very intuitive point."

"You like her, don't you?" She couldn't keep the accusation out of her voice. Will liked everyone until he didn't. She always needed a little proof before giving her heart to anyone, friend or lover. Jack took after Will.

"As a matter of fact, I do. I think she'll look out for him, the same way he looks out for her. She obviously cares about him."

"He's in love with her. She's damaged goods. I just think Jack deserves better."

"Her family gets killed in an accident, and her fiancé cheats, and you're gonna hold that against her? Maybe you could make a case she chose that guy, but her family, what'd they do?"

Maggie sat up and scowled at Will. She hated when he was the voice of reason. She hated it even more when he was right.

JACK KNOCKED ON JIMMY'S BEDROOM DOOR. HE'D been locked in there since they'd returned from church. "Hey, you got a minute?" Jack heard grumbling from the other side of the door, so he took that as a yes.

Jimmy sat at his desk working on the computer.

"How's it going?" Jack asked.

"How's what going?" Jimmy asked, not looking up from the screen.

Jack had enough. "What the fuck's your problem?"

"I don't have a problem."

Jack stretched out on Jimmy's bed. "Really? Because from where I sit, you're a spoiled little shit who can't spare a minute for his brother."

"Fuck off."

"Fine, then let's talk about Mom and Dad. Why didn't you come home last night? Or call? You know they worry, or can they fuck off too? And what about Trish? Have you told her to fuck off?"

Jimmy turned and glared at him. "No, you can fuck off. Everyone else is okay."

"You're behaving like a teenaged little shit. If I've done something, man up and talk to me about it."

"Why are you even here? You haven't spared a minute for me in years."

"You're full of shit, little brother. I've spent hours with you and dad working on the GTO. Who did you come to for advice on how to go down on a girl? You used to talk to me, and I'm sick of this passive-aggressive bullshit. Talk to me." Jack turned on his side and propped his head on his hand. Jimmy turned to look at him, and anger shot from his eyes, but he just scowled and turned back to the computer.

Fuck. He used to be able to piss the little shit off enough to talk to him, but Jimmy wasn't biting. Jack forced himself to calm down. "Was it a girl?"

Jimmy glanced at him. "Was what a girl?"

"The reason you stayed out all night? Did you get laid?"

Jimmy stood and used too much force to push his chair in. "None of your fucking business."

Not a girl, but he riled him. His indifferent demeanor was replaced with seething anger. Jack had no idea what he'd done to piss his brother off, but he planned on finding out. "That's a no." He paused then nodded. "I get it. You can't get it up."

Jimmy stopped pacing long enough to flip him off.

Jack turned on his back and clasped his hands behind his head. "Ah, broken dick, that'd make any guy pissy. You're young for that to happen, so it's probably psychological. Have you talked to Trish about it?"

"My dick works just fine, asshole." Jimmy's face reddened.

"Then why stay out all night and leave Mom and Dad to worry? If your problem's with me, why take it out on them?"

Jimmy shrugged. "That was an accident. Crane and I went on a bar crawl, and I got drunk and passed out at his place. I meant to call, kinda thought I had." Jimmy sat at the foot of his bed, his head dropping in his hands.

Jack hadn't been around enough to do anything to piss him off. His attitude had gotten worse over the years until Jimmy stopped talking to him altogether. Nothing Jack did made it better. Jimmy resented him, but he had no idea why. At least he had the decency to be miserable over upsetting their dad.

It didn't seem like Jimmy was ready to talk to him, so Jack backed off. He sat up and put his arm around Jimmy's shoulders. "Listen, if you go to Dad before he comes to you and tell him you fucked up, you're sorry, and it won't happen again, that'll go a long way toward derailing his anger." Jack stood and stretched. "Of course, it can't happen again."

Jimmy looked up at him with—if he didn't know better—gratitude and even managed a small smile and a mumbled "Thanks."

Jack opened the door. "I was just kidding about talking to

Trish. She'd probably write her thesis about you." He dodged the pillow that Jimmy hurled at him.

His dad fired up the grill while his mom relaxed on the patio and chatted with him and Trish. She looked happy, and Jack noted with satisfaction she'd worn the new earrings.

Jeff picked him up at six thirty Monday for their ten o'clock flight to Buffalo. Eight days till he'd see Em again. Eight long days.

Chapter Eighteen

F riday morning was hectic. Emily answered without checking the caller ID because she assumed it was Jack.

"I need an update," Meg barked into the phone.

She wasn't as far along with the new book as she would've liked. "I have a few chapters I can email—"

"No. Meet me in the city for drinks. I haven't seen you in ages, and I need an in-person conversation."

Emily furrowed her brow. This was a first. Meg had always conducted business with her over the phone, by email, or in her office. They'd never socialized before; although, Emily had invited Meg to her wedding. Crap, maybe they were passing because she'd missed her deadline. "Okay, when?"

"Tonight."

Jack would be in Maryland at the Merriweather Post Pavilion. They were scheduled to go on at eight thirty. She called him before each gig to wish him luck, but Emily didn't want to do that in front of Meg, so hopefully he'd be okay with a text and not blow it out of proportion.

"Where and when?"

"The Colonial Hotel, Upper East Side. Seven thirty."

"Okay." Emily's head dropped to the desk and landed with a thud. She needed to come up with a convincing story for Meg about Jack. Meg would take one look at her and know she was seeing someone, but Emily wasn't ready to share. Vince knew, but he'd figured it out on his own. She'd been meaning to call Eddie, but she didn't really know what to say. She didn't mind fudging the details with Meg, but she'd never lied to Eddie or Vince, and she wouldn't start now.

She was dating a rock star. How was she supposed to tell her friends that? What if they crashed and burned? Jack being away was different than she'd thought it'd be. Emily had imagined all those lovely hours she'd have to write, peppered in with a few phone calls and a daily Skype session. Instead, she found herself flitting away precious writing time daydreaming about Jack. She found it hard to knuckle down and, more often than not, found herself staring at a blank screen. Was this writer's block? She'd never had a problem concentrating before, and she had plenty of scenes outlined.

"Problem?" Ben asked, as he stood in the doorway of her office.

Emily didn't bother to raise her head. "Yes, and no."

Ben sighed. "Yes, a problem, and no you don't want to talk about it."

They knew her so well. She lifted her head off the desk and smiled. "Thanks."

Ben nodded and walked away.

Emily rushed home after work, changed into a long black skirt that fell just above her ankles, tights, and a short-sleeved hunter-green cashmere sweater. She finished off the outfit with black suede lace-up boots with a one-inch heel and a bold gold necklace and drop earrings. She hit a crap ton of traffic driving into the city but was only a few minutes late.

She spotted Meg at the bar, laughing at something the guy next to her said. Since it was Manhattan, they were both dressed in stylish business attire. His charcoal suit, white dress shirt, and red tie was a classic look. Meg's tailored red dress ended well above the knee, and Emily tamped down a pang of jealousy. The dress fit Meg perfectly, showing off her long, perfect legs. Her four-inch tan heels added to her five-foot-six height.

Meg turned as Emily walked up. "There you are, darling." She stood and kissed Emily on the cheek as she hugged her. The gentleman she'd been talking to now had a view of Meg's butt, and he didn't waste it. "Let me look at you." Meg pulled back and placed her hands on Emily's shoulders.

Emily was sure this was a ruse to give the guy extra time to ogle Meg. She noted the sparkle in Meg's crystal blue eyes and her smug smile. *Yup, giving him the chance to ogle.*

Meg turned. "Stefan, thank you so much for the drink." She tossed her perfectly coiffed and highlighted chestnut hair over her shoulder as she turned back to Emily. "Let's get a table."

Stefan followed their progress to the table Meg had chosen by the large windows that overlooked Fifth Avenue and Central Park.

Emily placed her small briefcase on the seat next to her and unzipped it.

Meg eyed her with concern. "What're you doing?"

"You wanted to talk about my book."

"I never said that."

Emily shook her head. *Shit.* "Okay, what did you need an in-person conversation to talk about?"

The bartender arrived with two drinks. She looked at Meg who shrugged. "Compliments of the gentleman at the bar." The bartender stepped aside, and Stefan waved and smiled. Meg blew him a kiss.

Meg took a sip of the martini. "Yum."

Emily didn't drink martinis, so she pushed the drink closer

to Meg. Meg would be taking a cab, so she didn't worry about her ability to drive.

"No." Meg's eyes widened, and she pushed the drink back toward Emily with her perfectly manicured fingers. "That's rude."

"I don't like martinis."

"Just take a sip. It's really good."

Emily sighed and lifted the glass to her lips and took the smallest possible sip. *Yuck.* She glanced toward the bar where Stefan sat watching them. She got the distinct impression he thought he'd be leaving with both of them. She sent a cold smile to disabuse him of that notion, which he clearly acknowledged with a shrug and resumed ogling Meg.

"Loosen up, let's have some fun tonight." Meg's eyes glinted with mischief.

If Emily didn't know better, she'd think that Nicki had possessed Meg. *But Nicki's on tour with Curt. Not here.* "Shouldn't we discuss my book?"

Meg took another sip of her martini. "Certainly, but I wanted to see you, see how you were doing."

"Well, I have six chapters." Emily opened her bag and laid the pages on the table.

Meg sighed. "Are you being dense on purpose, or are you looped from one sip of martini? I want to know how *you're* doing? After—we all know what happened, no need to rehash it. How you holding up?"

Emily was confused for about ten seconds and then it dawned on her what Meg was talking about. Sully. Not Jack. "I'm okay." She still had questions about what had happened with Sully, but they seemed to matter less. Which reminded her he should be returning from his trip this weekend, and she wanted his shit out of her place.

Meg studied her for a long minute then broke into a grin.

"You're seeing someone." She tapped her long red nails against her black beaded necklace. "Do tell."

Crap. Emily needed a drink but not the martini. She flagged down a server and ordered a glass of cabernet. "Yes, I'm seeing someone. We met a few weeks ago, rather unexpectedly, and it's new, so there isn't much to tell."

"Bullshit. You slept with him. Start with that." If Meg continued grinning like that, she'd pull something.

Emily held Meg's gaze. Meg didn't know anything. "I never said that."

"Darling, you didn't have to. You were with him when you called me three weeks ago to cancel our appointment. I could hear it in your voice; you sounded thoroughly fucked."

Emily almost spit out her wine. She took a few sips of water and smiled. It was better to give Meg a few juicy bits. "He's a musician." She couldn't help but smile when she talked about Jack.

Meg slapped her hand on the table. "I knew it. Oh, those musicians can get any girl out of her panties." She took another sip of her drink. "I slept with several in my twenties. Best sex I ever had." A dreamy look softened Meg's features, and she leaned in. "I slept with one of the guys from Alchemy Riot, although that was a lifetime ago, long before they hit it big. Then there was..."

Emily didn't hear another word. The idea that Meg could've slept with Vince weirded her out. She wanted to ask which one but thought better of it.

"Miss, compliments of the gentleman at the bar." The bartender placed another glass of red wine on the table. "1992 Sonoma Valley Cabernet, excellent year." He smiled and walked away.

When Emily looked to the bar, it wasn't Stefan who raised his glass but a man dressed in a navy button-down shirt. Before she could even react, he hopped off the barstool and headed their way. *Damn.* She looked at Meg who merely shrugged.

He stopped in front of Emily. "Hello, beautiful. May I join you?" He pulled a chair over.

"Actually, I'm in the middle of a business meeting. Thank you for the wine, but I need to get back to business." She threw Meg a look that said she'd better go along. She wasn't in the mood to make nice with some random guy who sent her a drink. Weren't guys supposed to wait for eye contact?

"Of course." He put the chair back and walked to the side of the bar where she'd be able to see him if she looked away from Meg.

"So, tell me all about this musician." Meg smirked.

Emily sighed. She'd never seen this side of Meg before. "His name's Jack."

"That's it?" Meg laughed. "How'd you meet?"

Emily shrugged. "Nicki dragged me to see a band."

"And?"

"And he's out of town right now."

"Okay, I get it. Not ready to dish. I'm just glad you're not pinning away for that bastard. But listen, kiddo," Meg reached for her hand. "You're vulnerable right now, so take it slow with this new guy."

Emily shook her head. Meg went from dish to concern faster than even Nicki. "Well, since he travels a lot, we have to."

"You trust this guy?"

"Yes."

Meg nodded. "Okay, I'll drop it. But please be careful, I've read enough romance novels to know this could end badly."

"Really, that's where you're getting your information?" Emily leaned in. "You know they're fiction, right?"

Meg smiled and patted her hand. "Right, like the titles of your first two books had nothing to do with anything that happened in your own life? And that Eddie and Sheryl aren't really friends of yours? Hmm?"

Emily's jaw dropped open, and she sat up straight. A chill ran through her. "What're you talking about?"

"So much of you is in your books; you aren't even aware of it." Meg lowered her voice. "You've turned tragedy into triumph. It's why your readers love you so much."

Emily had never consciously included anything in her books about her personal life. "I just used Eddie and Sheryl's names in that book, it wasn't their story. I checked with them first." Emily's face heated.

"Hey, it's okay."

Emily took a gulp of water. She'd never invade her friends' privacy by writing about what Eddie and Sheryl had gone through to be together. She hadn't realized, until this moment, that maybe that's why she wrote romances because theirs was so beautiful, and that Eddie shared it with her as part of her rehab had meant the world to her. Every session he'd tell her another part of it. It had kept her going back even when she'd wanted to give up. She was embarrassed to remember how often that had been. And Eddie had believed in her, that she could recover physically, like he had.

A server appeared and placed another drink on the table. "Compliments of the gentleman at the bar."

Emily seethed. *Oh, holy hell, can't a guy take no for an answer?* Emily looked at the guy in the navy shirt, but he'd moved on to a petite, black-haired woman, who giggled at everything he said. The server pointed to her right, and a guy raised his glass to her.

"Please thank him for me, but I have a boyfriend."

The server nodded, took the drink, and left.

Meg pulled the manuscript in front of her. A slow smile spread across her face as she tapped her forefinger over the title page. When she looked up at Emily, her eyes were misty. She'd never seen Meg choked up before.

"*No More Yesterdays*. I love it already." Meg nodded at her and began to read.

Emily had never watched Meg read one of her manuscripts before. Emotions crossed Meg's face like the tide flowed to the shore; anger to smiles to sniffles then to more smiles.

Emily glanced away, and the guy at the bar raised his glass to her so she quickly focused back on Meg. Watching Meg read was nerve-racking, so Emily allowed her mind to wander to her conversation with the Sullivans. A thread of an idea had begun to take hold. Emily had never considered giving up her job and writing full-time, but if she took the money, she could live off it for several months. Her next royalty payment wasn't due for over four months.

In the week since the Sullivans had called, Emily had dismissed the idea several times but kept coming back to it. Why shouldn't she get reimbursed? She needed to call them back before they called her again.

"Hey, gorgeous, have a drink with me."

Her head shot up. The guy from the bar stood at their table. She scowled at him. "I have a boyfriend, which I told the server to tell you. I guess she forgot."

"No, she told me. I'm okay with it."

Anger rose in Emily's chest. *What a dick.* She glanced at Meg who had stopped reading and gave the scene unfolding her full attention. "I'm not interested."

"I can be Mr. Right Now. After a night with me, you can decide if you want to go back to Mr. Not Here." He squatted down and rested his elbows on the table. "If you were mine, I wouldn't let you out of my sight."

Emily turned on him. "I'm not yours. I'm also not interested, which has nothing to do with the fact that I have a boyfriend."

"Come on, baby, what have you got to lose?"

Emily glanced at Meg, who quirked a brow at her.

His lips curved into a smug smile. "One drink."

When he touched her hand, Emily yanked it away. She needed to wash it as soon as possible. "You're going to be Mr. Call Me an Ambulance Right Now if you don't back off."

The dick left but not before adding, "Bitch."

Emily scoffed to herself. *Yeah, I'm the bitch.* She shook her head at Meg, who smiled at her. "What?"

"That was awesome." Meg's eyes glowed, and a satisfied grin crossed her lips.

Emily shook her head. If Nicki was home, she'd call her and dish, but no way she'd tell Jack about this. He was already irrational about Sully. Sean Sullivan never begged for anything from anyone. He'd made his decision and ended their relationship, and there was no way he wanted her back.

Chapter Nineteen

Jack woke Sunday morning still angry over the conversation he'd had with Em the night before. Why had she waited an entire day to tell him that two assholes had hit on her while she was having drinks with her editor? She'd said it wasn't a big deal, but it was to him. If Fletcher hadn't gotten caught so easily, he'd be watching over her now. He could've kept guys from hitting on his girlfriend. Guys who were there when he couldn't be.

The second fuckhead had said he'd never let her out of his sight if she were his. That cut Jack to the core. What he did for a living, what he loved, would keep them apart, and he worried she'd tire of him and move on to some other guy. Em wanted normal, and he'd never really considered his life wasn't normal before.

And now that Emily's ex was back, it was only a matter of time before he showed up.

Jack jumped out of bed. He took comfort in the fact that Em had been pissed that these guys interrupted. And telling asshole number two he'd be Mr. Call Me an Ambulance Right Now made Jack laugh in spite of himself. God, he loved her.

He'd be with Em on Tuesday, and then they'd have two days together.

They Skyped later that night after his gig, and she'd looked beautiful. She'd fallen asleep on the couch, so when he'd called her, her hair was all messed up, and she looked sleepy. He wanted to spend the rest of his life waking up with sleepy, messy-haired Emily.

Monday, he woke to the news that their gig that night was canceled because an overnight storm had damaged the roof of the Berglund Center. Jack shouldn't be happy about that, but he was. An extra day with Em. He'd just made it to the airport for the ten thirty flight to Newark. He'd left a voicemail and texted her his change of plans, but she hadn't responded. Since she was at work and didn't carry her phone around with her, Jack wasn't concerned.

He and Jeff checked into a motel a few miles from Em's place. They hadn't discussed it, and since he was trying to be patient, he'd wait for her to invite him to stay at her place. When they drove past her apartment complex, and Jack saw her car, he told Jeff to pull over. It was two thirty, and maybe she'd gotten his messages and left work early to surprise him. He checked his phone, but he she hadn't called.

His heart leaped in his chest. He ran up the steps and pushed the doorbell three times. A minute passed and she hadn't answered, so he called her. No answer. He banged on the door. *Fuck.* He needed to find the management office. Hopefully, they'd let him in.

Before he got down the steps, her door swung open. Emily stood there, shading her eyes from the bright sun, looking like death warmed over, in the world's ugliest pajamas—two sizes too big and a god-awful shade of blue.

"Jack?"

He closed the distance between them. "Baby, what's wrong?" Before he could pull her into his arms, she paled even further and bolted up the stairs. Jack took the stairs two at a time. By the time he reached the top, he could hear her throwing up. He ran down the hallway to the bathroom where Em was on her knees getting violently ill.

Jack stepped into the bathroom but stopped when she yelled, "Don't come in. Your cologne is killing me."

He knew she was sensitive to smells, but he'd worn this cologne the week they'd spent together and she'd been fine. Jack went to the kitchen, grabbed a towel, ran it under the faucet, and wiped it off. Em sat on the edge of the tub, head down. Jack knelt in front of her. "Better?"

"No. I can still smell you."

Then it dawned on him maybe she was pregnant. Warmth flowed throughout his body. His mom had been nauseated by most smells when she was pregnant with Jimmy. She'd been home on bed rest the last five months of her pregnancy, and Jack had taken care of her.

Jack ran a washcloth under cold water and placed it on the back of Em's neck. He went to the kitchen and grabbed a bottle of water from the fridge. He couldn't stop smiling. It wasn't planned, but he was ecstatic. "Here, drink."

Emily took the bottle but left if on the side of the tub. "No, I don't want to throw up again."

"You'll get dehydrated." Jack picked up the bottle, opened it, and handed it to her. "Please? Just a few sips."

She took a sip, swished it around her mouth, and spit it out in the toilet.

"Can I get you anything, crackers maybe? Or ginger ale?" He'd run out to the store if he had to.

"No, I just need to go to sleep. This is the worst migraine I've ever had."

Jack's heart plummeted to his feet. *Shit*. At least he hadn't said anything stupid. A profound disappointment settled in the pit of his stomach. "What can I do?"

She shook her head. After she brushed her teeth, Jack helped her into the bedroom. The blinds were closed, and she'd obviously been asleep before he'd shown up. *Fuck.* Em hadn't flipped the light on in the bathroom, so he'd bet she had light sensitivity too. He pulled the covers up and placed a kiss on her forehead.

The thud of a truck door had Emily burying her head under the pillow.

Jack left and pulled the door over. He went to the kitchen and made a list of items she needed, and then he called Jeff, who offered to take care of it. Em had a washer and dryer behind folding doors in the hallway, so he stripped out of his clothes, put them in to wash, and jumped in the shower to wash off the last remnants of cologne.

He wrapped the towel around his hips and walked into the bedroom. The steady sound of Em's breathing was a relief. At least she'd been able to get back to sleep. He crawled into bed next to her, and she stirred, trying to move away from him, but he held her tight. "Smell me."

She inhaled deeply, and he felt her smile on his neck. "You don't smell anymore." She nestled against him and went back to sleep.

An hour later, his phone buzzed with a text alert. Jeff was outside with the groceries. He inched his way out of bed, wrapped the towel around his waist, and went to let Jeff in.

Jeff unloaded the groceries while Jack put his clothes in the dryer. Jeff brought Jack's overnight bag, so he pulled on a pair of sweatpants.

"Anything else?" Jeff asked.

"No, thanks, man, I appreciate you going to the store. I didn't want to leave her."

"No problem," Jeff said with a rare smile. Jack followed him downstairs and locked the door after him.

Em was still asleep, so he went into the living room and

made a few phone calls. He'd packed his notebook in his suitcase, which was on its way to the next venue, so he went into Em's office for some paper. A crumpled piece of paper was on the floor by her desk, so he picked it up. He hadn't meant to look at it, but when he saw the business name, he did. Elegant Affairs. It was an invoice for $1,137 for tuxes rented for April twenty-second, Em's wedding date. But the wedding had been canceled, so why was the rental place sending her a bill? It was even addressed to her and not the fucker. Probably the only thing she hadn't paid for. Jack grabbed a notepad and stalked out of her office. He hadn't been snooping, but now that he knew about it, he'd have to bring it up to her later, after she felt better.

Jack worked for a while then crawled back into bed with Em. She hadn't stirred since he'd left, which was really odd for her. Jack was hungry, but he didn't want to disturb her. She stirred when his stomach growled in protest. Her hand caressed his belly.

"You better feed that thing."

She snuggled closer, and he loved it.

"What time is it?"

"Just after seven."

"Morning or night?"

"Night."

She bolted upright. "Shit, I never called out sick." She rubbed her eyes. "I can't believe I slept so long." She looked around. "Where's my phone?"

She seemed confused. Jack sat up and rubbed her back. "Calm down. Your stuff was at the top of the stairs. I'll get it."

Jack retrieved her cell and handed it to her.

"I can't believe I missed two days of work." She turned the phone on and waited impatiently for it to boot up.

"What day do you think it is?" Jack settled back in bed,

pulling her between his legs so she could rest up against his chest. He needed the contact.

"Tuesday."

"It's Monday."

She looked at her phone and tapped on the text messages. "I don't understand, you weren't supposed to be her till Tuesday." Emily paused as she read his texts. "Oh, how awful, I hope no one was hurt."

"It happened overnight when the place was empty. I jumped on the first available flight this morning." Jack kissed the back of her head. Her hair was matted from sleeping on it, but she looked much better than she had when he'd arrived. "How're you feeling?"

Emily relaxed back against his chest. "My head still hurts, but it's better than it was."

"Are you going in tomorrow?" Jack asked.

"I'll have to see how I feel in the morning. Once the migraine resolves, I'll still feel crappy for the next two days. My head always feels hollowed out after a bad one."

"Do you get them often?"

"It's been a few years."

"What triggered it?"

"Bad news in the mail."

Jack tamped down on his anger. She wasn't going to tell him about it. When would she trust him? He was her boyfriend; he was supposed to know about this kind of stuff. Jack's stomach growled again.

"I think I felt it kick. You should eat. It's getting angry."

Jack chuckled. She could always make him laugh even when he was pissed. Emily moved so he could get up. "What about you? What can I make you?"

"Nothing."

Jack turned to look at her. "When was the last time you ate?"

"Breakfast."

"That doesn't count. You puked that up." He leaned over and kissed her lips. "How about a sandwich?"

"I don't have any cold cuts. I was going to go to the grocery store after work today, but that didn't happen." Emily covered her face with her hands. "I'm sorry, Jack, you didn't exactly get the welcome you were expecting."

He sat on the bed. "To be honest, I was hoping for wild sex first thing."

"Yeah, me too. And no puke."

"Hey, you're sick, and I was kidding. Besides, we have plenty of food. Jeff went grocery shopping, so we're all stocked up."

"You sent Jeff to the grocery store? Isn't that above and beyond the duties of a bodyguard?"

"When I told him you were sick, he offered. He has a soft spot for you."

Em smiled. "You're in good hands with him, so I worry a lot less than I would if someone else was watching out for you."

"You worry about me?" He liked that idea; it meant she cared.

She kissed him on the cheek. "Course I do, the traveling, all those handsy women, your stalker. I'm glad you have someone to look out for you."

Jack kissed her lips. He wanted to do more, but she was still unwell, so he pushed all selfish thoughts aside. "You have to eat something. What can I make you?"

"Vegetable soup."

Jack thought for a second. "I could make chicken noodle."

"Not make, heat up. Vegetarian vegetable in the pantry."

Jack made a face. "Canned soup?"

"I know it's weird, but it's my comfort food."

She looked totally adorable sitting in bed, ugly pajamas

and all, wanting him to make her canned soup. He'd remedy her pajama situation sooner than later. "Okay."

Jack went into the kitchen, heated up her soup, and made himself a roast beef sandwich on a roll. When he returned with their meal on a tray, Emily had dozed off but woke as soon as he sat on the bed.

She sat up and Jack put the tray over her lap. "Mmm, smells good." She crumbled a few crackers into the soup and then took a spoonful. "Yummy."

He sat next to her and ate his sandwich. She finished before he did and eyed his sandwich. "Something you want?" He took a big bite.

She nodded and pointed to his plate.

"What will you give me for it?" It was hard to chew with his mouth closed since he was grinning like an idiot.

"You owe me."

Jack raised his brows. "Do I?"

"Yeah, I gave you that ice cream cone."

Jack's heart flipped in his chest. He remembered their playful banter over that cone and how it felt so normal even though they'd just met. That she remembered it also made him feel...wanted. Like it had meant something to her. "I always pay my debts." Jack handed her the plate.

She spent the next few minutes enjoying his sandwich. When she got to the last bite, she offered it to him. He smiled, opened his mouth, and she fed it to him.

Jack left to wash the dishes, so Emily called Ben to let him know she was still alive.

"Hold on," he said.

Several seconds passed before Ben was back on the line

with Jerry. Emily chuckled. She knew they weren't twins, but they sure acted like it.

"How are you feeling, young lady?" Jerry asked.

"Well, I'm sitting upright and on the phone, so better."

"She still sounds unwell to me," Ben said. "She should take the day off tomorrow."

"Agreed," Jerry said.

Emily shook her head. "We have two client meetings tomorrow," she reminded them.

"Young lady," Ben said. "Our company benefits include a generous number of sick days for a reason. You're sick. Take the day off. We're perfectly capable of handling client meetings. We're not doddering old fools. Yet." They were both sharp as tacks, and they genuinely cared about the health and wellbeing of all their employees.

"Thank you. I can change my day off to tomorrow—"

"You'll do no such thing. That was a scheduled day off, and you'll take it." Jerry's tone indicated he'd brook no further argument from her.

She was so lucky she'd found this job. She must be crazy to consider leaving it. "Okay, you win."

They both laughed. "We'd fully intended to, my dear," Ben said.

"Do you need anything?" Jerry asked.

She looked at Jack as he walked into the room carrying another bottle of water for her and smiled. "No, I have everything I need."

"Have you eaten? How about some takeout? I'll call and have them deliver some soup," Jerry persisted.

"No, I just had some, and I have plenty more." She grinned at Jack. Sully never would've made her soup. Germaphobe that he was, at the first sign she was sick, he'd have crashed at a friend's. That wasn't really fair; she'd understood his paranoia over getting sick. His office was extremely competitive, and sick days were frowned upon.

"We'll see you on Thursday. Feel better."

Emily dropped her phone on the bed.

"Have you told your bosses about me?"

Emily furrowed her brow. "No."

He looked hurt by that. "Have you told anyone about us?"

Shit. "Nicki knows."

"Nicki doesn't count."

Emily laughed. "Don't tell her that." At Jack's continued scowl, she added, "Vince knows, and I told Meg."

"What about Eddie and your other friends? Do you even think of me as your boyfriend?" Jack stood and paced the room. "I tell everyone you're my girlfriend. I'm proud of us."

"You know that's not it."

"Then why haven't you told them?"

"Told them what? That I'm dating a rock star? They'll want details." Emily sputtered. "I didn't tell anyone about Sully the first month we dated, not even Nicki."

"I thought she was your best friend."

"She is, but I'm a private person. I wanted to be sure there was something to tell."

"You don't think we have something real? Something to tell?"

Emily sighed. She'd known he wouldn't understand. "Jack, you said yourself that our relationship would come with difficulties. It hasn't even been a month, and except for a quick visit on Mother's Day, we haven't seen each other for almost three weeks."

Jack sat on the edge of the bed facing away from her. "You don't think we're going to make it?"

Emily huffed. "What do you want me to say? We met at your concert, I slept with you that first night, I don't want to share that with people."

"You don't have to tell them that."

"I'm not ready."

"To what, share details or admit to yourself there are details?"

Emily threw the covers back. "What do I owe you for the groceries?"

"What?"

"I stayed with you at your hotel in New York for a week, and you paid for everything. I visited you in Hartford, and you paid for everything including the bus tickets. This isn't a free ride."

"Baby, this is stupid. I have the money."

"And I don't, that's what you mean, isn't it?"

"Do you?"

"I live on a budget just like everyone else that's *normal*."

Jack ignored that. "Why should you if I can just pay? It doesn't make sense."

"I don't feel comfortable with you paying for everything. The clothes alone cost a fortune. Do you know how much that underwear cost?"

Jack shrugged.

"Seven hundred dollars. That's crazy."

Jack gave her a wolfish grin. "Worth every penny."

Emily growled in frustration. "I don't want you to think that I don't appreciate it, because I do. You've been very generous, but you need to understand that I've been on my own for a long time. It's not easy for me to have you swooping in here thinking you're just going to take care of everything."

"You think I'm trying to take over."

"No, I'm... I don't want to fight." Yet she'd picked a fight with him. She knew he'd take it badly that she hadn't screamed from the rooftops about their relationship. She'd met his friends and family, yet other than Nicki, he hadn't met any of her friends. Picking up her phone, she thumbed through her contacts until she got to Eddie.

"Hey, beautiful, what's going on?"

"Hi, Eddie, how are Sheryl and the kids?"

"Fine. What's wrong?"

"Nothing."

"Bullshit. Tell me."

When Emily didn't answer right away, Eddie swore. "You have a migraine, don't you? I can hear it in your voice. I didn't know you still got those."

"Not as bad as I used to, and this is the first one in two years."

"What happened?"

"Listen, I'm feeling better, okay, just drop it."

Eddie swore again.

"I wanted to tell you that"—she looked at Jack who turned to face her—"I met someone." Why did this feel so awkward? Meeting someone was good news.

"Emi, that's great."

"His name's Jack, and he's a musician."

Eddie chuckled. "I look forward to meeting your young fellow."

"Really, Eddie, young fellow? You're thirty-nine." Emily rolled her eyes.

"Is he older than me?"

"No."

"Then he's a young fellow who needs to be prepared for a going over. Vince and I decided we're not taking any chances. He will be grilled, and if he can't take it, then you'll have your answer."

Emily shook her head but smiled. She loved them both. "What are you going to do, take out your guns and clean them?"

"No, that was your father's way of dealing with the

undeserving youths that came calling. I'll just intimidate him with my size, tats, and scary piercings." Sheryl laughed in the background.

"That might work."

"I need the practice." Eddie's voice grew husky. "We're having a girl."

"Holy crap, the triple terrors are going to have a baby sister?"

"Yes. They're so excited." As if on cue, the volume on Eddie's side increased. "They miss their favorite aunt." She heard the unmistakable sound of toddler feet and then Nicholas. "I wanna tawk Unty Emwe."

"Hi, Nicholas," she said to her three-year-old nephew. "Someone has a birthday coming up."

"It's mwe."

"It is you. What would you like?"

Nicholas spoke for a minute, reverting to his baby babble, but Emily got the gist. He wanted a motorcycle like daddy's. His older brothers, Teddy, seven, and Michael, five, had motorized ones, and Nicholas didn't like being left out. He made kissy sounds, and then Eddie was back on the line. "Hey," he paused as the chaos receded on his end. "I got him one." She could hear the pride in Eddie's voice. He was madly in love with his wife and adored his boys.

"He's getting easier to understand."

"His speech therapist says he's doing exceptionally well. Sheryl does the exercises with him every day." Eddie cleared his throat. "Let's plan something, you can visit with the terrors, and I will grill your young man."

"Jack travels a lot."

"The next time he's in town, bring him over. In the meantime, please come for a visit before my sons destroy our home. Apparently, you tell much better stories than I do."

They planned a dinner for the following Monday. She'd

drive down after work, spend the night, and leave early the next morning to go to work. It was supposed to rain, and Eddie didn't like her driving late at night.

Jack was smiling when she hung up. "What?

"You'll make a wonderful mom."

Emily wasn't so sure about that. Sully had left it up to her to decide if they'd have kids. He'd said he was fine either way, but it was a lot of pressure to have the ultimate decision left up to her. It was entirely too soon to have this discussion with Jack, so Emily changed the subject. "Maybe we could plan a dinner with them when you're off that week in June." She didn't want Jack to feel like she was hiding him.

Jack made a face. "Yeah, we never talked about that week. I promised my folks I'd visit. It's Father's Day weekend, and we haven't had a long visit since Christmas."

Disappointment crashed over her. She'd been looking forward to spending that week with him. It'd be the most time they'd see each other since that first week in the city, and she assumed they'd spend it together. Like a normal couple. Except they weren't a normal couple and never would be. Emily sighed. "Oh."

"Hey, if you could take a few days off work, I could ask my folks if you can come."

She was blinded by Jack's smile, but her heart felt heavy in her chest. She remembered what he'd said on Mother's Day about wanting to be with all the people he loved at the same time, but Emily didn't relish the idea of spending that much time with his mother. An awkward few hours was one thing, but a long weekend? Emily couldn't contain her shudder.

"Cold?" Jack went to her closet, pulled out a sweater, and draped it over her shoulders.

Emily felt guilty for not liking Jack's mother but not enough to encourage his idea. "I don't think that's a good idea, but we'll see each other before and after." And Father's

Day was as awful as Mother's Day, and birthdays, and Thanksgiving, and Christmas... "Your mom doesn't like me."

Jack's smile faded. She felt like she'd just taken away his favorite toy. "She doesn't know you yet." He sat on the bed and rubbed her arm. "Think about it?"

Fuck. She didn't want think about it. She. Didn't. Want. To. Go. It was bad enough she had to adjust to this new type of relationship, where she never really felt solid about any plans they made, but this was too much to ask of her. "Maybe I'll visit you while you're there."

"Em, this isn't going to work if you're not willing to make an effort." Jack stalked out.

Not making an effort? Are you fucking kidding? This relationship was nothing but effort: phone calls at all hours of the day and night, arranging her life around his tour schedule. And where the fuck was Nicki when she needed her? Off on tour with Curt.

Emily ripped off the sweater and jumped out of bed. Losing her balance, she landed hard on her bad leg. *Motherfucker.* She couldn't even have a fight with her boyfriend without the past invading, reminding her she was damaged. Tears threatened, but she refused to give in to them. She had something to say, and she'd damn well say it dry eyed.

She used the bed to push to her feet and got her bearings before more calmly walking into the living room. Jack sat on the couch gently strumming his guitar. He wasn't wearing a shirt, and it was just about the sexiest thing she'd ever seen. Instead of letting it deflate her anger, she forged ahead. "That's not fair. You can't just say something like that and walk out of the room." In the past, she'd have given in and apologized.

Jack put his guitar back in the case. "I don't want to fight about this right now, you're still recovering."

"Well, when exactly will we fight about this? You're off again in two days."

Jack scowled at her. "And there it is. This is my fault because I'm on the road."

Emily shook her head. "I don't know what that means. This isn't about blame, Jack. It's about how huge of an adjustment being with you is. You said I'm not making an effort, but it's all effort. It's all new to me. Don't you think asking me to stay at your parents is weird? It's not like we've been together for years or we're engaged. My parents would've never allowed something like that." Emily sat because her thigh ached, and her head pounded with the angry blood that coursed through her veins.

Jack sat next to her. "I'm sorry, you're right, I shouldn't have walked out like that. It's just... Christie used to blame me when things didn't go her way. I kept waiting for you to blame me for what happened Friday."

Puzzled, Emily glanced at Jack.

"Those guys in the bar. If I'd been here, that wouldn't have happened."

"Even if you lived here, it's not like we'd be together every second of the day. Some guys hitting on me wasn't your fault. Why would I blame you?"

"Because I'm never around."

"Maybe part of the problem with you and Christie was that you did too much for her. No wonder she attached herself to you. You made things easier for her, took away the struggle. She had no one else to blame when success wasn't handed to her. You set yourself up to be the perfect excuse for her failure to succeed."

Jack nodded. "She said I never did enough to help her career."

"You can't fix everything. I know you want to, and that's honorable but impossible. It's one of the things I admire most about you. Remember when we left the Garden that first night? What should've taken a few minutes turned into ten because you stopped to talk to everyone. You knew everything that was going on with your crew. It impressed me that you cared about the people around you, so it doesn't surprise me that you've had the same crew for so long."

"Why do I get the feeling there is a giant but coming?"

"But I won't have you making decisions for me. I don't want or need that."

Jack exhaled, closed his eyes, and said in a soft voice, "What do you need?"

Emily took his hand, and when he looked at her, she saw fear. "I need you to support my decisions."

"I don't want you seeing your ex again."

Emily sighed. "Do you really think I want to?"

Chapter Twenty

J ack knew she didn't. But that didn't ease his fear that the fucker would be able to convince her to give him a second chance. Especially now that the reality of what their relationship would be like was playing out. He still hadn't figured out why he was pushing her, but he needed to soon before he did or said something to fuck this up.

How could he explain when he didn't understand himself? He stared at the floor. "No, but you might change your mind now that you see how hard it's going to be."

When she didn't answer, he slowly raised his gaze, afraid to see her rejection. But Em was smiling at him. "What?"

"Jack, I'll admit that I have no idea how we are going to make this work, but I'm made of stronger stuff than that. If we don't work out, it won't be because of him. I don't want him back, and even if you're right that he'll try and win me back, it'll never happen. I could never trust him again. But it's not just that. I realize now that we had a few major issues that I'd ignored. We probably could've worked them out."

Jack's heart stopped beating.

Emily stood and paced. "After it happened, I was so hurt,

so...shocked, that all I thought about was catching them. But now that I've had some time to step back, his reaction wasn't what I would've expected it to be. He didn't look guilty or shocked or even try to explain." She stopped in front of Jack. "You know what he said to me?

Jack shook his head.

A sad little laugh escaped her lips, and she scrunched her eyes closed. "He said 'We have to talk.' Can you believe that? Like there was anything left to talk about. He'd blown up our relationship, and he wanted to talk." Emily sat. "I think he realized what I only now understand. We did need to talk, but it's too late for that now." When she opened her eyes, sadness shone in them. "You don't have anything to worry about, Jack. Sully made his choice, and it wasn't me."

His heart expanded with empathy for her pain, and he couldn't explain to her why he felt the fucker would be back. Jack just knew he would be.

Jack woke early the next morning. Em had slept in his arms most of the night, only turning away twice, which he'd remedied by scooting over and spooning her. He was starving, so he got up to cook breakfast. He loved to cook, and Em needed a hearty breakfast, so he decided on pancakes.

Her kitchen was much smaller than the one at his house in California, but it was laid out nicely. He searched out the necessary items and mixed up the batter for pancakes. While the first batch was cooking, he put on a pot of coffee. He flipped the pancakes then washed their dishes from the night before. He heard Em come into the kitchen, and when he turned to her, his breath caught. Bare feet, messed-up hair, sleepy, and wearing his T-shirt. He opened his arms, and she walked into them, resting her head on his chest. It felt so damn good to hold her, to feel her warm body against his.

"Pancakes are burning."

"Shit." He opened the kitchen window. "Sorry." Jack

scraped the ruined pancakes into the garbage. He put the pan on the stove to cool off. "Coffee's ready."

Em got two mugs and filled each one. She poured cream in both and added two teaspoons of sugar in his. Their fingers brushed as she handed him his mug, which sent a jolt of awareness down his arm. That she remembered how he took his coffee made him smile. Christie only drank tea, so she didn't understand coffee. At all.

After breakfast, they went for a long walk. The dense, dark clouds, that weighed heavily overhead, threatened but never produced rain. He made chicken cutlets for dinner while Em handled the pasta. They worked well together in her small kitchen. She bumped into him playfully, and he loved it. She was still shaky from her horrible migraine, so the wild sex would have to wait, but he didn't care. He loved being with her. It was so easy, so relaxed. It reminded him of how his parents worked so well together.

They stretched out on the couch to watch a movie, but Em fell asleep, so he turned off the TV. He enjoyed the steady sound of her breathing and started her third book.

Jack woke after midnight and carried her to their bed. She'd changed into sweats, and even they were sexier than those hideous pajamas. She had an amazing body that needed to be covered in satin and silk, if at all.

He woke up when she moved away from him, but it was only to strip off her sweatshirt. The moonlight streaming through the open blinds illuminated her perfect breasts. Jack reminded himself that she was still recovering. She slipped the sweatpants off. Damn, she'd been naked underneath the whole time. He'd known she wasn't wearing a bra—guys could always tell—but no panties either.

He'd take care of his needs later, but right now, he had to taste her. He'd read that orgasms helped relieve headaches, so hopefully he could convince her.

Em lay on her back. He leaned up on one elbow, cupping her bare breast with his other hand. She moaned and arched into his hand, so he leaned down, moved his hand to cup her other breast, and took her nipple into his mouth.

"Oh."

Her body shifted closer to him. As his lips moved up her neck, his hand stroked a path down her side and across her hip, settling between her slightly parted thighs. He caressed her mound then slipped two fingers between her lips. Her moisture coated his fingers, and this time, he moaned.

He kissed her lips as he stroked her clit, and his tongue mimicked the movement of his fingers. Her hand trailed down his stomach and curled around his dick. Jack loved her touch, firm yet tender. He wanted her, but he wasn't entirely sure he'd be able to control himself, so instead, he slipped two fingers into her and worked her clit with his thumb. She convulsed around his fingers and moaned into his mouth as she climaxed.

Jack rolled onto his back, and she nestled into him, her fingers stroking his chest. He was painfully hard, but he'd leave it up to her what would happen next. He didn't want sex badly enough to cause her discomfort of any kind.

"Mmm, that was a nice way to wake up." Emily kissed his neck. Her tongue peeked out and licked his skin, which sent a shudder down the length of his body.

"That didn't go exactly as I'd intended."

"How so?" She kissed his jaw.

His blood continued its southern trek, making it hard to think. "I planned on going down on you, but you came too quickly."

Emily's giggle warmed him. "That's your fault, you're really good with your hands." She snuggled closer, throwing one leg over his. "And your mouth."

"It's been so long, are you sure you remember—"

Her hand stroked his cock. He'd been about to ask her something but lost it when her hand closed around him. "Yeah, that feels good." He knew it had to do with fucking, fucking and...oh right, his mouth. "Sit on my face."

She continued stroking him as she sat up and only stopped when she'd straddled his torso. Walking up on her knees, she settled her pussy over his face. After a deep inhale of the intoxicating scent of her arousal, Jack closed his lips around her. Her body shuddered as he swirled his tongue around her swollen clit. He needed to come, so he jerked it while feasting on her.

"Oh, yeah..." She swiveled her hips over his mouth, temporarily breaking contact as she gripped the headboard. "Jaaack?"

"Yeah, baby?"

"I want to suck your cock."

He immediately released himself and helped her turn around and settle over his face again. She leaned down, her knotted nipples grazing his abs. Then he was in her mouth, and her tongue moved up and down his length, as her hand grasped the base of his cock. "Yeah" was all he could manage. He had better things to do with his mouth, so he pushed his thumb inside her as he suckled and licked. She was so fucking wet, always so wet for him, and he couldn't get enough.

Emily sat up and ground her pussy onto his face, as she stroked his cock, her saliva providing all the lubrication necessary. His balls tightened, and her mouth was on him again, not a second too soon, as he erupted into her waiting mouth. He held her hips in place as her orgasm shuddered through her. He wanted every last drop.

She bucked over him. "Yes." Her cries echoed off the walls.

He helped her to climb off and pulled her into his arms. "I love you."

Wednesday morning, Jack woke alone. The rich smell of

bacon frying drew him out of bed. After a quick trip to the bathroom, he joined her in the kitchen. Em wore his T-shirt, which rose as she reached into a cabinet, giving him a delightful view of her bare ass.

He couldn't help the moan that escaped his lips. She was so damn sexy that Jack didn't think he'd ever get enough.

She turned and smiled. "Morning."

Em looked much better. Her color was back to normal, and her smile held no hint of discomfort or pain. He hated seeing her in pain, but she let him take care of her. That was progress.

Jack poured himself a cup of coffee and refilled hers. She tended to the bacon, so when the English muffins popped out of the toaster, he buttered them.

Christie had never cooked him breakfast. She detested cooking and would eat cereal or yogurt for every meal to avoid it. He'd convinced her to take a cooking class when they'd first moved to L.A., but she'd hated it, so Jack went alone. He enjoyed working with his hands. Music, of course, but also the car he, Jimmy, and their dad worked on together. Cooking was another outlet for his creativity. He enjoyed the process of creating a meal from scratch, from choosing the fresh ingredients to chopping the vegetables. He liked simple food but enjoyed experimenting with variations on his favorites. He'd hoped cooking would be something he and Christie could do together, another bond to form. Jack hadn't minded doing the cooking, but it would've been nice if they could've shared it.

"Do you want to eat here"—she pointed to the counter— "or in the dining room?"

"Here's fine." He couldn't resist grabbing her when she placed the platter filled with bacon and scrambled eggs on the counter. She went on tiptoes, and their mouths crashed together. Her lips tasted of mint and coffee.

"Mmm." She pulled back from the kiss, her eyes alight with desire for him. "We should eat first."

He reluctantly released her, and she hopped up on one of the tall stools. They shared a comfortable silence as they filled their plates.

"Thank you for this," she said, indicating their food.

"My pleasure." Jack frowned. "Em, I don't want money to be an issue between us."

"I was mad. I'm sorry. But I meant what I said about wanting to pay for the food. I don't want you to feel like you're my meal ticket." She smiled and waved her hand over the platter. "Literally."

Jack put his fork down and turned to her. "That thought never entered my mind. You're the most independent person I've ever met. But, I want to be able to help you, and if I see something that I think you'd like, I want to buy it for you without you biting my head off."

"Yeah, sorry. I overreacted."

"So, is there anything I can help you with?"

Emily's fork stopped midway then she placed it on her plate. "You saw the bill, didn't you?"

Jack put his hands up. "I wasn't snooping. I forgot my notebook and needed some paper. It was on the floor, so I picked it up, but Elegant Affairs caught my eye. Why are they sending you the bill?"

Emily dropped her head in her hands. "Because Sully told them to." Emily pushed her plate away. "Why would he tell the guy it was my idea to cancel the wedding? He cheated, that was his idea. You don't cheat three weeks before your wedding when you *want* to get married."

"Baby, don't work yourself up over this again. I'll pay it."

Emily's eyes darkened. "The fuck you will. I'm not a kept woman, Jack."

"That's not what I meant. Look, it's only eleven hundred

bucks, let me pay for it, then you don't have to deal with him again." The fucker obviously had a plan all along; although, for the life of him, Jack had no idea why that bastard would screw with her like this.

"It's a lot of money to me." She ground her teeth and clenched her fists. She took a few deep breaths. "You can't just swoop in here and fix this."

She was being stubborn. "Why the hell not? I have the money."

Emily shook her head. "We just agreed not to let this kind of stuff be an issue between us. I thought you understood that I have to deal with him. I appreciate that you want to fix this for me, but it's my problem. You have to let me take care of it."

"This bullshit has been dogging us since we first met, and I need it to end. How am I supposed to move on with you if this shit keeps cropping up?" Emily flopped on the stool.

His temper flared. *Why does it matter so much?* She admitted they'd had issues. "Why are you so hung up on this asshole? If I make you happy, the past shouldn't matter."

Emily's head snapped up. "Because you overwhelm me, and even when you're not here, all I can think about is you."

A ridiculously goofy smile spread across his face. She couldn't stop thinking about him, which made him insanely happy. "Let me pay the bill. We'll get him out of our lives, and you can pay me back if you want to."

"Absolutely not. I'm not paying the bill. This was his responsibility, and if he forgot, then he's the one who should pay." Her jaw set in that stubborn way he'd come to recognize as intractable.

"You haven't heard from him?"

"No. He was supposed to be back last Saturday, so I texted him about picking up his stuff, but he never responded. The guy at Elegant Affairs said Sully told him to send me the bill."

Jack pounded his fist on the counter top. "That fucker has

an end game." He stood and paced, but Emily stepped in his way and stopped him, putting his arms around her.

"I wish I didn't have to see him again, or to still be dealing with this crap, but the sooner I get in touch with him, the sooner it'll be over."

"What's his number, I'll take care of it."

"No, Jack."

His pulse hammered. "Why are you being so stubborn? Let me help you."

"Because it's my problem, and I'll handle it."

"I feel like you're pushing me away."

"I'm not, but I need to handle this, please..." She rested her head on his shoulder.

"I don't want you seeing him without me." Jack kissed the top of her head. He needed to keep his shit together over this before it blew them apart.

Chapter Twenty-One

E mily hadn't been able to contact Sully while Jack was staying with her. Jeff had offered to "visit" him, but Emily didn't want this escalating out of her control. Her boyfriend and his bodyguard were both control freaks. Okay, that was harsh. Jack worried about her when they were apart, and Jeff had an avuncular affection for her which was very endearing. Her dad had watched over the families of his fallen brothers and sisters in much the same way, so she understood.

Emily continued to text Sully several times a day, mostly to annoy him. He was avoiding her, but she couldn't figure out why he hadn't picked up the rest of his stuff. He'd have a new place by now, and surely, he'd want his favorite black leather recliner with heat and massage in his new place? If she was petty, she'd slice it up with scissors, but that wasn't like her.

It was, however, not above Wanda's behavior. That was the name Eddie had given her when she'd refused to tell him hers. Wanda was the first character she'd created and had become Emily's alter ego, who she'd drawn strength from while recovering from the accident. Wanda didn't take shit from anyone. She was an in your face, bitch-slapping, six-foot-tall blonde who wore five-inch spiked heels, miniskirts, and a black leather jacket. The jacket looked remarkably like the one Eddie still wore. He was a bad ass, and he didn't take shit from anyone, not even her. It was one of the things she loved about him.

When she'd started physical therapy, it had taken longer than she'd thought it would to see progress, so she'd stopped going. So Eddie had come to her room and had annoyed the crap out of her until she'd agreed to return. He'd told her about his accident, his three surgeries, and the tattoo artist that did the cover-up over his scars. He'd shown her pictures before and after the tattoo, and his scars were a lot worse than hers. Once she'd completed her rehab, he'd shown her the finished tattoo. It was cool, but she didn't want that. She'd never be able to wear shorts or skirts again. A tattoo covering her scars wouldn't change that. And no cute heels or any shoe that changed the angle of her ankle too much. The pins and screws ruled her.

MONDAY, AS SOON AS EMILY SHUT OFF THE ENGINE, the front door to Eddie's house crashed open. She was barely out of the car when her three nephews attached themselves to her legs.

"That's enough, boys," Eddie yelled, as he ran down the walkway. "Give Aunt Emily a break."

Three little Eddies pouted and released her but still crowded around her. They looked just like him from the jet-black hair to the azure blue of his eyes. Hopefully, baby girl Burris would take after Sheryl. She was a petite blonde with stunning green eyes.

"Now, boys, we talked about this. You have to be gentle with all girls. No roughhousing."

"Bwut Unty Emwe wikes it when we pway wif fer." Little Nicholas pouted. Nicholas was small for his age; Teddy and Michael towered over him.

Eddie picked up his youngest son and put him on his shoulders. "Nicholas, you can play with Aunt Emily but gently. I'll get that." Eddie took her overnight bag and the carrier that held the cake and cookies she'd made yesterday. Teddy and Michael held Emily's hands and didn't let go until they all walked into the kitchen.

Sheryl pulled a roast out of the oven. At five months pregnant, Sheryl glowed and had a well-rounded baby bump. Her petite frame was deceptively strong. She routinely beat Eddie at arm wrestling, and Eddie assured them that he didn't let her win.

She hugged Sheryl. "You look radiant. I'm so happy for you."

Sheryl pulled back and studied her. "You look glowy yourself." She winked at Eddie. "I want all the details about Jack. Eddie tells me he'll be joining us for dinner next time he's in town."

Eddie grunted. "Grill first, and if he passes, he can stay for dinner."

"I want a cookie." Teddy and Michael said in unison.

"Mwe twoo." Nicholas bounced.

Eddie put the cookies on top of the fridge. "After dinner." He turned and stared them down. All three boys burst out laughing. Eddie shook his head. "They used to be afraid of me."

"Who are you kidding, Eddie? You've never even raised your voice to the boys." Sheryl hugged her husband, who easily lifted her and kissed her full on the lips.

That sent the boys into fits of gagging and making vomit sounds along with a chorus of "ews" and "yucks."

Eddie set Sheryl on her feet and smiled proudly. "Still got it."

Grossing the boys out was one of his favorite pastimes and no easier way to do it than to kiss their mom in front of them.

Sheryl shooed the boys from the kitchen. "Go wash up, dinner will be in ten minutes. And help Nicholas."

Stomping feet went up the stairs, and the water faucet turned on full blast.

"It's good to see you, Emi. Sheryl's right, you do look all glowy." Eddie hugged her and kissed the top of her head. "Something you want to tell me?"

Sheryl swatted her husband's arm. "Pregnancy isn't the only thing that makes a woman glow." She gave Emily a sympathetic smile. "Your new boyfriend is in for it. He's been on the phone to Vince twice about it. Vince may even fly in if he can get away."

A ruckus broke out upstairs, so Eddie went up to intercede.

"Can I help?" Emily asked.

Sheryl looked around. "Nope." She gave Emily a knowing look. "Don't want to share the details just yet?"

Emily looked down. "Not really. He's great, but with everything that happened with Sully, I'm not sure I can still trust my instincts."

"Hey, we're family." Sheryl took her hand. "You couldn't have done anything that would make what he did okay. Take your time, and don't let Eddie and Vince pull that older brother routine on you. Tell us when you're ready."

Truth was, she liked the older brother routine. Riley always protected her.

The boys stampeded down the stairs and into the kitchen, followed by Eddie, whose T-shirt was spotted with water.

"I'm wungwy." Nicholas reached for his dad.

"Well, that's good, because dinner's ready." Eddie picked Nicholas up and put him in his highchair.

Emily was so blessed that Eddie and Sheryl had taken her into their family. They were both estranged from theirs. She and Vince were godparents to the three boys, and Eddie had asked them again for the new baby.

After dinner, Emily helped Eddie give the boys a bath so Sheryl could rest. They had dessert, and Emily made up three stories before the boys fell asleep. Teddy volunteered to sleep in his sleeping bag so Emily could have his room. Eddie tucked Nicholas in, kissing him on the head.

"What are you going to do after the baby comes?" Emily asked as they went downstairs. They had a three-bedroom split level.

"We're going to get bunk beds, and Teddy will move in. He sleeps on the floor in their room most nights anyway." The three boys were very close. When Teddy went to preschool, Michael cried for two days, and Nicholas was jealous that he couldn't go to school with his brothers.

They found Sheryl asleep on the couch, so they went into the kitchen. Eddie cut himself another piece of cake. "You want?"

"No, thanks, I'm stuffed."

Eddie licked icing off his fingers. "You make great cake, Emi."

"How's Sheryl really doing?" Sheryl seemed more tired than usual. Of course, she had three active boys, so it could be that.

Eddie smiled. "She tires more easily, but she's healthy, and so's the baby."

Emily smiled back. "A girl, I'm so happy for you." Eddie might look scary on the outside, but he was a sweetheart, and he'd always wanted a daughter who'd look just like Sheryl.

Eddie's face turned serious. "So, tell me about this guy."

Emily's smile faded. "What do you want to know?"

"How did you meet?"

"Nicki dragged me to a concert."

Eddie chuckled. "It's not like you to"—he cleared his throat—"move on so quickly." His smile faded. "I still think Vince and I should have a talk with that bastard. I can't believe—"

"Yeah, me either." Even though she now accepted her willful disregard for any qualms she'd had about their relationship, she was still blindsided by Sully cheating on her. Her misgivings aside, that still didn't make any sense. Emily wagged her finger at Eddie. "No talking." She knew that talking didn't mean talking. "You have your own family to protect."

Eddie scowled at her. "You, Vince, and Sheryl are *my* family."

She and Vince had been patients of Eddie's, but they'd formed a family of their own. Vince was a year older than her. His parents spent most of their time stoned, and they'd thought it was a great idea to dope Vince up and had gotten him high for the first time when he was seven. He hadn't seen his parents since he'd plowed their car into a tree and ended up in the hospital with a broken arm, leg, and three ribs.

Emily stood and put the dessert dishes in the dishwasher. When she turned, Eddie was rubbing his knee. "Still bothers you?"

Eddie smiled. "Storm's coming. I'm glad you're not driving in this."

He'd wrecked his car at night in the rain when he was nineteen.

"The nightmares are back?"

Emily nodded.

"Bad?"

"Worse than ever. I hear screaming and feel the heat."

Emily swallowed hard.

Eddie took her hand. "I think it's time you remembered."

Emily pulled free and stood. "I don't want to. One of the only saving graces was that I couldn't remember what happened."

Eddie's arms closed around her. "I think that your mind knows it's okay now. You'll never be able to fully let it go, but you've held it for too long."

"If remembering is the only way to do that, I'd rather not."

Eddie turned her to face him. "If you never remembered, that'd be fine, but it's not healthy to avoid it." Emily tried to look away. "Believe me, beautiful, I know. Not wanting to remember bad stuff caused more damage in my life. Damage that could've been avoided."

Emily leaned into him. Eddie had been through so much it made her heart ache. "I don't think I'm strong enough."

Eddie pulled back. "I didn't think I was either until I met Sheryl. I couldn't have done it without her love and support."

He was the bravest man she'd ever met. He'd slayed his demons and left them in a bloody pile. She felt like some of his immense courage passed to her and gratitude washed over her.

Eddie kissed the top of her head. "I'm beat. You need anything?"

"No." Something told her she had everything she needed.

"Goodnight." He walked into the living room and carried his still sleeping wife up to their room.

Emily shut the lights off and went to Teddy's room. She knew Eddie meant well, but she didn't want to remember, and she hoped he was wrong. At first, having no memory had been weird until the neurologist had explained that sometimes the brain didn't remember because it was trying to protect. Since her imagination could conjure up the most awful things, Emily prayed her brain continued to protect her.

Chapter Twenty-Two

J ack forgot to turn his phone off during soundcheck, so when it rang and he looked at the screen, his heart stuck in his throat. Wayne Ettinger wouldn't be calling him unless something happened to Christie. "I need a minute." He walked to the edge of the stage. "Wayne, everything okay?"

"Not Wayne, silly. It's me," Christie said, slurring every word.

"Why are you calling me?"

"I miss you, baby."

Fuck. He'd changed his number after the incident at Christmas. He'd only given it to her parents in case of an emergency. "Christie, it's over. I've moved on and so should you." Jack hated saying it—he didn't want to be cruel—but she needed to know they were over.

"No woman will ever be able to give you what I can, baby."

Ice clinked inside a glass. "Where are you?"

"Home."

"Home where?" She had to be at her folks' place since she was using her dad's cell.

"Home, home. You know, where every pathetic actress runs to when she loses her apartment."

She wasn't above lying, and he recognized the changed pitch in her voice. "Christie"—Jack paused trying to hold on to his temper—"I paid for a year in advance. You didn't lose your apartment."

"Pooh. Fine. I'm home for a visit. You think I'm pathetic." She sniffled loudly.

"You said that, not me."

"You didn't disagree with me." More sniffling.

Jack had to end this now. "You know very well that I think you're an amazing actor. I have to go. Please don't call me again." He disconnected the call and turned his phone off. He needed to get a new number.

EM HADN'T CALLED HIM BEFORE HIS GIG TONIGHT. When they got back to the dressing room, he realized he'd never turned his phone back on. Shit, three more calls from Christie and one call and two texts from Em. She sent him a picture of her from the neck down in one of the lace T-shirts she'd purchased, and luckily, no one was around when he checked it. He immediately moved it to a password protected folder on his phone. Her second text was: *R U OK? ;)* which made him laugh because he remembered their conversation in the cab about texting and poor grammar. She'd obviously expected a response to her picture.

He didn't bother listening to the messages. All he wanted to do was hear Em's voice. Before he could connect the call, Jeff knocked and opened the door. "Guys, we're ready for you."

Fuck. Meet and greet. "How many?"

"Ten." Jeff waited at the open door.

Their fans paid extra to get VIP access to the band, and they'd all agreed that on this tour they'd be donating the money to local charities in the cities they played. "One minute." Jack sent Em a quick text: *Sorry, babe, phone off. Love picture. Love you. Meet greet. Call U later ;)*

Before his phone was in his pocket, she responded with a "K". She must've been worried. Which meant she cared, which made him smile.

As soon as the meet and greet finished, Jack pulled out his phone, but before he could connect, Viv was next to him talking.

"Brian told me you needed a new phone number. Is everything okay?"

Her eyes were full of concern. She was a good kid. "Yeah, someone got my personal cell that shouldn't have it, so I gotta get a new number."

"I can take care of that for you. Here's one of the office phones, you can use it till I get your new number." She smiled brightly.

"Thanks, Viv, but I'll take care of it myself tomorrow." He turned to leave, but she stopped him.

"Jack, it's my job to help you guys." Her full lips formed a small pout.

"Actually, it's your job to help Brian. I appreciate it, but you have two days off, and you deserve them. I'll handle this one." He winked and smiled. He had no intention of handing his phone over to anyone.

"You're the boss's boss."

Viv seemed hurt, so Jack added, "You and Holden doing anything fun during the break?"

Viv's eyes widened, and she stammered, "Uh, what do you mean?"

"Hey, relax. That's Brian's rule, not ours. Touring is a

tough life, so if you and Holden are happy, then I'm happy." He winked at her. "It'll be our secret."

She smiled and left.

Jeff escorted the band to the SUV. He called Em as soon as his butt hit the seat. It was almost midnight.

"Hey. How'd the gig go?"

Just hearing her voice elevated his heart rate. "Great. Sorry it's so late. How was your day?"

Emily yawned. "Good. Got that new account. They need something by the end of the week, so since you're not coming in until later tomorrow, I'm going to go into the office. It was silly to take the day when you wouldn't be here until mid-afternoon. Gotta optimize my days so we can maximize our time together."

Fuck! He'd forgotten to text her he'd been able to get a flight at six thirty instead of the noon flight. Since he didn't want her to feel bad, he didn't mention it. "Okay." He was disappointed they wouldn't get to spend the day together. He missed her more and more each visit.

AFTER JACK CHECKED INTO HIS MOTEL, HE RAN SOME errands. Since Curt would be spending the break at Nicki's townhouse, they'd planned a double date, and they were happy to help him with his surprise for Em.

It had been a month since their first week in New York together, and they hadn't gone on any dates. He wanted to prove to her that they could have a little bit of normal together, and meeting another couple for drinks was a very normal thing. He'd show her they could have a normal, non-rock star date.

He gave Jeff the night off, which promptly elicited a "no

fucking way" from him. He'd be there but unseen. Even though Jack was technically Jeff's boss, there was no way to stop Jeff from guarding him especially when he was with Em.

They'd arranged to meet at The Vine and Barrel, a wine and whiskey bar, halfway between Nicki's and Em's places. Nicki told him to dress up, so one of his errands was picking up something appropriate to wear.

After he got the shopping done, he stopped and got a new cell number. The guy wanted to sell him the newest phone, but his was only five months old. He wasn't that much of a techie when it came to phones, but instruments and recording equipment were another story.

He texted his new number to the guys, Dex, Kevin, his folks, Trish, and Jimmy. Jeff had programmed his phone while they were still in the store. He called Em with the new number while she was at work, so she couldn't talk long. She was in the middle of a brainstorm and didn't want to interrupt the flow.

Just as he hung up, his phone played "The Trees." "Hey, Dad, what's up?" This was the third time he'd been forced to change his number since his split with Christie, and his folks weren't stupid.

"New number, huh?"

"Yup."

"Problem?"

Jack rubbed the back of his neck. "Christie called me the other night. That won't happen again."

"How'd she get the number?" Will asked.

"I gave it to Wayne and Carla in case of an emergency. Christie figured out they had it and called from Wayne's phone. I arranged for them to call Dex in the future if there's an emergency."

Will sighed. "I figured it had to do with her. How does Emily feel about this situation?"

"It's not a situation, Dad. I handled it, and it won't happen again. I know that you guys won't give her the number, she doesn't have Kevin's contact, and Dex sure as hell won't tell her. Handled." His dad's concern for Emily aside, he was a grown-ass man. "Em understood. She's had her own situations with her ex."

And she had understood. She felt sorry for Christie and had more empathy for her situation than most people, probably because of her experience with her friend Vince and his addiction.

"Emily is an amazing young woman, Jack. She's actually why I'm calling."

Jack knew his mom didn't like Em; although for the life of him, he couldn't figure out why. She'd always been fair-minded, but she was being unreasonable. Emily hadn't decided what to do the week in June yet, but Jack suspected he'd be splitting his time. "About Em, why?"

"We've been talking about it, and we'd like you to invite her to visit when you come in June."

Jack stopped and sat in the outside seating of a coffee shop. He expected he'd have to talk them into inviting her. Now that they'd offered, that would certainly help to convince Em. "Dad, that's great. I'd love that." He exhaled and felt a weight lift off his shoulders. In the past, he'd have told them he was bringing someone home, but what Em had said about her folks never allowing that had him wondering if he'd been an asshole all these years.

From what she'd told him about her family, it seemed that Em's parents were a lot like his. A sudden lump in his throat made it hard to swallow. Her folks were good people, and she'd had a great life with them. Just like he'd had with his family. If he'd lost them, he didn't think he'd have handled it as well as she had. Em had battled her way back from one of the worst things that could happen to a person except she'd just been a kid, so it was even more remarkable.

"Jack, is everything all right?" Will's voice ripped him out of his thoughts.

"Yeah, sorry. I'm seeing her later." After a quick catch-up about the family, Jack disconnected the call. He was so excited; the idea that he'd get nine days in a row with her if she agreed, sped up his pulse. Then he'd really be able to show her normal.

"WE'RE SORRY; YOU HAVE REACHED A NUMBER THAT has been disconnected or is no longer in service. If you feel you have reached this recording in error, please check the number and try your call again."

The receiver lands in the cradle with such force it bounces out and clatters to the floor. Fuck. Now what?

Nothing's working out the way it's supposed to, but then nothing ever does. Jack and I should be together, but we're not. It's that stupid whore's fault. What's Jackie thinking? He can't move on without me. We have a special connection.

What does she have that I don't? I gaze at myself in the mirror. Objectively speaking, I'm tall, blonde, and gorgeous. My tits are the perfect handful. What was it that asshole ex of mine used to say? Right, a walking wet dream; every man's fantasy. He used to hang back whenever we entered a room so he could see the envy in the eyes of every other man.

He only appreciated me for my looks and thought I was just another ditzy blonde, but Jack is all about what's inside a person. Of course, he enjoys the packaging as much as the next guy.

Men are always underestimating me. I need to burn off some of my anger, so I change into my jogging shorts and tight tank top. I pop my earbuds in and scroll to the song Jack wrote for me. Every time I listen to it, I'm more convinced Jack's soul is calling to mine.

His smooth voice sings to me.

"Not the welcome home I hoped for, baby. I've traveled so far. Please let me come home."

Yes, Jackie, come home to me.

Chapter Twenty-Three

On Wednesday during her lunch break, the Sullivans had called her again, but she hadn't decided yet, so she let the call go to voicemail. She couldn't get the idea out of her head to use the money to live on so she could write full time. It was a huge gamble. Meg had assured her that the readers would love more from her, but Emily loved her job at Bradford and Ross. They were like family; Ben and Jerry looked out for all their employees, but they were especially fond of her. As she was of them. They'd confided their story to her, and she'd been honored. It reminded her that even though other's lives might look perfect, they rarely were. Ben and Jerry were closer than any two brothers she'd ever seen.

On Thursday, Emily was so distracted with thoughts of Jack McBride that she struggled to concentrate on the task at hand—finishing copy for the Pets for Patriots campaign that B & R was donating for a fundraiser they were holding.

What was wrong with her? He was just a guy. But he wasn't. Jack was special, and she'd never met anyone like him. He was smart, talented, compassionate, and caring. Just thinking about him set Emily's pulse racing. She'd felt chemistry before, but this went beyond that.

She was equal parts nervous and excited for their double date with Curt and Nicki, and Emily appreciated the effort Jack was putting in to make their relationship more normal.

Before she left the office, she texted Sully again because he still hadn't responded to any of her calls or texts. Emily was tempted to donate it all just so she didn't have to look at it anymore. She wanted that chapter of her life closed so she could focus on her new relationship with Jack.

A rock star.

She was out of her mind.

When she got home from work, the opaque, black, thigh-high stockings and red-and-black-plaid skirt she'd ordered had arrived. Paired with a black chiffon blouse and her black suede lace-up boots, it was the outfit she'd pictured when writing one of the short stories for Jack. Except that skirt barely covered her butt, the thigh highs hadn't been opaque, and the boots had five-inch stiletto heels, but she hoped Jack wouldn't mind.

Emily wasn't sure she'd have the nerve to wear the outfit in public; it was more slutty than elegant, especially for The Vine and Barrel. She knew Nicki would love it. Since it was late May, it was warm to be wearing opaque stockings and boots, but once they got back to her place, the outfit wouldn't last long. He loved sexy underwear, and she wanted to be sexy for him.

Jack called to say he was running late, so she left to meet him at the bar. The twenty-minute drive seemed to take forever. Anticipation fluttered in her belly, and she had to blast the AC to keep from sweating. When she arrived, Nicki and Curt were seated at a high round table. She felt self-conscious and resisted the urge to tug the skirt down. It ended an inch above her knees, and even though the opaque stockings hid her scars, Emily hadn't worn a skirt this short in ten years. She always felt more at ease in pants, but on those occasions where a dress or skirt was required, even though the fabric reached her ankles, she still wore tights. It was the only way she felt covered enough.

When she approached the table, Curt whistled, which made her smile. Nicki playfully swatted his arm. His love for Nicki radiated off him like a disturbance in the atmosphere, and Emily had never seen Nicki happier.

Nicki tore her eyes off Curt and stood to hug her. "You look amazing, Emi. Is that new?"

Emily felt sexy so she turned in a circle which was so unlike her. It must be the outfit. Dressing in pants and long skirts had robbed her of this sexy feeling.

Curt looked down. "Jack called, he'll be another half hour."

"Oh." What if he was losing interest in her? He met hundreds of beautiful, stylish, sexy women. How could she compete with that? Maybe he was just trying to break it to her gently. But Nicki would've said something if Jack's interest was waning. *Damn.* She needed a drink to calm her nerves.

Curt raised his hand to the server, but Emily was too nervous to sit. "I'll go to the bar." She noticed a few guys staring at her, and even though she was flattered, that wasn't why she'd dressed like this. She'd done it for one very special guy who she hoped wasn't standing her up.

The bartender was helping another customer, so Emily—way more carefully than she needed to—sat on the bar stool. She had no interest in cultivating attention from any other guy. The lace tops of the thigh highs were meant for Jack's eyes and hands only.

She felt someone behind her, and then a large hand placed a glass of red wine on the bar. A deep voice said, "Have a drink with me."

Shit. She hadn't anticipated Jack not being here. When she turned, ready to blow the guy off, her mouth dropped open, but no words came out.

Brown hair, combed and parted, sparkling blue eyes, and that smile. He'd purposely lowered his voice when he spoke, so the shock of seeing him standing there, looking utterly delicious, in a navy blazer, sky blue button-down, and tan slacks, almost had her sliding off the barstool.

"I'm sorry, I'm waiting for my boyfriend." He looked so handsome she had a hard time keeping her breath steady.

He sat on the stool next to her. "Boyfriend, huh? Lucky guy. Are you sure he's worth the wait?"

His blue eyes sparkled which sent a shockwave down to her belly. Suddenly hot, she resisted the urge to fan herself. "Definitely." She smiled coyly. Her brain was so clouded with lust it had taken her a few seconds to realize this was a scene from one of the stories she'd written for him.

"Definitely, huh? Well, if I were your boyfriend, I would've picked you up. Certainly never let you walk in here dressed like that"—Jack's gaze stroked over her—"without staking my claim."

Emily smiled, but she couldn't keep up the pretense that she wasn't interested as her character in the story had. They hadn't been together in eight days, and she'd missed him. She slid off the barstool, being sure to let her skirt ride up a little so the lace tops of her stockings peeked out. She knew he'd seen because he gulped. She threw her arms around him, and when their lips met, she was lost to the fact they were in a bar, in public, with dozens of people around.

There was only Jack.

He groaned when she leaned into his body. He pulled back and whispered, "Baby, this isn't a good idea." His eyes were dazed and filled with desire.

Emily pouted. "I thought that was the idea."

Shock registered on his handsome face. "As much as I'd like to take you out back and fuck you up against the building, it's way too public," he whispered.

Emily grinned. The idea was so tantalizing that if he'd been into it, she wouldn't have refused him. At least one of them was thinking clearly. She liked seeing his shocked expression, so she said, "Maybe out back is empty?"

Jack narrowed his eyes then grinned. "It isn't. There's a clear view to the apartment complex, and they have patios."

"You checked out back?" Heat pooled between her thighs.

Jack raised a brow and smiled in response. He kissed her lips too briefly. "Yup."

His wicked smile caused her nipples to pucker, so she leaned into his chest.

Jack groaned. "Are we back to being us?"

Emily nodded. She was in serious trouble here. She should know better than to play games with Jack. There probably wasn't a sex game he hadn't played. Then, a most unwelcome thought took up residence in her mind. She shook her head to try and banish it, but it didn't work. What if he'd slept with Meg? The idea that they might have hooked up back in the band's early days turned her stomach.

Jack's hand waved in front of her face. "Hey, you okay?"

"Sorry. Yes, we're back to being us."

He took their drinks from the bar and escorted her to the table. "Might as well enjoy drinks with friends."

He was so thoughtful. This was a normal thing for couples to do. She missed Nicki almost as much as she missed Jack. She was used to having her to bounce ideas off of but found herself not wanting to interrupt Nicki's time with Curt.

Nicki smiled wickedly. "You two practically devoured each other." She winked at Jack. "At least you kept your head."

Emily sat next to Nicki, and Jack sat on the other side of

her. His hand settled on her thigh. "So, how's life on the road?" Emily asked.

Nicki's smile widened. "I love it. I would hate to be away from Curt—Sorry."

Curt put his arm around her. "I'm sure it's okay, babe, Emily knows what you meant."

His attention never strayed from Nicki. Until Curt, the guys Nicki had dated were mostly mid-thirties, but she'd told Emily that she didn't care that he was almost three years younger than her.

Jack's fingers teased at the hem of her skirt. Emily shifted closer and took a sip of her wine.

"Nicki says you're an amazing writer, too. Have you ever considered quitting your day job?" Curt asked.

Luckily, Emily had just swallowed her sip of wine. "Uh, no, not really."

"Why not?"

Everyone at the table stared at her, and Jack's hand stopped teasing her thigh. She took a deep breath. "Eighty-eight percent of writers have day jobs. I have to be able to support myself. Besides, I love working at Bradford and Ross. I'm lucky that I get to write for my job, too.

Jack squeezed her thigh. "I love your books. They're amazing."

Nicki had been telling her for years to give up her day job, but Emily hadn't received a trust fund when she'd turned twenty-five. Emily turned to Jack. "You have to say that 'cause you're my boyfriend."

He tilted her chin so she'd meet his eyes. "I'm saying it because it's true."

She wanted to look away, but he held her gaze with those tractor beam eyes of his. "Thank you." This was all new to her. She was used to Nicki cheering her on; they did that for each other, but the idea that Jack really loved her stories sent a warmth spreading through her. She had no doubt he meant it.

Nicki cleared her throat. "You two already put on one show. How's the new book coming?"

Emily somehow managed to tear her eyes away from Jack's. "Pretty good. I'm about a third done, and Meg loves the title." Emily always found the titles to be the hardest part. But with this book, it had come to her first, and she was writing the book around it.

"I suck at titles," Nicki said. "What is it?"

"*No More Yesterdays.*"

Nicki squealed. "I love it." She also gave Jack a wink.

Since their first week together, Jack hadn't asked her a single question about the accident, and Emily suspected Nicki told him. She wasn't exactly mad, but if she were being completely honest with herself, she was jealous that Nicki got to see more of Jack than she did. "Anyway, Meg had a few suggestions, but other than that, it's the usual problem."

Curt tilted his head to the side. "I'm new to all this writer stuff. What's the usual problem?"

"Never enough time," Emily and Nicki said in unison.

"You know, Em, I could help—"

Emily's head snapped to Jack so fast it cut him off. "Don't."

"I just want to help."

She swiveled her stool so she could face him. "I know that, but I'm not your responsibility."

A hurt look filled Jack's eyes. Damn. It always came back to this. He wanted her to be his responsibility, but it was too soon. Way too soon. Maybe someday, after they were married —Whoa. Where the hell had that thought come from? "Excuse me." She slid off her stool before Jack could stop her. Nicki followed, but Emily didn't stop until she'd pushed open the door to the ladies' room.

"Hey," Nicki said, rubbing her back. "What just happened there?"

Emily ignored her and wet some paper towels and dabbed her burning cheeks. She needed several deep breaths before she looked at Nicki. "The same thing that always happens. He's hurt because I'm not in the same place he is yet."

"You mean in love with him."

She swallowed hard. "Yes."

"Are you sure?" Nicki reapplied her lipstick.

Emily looked at her reflection in the mirror. "I think I'd know." She met Nicki's eyes in the mirror. "I miss you."

"I miss you, too." Nicki turned and they hugged. "Traveling has really sparked my creativity. I'm almost done with the book I started before we met, and I have ideas for two more."

"I'm so happy for you, sweetie. You deserve this."

Nicki pulled back. "So do you. You've been through so much. Jack's just trying to help."

"I know. But he helped his last girlfriend too much. He doesn't know when to stop. I don't want that to happen to us."

"It won't. You're Emily, not Christie. He loves you. Curt told me he's never seen Jack like this before. When you guys aren't together, he's cranky, and apparently, Jack's never cranky." She smiled. "Elliot says he's being a bitchy girl. He's so funny."

Great, now not only was the pressure to return his feelings growing, but she was making him cranky. Emily slumped against the counter. This wasn't the beginning of their two days together that she'd hoped for.

The door swung open, and two very tipsy women stumbled in, giggling. One nearly spilled her wine. Who brought their wine into the bathroom? *Gross.*

When they got back to their table, Jack and Curt stood. She smiled at Jack.

He dropped a featherlight kiss on her lips and smiled. "Sorry."

They finished their drinks with easy conversation and plenty of laughter. Seeing Jack had so scrambled her brain that she'd forgotten she'd driven here. Emily was glad she'd only had one glass of wine; otherwise, they'd have to leave her car. They waved goodbye to Curt and Nicki. Emily dug out her keys, but before she could unlock the door, Jack took them from her.

"Jeff will drive your car back, if that's okay?"

She hadn't seen him in the bar or waiting outside. Sneaky bastard. "That'd be fine."

Jeff smiled knowingly. "Didn't see me, huh?"

"No."

Jack unlocked a silver SUV, opened the door, and helped her in.

JACK'S HEART STILL HAMMERED IN HIS CHEST. HE'D never expected her to show up looking so...slutty: that plaid short skirt with the black not quite see-through blouse. And she wore thigh highs. His heart almost exploded out of his chest when she walked into the bar. He'd texted Curt to tell her he'd be late because he needed time to get himself under control.

He kept his speed five miles over the limit, because the last thing he needed was to get pulled over. He needed to fuck her soon; otherwise, he was positive his dick would explode.

They'd had the same idea, though. Her outfit was exactly like the one described in the story with the slutty professor. He was her student, and she'd offered to tutor him. Privately.

The twenty-minute drive did nothing to ease his discomfort, and she knew it. She'd pay for that sassy smirk of hers. When he finally pulled into the parking lot of her complex, he left the SUV running, helped Em out of the truck, and handed the keys over to Jeff. Jeff handed Emily her keys, and they walked hand in hand to her front door.

Emily flipped on the light switch as they went up the stairs. As soon as he reached the top step, he grabbed her and pulled her into his arms, sending her purse and keys crashing to the floor. Enough games. His lips took hers in a fiery kiss as he lifted her, and her arms and legs wrapped around him. He had her right where he wanted her—up against the wall. Except they were still dressed.

Her hands traveled down his chest as she undid the buttons of his shirt, stopping halfway so she could touch his bare skin. Her tongue explored his mouth, and any doubts that developed while they were apart vaporized. She wanted him as badly as he wanted her.

He tore his lips from hers. "I need you naked. Now."

She nodded as her hands left his shirt and undid the buttons on her blouse, but he stopped her. That was his job. When he pulled her away from the wall, she whimpered. He kissed her deeply then bit her bottom lip gently. "Don't worry, baby, we'll get back to the wall as soon as we're naked."

She smiled, and his heart flipped. Sexually, they were definitely on the same wavelength. His fingers deftly undid the buttons on her blouse, revealing a black satin push-up bra. As the tops of her breasts were revealed, he couldn't resist placing hot, wet kisses on her beautiful, creamy flesh.

Her head lolled back, and she moaned as he caught her nipple in his teeth. "Fuck, Jack, ohhh."

His girl liked it rough.

Jack dropped to his knees, kissing her exposed belly as he unbuttoned the final button. He grabbed her ass and pulled her to him, nipping her skin. She ran her hands through his hair, tugging. His fingers found the hem of her skirt, and he ran his hands up the backs of her thighs, not stopping until each hand was filled with a perfectly rounded cheek.

He sat back on his heels, taking in the highly aroused state she was in. Her lips were parted and swollen, and her eyes were dazed. He reluctantly let her ass go so he could push the skirt up her thighs, reveling the intricate black lace tops of her stockings. He didn't stop until he had the skirt bunched around her waist. Holy fuck. Her black satin panties were soaked, and her thighs trembled. He leaned in, using his thumb to push the drenched satin aside so he could taste her.

Her clit was swollen and warm on his tongue. He greedily drank from her as he slid two fingers deep. Her muscles contracted wildly around his fingers.

"Oh, yeah, baby, don't sto—"

Her juices gushed around his fingers and onto his tongue. He sucked her clit into his mouth, swirling his tongue around it. When the last of her tremors subsided, he stood, unzipped his pants, and pushed them and his underwear down to his knees. His cock burst forth, pointing exactly where it wanted to go.

Jack pulled a condom from his pocket and quickly protected them, as Em pulled off her boots and slid her panties off. She unclasped her bra and threw it aside. His hands cupped her full breasts, and she shuddered when he rubbed his thumbs over her distended nipples.

She pulled him down for a long, hot kiss. Jack's head spun with desire. Em broke the kiss and, with a wicked grin, pushed his jacket and shirt off his shoulders and down his arms. Jack shrugged them the rest of the way off.

"Fuck me now," Em commanded.

He lifted her and rested her back up against the wall. Still wearing the stockings, her long legs circled his waist, and her arms went around his neck. He slid into her wet warmth, her body stretching to take all of him. Em took his mouth in a fierce kiss, hot and wet and so filled with need that Jack locked his knees to keep them from buckling.

She nibbled a path to his ear and in a desperate whisper said, "Please."

Feeling steadier, Jack pulled out and thrust back into her. Em whispered words of encouragement as he fucked her.

Feeling his climax fast approaching, Jack eased off and took a steadying breath. "So fucking wet, so fucking tight." Em opened her eyes, their green depths glistening with passion. "So beautiful."

Her lips curled into an almost shy smile. Jack wanted to say more, but the primal need to possess her completely overrode his ability to speak. He thrust into her over and over. Every nerve ending tingled in anticipation. She nibbled her way over to his neck, nipping and biting gently. That drove him wild, and she knew it. He returned the favor, nipping her gently until he reached her shoulder. He opened his mouth on her soft skin and bit. *Mine.*

His balls tightened, and he came, thrusting as she tightened around him. His mouth stole her moans of pleasure as her climax shuddered through her.

Jack stood there with Em's body locked around his. She pulled back first and kissed him, a tender, emotion-filled kiss, and his heart skipped a beat. His body reminded him that he still had her up against the wall. Jack wasn't about to let her go, so he looked around. He couldn't slide to the floor because his pants were around his ankles.

The closest piece of furniture was a black leather recliner, but he didn't want to sit on her chair bare-assed.

Em tightened her arms and legs around him and whispered, "It's his."

Taking three steps, Jack flopped in the chair, still holding his beautiful girl. She rested her head in the crook of his neck. Her breathing was as wild as his. Normally, he'd never be so inconsiderate of someone else's property, but the fucker should've collected his shit by now, and since Jack didn't want to drop Em, the chair lost. He resisted the urge to wiggle. Barely.

She sat back and kissed him softly on the lips. "I missed you."

Those three words would have to do until she said the ones he longed to hear. Until she was fully his.

She nestled back into him, and her breathing steadied. "Did you fall asleep on me?" He kicked his shoes and pants off.

She snuggled closer to him. "Chilly."

"Come on, let's go to bed."

She scooted back, and with his help, she stood. Em picked up their clothes, and Jack scooped her up in his arms and carried her to the bedroom.

Jack went to the bathroom and cleaned up. Em joined him a minute later wearing a fuzzy pink robe. They shared the sink as they brushed their teeth. His heart expanded. This was normal.

JACK WOKE SUDDENLY WHEN EMILY SAT UP. "YOU okay, baby?"

"Shhh, I heard something."

Jack heard a shuffling sound.

Emily bolted out of bed, grabbed his shirt, and quickly buttoned it. "Someone's in the apartment." She slid her closet door open and pulled out a baseball bat.

Jack jumped out of bed, pulled on his pants, and went to

the door. This time, it sounded like someone tripped up the steps. "Stay here." He took the bat from her.

"Not a chance."

The light from the bathroom night-light illuminated the hallway in a yellow glow. As they started down the hallway, Jack gripped the bat tightly in his hand. He'd get one good swing to take the intruder by surprise.

"Ow!" echoed down the hallway.

"Shit." Em gripped his arm and stepped around him, moving ahead before he could stop her. She put her hand up to stop him but no way he was staying back. As he walked past the doorway to the kitchen, Jack saw a tall figure through the opening into the living room. He raised the bat just as Emily turned on the light, flooding the living room in bright light.

"Jack, don't." She grabbed his arm to stop him. "Sean, what the fuck are you doing here?"

The fucker, in the somewhat drunken flesh. He'd tripped over Emily's boots that were laying at the top of the stairs.

"Turn the damn spotlight off."

"You're drunk." Anger clouded her face. "Did you drive here like that?" She took a step closer which Jack hated. He suppressed the urge to pull her behind him. His hands held firmly on the handle of the Louisville Slugger.

"Of course not. I knew you'd never give me another chance if I did something that stupid." The fucker's eyes finally rested on Jack. Red washed over his fair skin, and he straightened to his full height, his expression a mix of shock and indignance. His lips curled into a sneer as he stepped closer. "Who the fuck is this?"

Oh, yes, please, come at me. Aside from not being shit-faced, Jack was a couple inches taller and in much better physical shape.

Emily stepped in front of Jack. "Who this is, is none of your business."

Jack was close enough to hear her intake of breath. She must've just registered the first thing the fucker said. Emily turned to look at Jack, her expression shocked. Shaking her head, she turned back to the fucker.

"How did you get in here?"

The fucker fumbled in his pocket and pulled out his keys. "Spare key."

She grabbed the keys from him, quickly taking her key off his ring.

"Hey." He stepped toward her but stepped back when Jack raised the bat higher. "Call him off, okay. I just want to talk." His eyes focused on Emily. "Who the fuck is this?"

Emily took a step toward him and raised her chin. "I didn't ask. I picked him up at the bar. He fucked me up against the wall." She tilted her chin toward the wall. "It was everything I thought it'd be and so much more."

The fucker winced.

Jack moved closer and wrapped his free arm around her torso. He looked the fucker up and down and smiled. "Want me to get rid of this guy?"

"No need. He's leaving. Now. And never coming back."

That seemed to snap his attention back to Emily, and again, he stepped toward her. "We need to talk."

Jack felt Emily's body tense. It wasn't exactly the same as her dream had been but close enough. "There's nothing left to say. Except get your shit out of my apartment by Monday, or I'm hauling it out to the trash."

"Hey, you're the one calling and texting me dozens of times the past two weeks." He glanced at Jack with a raised brow and a smirk.

Jack laughed. He would've loved to tell him that they'd been together for the past five weeks, but she'd said they'd just met tonight, so Jack wouldn't contradict that. She was sexy as hell when she was pissed and wearing his shirt.

"Yeah, about that." Emily stalked out of the room, returning a few moments later with the bill from Elegant Affairs. "I don't know what you're playing at, telling the manager to send me this bill. If your groomsmen or you were too stupid to cancel the tuxes, then that's on you." When he didn't take it, she slapped it against his chest, causing him to take a step back. "Now, get the fuck out before I call the cops."

"Hey, I had a key."

Emily growled at him. "You're an asshole. You cheat on me three weeks before our wedding, and you make out like any of this is my fault? Get out before I let J—this guy take a few swings like I know he's been dying to do."

Jack stepped forward and placed the head of the bat on the fucker's chest. "You heard the lady, fuckhead. Out. Now."

The fucker narrowed his bloodshot eyes but turned on his heel and retreated down the stairs. Emily went to follow him, but Jack stopped her. He went down, locked the door, and put the chain on.

Anger welled through him. Why hadn't she had the locks changed?

Chapter Twenty-Four

A s soon as Emily heard Jack engage the lock, she collapsed to the floor. How could Sully have thought it was okay to break into her apartment in the middle of the night? Powerful sobs wracked her body. She knew she'd have to deal with him, but right now, the thoughts swirling through her head caused her stomach to ache. What if she'd been alone?

Jack sat next to her and pulled her into his arms. "Shh, it's okay, baby. I'm here." She wanted to tell him how glad she was that he was here but couldn't speak through her sobs. She leaned against him, taking all the comfort he had to offer. What had Sully meant about taking him back? How could he think that was possible after what he'd done? She turned her face into Jack's bare chest and let the tears flush those thoughts away.

When she'd woken because she'd heard a sound in the apartment, she'd felt paranoid. Then she'd heard it again, and fear took over. Her father had taught her how to defend herself, but this was the first time she'd ever been in a situation where she'd have to use it.

The first hint that it was Sully was the overwhelming scent of his cologne. Then fear had been replaced by fury. She could've killed him.

Emily cleared her mind and repeated one of her mantras. The calming effects slowly took effect until she was all cried out and resting in Jack's arms. The calm before the storm.

"It's okay, baby, you're safe." He'd whispered it over and over to her while she cried.

She'd never felt safer. That raised a new wave of emotions. They'd only known each other five weeks. "I'm so glad you were here, if you hadn't..." She couldn't say it, couldn't think it. She lifted her head so she could see his face and was sorry she did.

Anger, bitterness, frustration, and hate. The muscles in his jaw tightened and released several times. He was trying to calm down, but it didn't appear to be working.

"You didn't have the locks changed." His eyes scrunched closed.

The accusation stung. Emily had no reason to think he'd be back after what he'd done. She'd gotten all the keys she'd known about back, so changing the locks hadn't occurred to her. Jack didn't understand, and she had no idea how to make him. His body vibrated with fury.

Emily stood, needing some physical distance from him. She didn't want to fight, but it seemed inevitable. She went into the kitchen for a drink. When she returned to the living room, Jack paced and was on his phone.

"Emily's ex broke in. I want an alarm system installed tomorrow." He disconnected the call and shoved the phone into his pocket. Emily stepped forward to protest, but Jack put up his hand. "Don't. I'm doing this, and that's final."

"That's final? Don't you think we should discuss this? I have no idea how much something—"

He opened his eyes. "I'm paying." Their normally bright

blue depths were clouded with anger. Some of it was obviously aimed at her.

Which pissed her off. "You can't just—"

"It's done." He strode into the kitchen and pulled out the bottle of Maker's Mark from the pantry. Jack poured himself a generous portion, drank it, then rinsed the glass and left it in the sink. "Let's get some sleep." He walked past her and down the hallway.

Sleep? She was too angry to sleep. How dare he? He had no right... But he was looking out for her. It was his thing, taking care of people. She'd known at some point this could be a problem between them. Emily took a few deep breaths. Yes, they'd get some sleep. In the morning, they'd discuss it like rational adults. He'd see that he was being high-handed and understand that this was her problem to deal with since it predated them. She calmly walked into the bedroom.

She crawled in next to him, and he turned off the light. He pulled her to his side, and she rested her head on his shoulder. At least they weren't sleeping on opposite sides of the bed. She closed her eyes and drifted off to sleep, nestled against the warmth of his body.

Emily woke to Jack's phone playing "Rooster." Grabbing it off the nightstand, he answered and then said, "Okay." Disconnecting the call, he sat up and swung his legs over the side of the bed. "Jeff's here. The alarm company will be here in half an hour. Get dressed." He walked out of the bedroom.

Anger had her instantly awake. So much for adult conversation. This was bullshit. No way she was letting this happen. She threw the covers off but sat on the edge of the bed. Her leg hurt, which only angered her more. She tried not to limp down the hallway. "What the hell do you think you're doing? We need to discuss this."

Jack faced her. "I told you last night what was going to happen. There's nothing to discuss."

"The hell there isn't." She was seething with anger, her head throbbed, and her leg pulsed with pain. She'd slept in one position to long. "You have no right—"

"I have every right, Goddamn it. That fucker didn't break in at two in the morning to talk!"

Emily slumped against the wall. That was what she didn't want to think about. Sully thought they would kiss and make up. Emily's stomach churned. The room started to spin, so she closed her eyes. Would he have tried to force her? She'd never been afraid of him, but she couldn't trust anything she'd known about him. How could she tell Jack that it wouldn't have happened? She wouldn't have let it. She should've told him last night that she was well equipped to protect herself. She'd never told Sully, and they'd lived together for almost a year.

This nightmare was spiraling out of control. Nothing was normal about this relationship. *How the hell are we going to make this work?*

Emily jumped when the doorbell rang. "It's Jeff. I need that shirt," he said as he walked into the bedroom. Emily followed, removing his shirt. She quickly dressed as Jack went to open the door.

When she returned to the living room, Jack was talking to Jeff. "We came down the hallway, and Emily realized who it was and kept me from bashing his fucking skull in." Jack sounded disappointed.

Jeff turned to her. "How did you know it was your ex?"

"His cologne. Then he said 'Ow,' and I recognized his voice."

Jeff nodded curtly. Emily bit her tongue and went to the kitchen. She needed coffee. Lots of it. After setting the coffee to brew, she decided she needed to stop the testosterone fest that was taking place in her living room. This was her home.

"Enough," she yelled through the opening above the

breakfast bar. "You two can't just waltz in here and take over." Her anger pushed her forward. Her father was a Marine, so Jeff didn't intimidate her with his Marine face. "You." She pointed to Jeff. "Leave. I need a private word with Jack."

Jeff turned and walked down the stairs. She waited for the click of the door before she turned to Jack. She took a deep breath. "I appreciate that you want to protect me, but you can't just have an alarm system installed. I don't own this place."

"Fuck." Jack slapped his hand against the wall. "This wouldn't be an issue if that real estate lady had found me an apartment."

Emily crossed her arms. "Oh really, why's that?"

Jack took a deep breath. "I get it. You wouldn't be moving in with me yet, but at least you'd have a safe place to stay. If I hadn't been here last night..."

All the anger drained from her body. Jack opened his arms, and when they closed around her, she felt safe and protected. "Okay, we're both angry and upset." She looked up at him. "I should've had the locks changed, but I got back all the keys I knew about, so it never occurred to me. I'm sorry."

He hugged her tightly to him. She'd felt cold since she'd gotten up. But now, she felt warm and safe in his embrace.

"Baby, I'm away so much. I worry about you. I told you he'd want you back." Jack rested his chin on the top of her head.

Emily pulled back so she could look up at him. "Yeah, you did. How'd you know?"

Jack pulled her over to the couch and sat, tugging her onto his lap. "Because"—he brushed a stray hair from her cheek— "you're the most amazing woman I have ever met. No way you loved someone who didn't have a soul. And no matter the screw up, that guy would try to get you back." His eyes were filled with love and worry. "I love you."

She closed her eyes and kissed him. A knock prevented them from more than a brief kiss.

"Jack, about this alarm..." She knew he worried. Nicki told her how he'd been acting, and she didn't want to add to his concerns. "Let me pay half."

Jack visibly struggled. "Baby, the money means nothing to me. I'll feel much better if I'm sure you're protected."

Emily didn't want him to constantly wonder when Sully would be back. And after last night, she was sure he would be. Sully never drank more than a couple drinks. He was unshaven, and his clothes were rumpled. She'd never seen him so disheveled, and she almost hadn't recognized him; his whole manner was off. She'd known as soon as she looked into Jack's worried eyes that she'd give in. It wasn't much, but it was what she could do to make him happy. "Okay."

He kissed her deeply until Jeff cleared his throat. "The guys will be here in five minutes."

Emily hopped off his lap. Jack stood, and it was as if a weight had been lifted off his shoulders. She didn't spare a second on regretting her decision. Swallowing her pride to ease his burden was a no-brainer.

"Emily." Jeff stopped her with a look.

Crap. She looked down. Maybe he wouldn't—

"Show me."

"Show you what?" Jack stood behind her, placing his hands on her shoulders.

"Her weapons."

Jack's hands tensed on her shoulders. "Em, what's he talking about?"

When Emily didn't answer, Jeff cleared his throat again. "No way a Marine left his daughter unprotected."

"Em?"

She avoided Jack's gaze. "I have a Beretta 92 in my nightstand. A Glock 19 in my office desk, bottom drawer, locked. And a Marlin 336 chambered in 30-30 Winchester under the couch."

"Get them." Jeff wasn't asking.

Emily retrieved her two handguns and then pulled the rifle from under the couch and laid them on the coffee table.

Emily spared a glance in Jack's direction. His stunned expression didn't surprise her.

"When was the last time you went to the range?" Jeff picked up the Glock and did a chamber check.

Emily looked down. "Six months."

Jeff shook his head. "Use it or lose it."

"I know." She finally looked at Jack.

Shock had melted into a small smile. "You know how to handle all these?"

Emily nodded. She'd planned on telling Jack about them, since he had a bodyguard, but the time hadn't been right. People could be weird about guns.

"Why didn't you tell me last night?"

Fisting her hands on her hips, she said, "Would you have let me protect you?"

"I... I'm not sure."

At least he was being honest.

"You made the right call, Emily. There was no time to debate who protects whom." Jeff whistled as he held the Beretta.

"He always had a fondness for the Beretta because it was the standard sidearm when he was in the Corps."

"I love it in stainless."

The doorbell rang, and Jeff went to answer it. Emily returned her firearms to their proper places.

"Jack, Emily, this is Gary Phillips, Ben Gardner, and Al Darcy from Sentry Alarms. We served together." Jeff smiled. "She's one of ours, her father was a Marine." Jeff's lips tightened into a line. "Asshole ex-boyfriend broke into the apartment last night. Let's make sure that doesn't happen again."

For the next half hour, Emily and Jack followed, as Jeff, Gary, and his installers went over every inch of her apartment. The system would be wireless, have twenty-four-hour monitoring, and an app for Emily's phone.

Gary opened the front door and inspected it. "Door's old, and I don't like the frame, not as sturdy as it could be. The deadbolt should be drilled deeper."

"The landlord would have to approve any changes like that." Emily pulled out her cell and called George Martin, the complex manager, leaving a message when she got his voicemail.

While they waited for approval, Gary discussed what he'd like to do. When Jack said price was no concern, Emily left the room. She couldn't afford it and didn't want to know how much Jack was spending on her. Instead, she made herself useful by brewing another pot of coffee and making sandwiches for the guys. She placed the coffee in a large thermos she kept for entertaining and brewed a second pot.

It was after nine when George got back to them. A new deadbolt was fine, but he'd need a key. Since the doors had to be uniform, they couldn't replace it or the doorjamb. Jack wasn't happy, but Gary assured him there was plenty that could be done so she'd be safer.

JACK WAS GLAD SHE HADN'T FOUGHT HIM OVER THE alarm or the cost. He knew she wanted to, had been gearing up to, but then she stopped. It pleased him to do things for her and to take care of her. He could do so much more, if only she'd let him. If she wanted to write full time, he could easily cover her expenses, but she'd already vetoed that in no uncertain terms.

He'd thought a lot about what she'd said about how much he'd done for Christie. He'd had resources to help her, and he'd been happy to do it. But Em had made a good point. Somewhere along the way, Christie began to say he wasn't doing enough and blamed him for not using his newfound celebrity to help her more. He was a musician, not an actor. If she'd wanted to make a record, he had connections that might have been able to help her, but he didn't know any Hollywood people and didn't really want to. He'd gone to enough red-carpet events with Christie to know he'd hate having to do that all the time. But if they'd stayed together, he'd have done it for her. He'd have done anything for her.

Jack walked up behind Emily and hugged her. He was relieved when she leaned into him. He didn't want to fight over this shit, but he still couldn't believe she hadn't changed the locks. *Shit, maybe I'm overreacting.* He'd call Elliot later and ask him; he'd let Jack know if he was being dick about this.

"I'm starving." Jack grabbed half a ham and cheese sandwich off the platter.

She playfully swatted his hand away. "Hey, those aren't for you."

He took a huge bite. "No?"

"No." Emily moved the platter out of reach. "They're for Gary and his men. They're going to be here a while, and since this job took precedence over whatever they had scheduled today, the least I can do is feed them."

I'm a dick. It never even occurred to him that these guys would have another job scheduled for today. All he'd cared about was keeping his girl safe. Everyone had someone they wanted to protect. "Shit, I never thought of that."

Emily turned and kissed him. "I got your back, rock star."

She picked up the platter and moved it to the breakfast counter, along with plates and mugs for the coffee. "Gary, I made some sandwiches and coffee for you and the guys, and help yourself to bottles of water in the fridge."

"Why don't you two grab some breakfast. I'll handle everything here." Jeff poured a cup of coffee.

"Thanks, man," Jack said. "What about you?"

Jeff smirked. "I ate at 0600."

"Em, why don't you pack a bag? After breakfast, we'll go to the motel and shower. Maybe we can catch a movie later."

"Okay."

Dex's ringtone blared form Jack's phone. "Hey, man, what's up?" Jack went into the bedroom and sat on the bed.

"It's Susan, Jack. I'll put you—oh, hold on." Dex's assistant placed him on hold. A minute later she came back on the line. "He's on with his wife, can you hold?"

"Sure," Jack said. "How you doing? Dex driving you crazy?" Jack knew the answer because he knew Dex.

Susan lowered her voice to a conspiratorial tone. "He's been on a rampage."

Something in Susan's voice had Jack thinking it had to do with him. Which could only mean one thing, but Jack hoped he was wrong.

He heard Dex yell, "Get off the line, Susan." There was a click, and then he said, "Your ex keeps calling me."

Jack rubbed his hand over his head. "Shit, sorry about that. I'll call her and tell her to back off."

"Please do." Dex hung up.

"That's what she wants." Emily zipped up her overnight bag.

"Who?" Jack flopped back on the bed. This was becoming a nightmare. He'd moved on. Why couldn't Christie leave him alone?

Em lay on her side next to him. "Christie."

"How did you know that was about her?"

"Isn't 'Another One Bites the Dust' Dex's ringtone? My dad played it at his victory barbecues when his team bested others during training."

Jack turned to face her. "Did you guys do a lot of stuff like that?"

"Yeah." She smiled fondly. "From spring to autumn, someone had a barbecue every weekend. When the guys were deployed, the families kept it up. My dad would make his famous chili recipe. It was always the first thing to go. His dad was a chef, and he made the best chili ever."

Jack kissed her. "I don't know what to do about Christie."

Emily looked down. "She wants you back."

"Hey..."

She smiled and their eyes locked. "I know you're with me now. But she's not going to go quietly."

Jack thought the same thing about the fucker, but he didn't say it. "You think I shouldn't call her?"

"It's what she wants. If you give into it, there's no reason for her to stop calling Dex whenever she wants to get to you. If you don't respond, maybe she'll get the hint."

He sat up and pulled her into his arms so he could kiss her properly. "How did I get so lucky?"

Em smiled. "I've been wondering the same thing."

JACK SIPPED HIS COFFEE. THEY'D STOPPED AT A diner near his motel for breakfast. Em had two strips of bacon left, and he wanted them. He took his fork and inched it toward her plate, but just as he was about to lunge, she picked them up and bit one.

"Too slow, rock star." She grinned as she chewed.

"Give me one."

"One of these?" she waved the bacon back and forth. "Nope."

"I'm still hungry."

Em smiled and handed over the bacon.

A short, brown-haired guy with a young boy stopped at their table. "Hey, Emily Prescott, right?"

Emily's smile faded. "Yes."

"Rich Harrison from Oakdale High, class of '07. Oh—"

She reached across the table and took Jack's hand. "Sorry, things are still fuzzy."

Rich grinned. "It's great to see you doing so well after..."

His son pulled him toward the door. "Dad, we're going to be late."

"Okay, Trevor." He turned back to Emily. "Maybe I'll see you at the reunion next year." Trevor successfully pulled his father out the door.

Emily put the rest of her bacon down. "Can we go?"

Jack settled the check, and they drove the three blocks to his motel in silence. She was hurting, and any questions he'd ask would only make her feel worse. He parked in front of his room.

Emily stared straight ahead. "I never think about her."

"Who?"

"The girl I used to be. It's like I've had two lives. I've been trying not to remember who I used to be."

Jack squeezed her hand. "Why?"

"Because she's dead."

He hated when she said things like that. "Tell me about her."

"No."

He locked his jaw and tried to hold on to his patience. "Why not?"

"Because you'd like her better. It hurts to remember all I lost."

Jack leaned over and kissed her gently. "I love you and always will."

"You can't know that."

Jack placed her hand over his heart. "I do. Knowing who you were won't make me love you less."

"You can't know that either."

"Someday?

"Maybe. Can we just go in?"

Jack sighed. "Of course."

As soon as they walked into the room, Emily asked, "Would it be okay if I showered first?"

"Sure." He assumed they'd shower together, like they usually did.

Emily took her overnight bag into the bathroom and closed the door.

Fuck. Back to that. She knew he hated it when she shut him out. Anger washed through him. Anger at her for shutting him out and for not getting the motherfucking locks changed. Anger toward the fucker for thinking he could get her back. *Newsflash, asshole, she's with me now.* Although, Em hadn't made that clear, had she? She'd said they'd just met. At the time, he hadn't thought twice about it. Jack assumed she was getting back at him for cheating on her. But what if she was just having fun with him?

Jack paced the small room because he needed to burn off his anger before they had another fight. Why hadn't she told that asshole that she was with him now?

They'd only met five weeks ago, but he'd been in love with her every single day. She'd only just said she missed him for the first time. A fear he'd been denying pushed its way to the forefront of his mind, and Jack wanted to punch something. She was so amazing, and he was away so much. His worst fear taunted him. She'd meet another guy, one with the normal life she wanted so desperately, and she'd dump his never-home ass. Bile rose in his throat.

He jumped when she touched his shoulder. "Hey, what's wrong?" Her hair was wet, and she'd dressed in jeans and a Stone Highway T-shirt.

"Sorry, lost in thought. Nice shirt."

"Gotta support the team."

When Jack didn't laugh, she dropped her comb and put her arms around him. "I'm sorry, baby, I just needed a few minutes alone. With everything that's happened, I'm feeling overwhelmed."

Jack didn't hug her back; if he did, he was afraid he'd never be able to let her go. "I hate it when you shut me out."

She rested her head on his chest. "I know. I'm trying to do better."

She was. Em hadn't hidden in the bathroom their whole last visit. Resistance was futile. He was hers. His arms went around her.

Emily sighed. "We can't seem to get a break, can we?"

Jack was an optimist, but even he had to admit that since that first week together, things hadn't gone as planned. He remembered the call with his dad yesterday, but now wasn't the time.

Emily leaned back. "What?"

"I didn't say anything."

"I know, but your heart rate picked up." She placed her palm over his heart. "What?"

"My dad called." Jack tried to calm down. If she said no, that would be a bad sign. "He and my mom wanted me to invite you to spend Father's Day weekend with us."

Emily raised a brow.

Jack shook his head. "I didn't say anything, I swear." He crossed his heart.

"I've been thinking about it."

Jack's pulse hammered in his ears. "And?"

"I don't think we can be that picky about how or when we get to see each other."

Jack's heart threatened to burst out of his chest. "Is that a yes?"

Emily smiled, and his heart flipped. "Yes."

"Thank you. I love you, baby." His lips found hers, and their tongues met and tangled. Joy spread throughout his body, and lack of oxygen made him dizzy.

Emily pulled back gasping for air. "One condition."

"What?"

Emily smiled that heart-stopping smile of hers that made him want to start planning out every day of the rest of their lives together. "Make sure your parents are okay with us sharing a room."

Jack exhaled. His folks had never said no to that. Then again, he'd never actually asked them. But she was coming no matter what, so Jack smiled. "Okay."

"Okay, you'll ask them, not okay they've never said no?"

"The difference being?"

She patted him on the cheek. "Baby, you don't get home all that often, and from the time I spent there, it was obvious your parents would like to see you more. Any way they can get you. They're a lot like mine were. My dad never would've allowed us to share a room unless we were married." Her hazel eyes shone, but she smirked. "Maybe not even then."

Jack scoffed. "That's different. I'm not their little girl."

"I don't think they'd allow Jimmy to have a girl sleep over either."

"You're saying they let me get away with it?"

"Yes."

Jack shook his head. "No way, not my folks. You saw how my dad was."

"Yes, I did. But I also saw two loving parents who miss you

terribly. Who are monumentally proud of you and might just let you get away with certain things because they're afraid you wouldn't visit otherwise."

Jack wanted to deny it, but Em was great at reading people, and he wanted to make her happy. "Okay, I'll ask."

She smiled and kissed him hard. In a matter of seconds, the Stone Highway T-shirt hit the floor, and her jeans didn't last much longer.

Later, Em lay curled up against him sound asleep. They hadn't gotten much sleep last night, and they still had the rest of the afternoon to get through. His girl had a fiery temper, and when they got back to her place, Jack hoped she wouldn't be *too* mad.

Chapter Twenty-Five

I t was midafternoon when Jeff called to say the installation was complete. As soon as they arrived, Emily's blood pressure skyrocketed. Sully's recliner and all the boxes that had been in her office were in a neat pile by the curb.

Emily unbuckled her seatbelt before the truck stopped. "You had no right," she yelled as she opened the door.

Jack grabbed her arm. "What the fuck are you doing?" The truck stopped, but he didn't release her.

"I told you I'd take care of this."

"You still can. Call him and tell him to come pick up his shit."

Emily ground her teeth together. Even for Jack, this was outrageous. Her body heated, and she took several breaths, but nothing stopped the mounting anger. She turned to Jack, seething. "How dare you?"

"How dare I? How dare he. He broke into your apartment last night. He left his stuff here to stay connected to you. I'm sure of it. I want it gone now," Jack said through gritted teeth. "The sooner he's out of your life—"

"He's been out of my life. How many times do I have to

say I don't want him back?" Emily tried to jerk free, but Jack held her arm. "Let me go."

Jack closed his eyes and inhaled. "Em, we agree on this. We both want him gone, so this doesn't have to be a fight." He loosened his hold on her arm. "We want the same thing."

Emily yanked her arm free. "Yes, we do. But, what I don't want is you arbitrarily deciding how that happens. You should've discussed this with me." They needed to settle this now.

"I should've discussed it with you? Why haven't you brought it up? Do you have a plan?"

"Yes." Emily's anger resurged.

"Then why didn't you share it with me?"

Her head snapped to face him. "Is that what this display is? You're mad because I didn't share my plan with you?"

"No, these guys were here, and Jeff wanted to know where the fucker lived so he could talk to him. I thought this was the better solution."

"You thought? Well, thank goodness you were here to do my thinking for me." She didn't know why she said it because she knew that wasn't what he meant, but she was so mad at him. Emily hated caveman behavior.

"You know I'm not like that. I just wanted to make this easier for you. You were so upset this morning at the motel, and you shut me out."

"You arranged this while we were at the motel?" Some of her anger faded.

Jack looked down. "No, before we left for breakfast. But, Em, if something happened to you, I'd never forgive myself. You refused to let Fletcher keep an eye on you."

"One thing has nothing to do with the other. You can't just make these decisions, we're supposed to be a couple, and couples decide things together. Instead, you ride in and solve the problem. I'm not Christie. I don't want or need that kind of help."

"Well, what was your plan? The one you didn't discuss with me? Or am I just some guy you're screwing, so I don't need to know?"

"That's not fair, you know that's not what's going on here—"

"Your ex doesn't. He thinks I'm just some random guy you picked up in a bar last night."

Emily sighed. She'd known that was a mistake as soon as she'd said it, but she'd wanted to hurt Sully. She'd been doing better, but seeing him again brought all her anger, humiliation, and rejection back to the surface. His shocked expression had been small satisfaction, but she hadn't considered Jack's feelings. "I'm sorry I said that. I wanted to hurt him, not you. Please forgive me?"

"That hurt." He looked straight ahead. "You should've made it clear that you've moved on. He's not done."

She took Jack's hand. "You're right." Her stomach burned with regret. "He may not be done, but I most definitely am." She touched his cheek, but he stared ahead. "Please look at me."

Jack faced her.

"I'm with you. I'll make sure he knows that."

Jack didn't smile.

Emily turned away. "I don't know what else you want me to say."

A car horn blast interrupted whatever Jack was about to say. He raised his hand, started the truck, and continued down the driveway to the back of the building, parking next to her car. He cut the engine and turned to her. "I'm scared."

"Of what?"

"Losing you."

"I don't understand."

"I know you don't. You have no idea how amazing you are. Guys are always looking at you. Those two assholes in the bar the night you had drinks with Meg. And last night. If I lived here, it wouldn't matter. The way things are now is how they'll be for the next eighteen months. I'm scared that while I'm away you'll meet someone and realize you can get everything you need from a guy who doesn't spend seventy-five percent of his time on the road."

Jack's eyes were closed, and he exhaled deeply. Emily touched his cheek, and he turned to her. She saw fear and sadness in his eyes. "I'm sorry, I thought I'd made it clear that if I wasn't with you, there wouldn't be anyone else. I wasn't ready for a new relationship, but we met when we met, and here we are." She cupped his face with her hands. "I know that we aren't on the same page yet, but it's only been five weeks."

She also saw his intense love for her, and it took her breath away. A lump formed in her throat and her chest tightened. Emily forced herself to continue. "You know that I like and care about you. It sounds silly compared to how you've expressed your feelings to me. But that's where I am." Emily had her own fears. "I know that's not enough for you. And I'm scared you'll meet some beautiful, perfect, undamaged..." Emily sat back. "And I'm afraid you'll give up before I'm able to catch up."

Jack pulled her to him, crashing his lips onto hers. Bright sun glared through the windows of the truck, illuminating them, its warmth having nothing to do with her body temperature rising. His heart thundered under her palms. Her body went limp, and all the energy it had went into kissing him, showing him that she was his and that, with or without him, no other man existed to her.

A whistle from far away barely pierced her consciousness. Then a louder woo-hoo. Jack regained his senses and broke the kiss, resting his forehead against hers. She moaned her dissatisfaction. She'd wanted the kiss to go on for eternity.

Jack's hands caressed circles on her back. "Emily Grace Prescott, I will never give up on you or us."

Drained and exhausted, she wished they could rewind time to yesterday when she'd first seen him in the bar. But everything that came after would've still happened, leaving her feeling like she did now. "I knew things wouldn't be easy, but I just didn't imagine they'd be this hard." How had her mom managed to keep it together all those years while her dad had been deployed? Five weeks in, and her world spun out of control.

"I love you."

She smiled and kissed him. Hand in hand, they walked to her apartment to face yet another challenge.

Gary walked them through all the upgrades they'd installed. Even though the landlord had forbidden installation of anything permanent, they'd changed all the window locks and added sensors. They also added another deadbolt to the front door that could only be unlocked from the inside and a wireless keypad. Gary assured her that Mr. Martin had granted approval. They'd wanted to install a motion-activated camera outside the front door, but Mr. Martin had said no to that as it would be an invasion on Mrs. Locke's privacy.

"Last thing we need to do is set your alarm codes, and we'll be on our way," Gary said. "Okay, four digits, please, and keep the code to yourself."

Emily stepped up to the keypad and punched in her code: 0421.

"Everyone who has entry to your apartment should have their own code, so if you have a cleaning service..."

"Just me." Emily smiled at Jack, but he looked away. *Shit.* "I meant just me that cleans. Jack should have his own code."

Jack smiled and punched in his code, but the display flashed error.

Gary frowned and punched a few keys. "Okay, try again."

Jack punched his code; again, error flashed across the screen. "If this thing isn't working properly—"

"No, it's working just fine. Each code has to be different, so unless you two picked the same code..."

Jack grinned. "Em, what code did you pick?"

"I'm sorry." She tried to hide her smile. "You heard Gary. I cannot tell anyone my code under pain of death."

Jeff stepped between them "Enough jocularity you two. One of you has to change your code." The restrained laughter in Jeff's tone belied his stern expression.

"I live here." Emily tilted her chin up.

"Fine, I'll change mine." Jack punched in a new code, and this time, no error message flashed.

"Great. The booklet has directions if you need to add any more codes or delete a user." Gary reached into his pocket and took out a card. "Or you can always call me."

Emily tucked the card into her pocket. "Thank you for coming on short notice."

Jack and Gary shook hands. "Yeah, I really appreciate it. Add twenty percent to the bill." Jack put up his hand to halt Gary's protest. "You guys did a great job, and I'm sure you had another client today. You did me a huge favor. I'll feel much better knowing she's more secure."

"Thanks, the guys will appreciate it." They shook hands, and Gary left.

She'd wanted to handle Sully on her own, but after what happened last night, seeing him so different, she decided it'd be better to deal with him while Jack was here. "I'm calling him." She grabbed her phone and dialed. She'd deleted his phone number and their texts the day she'd caught him, but she hadn't yet forgotten his number.

He answered on the fourth ring. "Hey, Emi, I'm—"

"Your stuff is out by the curb. Garbage pickup is Monday." Emily hung up. She didn't want him calling her Emi anymore, didn't want him calling her anything. She slumped on the couch. Jack was instantly next to her, cuddling her in his arms. She leaned into him, his strength and warmth a balm to her battered heart.

Hopefully, he'd pick up his stuff when she wasn't home. Maybe they could spend the night at the motel. Emily didn't think she could take much more.

When the text alert sounded on her phone, her heart pounded: *Bitch*.

Before she could respond, her phone rang, and she answered it.

"I'll be there in an hour." His voice sounded weak and defeated. For the first time in months, some of the anger and hurt she'd felt released their stranglehold on her heart, and she felt a little sorry for him. And that was the moment she knew the healing had begun. The moment she knew that someday, she'd be able to forgive him.

But not today.

JACK HEARD THE RATTLE OF THE TRUCK AS SOON AS it arrived. He watched out the window as the fucker and his fucker friends began to load up his shit. Even from the second story, Jack could tell the guy was broken. A niggle of sympathy worked its way in, and for Emily's sake, he let it flourish and refused to gloat. Jeff was parked across the street. Jack could handle himself, but he wouldn't take any chances with Em's safety.

Emily joined him at the window and took his hand. He knew before she said it that she was going to talk to him. Jack just hoped she didn't insist on doing it alone. Last thing they needed was another fight.

She squeezed his hand. "I'm going to make sure he knows I've moved on." She started to walk away but stopped when Jack didn't move. "You coming?"

His heart flipped, and together, they went out. His friends saw them coming and stopped loading the truck to walk toward them. *Really? Fine. Bring it.*

Emily stopped and turned to him. "No caveman crap. You're here as an observer only."

"Hey, don't tell me, they're the ones—"

"Jack William McBride, don't bullshit me. Your whole body tensed. I don't want this to escalate. Besides, I don't care about them. I care about you." Her eyes sparkled with emotion. "Please?"

"I can handle myself."

"I remember, but you're outnumbered."

Jack smiled. She was worried about him. He hadn't planned on telling her Jeff was still here, but he wanted to ease her mind. "No, baby, I'm not."

Instantly understanding, she looked around until she spotted Jeff. She sighed, in relief or frustration with him, Jack couldn't tell. She went up on tiptoes and kissed him briefly, too briefly, then stepped back and continued walking, stopping a few feet in front her ex and his friends.

"I knew it," the fucker said, smiling a smarmy salesman's smile. "This is his doing, you'd never do this to me."

"It's what I wanted."

The fucker's smile faded. "I don't know who you are anymore."

When Jeff walked up behind them, his friends went back to loading the truck. *Not as stupid as they look.*

"Make no mistake, Sean, this is *your* doing. What were you thinking, breaking in—"

"I didn't break in, I had a key."

"One that you shouldn't have had. You certainly didn't have permission to enter my home."

"It's my home, too."

Emily took a step toward him. "Used to be. Until you decided to blow up our life, our future."

Jack felt Jeff tense behind him.

"You were supposed to forgive me," he yelled.

Jack stepped next to Em; her face was red and tears threatened. He wanted to take her inside and end this, but he knew she wasn't done.

Her lips moved several times, but no words came out. "Forgive you? You planned this. You wanted me to catch you?" She shook her head, clearly not grasping what the fucker had done.

The fucker didn't deny it. He stepped forward but stopped when Jeff stepped next to Emily. He growled, "Yeah, that's right."

She swallowed hard, and her eyes scrunched closed.

Jeff's expression told Jack he'd protect Emily no matter what.

Tears rolled down her cheeks. "Why? What could I have possibly done to deserve such a...punishment?"

Venom poured from the fucker. His face turned ugly, and his fair skin reddened. "You needed to know."

"Know what?"

"That other women wanted me. That I was a catch and deserved your full devotion and attention."

Em's control snapped, and she stepped forward and pushed him, sending him stumbling backward. "Me wanting you wasn't enough?"

"You never got jealous. Other women would come on to me in front of you, and you thought it was funny."

"It was never funny. It was rude, appalling, and

outrageous. What did you expect me to do, pull their hair? You weren't responsible for their behavior. If I'd thought I had anything to be jealous of, we'd never have been together in the first place." Emily's hands fisted at her sides. "Why not just talk to me, tell me how you felt?"

"Tell you what? That I was so fucking jealous of every guy who looked at you that it was hard to breathe." His eyes narrowed to slits, and he shook with fury. "Jealous of every guy you talked to? That I loved you so much that the thought of losing you drove me crazy? You had to be so fucking independent. You never needed me. I went along with everything you wanted." He looked at Jack and glowered. "You're already on her hook. Well, get used to it, buddy. She'll never feel the same about you."

"What the fuck is that supposed to mean?" Emily took another step toward him. When Jeff put his hand on her shoulder, she shrugged him off.

"Just what I said, he'll always love you more than you'll love him."

"I loved you with everything I had!"

"It wasn't enough. It wasn't even close to how much I love you."

Emily stepped back as though she'd been slapped. "Is that how you justify what you did, that you loved me more? That's fucked-up bullshit."

"I'd have still married you."

Em's throat worked with the effort to swallow. "Gee, thanks."

"We could've been happy together. You're the one who ended it."

"How could you think I'd still marry you after what you did? In our bed? How many others were there?"

"It was only ever you for me since the moment I laid eyes

on you. I was done, other women ceased to exist. Baby, you know that."

Emily waived her hand in the air. "I'm not your baby. How many?"

He looked down. "Just her."

"I don't believe you."

Still looking down, he said, "This isn't how this was supposed to go. You were supposed to forgive me. We'd have postponed the wedding, but we'd have reconciled." When he looked up, seething hatred shot out of his eyes. The fucker took a step toward him. "This bastard ruined everything."

It took all of Jack's willpower to remain an observer. From the look on Jeff's face, his Marine discipline was stretched thin.

Em shook her head. "Reconciled? Are you fucking kidding me?"

"You forgave that drunken, entitled bitch who killed your family. All I did was—"

Jeff stepped between them. "Get your shit and get out of here."

Jack pulled her trembling body to his. Tears streamed down her pale cheeks, and she turned her head into his side as he guided her to the door.

"Good luck, buddy, you're going to need it," the fucker sneered.

Jack turned to see Jeff menace the fucker. His friends were smart enough to stay out of it. Emily openly sobbed, unable to contain her frayed emotions. Jack would've really enjoyed beating the shit out of him, but Em needed to handle it, so he suppressed his base urges to rearrange that asshole's face.

Once inside, she broke down. Tears and sobs tore from her. As the avalanche of her emotions overwhelmed her, Jack didn't know what to say to make it better, so he held her. He was glad she didn't shut him out. When she was done, her eyes were red and swollen, and tears stained her pale cheeks.

He cradled her in his arms, letting her rest her tired body against his. Her breaths evened out and she was still. He tried to gently adjust his position because his ass was numb.

She lifted her head and turned her worn out eyes to him. "What if he's right?"

Jack pulled her onto his lap. "Not a chance." He kissed her forehead. "You're the most caring person I've ever met. He was just lashing out."

Emily blinked slowly. "Things haven't been the same since the accident. I haven't been the same. I used to be different."

Jack smiled. "This is the version of you that I'm in love with. Everybody changes, baby. I'm not the same guy I was ten years ago."

Emily's wan smile made his heart ache. "Gradually, not in an instant."

"Baby, you lost everything. That would change anyone in an instant. But it doesn't mean you changed for the worse."

"What if I did?"

Jack shook his head. "Not possible. I know you have feelings for me, strong, scary feelings, and that makes you question everything you felt before."

Her eyes widened.

"I know because I feel the same way. I thought Christie and I would get married. I even bought her a ring, but then everything fell apart so fast. I tried to keep it together, but I couldn't." Jack's head fell back against the couch. "The day I realized that the future I'd been so sure of for so long wasn't going to happen made me question everything."

"I wish..."

"What?"

Emily shook her head. "Doesn't matter."

He held her face so she'd look at him. "Of course, it matters."

"I wish you didn't have to leave tomorrow."

Jack sighed. So did he. In all his past relationships, leaving was never easy, but it wasn't like this, like he left pieces of himself behind. "I'm here now."

She unbuttoned his jeans and gripped the hem of his T-shirt and pulled it up, kissing his skin as she went. "We never have enough time together." She palmed his chest.

With urgency, he relieved her of her T-shirt and bra. He cupped her breasts, kissing her mouth deeply.

A car backfired outside. Jack tore his lips from hers. They were on the second floor, but the blinds were open. He stood and carried her to their bedroom, laying her on the bed. He pulled her jeans off, quickly shucked his, and grabbed a condom off the nightstand.

She looked so beautiful, spread open and wanting him. He lay over her, slowly entering her. Her hands roamed over the muscles in his back and down to his ass and then slowly made their way up to his shoulders. He loved that her hands always moved over him, like she couldn't get enough. He couldn't.

JACK LAY AWAKE BECAUSE HIS MIND KEPT REPLAYING the events of the last two days. He wasn't one of those guys who liked to fight, but they had serious issues that they needed to work out sooner than later. It wasn't just Jack's insecurities about Em's feelings for him. Now that the fucker's shit was out of her place, he hoped that'd be the end of it, but he didn't think it would be.

"You awake?" Em asked.

"Yeah."

Em pushed up onto her elbow. "Have you been pumping Nicki for information about me?"

Jack tensed. "Huh?"

"I saw her wink at you Thursday night." Em rolled onto her back.

Jack relaxed. "I just wanted to know how to be a good boyfriend to a writer, so she's been giving me some pointers."

"Pointers, huh? Anything else?"

"Like what?"

"About my accident."

Jack turned onto his side. "Why would you think that?"

Em chuckled. "Because you, who has to know everything, haven't asked any questions since the first week we were together."

Damn, he hadn't realized that. "Not exactly."

"Jack..."

"She never betrayed your trust. I was miserable, and she took pity on me and pointed me in the right direction. I did a search on you." He'd felt ashamed at the time but not enough to let it stop him.

She sighed. "Did you get what you were looking for?"

"It definitely explained some things." Jack rolled onto his back.

"Okay." She turned and snuggled into his side.

"You're not mad?"

"I'm actually a little relieved. I'm sure you still have questions, but I don't like talking about it, remembering it."

"Will you answer my questions someday?"

A few seconds passed. She nodded.

Chapter Twenty-Six

After Jack left on Saturday morning for his gig in Tampa, Emily spent the rest of morning writing and then called the Sullivans and accepted their offer. She still wasn't certain about quitting her job, but she didn't need to decide that now.

And even though she didn't fully understand what went wrong in her relationship with Sully, it didn't matter so much to her anymore. He'd never shown any signs of jealousy. She'd known he'd gotten a lot female attention, and she hadn't been surprised when she'd met Tiffany at the company Christmas party that she'd gushed over him.

Early in their relationship, he'd told her that he liked that she was independent, but he'd thrown that in her face. She remembered the huge fight they'd had when she'd decided to cut her hours so she'd have more time for writing. It had never occurred to her to seek his opinion because they'd only been dating for four months.

Eight more days until she'd see Jack. She'd imagined being apart would get easier, that they'd make the most of their time together, and she'd get used to the large blocks of time until their next visit. So far, she hadn't. It took a couple days to adjust back to her normal life after Hurricane Jack blew through. This had only been Jack's third visit, and her baggage had blown up all over them.

Emily still hadn't told anyone at work that she was seeing someone, but she'd arranged dinner with Eddie and Sheryl over Jack's month-long break in August.

After their week together around Father's Day weekend, they'd be separated for over a month. And after their break in August, the band would be in Europe for six weeks. She wouldn't be able to visit him, and Jack wouldn't be able to fly to see her nearly as often, if at all.

On Tuesday, Emily and Cassidy walked out of the office just after five. As Emily approached her car, her spirits dropped. "Just great." She knew how to change a tire; her dad had made sure of that when she'd gotten her license, but she'd never needed to before. Emily opened the trunk to get the spare tire.

Cassidy stood between their cars. "That's not gonna help."

"Why?" She walked to where Cassidy stood. *Fuck. Just fuck.* The front tire was flat, too. What the hell had she driven through? She'd been rushed this morning but didn't remember running over anything. Now she'd have to call for a tow.

Cassidy unlocked her car and threw her stuff inside. "I'll wait with you."

Emily was still on hold, when Ben called out from the second story window. "What's the problem?"

"Flat tire."

"Flat tires," Cassidy corrected.

Emily shook her head. It had already been a long, frustrating day, and she just wanted to get home and soak in a hot tub. The tow would be at least two hours, and if they said two hours, it'd probably be closer to three.

She leaned up against the trunk. Ben, Jerry, and Jerry's son, AJ walked toward them.

Cassidy leaned over and whispered, "AJ is a total hottie. Dawn told me that he modeled in college."

Emily snickered. "He's also married. But yes, he modeled for a calendar for charity."

"How do you know that?"

"Ben told me."

Ben smirked as they approached. "I'm surprised you don't know how to change a tire, young lady." Ben waved his hand indicating his nephew. "AJ will have you good to go in no time."

Emily shook her head. "As it happens, I do know how to change a tire; unfortunately, I have two flat tires. Tow will be two hours."

AJ knelt and inspected the tire, mumbling something as he stood and moved to check the front tire. His grim face set Emily's nerves on edge. "Emily, your tires were slashed."

"What?" Emily pushed off the trunk and knelt by the rear tire.

"See here, that's a slash. You're gonna need two new tires."

Emily's head throbbed. Sully had been really pissed, but she couldn't believe him capable of this. But, then, she hadn't thought him a cheater, either. When would her past stop invading her present? Emily stood and kicked the tire. They weren't that old, and now she had to shell out several hundred bucks for new tires. She needed to call Jack.

"I'm calling the complex manager," Ben said. "Maybe security saw something."

"I need to make a call." Emily walked over to the steps and sat. Ben and Jerry watched her intently but allowed her privacy. Cassidy chatted with AJ.

She turned her phone over in her hands. Just hearing his voice would make her feel better, but he had a gig tonight, and she didn't want to worry him. Calling him to vent about her day would be selfish, but she really wanted to be selfish right now. It wasn't right to lean on him when he was a thousand miles away. He didn't belong to her exclusively; she had to share him with the world, but she didn't want to. Emily put her phone away.

She'd been so focused on Jack's fame and how she didn't want any part of it that she'd never considered how their time apart would affect her. She had feelings for him, deep, intense feelings. Would they be enough to help her deal with his lifestyle: the fame, the intrusion, and the photographers? But those things were nothing compared to the empty feeling, the loneliness, and the long nights without him.

A burning developed in the pit of her stomach. She had no idea what to do here, and her best friend wasn't around for her to talk to. She needed Nicki. She couldn't discuss Jack with her other friends since they didn't know about him.

Emily had promised not to shut him out. He hated it when she didn't talk to him about everything, even though that degree of openness was alien to her. She had doubts that she could ever be what Jack needed her to be. She didn't want to repeat her mistakes, so she pulled out her phone. After a few seconds of hesitation, she tapped Jack's picture, but it went straight to voicemail. Damn, soundcheck. She hung up without leaving a message because she didn't know what to say.

As she stood, her phone rang.

"Hey, baby, what's up?"

"Why do you think something's up?"

"You never call me from the car." When she hesitated, he said, "What's wrong?" His voice filled with alarm.

"I'm okay, really. I don't want to make the same mistakes again."

"Baby, just tell me."

"I'm waiting for a tow truck. My tires..."

"Em?"

Why was this so hard? "Were slashed."

"Are you sure?"

"Yeah, AJ looked at them."

"Who's AJ?"

"Jerry's son."

"Are you alone?" Alarm was replaced by panic.

"No. Cassidy, Ben, Jerry, and AJ are waiting with me. You know how my bosses feel about their employees."

Jack sighed. "Yeah, I do." She could hear him smile. "Tell me exactly what happened."

"I was leaving for the day, I saw I had a flat tire, then Cassidy pointed out that the front tire was flat, too."

"That's it? No one saw anything?"

"Ben's calling the complex manager, but if security had seen anything, I'm sure they would've let us know."

Jack swore. "You think it was the fucker?"

Emily sighed. "Maybe, but it's not like him."

"It's okay, baby. What did you mean when you said you didn't want to make the same mistakes again?"

Blood pounded through her head. "My first thought was to call you, but then I talked myself out of it."

"Why?"

"Because you worry, and you have a gig tonight, and there's nothing you can do."

"Em, I'm glad you called me, but I'll always worry about you. I love you."

She was in trouble here. Deep shit trouble.

I WOULD'VE LOVED TO HAVE SEEN THE LOOK ON THAT stupid whore's face when she found her tires slashed. Just thinking of tears streaming down her whore cheeks lifts my spirits. Once she realizes how vulnerable she is with Jack away all time, she'll smarten up. And if she doesn't, I'll just have to get more...persuasive.

Jack and I are meant to be together. How can he think he could move on without me?

I've dispatched another love letter. Men are so easy. A little flirting and a blow job, and they'll do anything for me.

JACK HAD RECEIVED ANOTHER LETTER WHEN HE'D checked into the hotel in Pelham, Alabama on Monday afternoon. It was addressed to him at the hotel, and they'd received it on Friday. The letter hadn't mentioned Em directly, only obstacles keeping him and the psycho apart. Obstacles that wouldn't stop her from being with him. The creep factor had been upped tenfold. He hadn't told Em about the letter, and Jeff had agreed.

But when she'd had her tires slashed on Tuesday, Jack felt in his heart that Emily was in danger. He'd talk to her about having Fletcher reinstated. If she said no, he'd do it anyway. She'd be pissed when she figured it out, but until then, it was the only solution Jack could see. He missed her so much, and if anything happened to her, Jack would never forgive himself.

Sunday morning, Jack and Jeff arrived at the airport to find the flight was delayed because of bad weather along the East Coast. Their flight arrived around one, and by the time Jeff dropped him off at Emily's, the storm that had kept them apart devolved to drizzle. Before he even started up the walkway, she opened the door and ran to him. He dropped his bags and lifted her in his arms. Their mouths met, and tongues clashed. "Baby, I missed you." Jack carried her toward the apartment.

"Bags," she said between kisses.

"Oh shit." He set her on the steps inside her apartment and jogged out to retrieve his bags.

When he got upstairs, she wasn't there. "Em?"

"Bedroom."

He stripped off his shirt as he strode down the hallway, stopping short when he reached the door. Emily lay naked on the bed. Jack wasted no time in removing his jeans and underwear.

"Bring that to me." She held out her hand. "Now."

He obeyed. She stood and kissed him and then pushed him to sit on the bed. When she dropped to her knees, his dick jerked in anticipation. Then he was in her warm, moist mouth, her tongue caressing him. "Damn, baby."

Over and over, she ran her tongue along the length of his cock, up and over the tip and back down the underside. As a warm-up to sex, a little oral couldn't be beat. "Em, stop." He needed to fuck her.

Instead of releasing him, she tilted her head up and winked. *Oh fuck.* She wanted him to come in her mouth. He cupped her head with his hand, stroking her hair as she sucked him off. His nuts tightened, and she grabbed the base of his cock, concentrating her tongue on the tip. "Gonna come, baby." And he did, in long spurts, all captured in that dirty, beautiful mouth of hers. She relished every drop, and when she released him, she licked her lips. She sat back, her neck and chest flushed with desire. He loved that blowing him made her horny.

Helping her up, he pulled her to him, resting his head against her breasts. Jack stroked her back as he cuddled her. Tilting his head to the side, he was treated to the lovely view of her amazing ass in the dresser mirror. "Does that mirror move?"

"No."

"Too bad." He scooted back on the bed, and she stretched out next to him. He grabbed a pillow and propped it under his head. Em used his shoulder for a pillow. Since they were laying across the bed, he couldn't pull the covers up over them, but from this angle, he could see them in the mirror. Emily was nestled into his side, an arm and leg thrown possessively across his body. She tilted her head and smiled up at him. "What?" he asked.

"So far so good."

"That was more than good, baby." His dick stirred in concurrence. Jack sat up and shifted so he faced the windows. "Sit on my face."

She straddled his chest, her pussy inches away from his eager tongue. He couldn't wait to taste her. He let her tease him for a bit and then grabbed her hips and held her in place as he opened his mouth on her. Her musky scent invaded his senses as his tongue laved her clit. He closed his lips around her and sucked her swollen nub into his mouth, swirling his tongue around it like she'd done to him. "Watch yourself in the mirror."

She stroked her breasts, tugging her nipples as he held her in place. "Oh," she moaned.

"That's it, baby, come for me." He sucked her clit hard then released it. "Then I'm going to fuck you." He couldn't get enough of her; he licked and sucked, her moans egging him on.

With a wail-like cry, she came, her body trembling from the crush of her orgasm. He licked her until she begged him to stop. He scooted out from under her and then bent her forward so she was on all fours, facing the mirror. Grabbing a condom, he protected them. He used her juices to coat his dick and then, without warning, thrust into her hard.

"Fuck, yes, baby," she moaned.

Em took the words right out of his mouth. Every time he

pushed into her, she pushed back. He leaned forward so he could kiss her back, nibbling her shoulder. "You like that, don't you, baby? You like it when I fuck you hard."

"Yes. Hard, fuck me hard."

He straightened and did just that, impaling her with his cock, watching her tits jiggling in the mirror, the look of pure ecstasy on her face, and he was lost. She tightened around him, and as he pounded into her, Jack came with a primal growl. He pulled out, disposed of the condom, and returned to bed, pulling her limp body up next to his. She snuggled closer as he yanked the covers up over them.

Her breathing evened out, and Jack felt sleep pulling him under. "Another One Bites the Dust" wafted through the air. *Shit.* His phone was in his jeans pocket on the floor, and it was Dex. It was also Sunday. He deserved a day off, so he ignored it. As sleep continued to pull him, the song busted into his consciousness again. *Fuck.* He slipped out of bed, careful not to wake Em.

Grabbing his jeans off the floor, he answered just in time. "Dex, what's up?"

"Wayne Ettinger called, needs to speak to you."

"Shit." Jack rubbed a hand over his face. "Thanks, Dex, appreciate it." His heart pounded.

"Everything okay?" Emily asked.

"Christie's dad wants me to call him."

Emily pressed her body up against his back, her arms circling around him. "Want privacy?"

"No."

She snuggled closer and rested her cheek on his back.

Jack took a deep breath and dialed Wayne. His heart pounded and his throat tightened up. He prayed—

"Jack, thanks for calling me back."

"What's up?" Jack held his breath.

"Christie says she's ready to go into rehab."

Jack exhaled, and his throat relaxed. "Thank God. That's great. I was afraid you were calling for another reason."

"Sorry, I should've led with that." Wayne cleared his throat. "Listen, there's just one thing..."

Jack had promised, and he'd honor his promise. "Wayne, don't worry about it. Whatever it costs, I'll pay."

"It's not that, but Carla and I really appreciate it."

"What then?"

"Christie will only go if she can see you first. She wants to make amends. Will you come?"

Jack's heart hit the floor. She'd given up calling Dex by the end of last week, and obviously, she'd come up with a new plan. "Wayne..." What could he say? That Jack thought this was just a way for Christie to see him, that she wasn't serious about getting the help she needed? But, what if she was? He leaned back into Em's embrace. He needed to discuss this with her.

"Jack, please? I know she's been harassing you, but she's our baby. Please come?" The strain in Wayne's voice was evident. It had been horrible for them, watching helplessly as their little girl sank deeper into drug and alcohol use. Jack knew how they felt. Emily tapped him on the shoulder. "Hold on." Jack muted the call.

Emily sat next to him. Her beautiful hazel eyes shimmered with unshed tears. "You have to go." Leaning in, she kissed his lips gently.

Knowing he had her blessing melted his hesitation. He wiped away a single tear that rolled down her cheek and kissed her nose. "Wayne, I'll call you back when the arrangements are made."

Wayne heaved a sigh of relief. "Jack, thank you."

He dropped the phone on the bed and then pulled her into his arms and kissed her, pouring all his love into the communion of their lips. Tears welled in his eyes. Hopefully, this time, Christie would accept the help and be able to break free of the devastating hold of addiction. "Thank you. Gotta call Jeff."

"Do what you have to. I'll start dinner." She grabbed his T-shirt and slipped it over her head. Before leaving, she turned and smiled.

Jack called Jeff and let him know the change of plans and then made the necessary arrangements. The first flight to John Glenn International was Monday morning at 6:25, and Jack reserved an SUV for the sixty-mile drive to Mount Vernon.

He found Emily in the kitchen at the stove. "Smells good." He snaked his arms around her. "I'm starving. What's cooking?"

Emily leaned back. "Roasted chicken, spicy rice, and balsamic carrots."

"No you?" He kissed her neck just below her ear.

"I'm dessert."

And just like that, he was hard.

After dinner, they watched a movie, then made love, and Em fell asleep in his arms, but he still woke every time she moved away from him.

The next time Jack woke, Em was rubbing his chest. Moaning, he grabbed her hand, brought it to his lips, and kissed it. "Morning."

"Morning. I need my hand back."

With one final kiss, he released her hand which trailed down his chest, stomach, and groin, finally curling around his erection. He grabbed a condom, which she took from him, opened it, and rolled it on, and then she slowly sank onto him.

She joined him in the shower and made him pancakes while he packed up his stuff. They ate in silence, whether because he was leaving or that it was three thirty in the morning, he wasn't sure.

Their flight arrived a little after eight, and it took them

almost three hours due to rush hour traffic to get to the Ettingers' home. With every passing mile, he prayed and hoped in his heart that Christie was serious about getting help.

Jeff parked, and Christie ran out of the house as Jack got out.

"Baby, I'm so glad you came. I've missed you." She jumped into his arms, so he had no choice but to catch her. Her lips covered his.

"Stop." Jack tried to put her down, but she wouldn't let go. "I told you, I've met someone." The coffee they'd stopped for soured in his stomach.

"No woman can—"

"I'm in love with her." No reason to drag this out. The therapist he'd seen at the end of their relationship told him to be honest, and that he couldn't give her any hope.

The crushed look on her face lasted only a few seconds before she masked it. "When I get out of rehab—"

Jack shook his head. "Christie"—he paused until she met his eyes—"it's over. It's been over."

She collapsed on the ground, tears streaming down her cheeks. Christie's parents stood in the doorway, and Jack noticed a neighbor gawking at them.

He extended his hand. "Let's go inside and talk."

When she made no move to accept, he reached down and pulled her to her feet. She leaned into him and sobbed uncontrollably, so Jack carried her inside and set her down on the couch. He grabbed a few tissues and handed them to her.

She sniffled, blew her nose, and looked up at him. "Please, can't you give me one more chance? Give *us* one more chance?" Her blue eyes, that had always captivated him, held hope and lust.

He felt pity but nothing else. Jack assumed her parents went into the kitchen to give them privacy but wished they hadn't. He'd lain awake last night, hoping her request to see him wasn't an attempt to get back together. There were no more pieces left to put back together; she'd destroyed them all. He shook his head. "Your dad said you wanted to make amends and then you'd go to rehab. Were you lying?"

An expression flitted across her face for a split second before she spoke. "No, I'm ready to get help. I am sorry, Jack, for everything. You're the best thing that ever happened to me. Please give me another chance."

He wanted to believe her words, but he'd seen the look and knew she was lying. His heart felt heavy. There'd been a time when, desperate to believe her, he would've ignored the expression. But no more. He couldn't, wouldn't, do this again. "It's over, and it has been for a long time. You need help. Please go into rehab, but there won't be an us for you to come out to. You have to do this for you."

Anger flared in her eyes, and she stood and slapped him. "You never loved me. You used me."

He walked out. He'd loved her with everything he had. Then he remembered what that fucker had said to Em last week. That it hadn't been enough. In Jack's case, he realized for the first time that it was true. He could never love her enough to fill the hole inside her.

Needing to hear Em's voice, he pulled out his phone. "Hey."

"Hi. You okay?"

He heard her office door close. "No."

Emily sighed. "I'm sorry. I was really hoping she'd get help."

"Yeah, me too."

"Jack?" He turned. Wayne and Carla stood there, tears welling over.

"Baby, I've got to go. I'll call you later. I love you."

Carla stepped forward. "Please don't leave yet. She needed

to know you weren't getting back together. Once she gets used to the idea..." She looked down.

Jack couldn't fault them for laying a guilt trip on him. Christie was their daughter, and they were losing her. If she didn't get help, she'd be lost to the world. Addiction would consume her, like so many people before her.

Jack nodded and walked slowly back to the house. They spent hours trying to convince her to get the help she needed. In the end, she refused. He left feeling exhausted, depressed, and angry that he'd wasted the time that he could've spent with Em.

Christie's parting words still echoed through his mind. "We're not done. We'll never be done."

Chapter Twenty-Seven

The following Thursday, Emily waited nervously for Jack to arrive. His flight landed two hours ago, so he'd be calling her soon to pick up the key. She'd offered to leave the key under the mat since he was staying with her this week, but he'd vetoed that idea. Well, until they left Friday morning to spend four days with his family. Her nerves were frayed over that. She kept reminding herself that they were nice to invite her, especially after the stellar first impression she'd made.

She'd taken off Thursday through Tuesday. Jack was leaving next Friday for the month-long run, and they wouldn't be able see each other.

She'd been surprised when he'd told her he'd planned to spend so much time at his parents' instead of taking a real vacation to an island with sunshine, beaches, and tropical drinks like Curt and Nicki were doing. He'd explained that he traveled so much that his idea of a vacation was to be home. That made perfect sense to her. Maybe this crazy relationship could work. She jumped when her cell rang. "Hi, baby."

Jack's voice cut in and out. "Sorry...traffic...soon." The line went dead.

It was ridiculous how nervous and happy she was to see him. She'd put in a dozen extra hours the last week at work so she'd be able to finish everything before she left on vacation. With Jack. Nine days together. He'd be all hers. And his family's. She could deal with that.

Chimes alerted her to a text message from Jack: *In the parking lot, black SUV, missing you.*

Emily sprinted out of the office, barely getting out to Cassidy that she had to get something from her car before she was out the door. Seeing each other for the first time in over a week in the parking lot of her office wasn't ideal, so Jack had agreed to wait in the car.

She opened the door and climbed in the front seat. His blue eyes sparkled as he reached for her, or had she lunged toward him? No matter, she was in his lap, kissing her boyfriend. He tasted of mint and coffee, and she couldn't get enough. The interior smelled of his cologne and that unique combination of soap and wind.

A sudden knock startled Emily, and she hit her head on the roof of the truck. "Ow." She turned to see Ben smiling through the closed window. *Oh crap.* He crooked his finger at them.

"That's my boss." He helped her off his lap and back into her seat. She smoothed her hair down and checked her makeup in the mirror.

Jack got out and walked around to her side, opening the door, and offering his hand. Jack put his arm around her.

"Ben Bradford, Jack McBride."

Jack shook Ben's hand. "Nice to finally meet you, sir. Emily's told me all about you."

Ben smirked back. "Really, because I've heard nothing about you." He quirked a graying brow at her. "Come in, my brother and I would like to talk to you."

Emily would've protested, but Ben cut her off. "You should've told us you were dating a bona fide rock star."

Emily was sure her chin hit the pavement. "How do you—"

Ben addressed Jack. "Emily doesn't think an old geezer like myself would recognize a rock star." He chuckled. "We are a marketing firm, it's our job to have our fingers on the pulse of pop culture."

Emily's feet finally got the message from her brain to move. She followed behind Ben, taking Jack's hand. "I wouldn't use the word geezer."

Ben looked over his shoulder. "What word would you use?"

"Codger."

Ben laughed. "That's my girl. Come on, stop stalling."

When they walked into the office, Cassidy glanced up and gulped. "You're Jack McBride," she screeched.

This is like a nightmare. Emily hadn't been prepared to introduce Jack yet, let alone getting caught making out like a schoolgirl with him in the front seat of his truck. Definitely a nightmare. Or a daymare.

"Oh my God, you're like my favorite singer. I love your band," Cassidy gushed. She grabbed a pen and paper and thrust them at Jack. "Can I get your autograph?"

Emily's head dropped to her chest. Her cheeks flamed. "Cassidy..." At least her friend hadn't asked Jack to sign her cleavage.

"I'd be happy to," Jack said with practiced, rock star ease.

And he was at ease, not at all embarrassed or put out, so Emily relaxed. She'd been embarrassed that Cassidy made such a fuss, but Jack took it in stride. She'd seen him in action with other fans, but she hadn't been friends with them. The weirdness faded, and she smiled. He really was a natural.

Cassidy's screech had caused other women in the office to

rush to the reception area, practically knocking each other over for a better look. Jack just spoke to each in turn, signed autographs, and took a few pictures. Emily looked on still amazed and aware that Ben watched her closely.

"What's going on out here?" Jerry asked.

Ben smirked at his brother. "This is Jack, Emily's new boyfriend."

"Boyfriend eh? Ha, you owe me a dollar, Benji."

Ben scowled at his brother. He hated when Jerry called him that, which was probably why he did it. Now that the bosses were watching, his fans receded, and Emily stepped next to Jack and took his hand. "You had a bet going?" She tried for a stern tone, but it was impossible to pull off through her smile. "You two have a problem," she scolded, still smiling.

Ben put his arm around Jack's shoulders. "Come into our office, young man, we have some questions for you."

Jerry nodded in agreement. They walked to the door, but Jerry stopped her. "Don't you have some work to do?" He closed the door, leaving Emily to stare at the woodgrain pattern that always resembled a spooky face.

Oh shit.

JERRY SMILED TO HIMSELF. THE LOOK ON EMILY'S face as he closed the door was priceless. He and his brother had suspected she was seeing someone new, but Jack McBride was a shock. Stone Highway was just about the tip of the top of the music industry. Jerry liked their music; it had a melodic quality that he appreciated, and the lyrics actually made sense. Unlike some of their contemporaries, Stone Highway didn't just produce noise.

Jerry stopped at the bar. "Would you like some water?"

"No, thank you."

Polite too. He liked that. Emily was a good girl, and she deserved someone who would treat her with respect. "Whiskey?"

"None for me, but you go ahead."

He shared a look with his brother. Good, not a day drinker. Some of those musicians were into all kinds of bad behavior. They couldn't be too careful with their Emily.

"Have a seat," Ben offered.

Jack took one of the club chairs that faced Jerry's desk and angled it so when he sat, he could see both men.

Whoever got in first moved the chairs to face their desk. They loved watching someone new come in and decide how to sit without offending one of them. Most chose to stand.

Jerry settled behind his desk.

"So, tell me, how many girlfriends do you have?" Ben asked.

Jack smiled. "Just Emily."

"So, no girl in every city?" Ben pressed.

"No sir. Emily's it for me."

That shocked Jerry. A glance at Ben confirmed his shock. They were half-brothers and usually on the same page. Based on how the ladies in the office responded to him, Jack was used to female attention, but he'd done it with a certain detachment. He doubted the ladies even realized it, but Emily had. This guy might just be worthy of her.

"Any kids?" Jerry asked. Some of these guys had more baby mommas than could be counted on one hand. Of course, in his day, they were called wives.

"No."

"Are you sure?" Jerry asked.

Jack smiled. "As sure as any man can be."

Huh. He'd meant to rattle him with that question, but Jack didn't rattle. Ben had been busy on his computer, but now he looked up and cleared his throat.

"So," Ben said. "What do you do when you're not on tour?"

"Touring eats up about seventy-five percent of my time, so when I'm home, I like to be home. I have a studio in my house, so I'm always working on a new song."

"That'd be your house in California?" Ben asked.

Jack nodded.

"How do you expect to carry on a relationship with our Emily if you live across the country?" Ben rocked back in his leather chair.

"Actually, that house is on the market, and I'm looking for a place in the city. We'll be visiting my folks this weekend, and hopefully, by Tuesday, the real estate agent will have a few places for us to look at."

"Us?" Jerry asked.

Jack held his gaze. "Emily's not ready to move in with me, but I'd like her to help me pick out the place, since she'll end up there eventually."

So, he had long-term plans for this relationship. Jerry held his smile in check. He liked this guy, but he could tell Ben was skeptical.

Ben narrowed his eyes. "What exactly are your intentions?"

Jack didn't hesitate. "I want to marry her, sir."

Ben sat back and smiled.

Even though they had different mothers, since they'd met, he'd always felt like he had a twin. To a casual onlooker, their grilling this young man might seem odd, but Emily was like a daughter to them. And after the havoc their own father had wreaked on everyone in his life, especially his wives, children, and employees, they'd been determined not to let history repeat itself.

When Ben stood, Jerry knew he was satisfied. Ben offered

Jack his hand. "Well, it's been a pleasure to meet you, young man."

Jack stood and accepted his hand. "It was a pleasure to meet you as well. I hope you got what you were looking for."

"Young man, if I hadn't—"

"Ben, enough." Sometimes he needed to be reminded that Emily was a grown woman. And making threats wasn't legal.

Ben shot him a "fuck you" look, which Jerry responded to by brushing his hair back, giving Ben the finger.

"I understand," Jack said. "Emily told me you were like a family here. I can see that you love her, and after what happened, she needs protecting."

Jerry's temper rose in an instant. "That motherfucker..."

Jack's eyes widened.

Ben chuckled. "What? You think your generation invented that word?"

Jack looked down but that didn't hide his smile. "No, sir."

Jerry shook his head; young people today thought they invented everything. They couldn't imagine a world that existed before they did. At least not where people were intelligent, creative, and didn't live in caves.

Ben hit the intercom button. "Emily, please come in."

Ten seconds and a quick knock later, Emily walked in. From the look on her face, they were in trouble.

Emily narrowed her eyes and pointed at Ben then Jerry. "What have you two been doing in here?"

"None of your business, young lady, and I'll thank you to remember that we are your employers and, as such, deserve not to be spoken to—"

"Cut the crap, Jerry. You spent the last twenty minutes grilling my boyfriend, that's hardly the duty of an employer." She grinned at him.

"Yes, well, it's every father's duty." Jerry choked up and turned to cover, noticing that Ben did the same.

"I appreciate it." When he looked at her, she smiled. "Thank you." Emily cleared her throat. "Now, if you're done, I'll say goodbye to Jack and get back to work."

Ben looked at his watch. "It's almost lunchtime. Why don't you two go out to lunch a little early."

"Sounds like a great idea to me." Jack pulled her into his side, his arm curling possessively around her waist.

"I can't, I have—"

"Young lady, we'll tell you what you have left to do. That is, if you think our feeble minds are still capable of running our business."

Emily closed her eyes and slowly inhaled. She always did that when she was frustrated with them. "Sir, thank you, sir."

Ben tutted. "You know very well, young lady, that the 'sir sandwich' is reserved for those who outrank you."

Jack laughed, and Emily playfully shook her fist at him. "You're not helping."

He pulled her into his arms and kissed her. "I like these guys."

"Yeah, me too. I'll keep 'em."

"Enough of that, you two." Jerry ushered them toward the door. "Go have lunch. And don't rush back." He winked at her as he closed the door behind them.

JACK SAT ACROSS FROM EM IN THE SMALL ITALIAN restaurant and felt more relaxed than he had in days. He'd missed her so much, but now they had over a week together. She had to work tomorrow but took Friday, Monday, and Tuesday off so they could spend time with his family. He hadn't expected her bosses to grill him the way they had, but he obviously passed.

Em sipped her wine. "What?"

Caught smiling like an idiot again. "I like your bosses. It's clear they love you."

"Yeah, I'm sorry about that."

"About what?"

Em rolled her eyes. "That they questioned you like that."

"What makes you think they asked me questions?" Jack sat back, he'd missed talking to her in person. Over the phone she was more distant, uncomfortable even.

"Because, I know those two curmudgeons."

"I thought they were codgers?"

Emily smiled. "They are, but they can take a little getting used to."

Jack leaned in and took her hand, bringing it to his lips. "I think it's nice. You told me they think of their employees like family. That's what we try to do. The band, I mean."

"I think you succeed quite nicely." Em sipped her water. "They've been so good to me. When I first started, my aunt and uncle had moved to California, so I had nowhere to go for Thanksgiving. They asked everyone what their plans were, and I didn't have any." She smiled. "It was Ben's turn to host that year, so he invited me on the spot."

Jack's chest tightened, the way it did every time she spoke of being alone. "What about Nicki?"

"Her family's idea of the holidays is a trip somewhere. I think they went to Scotland that year."

He hadn't meant to look or be obvious about it, but when she leaned forward, her blouse dipped, and he got a peek of burgundy lace. Damn. He wanted her, maybe she'd—

Emily waved her hand in front of his face. "Earth to Jack." His head snapped up, and she smirked at him. "Really, Jack, you've seen me naked."

Why did she have to say naked? His mind instantly conjured her naked and riding him. He tried to casually adjust himself. He leaned forward, trying not to crush his dick. "Baby, it's been nine days."

She tilted her head and counted on her fingers. "So it has."

He knew she was busting his balls, that she wanted him as badly as he wanted her. "If you lived closer, we'd have satisfied a different hunger."

He could tell she was picturing exactly how they'd satisfy themselves. When the waiter arrived with their salads, she was startled. She licked her lips. "Mmm, I'm starving." Then she leaned forward and whispered, "For you."

"Mean, you're mean." He picked up his fork and took his frustration out on the salad, stabbing repeatedly, unable to get the damn lettuce to stay on the fork.

"Sorry."

He knew she wasn't. "I want to rip that blouse off you and —" he whispered. He glanced at the table next to them, but the mother was busy cleaning up a spill. He struggled to find a word other than fuck. "Have you."

Emily sipped her water. "I like this blouse." She tapped her forefinger on her chin. "But I do have a gray one that gaps. Next time I wear it, you can rip that one off."

Shit, now his dick was hard. He hoped she was serious. He'd jerk it to ripping her blouse off as soon as he got home. Home. Her home. She'd insisted he stay with her and that getting a hotel was nice of him but a waste of money. He was so fucking happy he thought his head might explode. Hopefully, she'd wear the gray blouse to work tomorrow.

"Did you ask your parents about the sleeping arrangements?"

"You were right. They'd prefer if we slept in different rooms." His dad had seemed shocked that he'd asked, probably because he never had before. "I'll be sleeping with my brother. You'll be in my room. I hope you appreciate my sacrifice because Jimmy farts. A lot."

"I'm sure I can find a way to make it up to you."

He pictured her smirking lips taking his dick in her mouth. Shit. He forced that thought out of his head and concentrated on his salad.

After their leisurely lunch, he drove them slowly back to the office. He managed to get stopped at every red light.

"What time will you be home?"

"Not sure. I have copy that has to be finished tonight. I'd planned on working through lunch."

Damn, if he'd known that, he would've taken her to the diner across the street. "Why didn't you say something?"

"I meant to, but then the gruesome twosome insisted we take our time. You don't decline when they tell you to take a long lunch."

Jack parked and cut the engine. "Key?"

Emily chuckled. "Oops. Here." She pulled the key out of her pocket and handed it to him. He knew it was only temporary, but it was the best gift he'd ever gotten.

"Let me know when you have a better idea when you'll be home. I'll make dinner."

"You're a good boyfriend." She kissed him and got out.

He'd have a surprise for her when she got home. Jack had done quite a bit of shopping: silk lingerie, bras, panties, and cute pajamas. Not that she'd be wearing them anytime soon. He planned to do more shopping tomorrow while she was at work. Maybe they could have lunch together again.

She called at four thirty to say that she'd hopefully be home around seven. At six thirty, she called to say that she'd be at least another hour. At seven forty-five, she called and told him to eat without her. Her computer had crashed and she'd spent the last hour waiting for IT to call her. At eight forty-five, she was on her way home.

When he heard her key in the door, his pulse raced. He

needed her so badly, but that would have to wait because she sounded exhausted when she called.

"Hi." He opened his arms and hugged her. Her lips devoured his. Forcing himself to break the kiss, he slid her purse strap off her shoulder. "How does a hot bath sound? Or would you like to eat first?"

A funny smile crossed her face. "Jack, I...haven't cleaned the tub in weeks."

"I took care of it."

"You scrubbed my tub?"

He shrugged. "My arms aren't broken. Dinner or bath?

"What's for dinner?"

"Beef and vegetable stir fry with brown rice."

Emily whistled. "Wow, you do like to cook, don't you? Dinner wins."

Jack smiled. "Go get undressed. There's a present for you on the bed. Put it on." He busied himself with opening and pouring wine so he wouldn't picture her getting naked.

"Jack, it's beautiful."

He turned to see her standing in the doorway to the kitchen, the silk burgundy robe covering her naked body. "You're beautiful." He handed her a glass of wine. "To time spent together."

She smiled, raised her glass to his, and clinked. "To us."

Us. His heart fluttered in his chest. *Us.*

"I have a surprise for you, too," Emily said between bites of stir fry.

Jack's mind went dirty. Sitting at her dining room table, he pictured himself sweeping the dishes off the table, bending her over, and—

"Don't you want to know the surprise?"

"Yes, please."

"Well, I've been putting in extra hours for the last week,

and the reason I had to finish the copy I was working on today is because I was able to get a comp day off tomorrow."

"Comp day?" That didn't sound the least bit sexual.

Emily smirked at him. "Yes, Jack, in the working world that means I got tomorrow off for working longer other days."

His heart leapt in his chest. "You're off tomorrow?" An extra full day together?

"Yup."

He pulled her onto his lap and kissed her. "I love you."

"I don't know what you planned for tomorrow, but I thought we could make chili. I know your parents didn't want us to bring anything, but I'm a guest, so I'd feel better if we contributed something." She kissed him. "It's my dad's recipe."

"Em, I'd love that." She wanted to make her dad's chili recipe with him; he loved her more every damn day.

"We have to go to the grocery store first thing. We always simmered it all day."

A very normal thing to do. But first, she needed to finish eating and relax. "Finish eating and then into the bath."

Jack washed the dishes while Emily soaked in the hot bubble bath. When he was done, he grabbed his wine and knocked on the partially closed bathroom door. "May I come in?"

"Of course." Her head rested on a bath pillow, eyes closed, bubbles up to her neck, looking stunningly beautiful as always. "I can't believe you scrubbed my tub."

He sat on the side of the tub. "I grew up doing chores. When I was six, my dad started McBride Plumbing, so he worked all the time. Trish was two and my mom was pregnant with Jimmy." He laughed at the memory. "Although that's not what I called him."

"What did you call him?"

"Jack Jr." He refilled Emily's glass. "I went through a

phase where I thought all babies should be named Jack, and since they were younger than me, I added junior. It started when my mom was pregnant with Trish." Jack shook his head. "She was supposed to be a boy 'cause I wanted a baby brother." He sipped his wine. "But after she was born, I was glad to have a sister."

Emily's laugh echoed through the bathroom. "How cute." Her eyes fluttered closed.

"Okay, out of the tub before you fall asleep."

"Mmm, I think I did." She stood and Jack wrapped a bath sheet around her.

Twenty minutes later, she was fast asleep nestled into his side. He was so excited that he had a hard time falling asleep. An extra day together making chili, and then four days with his family. Jack was sure their rocky start was behind them.

Chapter Twenty-Eight

Emily woke early the next morning in the most pleasant way possible—with Jack between her thighs. Jack went out for bagels while Emily put on the coffee. After breakfast, they went to the grocery store to get the ingredients for her dad's chili recipe.

It amazed her that Jack was comfortable in every situation. He looked as natural shopping for groceries as he did on stage singing to tens of thousands of fans. He took everything in stride. Emily wished she could be like that. "So how many people will be at this barbecue?"

"I'd guess around a hundred."

Emily stopped short and Jack bumped into her. "Please tell me that's a joke."

Jack shook his head. "I told you I had a big family."

"Yeah, but you didn't say they'd all be there. I thought it was your immediate family."

"It will be. Most everyone lives in a four-town radius. A few might not come, but my folks do this every year, either on Mother's Day or Father's Day, depending on my tour schedule. It's the only time I get to see all my cousins."

"Oh."

"Em, if you'd rather not go, we can—"

She smiled and touched his cheek. "No. It's fine. I was just surprised at the sheer number of McBrides is all."

"Not just McBrides, my mom's side of the family, the Donoghues, and both sets of grandparents. Last I heard, all my aunts and uncles were coming and all but a few cousins. Many of the married cousins have kids or one on the way, so it'll be quite a shindig."

"Wow." *Suck it up, Prescott, you said you'd go. Smile. Bigger.*

"Em you okay? You're smiling weird."

Too big, too big. Emily relaxed her facial muscles. "Sounds like fun."

They started the chili as soon as they got home. Emily went to her office to dig out her dad's recipe. She'd had it laminated because it was in her dad's handwriting. Jack chopped the peppers and celery while she handled the garlic and onions. Emily sautéed the vegetables while Jack browned and drained the meat. Once all the ingredients were in the stock pot to simmer, Jack washed the dishes, and Emily made them sandwiches for lunch.

"We forgot the chili peppers," Jack said.

"No, we'll cook them separately, then they can be added to taste."

"Did you make this often?"

Emily stopped spreading the mayo. "All the time. My dad was an only child, and his parents were both over forty when they had him. His dad passed when he was seventeen and his mom a year later. He found a second family in the Corps, more brothers and sisters than he could've ever hoped for. We were like one big family."

Tears pricked her eyes, but these were happy memories. "We always had the first barbecue, and the chili was always the first thing to go. I always helped my dad make it. It was kind of our special thing." Jack's arms encircled her, and she leaned back against him. "This is the first time I've made it since..."

Jack turned her and tilted her chin up so she had to look at him. "I'm honored that you let me be a part of this."

Emily could only nod. If she spoke, she'd lose it. When she stepped back, Jack's shirt was wet where her face had rested against his chest. "Sorry, I didn't mean to use you as a tissue."

Jack looked down at the wet dots and shrugged. "I'd go through ten shirts if I needed to. Let's eat, I'm starving."

After lunch, Emily packed for their weekend. Jack walked in with two duffel bags. "Here, pack these." He opened one bag and pulled out a dozen sets of bras and panties. "I washed them all, so you're good to go." Jack wagged his brows up and down.

Emily sorted through the pile of bras in satin, lace, and mesh. The matching panties were in various cuts from thongs to boyfriend panties. All expensive. Jack pulled more and more out of the bag. By the time she'd matched up the bras and panties, her bed was covered in lingerie from black to white and all the colors in between.

Her eyes widened at the mass of silk and satin. "Are you insane?"

"What? I like you in nice things."

"I'm not bringing any of this to your parents' house."

"Of course not, bring these." He took out several sets of pajamas, all long pants and tank tops.

"I have plenty of pajamas, Jack."

"Yeah, I've been meaning to talk to you about that. They're ugly."

Emily huffed. "My pajamas aren't ugly." She knew they weren't pretty, but they were pajamas, so who cared?

"You're too beautiful to wear ugly pajamas."

"What difference does it make? Whenever we sleep together, I'm naked or wearing your T-shirt."

"I do like you in my T-shirt, but humor me."

Emily shrugged. "Okay." If it made him happy to see her in non-ugly pajamas, then so be it. But now that Jack had emptied one bag that contained all stuff for her, that didn't leave him with a lot of clothes. "Why do you have so little with you?"

He smiled. "This is plenty for here. I keep clothes at my parents' house, still have my old room."

She went back to packing. "It must be nice to have a home to go back to."

Jack nodded.

Emily shook off the melancholy that dogged her the last few days for the hundredth time. Jack was here, and they'd be together for the next week. She wouldn't waste another minute on feeling sorry for herself.

While Jack dried the pots, she slipped into an emerald green baby doll with matching thong. Barefoot, she padded into the kitchen and put her arms around him. She rubbed her breasts against his back.

He stood still. "You're not wearing a bra."

"Nope, but I am wearing something new." Jack tried to turn but she stopped him. "Guess?"

"What do I get if I'm right?"

"Me."

"What if I'm wrong?"

"Don't be wrong."

Jack moaned. His breath stuttered in and out, and his skin warmed. She loved that he was as affected by her as she was by him.

"Is it made of silk, lace, or mesh?"

"Yes."

"Is it a solid color?"

"Yes."

"Is it a color between black and white?"

"Yes. You're good at this."

"I really want to win. Okay, last question. Are you naked underneath it?"

Being this close and teasing him teased her too. Her nipples were painfully hard, and she'd already soaked through the skimpy thong. Everywhere her skin touched his burned. "Yes."

Jack turned, and she stepped back so he could get the full effect. The emerald silk brought out the green in her eyes. She'd put her hair up in a clip, with tendrils falling loosely around her face and shoulders. His eyes darkened, and a slow, wicked smiled curled his lips.

"I saw that color and knew it'd be stunning on you." His throat worked with the effort to swallow. "Stunning doesn't even come close to describing how beautiful you are." He lunged forward and swept her off her feet, carrying her into the bedroom.

He lay her on the bed. Grabbing his duffel bag, he pulled out a pair of stockings. "Tie me up."

Shock rushed through her system. She wasn't into bondage, and there had never been any indication that Jack was either. "I'm not into that." She wanted to please him more than anything, but they'd never discussed this.

Jack laid the stockings on the pillow next to her. "Not even a 'little b'?" His eyes sparkled with mischief.

Her brain rushed back to the conversations they'd had the night they met, when she described one of the scenes she'd written. A poor fellow who couldn't keep his hands to himself while his girlfriend stripped for him. "Are you saying you won't be able to keep your hands to yourself while I strip for you?" Nerves didn't have time to rise because Jack hauled her into his arms, his erection digging into her belly as his lips crashed down on hers.

His hands cupped her ass, and she was so tightly pressed against him she could barely breathe. She could do delicious things to him if he was tied up. She placed her palms on his chest and used all her strength to push him away. He didn't budge.

She bit his lip. His hands roamed over her back and around to cup her breasts. He rolled her nipples between his thumb and forefinger. She gasped with pleasure. Oh fuck. "Enough."

Jack released her instantly, his face shrouded in doubt. "I'm sorry, I—"

"Oh, you're going to be sorry." She kissed his puzzled lips gently. She rubbed his dick through the thick jeans, but she needed to feel his skin. She undid the button and thrust her hand down, her fingers curling around his hardened flesh. She gave him an aggressive squeeze. His sharp intake of breath pleased her. "Now, you stand still while I undress you. If you move. I'll punish you."

Jack nodded.

"Good boy. No talking."

She stroked him a few more times before removing her hand and trailing her fingers under his shirt. She lifted the hem, kissing as she exposed his abs and chest. His skin was warm and tight over his muscled torso. The dusting of hair on his chest tickled her lips. When she licked his nipple, he swayed and then planted his feet wider. "Good boy."

She rewarded him by unzipping his fly but didn't free him yet. "Better?"

He whimpered.

She smiled and lifted his shirt over his head and tossed it away. "How 'bout now?" She caressed his biceps, loving the feel of his muscles. Her fingers played over the lines of his Celtic tattoo.

He looked down and back up at her and moaned.

"Too confining?"

He nodded vigorously.

Emily slid her hands between his jeans and underwear, caressing him, and he groaned. She kissed his jaw up to his ear. "Do you want me to fuck you?"

His cock jerked beneath her palm. "Yes."

"Tsk, tsk, tsk." Now, she'd have to punish him. She made eye contact and then slowly lowered her gaze down his chest, abs and stomach and rested at his groin. The tip of his dick peeked out from the waistband of his boxer briefs. That must be uncomfortable.

She got off the bed and dropped to her knees, pulling his jeans off as she descended. He stepped out of them. Looking up, she leaned in and licked his cock through his underwear. A bead of fluid emerged from the tip. She wanted to lick it off but not yet. He needed to be punished. She cupped his ass as she continued to lick him through the cotton fabric.

His hips moved forward every time she moved back. "Are you trying to tell me something?" she asked, addressing his dick.

Jack grunted. She smiled and looked up at him. "Pussy got your tongue?" Jack groaned as if in pain. "Oh, right, I forbade you to talk."

Her body throbbed with need. She was in as bad a shape as he was, but it was too soon to let him know that. She moved to stand, but Jack stopped her with a hand on her shoulder.

"Please," he whispered. His eyes pleaded with her.

Emily shook her head. "Whispering counts." She pushed to her feet as her hands slid up the silk baby doll, and she cupped her breasts. Her eyes closed and her lips parted. She let her head fall back as she tweaked her nipples.

Jack grunted and hauled her up, kissing her with a ferocity that startled her. His lips took, and his tongue gave back. He ground his erection into her belly. She was so lost in the passion of his kiss she forgot she'd gotten the reaction she'd been waiting for. She enjoyed his lips and hands for another few seconds before tearing away from him.

She pulled his underwear down, and his cock burst out, nearly hitting her in the face. She opened her mouth and leaned in but didn't take him between her lips. Instead, she stuck out her tongue until it was a hairsbreadth from the tip of his jutting cock. She swirled her tongue around but didn't touch.

This time when Jack grunted, he didn't speak.

"Good boy. Now, lie on the bed and spread your arms. I'm going to strip for you, but you've been naughty, so I'll have to incapacitate you."

Jack stretched out on the bed, arms spread. Emily knelt on the bed and picked up one of the stockings. "Silk?"

He nodded.

"Nice." She ran the stocking along his leg, over his cock, and up his chest. He lifted his arm, and she wrapped the silk around his wrist and then around the bedpost, tying the ends. She repeated the process with his other wrist. She sat back and admired the beautiful sight of Jack tied to her bed. "Delicious."

Jack thrust his hips up.

"Something you want?"

Jack's lips moved, but he didn't speak. His eyes scrunched closed. He opened his mouth and bobbed his head up and down.

Emily tapped her chin. "Oh, you want me to take your huge, hard cock in my mouth?"

Jack's whole body nodded.

She did. She was amazed at her restraint in making him

wait so long for what they both wanted. But she wouldn't let him come. Yet.

She felt his upper body flex as he tried to move his arms. She smiled up at him. "You really can't keep your hands to yourself."

His hips thrust up, so she leaned down and took him in her mouth. Emily loved his spicy scent. The saltiness of his skin combined with his unique smell intoxicated her. She almost forgot she wasn't going to let him come. She still had to strip for him, so she forced herself to sit up and licked her lips. Jack's arms pulled against the stockings.

She crawled slowly off the bed, giving him a view of her ass. He moaned, and she smiled. She was nearly at her limit of how much teasing she could take before he was inside her. With her back to him, she wiggled and slowly bent over, taking the thong down.

"Oh fuck."

She barely heard him, but she stood and faced him. "Did you say something?"

He shook his head wildly.

"Hmm. Must've been the wind."

Jack nodded in agreement. His eyes screamed please.

She crossed her arms, and her fingers nudged the straps of silk down her arms. Jack's eyes widened at her bared breasts, and her nipples tightened. She let the emerald silk fall to the floor.

Jack tugged the stockings, and the ties around the bedpost opened, freeing him. He extended his arms out to her. She sashayed to the side of the bed, grabbed a condom, and crawled onto him, straddling his hips. His fingers dug into the soft curves of her hips.

Tearing the condom open with her teeth, she handed it to him, and he rolled it on. Emily positioned herself and slid onto him. "So good." Her eyes fluttered closed as she focused on the sensations from their joined bodies.

"Can I talk yet?"

"Uh-huh."

He sat up and kissed her, his lips warm and moist against hers. "That was incredible. I need to fuck you so badly."

"I need that too." She gulped for air.

He flipped their positions so she was under him, and he pulled out and slammed back into her, causing her vision to blur. He brought her legs up, hooking them over his shoulders. "Ready, baby?"

Emily nodded, and he pulled out slowly, allowing her to feel every inch of him. "Ah, yes."

Slam, pound, thrust, he did it all. She was so close; a few more thrusts, and she'd come. He pulled out and flipped her over. "On your knees. Face on the bed."

She pulled the pillow down and turned her face to the side. She could barely see him from the corner of her eye. He rubbed his cock between her lips, teasing her clit. "Jaaack."

"I know, baby. I can't hold off anymore either." Grasping her hips, he slammed into her. He pulled out and pushed back in hard, driving her over the edge. She turned her face and screamed as her orgasm broke. With two brutal thrusts, Jack followed, a primal yell escaping his lips.

Jack pulled out, and she collapsed on her side. Seconds later, he was behind her, encircling her in his strong, warm embrace. He kissed the back of her head. "I love you, Em."

Emily shoved her apprehensions aside about visiting his family; it had to turn out better than last time. There was no way it could turn out worse.

Chapter Twenty-Nine

J ack woke early on Friday and knew as soon as consciousness took hold over him that Emily wasn't in bed. Last night had been unbelievable. Twice more, they'd reached for each other during the night. Each time he'd felt a little more of her wall crumble.

She no longer waited for him to fall asleep to move away from him. It took a few tries, but she adjusted until she was comfortable, and then he'd settle next to her. Maybe he'd told her he loved her too many times, but he couldn't help it. He reminded himself daily that even though they'd known each other for eight weeks now, they hadn't spent eight weeks together.

She'd told him that love crawled up on her, and she'd never fallen like a stone off a mountain. She had a way with words that eased his restlessness. When she'd agreed to go with him to visit his family, a contentment washed over him the likes he'd never experienced. He knew she was doing it for him because she cared. He also felt her tension increasing the closer they got to leaving. He'd do whatever he could to make it easier for her. He'd stick with her, no matter what.

Christie had grown to hate visiting his family. She'd gotten to the point where she'd go but wouldn't interact with anyone. She had a career to consider, and he was being selfish for taking her away from it. At least that's what she'd told him during those last awful months before he'd finally had enough.

Jack rolled out of bed and strode to the door, crashing into Emily. They collided with such force she fell backward, but he caught her around the waist. "Don't worry, baby, I've got you. I won't let you fall."

She threw her arms around his neck and kissed him. When she pulled back, she whispered, "I know."

Jack's heart constricted. "Em..."

"Sorry, had to pee." She took his hand and walked back into the bedroom. "We don't have to get up yet." She turned to him. "Unless you want to."

"No." He could barely contain his smile. They wouldn't have the luxury of waking up together while visiting his family.

Emily snuggled into his side, and Jack wrapped his arm around her. "You asleep?"

"Unh-unh."

"I have questions, but if you aren't ready yet..."

Em adjusted so she lay on her back. "I don't think I'll ever be ready. I've been thinking about it, and this probably isn't a normal relationship for you either."

Jack liked that she thought about him. "Yeah, but—"

Em covered his lips with her fingers. "We've both had to make adjustments, and we'll figure out our normal together."

The sun was still low in the sky, but the soft light that spilled in allowed him to see her beautiful smile. She hadn't said the words he longed to hear yet, but this was future talk. He thought back to that morning she'd come to his hotel room after breaking it off with him. She'd said she hadn't come to leave him again, but part of him was scared she would.

But she'd been true to her word. Even through uncomfortable family gatherings, a stalker, her ex breaking in, his ex trying to get back in his life, and his career, Em had stood by him. And Jack had never been happier.

"What do you want to know?"

"Anything?"

"Sure. If I'm not ready, we'll move to a different topic."

He had many questions, but since they'd made chili yesterday, and she'd told him stuff about her dad, one stuck out. "Tell me about the Boyers."

Emily relaxed and snuggled back into his side, resting her palm over his heart. "Uncle Griff and Aunt Ellen were my parents' best friends. We lived next to them on the base in Bridgeport. We were stationed there for the last three years before my dad retired. At the time, that was the longest we'd ever been in one place."

"You were born in California?"

"At Miramar, near San Diego. We'd moved five times before we were at Bridgeport. Anyway, Uncle Griff and Aunt Ellen have twin daughters, Michelle and Erin, they're four years younger than me. Riley and I used to babysit them when our parents would go out together. They used to live in Oakdale, too."

"Where are they now?"

"They moved back to California when the twins decided to go to Washington State University. After everything that happened with my family, Uncle Griff and Aunt Ellen couldn't stand being so far from their kids."

"How old were you?"

Emily turned onto her other side, so Jack spooned her. "Twenty-two. I'd just finished my sophomore year of college. Because of the accident, I'd missed my senior year and graduation, so I got my GED, and once all the surgeries were done, I didn't leave the house much because I was so self-conscious about my leg. Eddie and Sheryl would come every weekend so Eddie could continue as my therapist." Emily laughed. "Anyway, one day, Eddie and Vince visited without Sheryl. I knew I was in trouble as soon as they got out of the car."

"Why?"

"They looked...determined. Eddie said it was time to shit or get off the pot and that I needed to stop feeling sorry for myself and return to the land of the living."

Jack shifted. "After everything you'd been through, that seems kinda harsh."

"It was what I needed to hear. My aunt and uncle had been saying the same thing, only nicer, and that hadn't worked. I couldn't see anything but what I had lost. Eddie has a way with words. He doesn't suffer fools, and he doesn't take shit from anyone. He's also the kindest and most gentle person I've ever met. Eddie told me if I didn't start looking forward instead of backward, my leg and my life would never get any better. Then he said that Sheryl was pregnant, and I needed to be able to play with my little niece or nephew. He also asked Vince and me to be godparents."

Em had said she'd have never survived without them, and now Jack understood. "I cannot wait to shake their hands."

"I should probably warn you that they're planning on vetting you."

"Vetting me?"

"Yeah, asking you tons of questions that are none of their business, but they think they are."

Jack smiled. Em obviously loved Eddie and Vince, and they loved her. She may not have any blood relatives, but she definitely had family. "I'm not worried. I'll answer any questions they have. Why didn't you go when the Boyers moved?"

"Because I'd worked really hard to build a new life here, and I didn't want to start over again."

"They just left you?"

"I'd overheard them talking one night after the twins had gotten accepted. They wanted to move so they could be closer to their girls but knew I'd never go. I couldn't let them stay here for me. I wasn't really getting on in college very well anyway, so I just never went back."

Jack scoffed. "I don't believe for one second that you didn't do well in your classes."

"It wasn't the classes. I had hard time adjusting to being around so many young people. I felt so much older than everyone else, and everything they thought was so important seemed so silly to me, so I isolated myself. Anyway, I got a job, told them I was moving out, and they should go to California."

"They didn't argue?"

"Of course. But they'd sacrificed enough for me, and I was so very grateful for everything they'd done, but I couldn't let them do this." Emily sniffled. "After weeks of them trying to convince me to stay in college, Uncle Griff said he could see that I'd made my decision and nothing would change my mind. He said I was just like my dad, and that he'd never won an argument with him either."

"Do you keep in touch?"

"Yes. They were going to fly in for the wedding. He still travels a lot and stops in to check on me a few times a year."

Jack would ask Jeff to locate the Boyers. Maybe he'd visit them when the tour took him to the West Coast. "Was your mom an only child, too?"

Emily tensed. "Yes."

"When did her parents pass?"

When she didn't answer, Jack thought she'd fallen back to sleep until a hot tear landed on his shoulder. "Em?"

"They didn't. Can we stop now?"

Anger surged through him. Her grandparents were alive? Why hadn't they taken her in after the accident? "Of course."

JACK WENT FOR A RUN WHILE EM DID YOGA. HE pounded the pavement until he couldn't breathe and every muscle in his body ached. It did nothing to squelch the waves of anger that continued to roll through him. As much as he wanted to know every detail, he wouldn't invade her privacy again. He'd just have to wait until she was ready. By the time Jack returned to her apartment, his temper was under control. For now.

They shared a shower, another luxury they wouldn't have for the next four days.

On the drive to his childhood home, Emily spent most of the way staring out the window. Once they entered Pine Hill, Jack pointed out local attractions: the first bar they'd played, the high school they'd attended, and the best ice cream shop on the planet. She gave him her full attention, asked questions, and smiled.

Jack pulled into the parking lot of the liquor store and parked. "I want to get my dad a case of Seaquench Ale."

"I thought you were having the liquor delivered tomorrow?"

"I am, but this is for my dad. I got him into it, but he won't buy it for himself."

Emily smiled. "You are so damn sweet, Jack McBride." Emily turned and looked at the huge pot of chili. "I'll wait here."

"Okay." He kissed her quickly and got out before she could say anything about public displays of affection.

When they were only a few blocks from his folks, Jack

pointed to the left. "See that white house with the green shutters?"

"Yeah?"

"That's where it all started twenty-one years ago."

"What started?"

"My obsession with music." Jack pulled over and put the truck in park. "My piano teacher, Mrs. Wagner lives there." Jack smiled fondly. "She was a music teacher in the high school and the organist at St. Al's." He turned in his seat. Emily faced him, eyes shining. "When I was eight, my mom was home after having Jimmy. I wanted piano lessons, but my mom wasn't working, and money was tight. One day, I walked here and knocked on Mrs. Wagner's door. I said I wanted to take piano lessons but didn't have any money. Was there anything I could help with in trade for the lessons."

Emily placed her finger over his lips. "Stop for a second. I'm overwhelmed with how frickin' cute this story is." She closed her eyes, still grinning, and took a few deep breaths. "Okay, go."

Talk about cuteness overwhelm? "She said the yard needed raking. As you can see, it's a decent-sized lot, so she figured if I did the entire yard that would be worth three lessons."

"Aw." Emily looked past him. "Oh."

He'd meant that to be a nice story. "What?"

She pointed. Mrs. Wagner hobbled down the walkway, the front door still open. She had to be in her sixties, not that old, but as she hobbled along, she looked frail.

Jack jumped out of the car. He crossed the street and met Mrs. Wagner as she bent to pick up the newspaper.

As she stood to her full height of five feet eleven, her eyes brightened when she saw him.

"Jack McBride." She flung her arms around him.

Jack hugged her back. "Mrs. Wagner, how are you?"

She pulled back, studying his face. "Jack, after all these years, I think you can call me Kathy."

Up close, she no longer looked frail, and relief washed through him. "Okay, Kathy. How are you?"

"Oh, I'm fine."

"You don't sound so sure."

Kathy smiled fondly. "I suppose you saw me limp my way down the walk." She exhaled deeply. "Stupid me, missed a step coming down the stairs this morning and turned my ankle."

Jack's face must've shown his concern, because Kathy shook her head. "I'm fine, really, just a little stiff, been resting my ankle."

Jack realized that Em stood next to him. "Kathy Wagner, this is my girlfriend, Emily Prescott."

Emily shook Kathy's hand. "It's a pleasure to meet you."

"What a lovely young lady." Her eyes beamed. "Do you have time for a chat and some brownies?"

Jack looked at Em, and she smiled and nodded. "You had me at brownies. Mrs. Wagner—sorry—Kathy makes the best brownies ever. Always the first thing to sell out at the church bake sales."

They spent the next hour catching up. Emily asked Kathy questions about what Jack was like as a little boy. Kathy was more than happy to sing his praises. Even though Jack was used to being flattered, that Kathy held him in such high regard had him almost embarrassed.

They arrived at his folks' house just after one. He'd planned to spend the next few hours in bed, but his dad's truck in the driveway shot that plan to shit. "I didn't expect my dad to be here."

Emily grinned wickedly at him. "What did you expect?"

"Sex." He pulled in and parked in front of the garage.

"In your childhood bedroom? I don't think so."

"Please tell me you're kidding." He'd agreed to not sleep

together, but four days together with no sex? He'd lose his mind being around her.

"Jack, your parents trust us to behave ourselves while we're staying in their home. Having sex when they aren't here wouldn't be right."

Shit, he couldn't tell if she was kidding. She certainly looked serious. "Em, come on, really?"

Her smile broke wide across her beautiful face. "I don't have that kind of self-control."

He unbuckled her seatbelt and pulled her onto his lap. "Neither do I." She crashed her lips onto his, and he was lost. Lost to the fact that they were in his parents' driveway, in broad daylight, making out like teenagers.

"Ahem."

Jack turned. "Hey, Dad." He helped Em back into her seat.

"Jack, Emily." Will stepped back as Jack opened the door.

He hugged his dad. It was good to be home. "You're home early. Everything okay?" His dad looked healthy, but...

Will smiled. "It's not every day my son comes home for four days." He pulled Jack back into a hug. "I'm so glad you made it."

Jack cocked his head to the side. Something about the way his dad said that troubled him. "Of course, why wouldn't I?"

Will glanced down and shrugged. "I found an original emblem for the GTO. Got a good deal on it too."

Emily walked around the front of the truck carrying the chili pot. "I'll get that." Jack took the heavy pot from her. "We made chili."

"You didn't need to bring anything. You're paying for all the booze."

"I'll be here all weekend, and I wanted to contribute," Emily said.

Will smiled. "It wasn't necessary but very thoughtful.

Thank you." He took the pot from Jack. "I think this'll fit in the refrigerator in the garage."

Jack grabbed the case of beer off the backseat, hauled it onto his shoulder, and took Em's hand. "Come on."

It took a little rearranging, but Will fit the pot in.

"Here." Jack set the beer on the workbench.

Will rubbed the back of his neck. "Jack, you don't have to do that."

He put six bottles in the door of the refrigerator. "I know."

Will shook his head. "Thanks, son."

Jack turned to the GTO. "How's it coming?"

"Great. Check this out." Will popped the hood, his voice filled with pride.

"If you guys are hungry, I could make some sandwiches."

Jack and Will turned at the same time. "Sorry, Em—"

Emily put up her hand. "Don't be, Jack. This visit is about you. Your dad took the afternoon off to spend time with you. Enjoy it." Her smile was genuine with no hint of resentment. "Now, what'll you guys have?"

Will hugged her. "There's a ton of cold cuts in the kitchen. Ham and swiss for me."

"Me too." Jack's heart fluttered in his chest. "And extra pickles."

"Extra pickles, Will?"

"Please."

She nodded and Jack watched her walk out the door toward the house. He leaned up against the workbench, eyes closed, heart pounding.

"You okay?" His father's hand gripped his shoulder.

For several seconds, Jack couldn't speak through the lump in his throat. He opened his eyes to see his dad's eyes filled with concern. "Yeah. I'm fine." He inhaled and exhaled deeply.

"I didn't think it was possible to be more in love with her, but I just keep falling."

Will nodded. He grabbed two cold beers and handed one to Jack. "That's how it is with your mother. Even after thirty-two years of marriage, I love her more every day."

E mily stood at the counter and smiled. Jack and Will were so much alike.

"Hi," Jimmy said as he entered the kitchen.

Emily turned and smiled at him. "Hi. Want a ham and swiss sandwich?"

"Sure. Where's the prince?"

Emily hid her smile. "Jack's in the garage with your dad."

"The prodigal son..."

"I know how you feel." Emily pulled out two more slices of bread. "When I was a kid, first day of school, once the teachers found out I was Riley Prescott's little sister, I got to hear about how great he was."

Jimmy pulled out a chair and sat. "Yeah."

"Thing was, it wasn't his fault, you know. He was just being him. He was smart, funny, athletic, friendly, and outgoing. He was good at everything. It all came so easily for him." Emily packed up the cold cuts and put them in the fridge. "He was four years older, and when he decided to go to university in Connecticut, I was devastated. I was mad at him for a long time."

"I couldn't care less that Jack left."

"Really? Wow, then you're a better person than I was. First time he came home for Thanksgiving, I wouldn't even talk to him. Riley and I had always been so close. When our dad was deployed, he'd have tea parties with me. Even at nine, Riley had a very developed sense of taking care of people."

"Did you ever talk to him again?"

"Of course, it was impossible to stay mad at him. He explained to me why he chose to go away to college, and at the time, I didn't really understand it, but I was just glad it wasn't 'cause I was a pain in the ass."

"Why'd he leave?"

"He always felt like he lived in our dad's shadow." Emily smiled. "Our dad was amazing. He always had time for us, all his men, and their families. They could call him anytime, and he'd be there for them. Even after he retired, they knew they could still reach out to him, and many did."

"That's nothing like my situation."

Emily sat next to him. "You could spend all your time hating Jack, resenting living in his shadow, or you can put your effort into being the best you that you can be."

Jimmy's head snapped up. "I don't hate him."

"Jack thinks you do."

Jimmy took a deep breath. "When he moved to the city, everything changed. He hardly ever came home, and when he did, it was only for a few hours. He'd always had time for me, then suddenly it was like I didn't exist." Jimmy shrugged. "I missed him."

"Yeah. I missed Riley too, but at fourteen, I didn't understand how hard it had been for him. All I could see was that he'd left me. I'm sure Jack being famous only made it more difficult for you."

Jimmy glanced at her. "I never told anyone this. I probably shouldn't tell you."

"I'm a good listener."

"The first girl I ever...you know...told everyone at school the next day she'd done it with Jack McBride's brother. It was like I didn't exist."

"What a bitch."

"Don't say anything, okay?"

"Never."

Emily texted Jack to let him know the sandwiches were ready.

Jimmy took his plate, but before he could leave, Will and Jack walked into the kitchen.

"Hey, Squeak." Jack grabbed Jimmy and tried to hug him, but Jimmy pushed him away.

"Don't call me that."

"Where you going with that plate?" Will asked.

"Nowhere." Jimmy plunked the plate on the kitchen table and sat.

Jack dropped a quick kiss on her lips and sat. Will smiled and looked away.

"What?" she asked, sitting between Jack and Jimmy.

Jack grinned. "Nothing."

Emily shrugged. It never ceased to amaze her how quickly hungry men could make food disappear: sandwiches, chips, and pickles vanished with lightning speed.

Jack's cell rang. "Hey, Dex. What's up?" His face clouded over, and his eyes closed. "I'll call her. Dex, listen, I know this shit is outside the scope of a manager, so I really appreciate it." Jack disconnected the call but stared at his screen. He stood and exhaled slowly.

"Jack?" Will said.

Emily stood and put her arms around him. "Is it Christie?"

Jack swallowed hard. "Her friend Amber called Dex. She said that she found Christie on the floor of her apartment.

She's been taken to the hospital. She told Amber the only way she can win me back is to stop using, so she quit cold turkey."

"I thought you were done with her?" Will said.

"I am. I've told her it's over, but she won't let it go. It's like she's obsessed." He glanced at Emily, and she knew they both thought the same thing. Even though Jeff had cleared her, she might be Jack's stalker after all.

"Then why are you calling her?"

"Not her, Amber. She's alone in this, I mean, I have to help her, right?"

Will stood and put his hand on Jack's shoulder. "Son, you've done everything you can to help Christie. This is just another attempt to prey on your good nature." Will sighed. "I know you don't want to hear this, but Christie is a user. I don't just mean of drugs but of people. You let yourself get taken advantage of because you loved her. But this has to stop. If she truly wanted your help, she'd have gone into rehab instead of trying to quit on her own. This is just another attempt to get you to rush to her."

Jack's arms tightened around her. "You really think she's capable of something like this?"

"Yes. Users use people, Jack. I know you loved her, and part of you may still, but you cannot save everyone. She did this to herself, and she has to pull herself out of it."

"I thought you guys liked her?"

"We did, at first. But once you moved to California for *her* career, she changed, or maybe she just showed her true colors. Either way, it doesn't matter. Last Christmas, you ran out of here a week early because she called with some crisis. Your mother and I vowed never to interfere in our children's love lives, but Jack, you have to stop this; otherwise, you'll ruin what you have."

Jack's hold tightened, and Emily was glad that Will had been the one to say it. Jack saw the best in people, and his willful blindness was the reason Christie had been able to manipulate him. But Jack let it happen.

Emily had supported him in going to see Christie, but that hadn't worked out how Jack had hoped. A small part of her had thought Christie was using rehab as a ploy, but she hadn't wanted to believe it. But she also wasn't a fool and wouldn't fall for that bullshit again. Vince told her that addicts were masters of lying. Emily knew that Christie would do anything to get Jack back. Anything.

"Em..." Jack's eyes held tears.

"I think Will's right."

Jack nodded, his throat worked with the effort to swallow, and he scrunched his eyes closed.

Emily's heart ached for him.

When he opened his eyes, she saw his acceptance. "I'm going to call Amber, but I'm not going anywhere."

Will put his arms around both of them, and Emily felt accepted.

Jack went into the living room to call Amber, returning a few minutes later. "She's going to call Christie's parents. I told her there was nothing more I could do."

Emily opened her arms and Jack accepted her comfort.

"Don't say anything to Mom, okay?" Jack looked back and forth between Jimmy and his dad.

Jimmy nodded.

Will closed his eyes and sighed. "Okay, but if you get another call..."

"Understood," Jack said. He hugged her close to him and his body relaxed into hers.

Will cleared his throat. "Come on, boys, let's work on the car."

Emily caught Jack's hopeful glance at Jimmy.

"Jimmy?" Will asked.

"Yeah, okay."

"I'll be right there. I want to get the bags from the car," Jack said.

Emily followed Jack up to his room when he returned with their bags. Vintage Soundgarden and Foo Fighters posters hung on Jack's bedroom walls. A navy comforter covered the full bed, and the oak furniture shone as if it were polished regularly.

"Here ya go." Jack deposited her laptop bag on the desk. He pulled her into his arms and kissed her. Jack cupped her face and gazed deeply into her eyes. "Thank you, baby."

She smiled and rested her head on his chest. "I'm happy to do it."

"Jack," Will yelled from downstairs. "Your mother will be home in a few hours."

"Coming."

"Go. I'll settle in."

"You're amazing."

She unpacked her laptop and worked for ninety minutes. She was happy with the progress she'd made the last two weeks, so any writing she got done this weekend would be a bonus. She went down to the kitchen and set the kettle to boil because she knew Jack's mom liked tea. Emily searched through several cabinets until she found her stash. Earl Grey, chamomile, oolong, white tea, and several herbal teas. She took out the Earl Grey and berry herbal tea.

When the water started to boil, she turned the flame down to keep it warm. She heard Mrs. McBride's car and watched as she walked to the open garage door. "Jack," she exclaimed.

Emily's stomach fluttered. She wanted to start fresh with Jack's mom; they'd gotten off on the wrong foot.

"Don't you dare set foot in this house till you've washed that grease off your hands, James." Mrs. McBride walked through the screen door. "Emily, we're glad you could join us."

Her words were nice but sounded forced. Emily had her work cut out for her. "Jack told me you like tea, so I thought after a long week you might enjoy a cup." She pushed away from the counter.

"Oh, thank you, dear...that's nice of you."

Emily's heart sank. It was going to be a long four days. Only like three and half now. They'd be leaving Tuesday morning after Jack's parents left for work. Barbara Callow had arranged for them to see three apartments in the city. Emily hoped Jack didn't bring that up again.

Emily left Mrs. McBride to the peace and quiet of the kitchen. She'd been teaching eleventh graders all week, in the home stretch of the school year, and she needed time to unwind, so Emily tried not to take her distance personally.

She'd made it to Jack's bedroom door before she heard her name. She turned, expecting Jack, but it was Jimmy. Their voices were so similar it was eerie. "Hey, Jimmy."

Jimmy frowned as he stopped in front of her. "You okay?"

Emily looked away. "Yeah."

"Hey, you can talk to me."

Emily exhaled deeply as she met Jimmy's eyes. "Your mom doesn't like me."

Jimmy pushed her into Jack's room and closed the door behind them. "Never say anything private in the hallway. It's like a direct line to the kitchen." Jimmy looked around. "This room looks exactly like it did the day Jack left. It's like a fucking shrine."

"Or it's a place Jack can always come back to. I wish I had that." Emily flopped on the bed. Her leg throbbed. She glanced out the bedroom window. Thick black clouds rolled in. Maybe the barbecue would get rained out. She smiled but then felt bad. Jack had been looking forward to this for weeks.

Jimmy leaned up against the desk. "I've been thinking

about what you said, and you're right; none of this is Jack's fault, but it's hard not to blame him."

Emily smiled. "It wouldn't hurt if you didn't love him. You felt left behind, and you had the added frustration of Jack's fame. Honestly, I don't know how well I'll deal with it. I'm so proud of him, but I don't want to be pulled into it. Any advice?"

Jimmy's smile dipped. "Jack McBride's girlfriend will get pulled in, so you better prepare." Then his smile grew, but he looked like he was trying to contain it. "Stone Highway's the hottest band in the world." His smile dipped again. "Does Jack really think I hate him?"

Emily nodded. "He loves you. You've shut him out, and he doesn't understand why, but he'll never give up on you."

Jack walked into the room. "Hey."

Jimmy pushed away from the desk, grabbed Jack, and hugged him. "She's amazing." He winked at Emily and released Jack. "Don't fuck it up."

Jack looked dumbfounded as Jimmy left. "What was that all about?"

"Maybe he has a new perspective." Emily stood. Discomfort rolled through her. She'd have to prepare. *Am I really gonna do this?* With her emotions in turmoil, Emily needed to be alone.

"Please, don't." Jack stopped her before she could walk out.

He stood so close she could feel his body heat.

"If you're upset, talk to me. Please don't shut me out."

Shit. Isn't that what I just told Jimmy he'd done? "I've got to figure it out on my own." She wouldn't complain to Jack about his mother. Or his fame. Not again.

"Is it my mom?"

When she didn't answer, Jack said, "I'll talk to her."

Emily moved away from him. "Please don't. You can't fix this, Jack."

"You won't let me try?"

"Whatever her problem is, it's with me, not you. Promise?"

She watched him struggle, knew that he wanted to argue, wanted to fix this. "Okay."

"Thank you. I'm going to see if your mom needs help with dinner." Jack wouldn't give up on Jimmy, and for Jack, she wouldn't give up on his mother.

When they walked into the kitchen, Trish and Brad had just arrived.

"Trish." Mrs. McBride wiped her hands on a towel and embraced her daughter. "You made good time. I didn't expect you until after dinner."

Trish smiled. "Can I help?"

"You can get the salad together." She turned back to the stove.

"Hey, sis." Jack hugged his sister, lifting her off her feet before putting her back down. "Brad," he said, extending his hand.

"Good to see you, Jack."

Emily stepped forward. "Anything I can do to help?"

Mrs. McBride didn't turn from the stove. "No thank you, dear. Trish and I have it covered."

She had to get out of here. "Okay, then I'm going for a walk." Maybe she'd walk all the way back to New Jersey. But she'd promised Jack, so she needed to suck it up. Jack followed her out the screen door. She took his hand. "I don't want to talk about it."

Jack didn't push it, and they walked around his neighborhood in silence. *How the fuck am I going to get through this awful weekend?* Why invite her only to alienate her? For Jack, of course.

Three blocks from his childhood home, Emily stopped in front of a lovely bi-level. It was set back from the street, and the landscaping was well maintained. The two-story white house had brick around the bottom half and deep red shutters. The paving stone driveway led to a two-car garage.

Jack turned her to face him. "What?"

"I like this house. The brick sets if off from the other houses."

"Yeah, I liked it too. That's why I bought it."

"When?"

"Last summer when I was home, I saw it was on the market." Jack pointed across the street. "See that gray house on the next street?"

Emily could just see the back of the gray house between the two houses across the street. "Yeah?"

"That's Elliot and Siobhan's house. It's a great neighborhood, good schools, all in all a wonderful place to raise a family." Jack's grin was epic.

"Oh." She couldn't handle another uncomfortable conversation right now. Kids, houses, all too soon to be talked about. Of the eight weeks since they'd met, they'd only spent seventeen days together.

Jack took her hand, and they continued walking. He also took the hint and dropped the subject. Emily knew it wasn't easy for him, and she was glad he was making an effort. When his phone rang, Emily knew her respite was over.

"Hi, Dad. Okay." Jack snapped a picture of her before putting his phone away. "Dinner's in fifteen minutes."

Emily smiled. "We'd better get back then."

JACK SAT AT THE DINNER TABLE, BUT THE conversation washed over him. His brain finally got the message his heart had been sending. He wouldn't risk losing Emily because of Christie. If she ever went to rehab, he'd pay, but there was nothing else he could do for her, and he'd told Amber that. He'd figured out a long time ago that Christie was manipulative, but he hadn't realized his folks had. He'd loved her and naïvely thought that was enough. It wasn't. Love was the building block of a relationship, but it needed trust, support on both sides, give and take, and common goals to hold it all together. Like his parents had. Like he wanted to have with Em.

Realizing how deeply in love he was with Em rattled him. The fact that she hadn't shared how she was feeling yet was all he could focus on. Realistically, he knew it was too soon, but with a month apart looming in front of them, he didn't care about being realistic. He was feeling increasingly desperate but still hadn't figured out why.

Dinner had been tense. His mom wasn't nasty, but she was polite, which Jack knew from Christie was almost as bad.

Everyone hung out in the family room after dinner. Brad and Trish sat on the love seat holding hands. Jimmy stretched out on the floor, and his folks sat on the couch next to Jack. When Emily walked in, she sat in one of the club chairs.

"Emily, I hope you'll be joining us for church on Sunday," Will said.

"Of course."

Maggie smiled. "I'm sure Jack told you we dress for church, so I hope you brought something appropriate to wear."

Em's eyes widened as she looked at Jack.

"Shit."

"Jack," Will said.

"Sorry. I forgot to tell Em that we dress for church."

Emily laughed. "I won't be naked."

Maggie stood. "Jack means that we expect him and his girlfriend to dress appropriately. No shorts, jeans, or T-shirts."

Emily's face reddened. "I only brought jeans, but I have a light sweater I can wear."

"Mom, it's not really a big deal, is it?"

"No, of course not. I'm sure your sister or I have something that will work. Trish?"

"Emily's taller, but I have a long skirt that should fit." Trish stood and extended her hand to Emily. "Might as well try it on now."

Fuck. This was his fault. He knew the rules. Nothing his mother or sister had would be long enough for Emily to feel comfortable. "Trish—"

Em pasted a smile on her face. "It's okay. I'll try it on."

Trish rolled her eyes at Jack. "What's the big deal, it's just a skirt. Sheesh. Let's go."

As soon as the women left the room, Jack stood and paced. "Fuck."

"Jack, language."

"Come on, Dad, Mom's not here. This is all my fault. I'm so stupid."

"Your sister will lend Emily a skirt."

Jack sat in the chair Emily vacated. "You don't understand. Emily was injured really badly in the accident. She has bad scarring on her right leg, and she's very self-conscious about it. I'm not sure she even owns a skirt." Jack knew she owned at least one, but he wouldn't think about that.

Will sat forward. "How bad?"

"Mid-thigh down to her ankle. Bad." *Stupid fuck.* He should've remembered to tell her to pack a pair of slacks. He'd fix this.

"Fuck." Will sat back and didn't ask any more questions.

A few minutes later, the women returned to the room, bringing silence with them. She'd told them, been forced to.

And it was his fault. He pulled her onto his lap. "I'm sorry, baby," he whispered.

She nodded.

"Hey, if you have to do some writing..."

"No, I'm good."

Jack was trying to give her an out. "You put in so many extra hours so you could be off yesterday I'm sure you fell behind on your writing."

Emily smiled. "Nope, I got ahead of where I wanted to be, so I'm free all weekend."

Jack kissed her deeply, not a porno kiss but with passion, until his father cleared his throat. "Sorry, I just had to."

Em shook her head at him. "Jack, I didn't come here to hide in your room. I did what I had to, to be where I needed to be, to not fall behind. No big deal."

But it was. To him and to his mom. He could see from her expression that she was impressed. The last year with Christie, she'd do just that. Headaches, running lines, whatever, anything to avoid his family. If earlier he'd slipped deeper in love with her, now he was falling from the sky. Em was *it* for him.

AFTER A FEW INTENSE ROUNDS OF POKER, WILL AND Maggie went up to bed. Brad was sleeping on the pullout in the den, and he'd been up early, so he begged off. Emily played a few more hands then went up to bed.

That left him, Trish, and Jimmy. Jack expected Jimmy to bolt, but he hung out, playing Go Fish, like when they were kids. It had been a long time since the three of them had just hung out like this, and Jack loved it.

Another thirty minutes, and they were done. He went up to say goodnight to Em, but the door was closed and the light off. It was ridiculous how disappointed he felt at not getting to kiss her goodnight. He went into Jimmy's room and changed into his pajamas. When he got back to Jimmy's bedroom after brushing his teeth, the door was closed. *What the fuck?* Screw it, he'd sleep on the couch.

Jimmy opened the door. "Sorry, phone call."

Jack lay down on the cot and pulled the sheet up. Jimmy clicked off the light.

Jack couldn't sleep. His beautiful, sexy girlfriend was only a few feet away and he was stuck in his brother's room. After Jimmy fell asleep, he planned on sneaking into her room.

"You asleep?" Jimmy asked.

"No."

"I've been a dick. I'm sorry."

"Okay."

"That's it? Just okay?"

"What do you want me to say?"

"I missed you when you left. You hardly ever came home, and I was mad. We used to do stuff together, and then you were just gone. I felt like I didn't matter to you anymore."

"I'm sorry, Squeak. I had no idea." Jack turned on his side, facing Jimmy's bed. "Why didn't you say anything?"

"I'm telling you now. Does that count?"

"Absolutely. You're my brother, and I love you."

"Love you too, bro. And Jack?"

"Yeah?"

"Don't forget about the squeaky floorboard outside the bathroom."

"Thanks." It was after one when Jack snuck into his bedroom, careful to avoid the loose floorboard in the hall. He stripped out of his pajamas and crawled into bed next to Em. She was on her side, so he spooned her.

"Jack William McBride, what the fuck do you think you're doing?"

He ground his groin into her back; he was already hard, but when she said fuck, his dick jerked. "You said fuck, so you must have some idea."

She turned, trying to face him. The moonlight spilled in through the open curtains. "We're not doing this."

He kissed her lips and cupped her breast, her nipple hardening under his palm. "It feels like we are."

She moaned and kissed him back, her fingers curling around his dick, stroking him. "What if we get caught?"

Jack helped her out of the tank top. "We won't if you keep it down."

She bit his lip. "You're not exactly quiet."

He sat up. "It's not like my dad's going to bust in on us. If we get caught, he'll talk to me privately." He knelt on the bed and slid her pajama bottoms off. The moonlight covered her in an ethereal glow that sent shivers up his spine. He'd never seen anything more beautiful in his whole life. He opened the nightstand and pulled out a box of condoms, and ripping one open, he rolled it on. He settled between her thighs, covering her in kisses on her chest, neck, and finally her lips.

"How long have those been in there?"

"Since we got here." He slid inside her slowly so she could feel every inch of him.

"You planned this all along, didn't you?"

"Yes." His lips ended all communication that involved words. He showed her with his body just how much he loved her. His orgasm built slowly as he brought her to climax twice. When he finally came, tears formed behind his closed eyes.

The alarm he'd set on his phone went off at four forty-five. Even though it was Saturday, his dad would be up at five. Em was snuggled up against him with her head on his shoulder. Jack slid out of bed without waking her. He dressed, dropped a kiss on her lips, and left. He avoided the loose floorboard. His folks' room was at the other end of the hallway, and the door was closed. Jack snuck back into Jimmy's room. He had an errand to run after they put up the tents. He drifted back to sleep wishing he was still with Emily.

Jack covered his head with the pillow. Jimmy had been farting in his sleep for the last hour. This was punishment enough if he were to get caught. Needing relief, Jack got up and showered. The enticing scent of pancakes and coffee had his stomach growling. Em stood at the stove, and his dad sat at the kitchen table reading the paper and sipping coffee.

Jack hugged her from behind as she flipped the pancakes. "Smells delicious."

"You're just in time."

"My dad was here first."

"I've already had some, but if Jimmy and Brad don't get up soon, I'll have seconds."

Jack poured himself a cup of coffee and refilled his dad's. Emily handed him a plate stacked high with pancakes. Jack poured syrup over the top and dug in.

His father looked at him over the top of the newspaper. "How'd you sleep, son?"

"Okay."

"You showered?"

"Yup."

"Rookie. It's going to be ninety today, you'll need another after we get that tent up."

Jack had showered for another reason, and he was pretty sure his dad knew why. "Wish you would've let me pay to have the party company set it up."

"Waste of money. There are four, able-bodied men in this house." Will checked his watch. "Where's your brother?"

"Still sleeping when I got up."

Brad walked into the kitchen. "I smell pancakes."

Emily handed him a plate. "Welcome to pancake nirvana."

Trish yawned as she walked into the kitchen. "Emily, you need some help?"

"Nope. Pancakes will be about five minutes."

"Trish can have mine, I'll wait."

Jack smiled at his sister. "Aw, sounds like love to me."

She smacked Jack on the arm. "Shut up."

Trish and Brad exchanged a look, and both smiled and looked away.

Maggie walked into the kitchen, finger combing her hair. "Will, why'd you let me sleep? You know we have a hundred things to do before the families arrive." She stopped dead when she saw Emily at the stove.

Disappointed, Emily looked away. "I didn't mean to step on your toes, but I was up early, so I made breakfast."

Jack glared at his mom.

"That was very sweet of you. Thank you." She poured herself a cup of coffee.

"They dropped off the tent, tables, and chairs an hour ago. Get your brother up," Will said. "We need to get everything set up before my father gets here and starts giving directions on how to do it *the right way.*"

Jack laughed. His grandpa owned McBride and Sons Roofing. All his sons had joined the family business except his dad. Grandpa was used to being in charge, which was one of the reasons his dad had turned his back on the family business. He wanted something that was his own.

Jack had to get a move on if he wanted to pull off his surprise for Em.

Chapter Thirty-One

E mily watched through the kitchen window as the guys set up the tent and tables. By the time they were done, they were all dripping with sweat. Jack beat Jimmy to the door, which apparently won him the first shower.

She and Trish laid out the paper plates, cups, napkins, and plastic cutlery. Emily regretted her choice of jeans. Even though the humidity was low, there wasn't a cloud in the sky. The sun beat down, its unrelenting heat burning the ground.

Jack grabbed her around the waist and lifted her. "Hey, stop that, I'm gross." Sweat trickled down her temples.

"Not gross, beautiful. And wonderful."

He put her down, and she turned in his arms. "Wonderful?"

"For coming. For helping. For everything."

She placed her palm on his forehead. "Heatstroke?"

Jack just smiled at her. "I have an errand to run. Need anything?"

"More ice. We used up what was delivered, and there are still two coolers that need ice."

"On it." He kissed her and strode toward his truck.

Dressed in a pair of cutoffs and a white T-shirt, he looked sexy as hell. She forced herself to look away before she got caught drooling over their son. Mrs. McBride had thawed slightly, and Emily didn't want to give her any cause to refreeze.

A honk alerted her to Jack's return. He'd been gone for almost two hours, and his relatives were due to arrive in just over an hour. Will, Jimmy, and Brad helped Jack unload the truck. He'd gotten enough ice to start his own ice age.

Emily stirred the chili and lowered the heat. His mother and Trish sat at the kitchen table, slicing the toppings for the burgers.

Jack sauntered into the kitchen. "Hey," he said taking her elbow. "I got you something. Come upstairs."

Emily shook her head. "Haven't you spent enough money on me?" He'd paid for the alarm system and the expensive clothes, lingerie, underwear, and pajamas. She didn't need anything else. Jack carried a large pink and black shopping bag. The last thing she wanted was his mother thinking she was a gold digger.

He placed the bag on the bed. He pulled out two large boxes and one small box. "Okay, don't get mad, but it's my fault you don't have anything appropriate to wear to church tomorrow, so I fixed it. He pointed to the large boxes."

Emily opened the first box and pulled out a long white gauzy sundress with a fine silver-threaded Aztec design over the bodice. She held it up to her, and it fell just below her ankles. It would go perfectly with her strappy flat silver sandals. She looked up at Jack's expectant face. "Jack, it's perfect. How?"

He grinned. "I made a note of where your waist and shoulders matched up to me. The shop owner's mother was able to hem it on the spot."

She flew into his arms and kissed him hard on the lips. "That's the sweetest thing anyone has ever done for me."

"There's more," he said, pointing to the other box. "Open it."

She laid the sundress on the bed and opened the second box. Another long sundress in a deep peach. "Jack, it's beautiful, but I only need one for church."

"This is for today, it's going to be hot, and since you can't wear shorts, I thought you'd be more comfortable in this." Jack held the third box, rolling it nervously in his hands. It was oblong and obviously from a jewelry store. "Okay, you took that well since I'm still in one piece. Now, don't get mad, but I saw this in the window, and I wanted you to have it."

He handed her the box, and she lifted the lid and slid out the black velvet box inside. When she opened the lid, her eyes nearly popped out of her head. A platinum, double heart pendant, encrusted with diamonds and inlaid with rubies on a fine box chain. She was already shaking her head when she looked up at him. "Jack, it's beautiful, b—"

"Don't say but. I wanted you to have it. It has a special meaning." He took the box from her and removed the necklace. He opened the closure and put it around her neck. It nestled just above her breasts, next to her heart. He moved around so she could see it in the mirror. "The outside heart is yours, this red heart inside"—Jack traced the inner heart with his finger—"is mine. You've captured my heart. It's yours."

Emily leaned back on him for support.

"Oh my God, that's the sweetest thing ever." Trish's not so whispering voice came from the hallway.

"Trish, how old are you?" Jack walked to the door and looked out. "Mom?"

Jack stepped back as Trish and his mother walked in. Trish pulled Emily into a hug. "He was always such a sweet boy. All my friends had crushes on him." She picked up the peach dress and held it up to her. It was several inches too long. "Jack, this is lovely. I think you missed your calling," she teased.

"Why were you listening in the hallway?"

Trish laid the dress on the bed and rolled her eyes at her brother. "Because you walked in with two bags from the most expensive boutique in Pine Hill, and I wanted to know what you bought." She looked at Emily. "The necklace is beautiful."

Emily stroked the hearts with her fingers.

Jack shook his head. "Mom?"

Maggie McBride looked down, having the decency to look guilty at being caught. "Jack..."

Emily stood next to Jack. "It's okay, they'd have found out anyway." She hoped that since she didn't make a big deal out of it, he wouldn't either. She didn't like being snooped on, but she understood it. If Nicki had been here, she would've done the same thing.

Jack hugged his mom and sister and gave them a stern look. "No more eavesdropping."

After everyone left the room, Emily changed into the peach sundress. From the clamor outside, she knew the families were arriving. With one last deep breath, Emily left the sanctuary of the bedroom to face Jack's enormous family.

Jack introduced her to what seemed to be an endless line of aunts, uncles, cousins, and their kids. She tried to stay calm under the pressure of their stares and whispers. Jack had only brought two girls home in the past, so she was a novelty.

Emily felt a tap on her shoulder, and when she turned, Buzz stood there with a huge grin. "Buzz." She threw her arms around him. With the chaos of Jack's family, she'd forgotten that Buzz and his family were coming.

"Emily, you look lovely." He hugged her back. "Mom, Dad, Stephanie, this is Emily, Jack's girlfriend." Emily hadn't seen Buzz look so relaxed before, and his brown hair was longer than she'd seen it. He was laid-back but always seemed to carry some tension.

Buzz's mom stepped forward and hugged her. "Buzz told

me what you did for him. I'm so grateful he has such wonderful friends."

"Mel, what'd Emily do?" Emily hadn't noticed Jack's mom standing next to her.

Will stood next to Maggie. "Garth," he said, shaking his hand.

"When Buzz was having a bad night, and he couldn't get in touch with his sponsor, Emily put Buzz in touch with a friend of hers who's in recovery." Buzz's dad and sister also hugged her.

A look passed between Jack's parents, which made her smile. Her parents, too, had a way of communicating with just an expression.

By two, the yard was packed. Buzz hung out with her while Jack reconnected with his cousins. "It's quite a lot of people, isn't it?" she said.

Buzz nodded. "Sure is."

Emily turned to look at him. "You doing okay?"

Buzz smiled and looked at his can of soda. "Yeah. You know, I really don't miss it that much, drinking, anyway. I never really liked the taste of alcohol." He looked at her, his brown eyes filled with gratitude. "I really appreciate you hanging out with me."

Emily laughed. "And here I thought you were the one hanging out with me."

Elliot and Siobhan walked up the path on the side of the house. "You're late," Buzz said with a smirk, as he and Elliot fist bumped.

Elliot shook his head, sending his unruly curls flying and his smile turning to his signature smirk. "First of all, you're not late to a barbecue unless they've run out of food or beer." Elliot hugged Siobhan to his side. "And second, you know the McBrides and Donoghues descend like a swarm. Didn't wanna wait in line."

Siobhan looked up at her husband with a smile.

Buzz laughed. "Been looking forward to this, so I jumped the line."

Jack's cousins set up the volleyball net. This year, instead of picking teams, all the games would be the McBrides versus the Donoghues. That put Buzz and Elliot on Jack's team. After a few minutes of good-natured ribbing, the game started, and Jack scored the first point. It went downhill from there for the Donoghues.

Emily was grateful for the light sundress. Even under the shade of the tent, it was hot. When Jack took his shirt off, a very obnoxious wolf-whistle came from the next table.

Siobhan crinkled her nose. "That's Jack's cousin John's wife, Paulette. She's always had a thing for Jack. At their wedding, when Jack danced with her, you know, 'cause he's Jack and always tries to be nice, she grabbed his ass."

Elliot walked over, opened a bottle of water, and poured it over his head.

"She'd just exchanged vows and she's molesting Jack?" Emily shook her head. "What's wrong with the cousin?"

Elliot laughed. "Pussy whipped. John's always been on Paulette's hook."

Emily sat on her hands. "I have the most overwhelming urge to slap her."

Elliot shook his head, spraying them with water. "I'll give you a hundred bucks if you do."

"E," Siobhan chided.

"What? She's a bitch."

Siobhan didn't disagree.

The chili they'd made was gone an hour after it was set out. Emily felt a deep satisfaction over that. Her dad had always been proud of his recipe.

Jack's family was huge, and since she was his girlfriend, the scrutiny continued. Especially Paulette, who thought out loud that Jack could do better. Every chance she got, Paulette cornered Jack in conversation. When she insisted that Jack take a picture with her and her kids, who missed their "Uncle" Jack, Emily had enough. She purposely stepped in front of John as he dutifully took the picture his harpy wife insisted upon.

Elliot roared with laughter while Jack suppressed a grin.

"Oh, you were taking a picture. Sorry." Emily smiled sweetly at the harpy. "Jack, I need your help with the chili pot."

She felt bad when the harpy turned her venom toward John, but he'd married her, so he must be used to it.

Jack grabbed the pot, and Emily followed him into the kitchen. The pot hit the sink with a *thunk* as Jack turned and grabbed her, pulling her in for a deep kiss. She melted into him.

"Thank you. John's a good guy, but Paulette is..."

"A venomous harpy and a succubus bitch?"

His chest vibrated with laughter. "Exactly. You always have the perfect words."

Her lips curled into a smile. "I *am* a writer."

"Yes, you are. How about you write us a scene, where I carry you up to my room and make wild, crazy love to you while the barbecue continues." Jack groaned and made an adjustment. "Damn."

Emily rested her forehead against his chest. "Well, it'd be very naughty, but we'd get caught. I give it five minutes before Paulette comes looking for you."

The screen door opened then slammed shut.

"I saw what you did, Emily. That was freakin' awesome." Jimmy hoisted himself up on the counter.

"Why, whatever do you mean?"

Jimmy snorted. "You ruined Paulette's picture with Jack."

"Oh, that. Yeah, I did." She smirked at Jimmy.

"She's a keeper, Jack."

Jack leaned back and tilted her chin up. "She sure is."

Two minutes early, Paulette walked into the kitchen. "There you are, Jack. John Jr. needs his Uncle Jack to play monster."

Emily tensed, and he tightened his arms around her. "Don't you think John should do that?"

"I can't find him."

The stars aligned in the most perfect way when John walked into the kitchen from the living room. "Who can't you find?"

Jimmy burst out laughing.

Jack cleared his throat and tried to hide a smile. "You. Your son wants to play monster."

John shook his head. "Baby, I told you I needed to use the bathroom." He grabbed his wife's hand and pulled her out of the kitchen.

"Looks like he's finally growing a pair." Jimmy jumped off the counter and looked at the pot in the sink. "Oh, the chili's gone?"

"Yes, but I put some in a container and hid it in the back of the fridge."

"Score."

Will popped his head in the kitchen. "Come on, boys, it's the annual whiffle ball game. We need to continue to kick Donoghue butt."

"Be right there," Jack said. Jimmy followed Will out the door. Jack kissed her one last time before pulling her out the door. "You can cheer us on."

After the highly competitive whiffle ball game, in which team McBride crushed team Donahue ten to three, Will fired up the grill for the second time. She and Jack sat with Buzz and Elliot and Siobhan, who smiled at each other like newlyweds.

John came over and enlisted the guys for another round of volleyball.

"Go," Emily said. They watched as Jack set up a volley that Elliot spiked over the net. They chest bumped in celebration.

Emily glanced at Siobhan who had a perpetual smile on her face. "You look happy."

"I am," she gushed. "For the first time ever, when Elliot leaves next Friday, I'll be going with him." Her smile grew wider. "I'm so excited."

Emily hugged her. "Elliot's so much happier than the day I met him."

Cheering from clan McBride drew Emily's attention back to the game. Elliot scored another point and high-fived one of Jack's cousins.

"I've never seen Jack happier either," Siobhan said. She smiled and looked down.

Emily didn't know what to say to that, so she pushed to her feet and gathered up the plates.

Siobhan stood and wobbled a bit.

"Sit. I'll take care of it. You look exhausted."

She smiled gratefully. "Thanks."

She'd noticed that Siobhan hadn't had any alcohol. Since Emily wasn't one to pry, she didn't push it, but she expected an announcement from camp Black.

She walked past Paulette's table, where Paulette was undressing Jack with her eyes. Emily walked to the trash and dumped the plates. She walked back slowly, stopping directly in front of Paulette, blocking her view.

"Hey, I'm watching the game."

"Really, because your husband's over there." Emily pointed to where John knelt on the sidelines tying his daughter's sneaker. "The game's in time-out."

Paulette stood and stepped to the side.

Emily stepped in front of her again. Paulette was

disgusting, and she didn't even try to be discreet. "How about you pay attention to your family and stop eye-fucking my boyfriend?" Emily turned and walked straight into Will and Mrs. McBride. From the expression on their faces, Emily knew they'd heard her. She only noticed Jimmy when he burst out laughing.

Mortified, she ran into the house, taking refuge in the bathroom. She splashed her face with cold water, but it did nothing to cool off her embarrassment. Will had liked her, too. Mrs. Doesn't Like Her was probably demanding Will have her removed from the house immediately, never to be invited again. John was her nephew, and blood was thicker than water. Emily wanted to kick something. She'd hoped to change Mrs. McBride's opinion of her by coming this weekend, and all she ended up doing was cementing her dislike, proving that Jack could do better.

Again, she toyed with the idea of staying in the bathroom forever, but there were over a hundred people outside, so she wouldn't be rude and hog it. After a few deep breaths and a long pep talk, Emily opened the door. Will and Mrs. McBride stood there, and Emily couldn't contain her groan. "I'm—"

"Come here." Will ushered her into the den, and Mrs. McBride followed and closed the door.

Emily swallowed hard and turned to face the music. "I am so sorry, I—"

"Are you kidding? That was awesome," Will said. "No one has ever talked to Paulette like that. She's been drooling over Jack since John introduced her to the family nine years ago. Frankly, it's disgusting."

Mrs. McBride stared at her, almost as if she were picking her apart.

Will looked at his wife then back at Emily. "Paulette grabbed John and the kids and took off. Said she wouldn't come here again until she got an apology."

Emily tilted her chin up and met Mrs. McBride's green stare. "The last thing I wanted was to cause a problem with your family, but I'm not going to apologize." Paulette had no respect for her husband, his family, or her. She could've chosen her words better, but she wasn't sorry.

Will put his hand up. "No need, we can't stand that woman." He hugged his wife to his side. "You did us a favor. Let's hope she keeps her promise."

A slow smile spread across Mrs. McBride's face. Emily was sure it was the first one aimed at her. "Emily..." Mrs. McBride stepped forward and embraced her. When she pulled back, her green eyes had softened and held tears. "Thank you."

A lump formed in Emily's throat. If she didn't know better, she'd think Jack's mom was starting to like her.

Will put an arm around each of them. "Let's get back to the party."

As they walked outside, Jack ran up to them. "What happened?"

"Emily told off Paulette." Will hauled Jack into a hug, and his mom kissed his cheek, and then they returned to the party hand in hand.

Before she could apologize to Jack, Elliot appeared, lifted her, and swung her around. "You are my favorite person. Ever."

"Put her down," Siobhan said, as she swatted Elliot.

He set Emily down and pulled his wife into his arms, resting his hands on her stomach.

"What happened?" Jack repeated.

"I'll tell you what happened," Elliot said. "Your girlfriend just told Paulette to stop eye-fucking you."

Jack turned to her, eyes wide. "You did?"

Emily nodded.

Jack pulled her into his arms, bent her over backward in a

low dip, and kissed her. He didn't let up until Elliot yelled, "Get a room."

He cupped her face between his palms. "I love you."

WHEN THE SUN DIPPED BEHIND THE HORIZON, LARGE Tiki torches were lit all around the yard. The inside of the tent had been strewn with tiny white lights, providing a romantic setting.

Jack sat with Emily on a lounge chair. Elliot and Siobhan were back together and happier than he'd seen them in years. Curt was head over heels in love with Nicki, and it was quite clear that she felt the same. Buzz was nine months sober and getting stronger every day. The band was tighter than ever, and the tour was their most successful. But all of that paled in comparison to his love for Emily.

He'd been so happy when she'd agreed to spend these four days with him. She'd given it her all, too. No hiding in their bedroom or sulking on the couch. And for the first time in years, Jack hadn't felt compelled to defend his girlfriend's actions.

He'd drunk more beer today than in the last month, but he wasn't drunk. Not too drunk anyway; he hadn't put his foot in his mouth.

A warm breeze fluttered by, and Em shivered in his arms. "Cold?"

"A little but too comfortable to move."

He ran his hands up and down her bare arms. She looked even more lovely in the peach sundress than he'd imagined, and her skin glowed with a touch of color from the sun.

"Jack..."

"Yeah?"

"I just...I wanted to tell you that..."

It wasn't like her to be at a loss for words. He turned her to face him. She looked troubled. He'd fix whatever it was. "Hey, it's okay. You can tell me anything."

Em's eyes sparkled with emotion, and she pressed her lips to his. His heart leaped in his chest.

Her fingers traced the outline of the heart necklace. "I'm honored to have your love." Her voice was raspy, and she swallowed hard. "Thank you for this." She waved her hand around. "It's been so long since I've felt like I belonged."

He pulled her to him. They might have only known each other eight weeks, but he knew when she was overwhelmed. His family was loud and boisterous, and he always had a great time when they all got together, but Emily hadn't had that in ten years. He'd planned to stay with her, but she'd told him to go and have fun, so he had because he'd known she'd meant it.

His mom had warmed toward Em after what Jimmy was calling "The Greatest Smackdown Ever." Christie had always thought it was cute that Paulette had a crush on him. At first, he hadn't thought much of it, but as Paulette got more vulgar over the years, it sickened him. John was a good guy, but he'd always been shy. He'd told Jack that when Paulette had agreed to go out with him that he was lucky. Paulette enjoyed John's undivided devotion and fostered his insecurities. She knew better than to belittle John in front of his family, but Jack had no doubt she did it when they were alone.

One day, his cousin would realize he was the one who could do better and divorce that bitch. John loved his kids and doted on them, and they'd always be his. But Paulette was living on borrowed time; she just didn't know it. She was too busy overestimating her beauty.

"I'm glad you had a good time." He kissed the top of her head. She fit so well in his arms, no matter the position. They were perfect together, and she was finally seeing it. "Do you think I'll be honored with your love soon?" *Fuck.* As soon as the words left his mouth, he'd known it was the wrong thing to say. He hadn't meant it how it sounded. Emily tensed in his arms; he'd ruined the moment. "I'm sorry, baby. I don't know why I said that." Too much alcohol loosened his resolve to give her all the time she needed and to stop pressuring her.

She sat up and swung her legs over the side of the chair. "You said it because you feel it." She put her hand over his heart. "I'm sorry."

"Don't apologize for not being here yet." He covered her hand with his.

Jack sat up and swung his leg around so she was nestled between his.

She leaned back on him and took a deep breath. "When you came after me, saying that you knew the timing sucked but the opportunity was now and we had to grab it, I was terrified because I knew you were right. It was our one chance to see if we belonged together."

"What you're saying is you miss me when I'm gone, and when we're together, it's amazing but too short, and you can't imagine your life without me."

Emily turned and smiled at him. "No wonder you're an amazing songwriter. You boiled things down so succinctly. I suck at that."

He tried not to think about her sucking anything. "You're an amazing copywriter, so that can't be."

Emily chuckled. "You'd think, right? I tried to write a song."

"Really? How is it?"

"So far, it's 25,624 words."

The noise level elevated as Liam, Ethan, and Thom, three of his cousins, strode toward them. "Jack William McBride," Liam said in an exaggerated brogue. "A bunch of us are going to Brick Tavern. Come with us."

"Did we run out of alcohol?"

"Not yet, but we're still here. Pool."

Oh shit, a pool competition with his cousins could last hours. And sounded great.

"Go," Emily said. "Have fun with your cousins."

"But—"

"I'll be fine. I'll help clean up then I'm going to bed. I'm beat."

"We like her, Jack."

To emphasize this, Ethan yanked Emily off the chair and whirled her around the patio before bringing her to a stop where Jack stood.

Jack put his arm around her. He knew his cousin was just having fun, but every nerve ending in his body went possessive.

"Let's go, Jack. The little lady gave you her blessing."

He turned to her. "I'll be back late." Jack kissed her deeply.

His cousin Betsy offered to drive since she had the late shift at the hospital. She hadn't been drinking, and her truck was big enough to hold them all. Jack assured his dad he'd get everyone cabs home.

He grabbed Jimmy on the way to the truck. "Come on, Squeak, join us."

"Jack…" Will said from behind him.

"Don't worry, Dad, I'll look out for him."

Will nodded. "Be safe."

Jack yelled over his shoulder, "Don't wait up."

They were off for yet another epic competition.

Before he and Jimmy left the bar, Jack ensured all his cousins were in cabs. He'd pay for it tomorrow, but he had a fucking blast with his cousins and, more surprisingly, with Jimmy.

Jimmy had eased off busting his balls, and he suspected that Em had something to do with it. No crass jokes about him being the prodigal son or the prince. They'd had a nice conversation last night even though it had been quick.

It was after one when they walked in the kitchen door. Their dad sat at the table. "Everything okay?" Jack asked, stumbling slightly through the doorway.

Will looked up from the crossword puzzle. "Yup, just waiting for you boys to get home."

"Dad, I told you not to wait up." Jack slurred only slightly this time. He grabbed a glass of water and sat.

"You're still my kids." He folded the paper and placed it on the recycling pile. "You look like you had fun."

Jimmy snickered; he was a sloppy drunk. Then he looked as if he'd just solved a great mystery. "Fun *is* fun." He put so much emphasis on the word is that he sounded like Ren from the cartoon.

Jack had never heard anything funnier or truer. *Truwer. Truwwer.* Funny how a word sounded stupid if it was said slowly enough. What a great night!

"I'm glad you guys had a good time, but keep it down. I'm going up. Remember, church at noon. I expect you both to be sobered up by then." As Will turned to leave, a loud scream shattered the silence. "What the hell?"

Emily. Jack darted out of the chair so fast it fell over. "Coming through." Will stepped out of the way as Jack took the stairs two at a time. By the time he'd gotten to the top, another scream echoed through the hallway. His mom and Trish were standing half-asleep in their bedroom doorways.

Jack opened the door and flipped on the light. Emily sat upright in bed, tears streaming down her cheeks, hair a tangled mess. The blanket was on the floor, and the sheets were pulled from between the mattress and box spring. She was shaking her head, but Jack wasn't sure she was awake. He ran to the bed, sat, and pulled her into his arms. "It's okay, baby, it was just a bad dream." Jack smoothed her hair down and rocked her gently. She slumped against him, all the tension draining out of her body.

In the doorway to his room stood his folks, Trish, Jimmy, and Brad.

"Is she okay?" his mom asked.

As if just realizing her surroundings, Emily sat up and looked around the room, and when she saw his family in the doorway, she covered her face with her hands. "Oh God, I'm so sorry."

Jack adjusted on the bed so he sat between her and his family. "Hey, it's okay."

"No, it isn't. I woke up the entire house."

Jack felt his mother's hand on his shoulder. "It's fine, Emily. Don't worry yourself." Em looked up at his mother, her eyes filled with tears and her face red. She leaned forward and buried her face in his chest.

He looked up at his mom. "She'll be okay." He made a gesture with his head, hoping his family would understand.

They did. His mom backed away, and his dad ushered everyone out of the doorway, closing the door behind them.

She still wore the necklace he'd given her that morning. He hoped she never took it off.

Em made no move to get away from him. Two months ago, she'd have vaulted past all of them to get into the bathroom and shut him out. Instead, she let him comfort her. If she didn't want to share her dream, he'd deal. At least she hadn't run. When she calmed down, he grabbed some tissues. "Here."

She dabbed her eyes. "Thanks." Lying back against the pillows, she covered her eyes with her arm. "Your mom hates me."

"No, she doesn't." He was sure of it.

"I'm a mess. If it's not one thing backing up on me, it's another."

Jack kicked off his sneakers and stretched out next to her. He wanted to make love to her and show her none of that mattered to him. The door was ajar, and he was pretty sure his parents were waiting up. "Was it the accident again?"

Emily nodded. "They lied to me."

"Who?"

"The doctors."

"About what?" A heavy feeling settled in the pit of his stomach.

"They didn't die instantly. They suffered."

"You don't know that." Jack knew she did.

"When I saw Eddie a few weeks ago, I told him about my nightmares and how each one was worse than last. He thought they might be memories finally making their way to the surface. I didn't want it to be true. I didn't want to remember."

All of his abilities as a songwriter failed him. "Fuck."

"Yeah." She rolled on her side and faced him. Her eyes held a hollow look, like she wasn't in there. "I remember it all. The piercing squeal of the brakes, how the truck fishtailed, and my dad yelling 'Hold on.' He tried to avoid her, but she must've woken up at the last second and swerved into us instead of away. The truck rolled over, and I remember the sensation of free falling. Riley's seatbelt snapped, and he crashed up against me. My mom was crying, and my dad screamed 'Riley, Emily, you okay?' My mom begged God to let us be okay."

Fresh tears welled in her eyes, and she swiped at them. She swallowed hard a few times, and her breathing was coming in short pants. "Then my mom stopped crying. She said 'Ry, I love you. I love you all.' My dad tried to release the seatbelt, but he screamed in pain. Then he said 'Everything will be okay, Em.' Then silence. I must've passed out, and when I came to, Riley was crumpled on top of me, and there were people outside the truck trying to open the doors."

She rolled onto her other side and drew her knees up to her chest. Jack spooned her, holding her tightly. After a few minutes, her breathing steadied, so he carefully got out of bed. He tiptoed to the door and stepped into the hallway. His folks' door was open, and his dad gestured to him.

His mom was on the bed, and when his dad joined her, she leaned up against him. "How is she?" Will asked.

Jack stood in the doorway. "Asleep, for now." He looked down at the floor but refused to pussy out about this. He needed to be with her. "The nightmares started up again after that fu—her ex cheated on her. They've been getting progressively worse, this one was..." He swallowed hard. "She doesn't have them when we're together."

"She didn't have one last night," his mom said.

Will raised a brow but said nothing.

"She doesn't have them every night. She had a great time today and was happy to be included in our family. The chili we made was her dad's recipe. It's the first time she made it without him." Jack knew he was rambling. He walked in and stretched out on the floor. He was emotionally exhausted. He just wanted to be with his girl.

"Why did you ask if you could share a room this time? You never have before," his mom asked.

Jack wiped his hands over his face. "Em wanted me to. She said her folks wouldn't have allowed it. She wants you to like her." His head throbbed. "I should've asked in the past. I was wrong to assume you'd be okay with it. I'm sorry."

The bed creaked, and his mom knelt next to him. "Yes, you should've, and we should've told you how we felt about it."

"Why didn't you?" Jack sat up to face her.

"I guess we were afraid you wouldn't visit as often if we said no."

Jack chuckled. "That's what Em thought." He stood and

helped her up. "It wouldn't have stopped me from coming home. I love you both. I couldn't have done any of this without your unstinting love and support." He hugged her. His dad joined them, wrapping them both in his arms.

His mom kissed Jack's cheek. "Go to her. Just remember your baby sister and brother are across the hallway from you."

Chapter Thirty-Two

The room was dark when Emily woke. She was on her side facing Jack, and his arms held her firmly to his chest. Damn. They must've fallen asleep after her nightmare.

"Jack," she whispered, shaking him gently. "You gotta leave."

He moaned in his sleep and rolled onto his back, tucking her into his side. The steady rise and fall of his chest continued.

Damn it. She lifted her head but couldn't sit up. "Jack." She put her hand on his chest and rubbed. That always woke him up.

"Mmm. Lower." Moonlight provided enough light that she could see his smile.

"You can't stay here. I think your dad knows you slept here last night." He hadn't said anything to her, but she knew he knew. "Jack."

His hand covered hers, and he guided it down his stomach. He was naked. He'd been dressed when she'd fallen asleep. "Jack. You have to get dressed and leave." She tried to move away, but even in this sleepy state, he didn't let her go.

"I have permission."

"Permission for what? From whom?" If this conversation went on much longer, she wouldn't be able to fall back to sleep.

"My mom and dad."

His hand covered hers, which rested on his erection, but she didn't curl her fingers around him. He was horny and didn't know what he was saying. "Bullshit."

"Not bullshit. Permission. If you're not going to touch me properly, I guess I'll just have to do it myself." He moved her hand away.

"Jack, come on, you're just horny and sleepy. No way they gave you permission."

"They did. They felt awful after your nightmare. I told them you don't have them when we're together."

From the shifting of his arm, Jack wasn't holding back. She put her hand over his forearm to stop him.

"Be my guest." He released his grasp. "Oh, and I apologized for not asking permission in the past."

"You did?"

Jack moaned and sat up on his elbows. "Yes. It was wrong. I have younger siblings, and I should've known better. Can we please have some form of sex now? I'm more than ready." He tilted her head and kissed her. "We just have to keep it down."

She ducked under the covers and crawled between his legs. She stroked his thighs, letting the tops of her hands gently nudge his balls. She leaned down and took him in her mouth.

"Oh fuck, yeah."

He was rock hard, and his salty skin tingled on her tongue. Jack threw the covers off, and the sudden change in temperature had goose bumps forming on her skin. His head lolled from side to side on the pillow. She cupped his balls in her left hand, grasping the base of his cock in her right and stroking him with her tongue.

"Gonna come." His hips lifted off the bed as he exploded in her mouth. A low primal grunt rumbled through his chest.

Emily crawled up, pulling the covers over them as she settled next to him. She tangled his chest hair in her fingers, caressing his pecs. His hand covered hers.

The next time she woke, soft daylight crept into the room, and Jack was between her thighs, his mouth gently teasing her. His hands stroked down her legs, and Emily couldn't stop herself from tensing. His mouth moved to her right leg, placing open-mouthed kisses down her thigh, over her scars. Bile rose in her throat. "Please stop." He sat up. She moved her leg around him and rolled onto her side. He stretched out behind her, cradling her against him.

She didn't ask him why because she knew. He wanted to be able to touch all of her when they made love. Every inch.

"Explain it to me," he whispered.

She shook her head. She couldn't. Wouldn't. How was she supposed to tell the man who was in love with her that his touch made her physically sick? The layers of her damage just kept revealing themselves, like peeling an onion.

"I love you."

"I know." It wasn't what he wanted to hear, but she needed to be damn sure before she said it back. But she wasn't there yet. He deserved nothing less than her total heart. "I'm sorry."

"No, I'm sorry. I should've stopped when you tensed, but I was a dick and pushed it. Won't happen again."

What held her back, she didn't know. But she did know it had nothing to do with trust. She inched closer to him. In his arms, she felt cherished and protected.

EMILY'S EYES DRIFTED OPEN AS SHE INHALED THE warm, rich scent of coffee.

Jack held the cup under her nose. "Wake up, sleepyhead, breakfast's ready."

She sat up and looked at the clock. She'd meant to get up earlier. "I was going to make breakfast." A languid stretch helped ease her muscles into waking.

"No need. My dad was up and out first thing. The party company picked up all the rentals, and he got bagels." He took a sip of her coffee.

"Hey, I thought that was for me." She thrust out her bottom lip.

"You'll have to do better than that if you want this coffee." He took another sip. He was still in his pajamas, his hair tousled, sporting beard shadow and looking totally adorable.

She leaned in and kissed him passionately. "How about now?"

"It's yours."

She took a long sip. "Thank you." She put the cup on the nightstand and scooted out of bed. Jack held out her pajama bottoms. She pulled them on and stretched again. Her stomach rumbled, so yoga would have to wait.

After church, Jack changed out of his charcoal slacks and white button-down shirt into black shorts and a gray T-shirt. Normally, his dad did grill duty, but since it was Father's Day, Jack took over.

Emily helped Trish and Maggie set out leftover potato and macaroni salads, as well as a green salad. Will showed Brad the progress he'd made on the GTO. Jimmy set the table on the patio. It was cooler than the day before, so they ate outside.

Brad and Trish left after lunch to spend the rest of the day with his father. Jimmy's internship at Cone and O'Neill Architects started on Monday, so he went to his room to double-check his portfolio. Jack and Emily cleaned up, and his parents lounged on the patio, sharing a glass of wine.

Emily's phone rang. Her brows drew together as she answered. "Hi, Meg."

"Hey, kiddo. How's your rock star?"

She looked at Jack. She'd only told Meg Jack was a musician. "Huh?"

"Drop the innocent act. Nicki inadvertently spilled the beans."

Her eyes widened and Jack looked at her questioningly. "Nicki?" Oh shit. She wouldn't have told Meg about Jack, but she would've told her about Curt. Emily sighed. "He's fine." Something in Meg's tone set the hair on her arms up. "I don't have any more pages for you yet." It was odd that Meg called her on a Sunday.

"I'm not calling about your book."

Jack's parents came in from the patio.

"Then why are you calling?" She pulled out a kitchen chair and sat.

"What do you know about Jack's past?"

Meg wasn't known for subtlety. Emily looked at Jack, who sat next to her. "That it's in the past. Meg, it's not like you to be anything other than direct. You're scaring me, so just say whatever it is you called to say." Emily's nerves were stretched to the breaking point, and she couldn't take the intrigue.

Meg took a deep breath and sighed. "I have a friend who's an editor at *New York Entertainment* magazine. She got a call from Christie Ettinger, she wants to give an exclusive interview, where, from what my friend said, she'd announce her due date."

"Due date for what?" Emily rubbed her forehead.

"Come on, kiddo, don't make me say it."

"Just fucking say it, Meg." Too late, she forgot Jack's parents were in the kitchen.

"She's pregnant."

"Did she say that?" Emily closed her eyes and inhaled deeply. Jack's hand covered hers.

"Not exactly, she implied—"

"It's not his." She squeezed Jack's hand.

"How can you be sure?"

Emily looked at Will and Maggie; they obviously understood the conversation. "I just am."

"Hiding your head—"

"I'm not. I know him, okay, he wouldn't..." What? Have sex with his ex after their breakup? Plenty of people did. Nicki, for one. But Jack wouldn't have. She knew he'd seen Christie in April before they'd met. And he'd left early during their last visit, to see her, but he wouldn't have slept with her then because he was with her now. She waited for the rush of fear, but it never came. No, he didn't sleep with her last week. And it was highly unlikely if he had that she'd even be able to tell she was pregnant.

"Emily, are you still there?"

She opened her eyes. "Yeah. Thanks for the heads-up, Meg. Make sure you tell your friend to have any story fact-checked."

"You're that sure? Even after what your ex did?"

"Jack isn't Sully."

"I envy you. I wouldn't be able to be so trusting if I were you. Emily, I'm sorry to have upset you, but I don't want you to get hurt again."

"I know. I appreciate your concern. Thanks." Emily closed her eyes and disconnected the call. She took a few deep breaths to try to calm her thumping heart.

"Em?" Jack's hand stroked hers. "Talk to me."

She wished they were alone. "Meg got a call from a friend at *New York Entertainment* magazine." She opened her eyes and met Jack's. "Christie implied she was pregnant and wants to give them an exclusive."

"Em, I haven't slept with her since we broke up. I swear." His eyes implored her to believe him.

She touched his cheek. "I know." Emily stood and paced the kitchen. She grit her teeth, her body warmed, and her mouth went dry. "Okay, maybe it's true, maybe—"

The chair legs screeched over the tiled floor. "I thought you believed me?"

"I do." She closed the distance between them and put her arms around him. "I know it in my heart. But we need to figure this out. I can see three possible scenarios." She pulled free from Jack's embrace. "A. She's pregnant, it's not yours, but she's not above implying it is. The way Meg worded it, it seems there were a lot of implications. She didn't come right out and say it was yours." She looked at Jack's parents, but she couldn't worry about them right now. "Maybe she's trying to break us up? But that won't happen.

"B. She's not pregnant, and she'll put off the interview long enough for rumors to spread. She'd have to fake a miscarriage to cover the fake pregnancy. The only reason to do that would be to try to damage your image. But no one will believe it. You're honest and genuine, and anyone who's ever met you knows that."

"To what end?" Maggie asked. "Why try to damage Jack's reputation?"

"To get back at him for moving on."

"I thought you hadn't talked to her since you got a new number?" Will asked.

Jack rubbed the back of his neck. "Her parents called Dex last week. She'd agreed to go into rehab but wanted to see me first."

"And you went?" Maggie asked, anger darkening her green eyes.

"What choice did I have? If she was serious about going into rehab, how could I say no?"

Maggie's fists clenched at her sides. "She knows exactly how to manipulate you."

"If there was even a small chance, I had to do what I could."

Emily stood next to Jack and took his hand. "We discussed it, and I agreed he should go. I suspected it was a manipulation, but like he said, even a small chance was worth the risk."

He put his arm around her and hugged her to him. "I'm sorry about this." Jack pulled out his phone. "I'm calling her."

"No," Emily and Maggie yelled.

"Jack, that's what she wants. That's option C. You told her to move on and not contact you again. There are plenty of newspapers in California. Why not call one of them? She's desperate. She had no way of knowing you'd find out so soon. Maybe she'll regret it and just drop it. She didn't really say anything yet. Give her the chance to get out of this gracefully. If this blows up, she won't have a career to go back to." Emily sighed. "Or maybe she'll have a bigger one. I don't pretend to understand how Hollywood works."

Drained, Emily dropped on the nearest chair. She would've liked to go for a walk, clear her head, and have a few minutes to herself, but Jack needed her. He still looked shocked, and she knew how he felt. Even though that relationship ended eight months ago, he just couldn't believe that someone he'd loved could do something so hurtful. Maybe tomorrow, they'd get a whole day without this bullshit.

MAGGIE STOOD IN THE KITCHEN AND WATCHED JACK leave with Emily. She'd always been so proud of Jack; he'd always been a sweet, kindhearted child, and he'd grown into a man of infinite compassion. She wanted to rip Christie's face off. How dare she do this, after all Jack had done for her? He never said so, but Maggie knew he paid her way—all those fancy clothes and lessons she simply had to have. She'd never interfere in Jack's private life, but she'd seen enough to come to dislike the girl intensely.

Christie had been so sweet when Jack had first brought her home to meet them. Maggie had liked her immediately. After they'd moved across the country to California for her career, Christie had changed. And not just her clothes. Her entire personality changed, and Maggie no longer saw the sweet girl she'd been.

"Well, that was something."

"Really, Will?" Maggie turned to her husband. "Is that all you have to say? Jack's ex is faking a pregnancy, and that's the best you can do?" Sometimes her husband's calm demeanor pissed her off. It took a lot to set him off. This should've done it.

"Magpie, my love"—Will pulled her into his arms—"I meant that Emily didn't doubt Jack for an instant. Didn't even ask him if it was possible. After what she's been through, I think that's rather extraordinary, don't you?"

She had to admit she was impressed. That poor girl had been through so much. When she'd shown her and Trish the scars on her leg, Maggie's heart broke. She couldn't even imagine what it would be like to be left with such a reminder of a horrific accident. Even though she'd been resistant to her, Emily still came this weekend and participated. She'd expected her to hide in Jack's room, the way Christie had. She rested her head on Will's chest. "I think Jack finally met someone who will take care of him the way he takes care of others." Tears filled her eyes. She loved all her children, but Jack had left home at so young an age she never stopped worrying about him. It didn't matter that he was twenty-nine.

Trish was the most like her, very grounded. Maggie was sure that Trish and Brad would be announcing their engagement soon. Jimmy and Jack took after Will. Jimmy seemed to finally be forgiving Jack for leaving home. He'd only been twelve and worshiped the ground Jack walked on. Jack always made time for him until he'd moved. "We've been extremely lucky, Will."

"That we have, my love. That we have."

Chapter Thirty-Three

As I sink down on his cock, I imagine it's Jack I'm fucking.

"You're so fucking wet, baby. Play with your tits."

He's lying there with his hands behind his head, expecting me to do all the work. Jack wouldn't do that. But until we're together, I have needs. I pinch my nipples between my fingers and roll them.

"Oh yeah. Play with your pussy."

My hand travels slowly down my firm belly, to my aching clit. I stroke it back and forth.

"Spread your lips. I want to see."

I obey, and he rewards me by using his thumb on my clit. I feel my orgasm building, but just before it consumes me, he removes his hand.

"Fuck me hard, baby."

I ride his cock hard while he gropes my tits like a teenaged boy.

"Come on, baby, make some noise."

I open my eyes and stare down at him. I'm not a screamer, but that's what he likes, so I find my motivation. "Oh, yeah. Yes, oh, yes."

He smiles up at me, so I continue.

"You're so fucking hard, baby. I wanna suck your cock." I'm saying the words to him, but all the while I'm picturing Jack. His blue eyes are lighter than Jack's, but I focus on them anyway. "Oh, fuck!" I come so hard I collapse on top of his chest.

"Hey. We're not done yet."

I push up and fuck him hard. If Jack and I weren't already destined to be together, this guy wouldn't be...NO! Stick to the script. This is just fucking. Jack's the one for me.

These last two months have been difficult, but the rewrites are done. In a few weeks, Jackie will be in L.A.

I smile. And that groupie whore can't fly.

JACK WAS AWAKE WHEN HIS ALARM WENT OFF AT five twenty-five. He'd been awake for hours. The intensity of his love for Em scared him. And it had only taken him two months to figure out why.

Fear spiked his blood.

Erica. The first great love of his life, and at nineteen, he'd thought she was *the* great love of his life. He'd fallen fast and hard for her, too. She'd been three years older and so much wiser, and Jack had trusted her completely. He'd wanted to spend every minute with her, and he realized now his love for her had bordered on obsession. There always seemed to be a part of her that she'd kept to herself, but Jack had ignored that.

He'd also blown off Elliot's dislike of her because Elliot didn't like many people. But Jack should've listened. When Erica had lost her apartment because the building had been sold, Jack had jumped on the chance to move in with her. He'd offered for her to move in with him in the apartment the four of them shared. It had two bedrooms, which meant that two of them slept on the pullout couch. He'd told her it would be temporary until they could get a place of their own.

He wished he could forget how she'd laughed in his face. How that sound had shattered his heart. She'd said his apartment was a shithole, and she'd had a much better offer. Jack remembered how his heart had beat so hard he'd thought it might blow a hole in his chest. Erica hadn't loved him, not the way he'd thought. She'd said she loved him, but she also loved many guys and fucked them all, and he was sweet, but she wasn't the type to be tied down to one person, and Jack was. That he'd been fun. *Fun.*

Never before had he been so betrayed. He'd been played for a fool, and it had taken Jack years before he was over it. He realized now that maybe he wasn't. He'd loved Sandra and Christie, but everything that happened with Erica had colored those relationships.

Sandra...she'd called him while he was on tour and broken up with him. Said she wasn't going to waste her life waiting for him to show up. Since he'd met her while he was on tour, he'd thought she'd understood. And maybe she had, but she'd met a guy who lived near her, and Jack was out.

He'd thought he'd found the solution to his career being an issue when he'd met Christie. She was an actress, and she'd understood what it took to succeed in a creative field. There had never been any recriminations over how often he was gone. There had been others though. Again, one's he'd never seen coming.

He realized that his pushing Em to return his feelings was his way of trying to control the situation. The situation being his career, and until she loved him back, it would be their biggest obstacle. Jack couldn't lose her. He wouldn't.

Emily stirred next to him, lifting her head. "What time is it?"

"Early. Go back to sleep." Jack sat up and adjusted the

covers over her. He stood and dressed in sweatpants and T-shirt.

"Where you goin'?" She snuggled deeper into the bed.

"I'm gonna make breakfast for my dad."

"So sweet."

Jack hurried downstairs. He grabbed the paper off the front walk, put on a pot of coffee, and started the bacon. His dad was in the basement working out.

Will came up the stairs. "Maggie, you didn't have to— Jack? What's all this?"

"Morning. Bacon, scrambled eggs, toast, coffee. Paper's on the table."

Will smiled. "I'll be down in ten minutes."

Just as Jack plated the eggs, his dad walked back into the kitchen, freshly showered and dressed in his standard work attire: jeans, navy McBride Plumbing and Heating T-shirt, and work boots. "Coffee?"

"Please."

Jack placed the toast on the table. He grabbed a plate of eggs and bacon for himself and sat across from his dad.

They ate in silence for a few minutes. Will finished a second helping of eggs and sat back, sipping his coffee. "You always did make the best scrambled eggs. What's the secret?"

"Butter. It makes everything better." He cleared the plates from the table and poured more coffee. "Sorry about yesterday."

"Not exactly a conversation you wanted to have with your girlfriend ever, let alone in front of your parents, huh?"

"Yeah." Jack's anger reignited. How could Christie do such a thing? Jack didn't give a shit about his image, but to fake a pregnancy? She certainly didn't look pregnant when he'd seen her, but neither did Siobhan, and he was pretty sure she was. Elliot had been walking around with a goofy grin for the last two weeks. Every time Jack asked what was

up, he'd wipe it off his face as best he could and say nothing
was up.

"Emily took the whole thing well, don't you think?" Will
asked.

She hadn't doubted him for a single second. That erased
all his anger. He had no control over what Christie did. Emily
believing in him meant everything. A goofy grin of his own
spread across his face. "Yeah, she did. I just wish..." *That she
loved me.*

Will put his mug down and smiled. "You've never been the
most patient person. She needs time, you've only known each
other a short while. After everything that girl has been
through, it's no wonder that she's scared."

"Scared? Of me?"

Will stood and poured more coffee. "Even as a child, you
had a singular focus when something caught your interest."
Will smiled. "Remember your piano lessons? You wore out
that keyboard we bought you till we finally had to buy a real
piano. Kathy Wagner always said you were her finest student."

"She's a great teacher." That piano still sat in the living
room. He was glad his folks hadn't sold it when he'd moved
out. He'd love to have it in his home when he and Em got
married and moved to Pine Hill. She'd loved the house, the
outside anyway. He wanted to show her the inside, but he
didn't want to inconvenience his tenants.

Will sat forward, resting his hands on the table. "But, Jack,
give the girl a break. Your life is very complicated. She
obviously isn't comfortable with that aspect."

All his insecurities bubbled to the surface. "What if she
doesn't..."

"Jack, she's been through a lot, and well, that ex of hers..."
Will clenched and unclenched his fist. "She needs time and
patience. It took weeks and weeks of convincing before your
mother agreed to go out with me."

"I thought it was love at first sight?"

Will smiled. "It was for me. Your mom is more...practical." Will stood and rinsed his cup. "Just remember, Jack, actions speak louder than words. I don't think you have anything to worry about."

After his dad left, Jack took a quick shower before returning to the kitchen and cleaning up the dishes. By the time his mom came downstairs, Jack had Earl Grey steeping, an English muffin ready to toast, and eggs over easy in the pan.

"Jack, why are you up?"

"I had breakfast with Dad, worked out, and now, your favorite breakfast. Ta-da." Jack grabbed her and twirled her around the kitchen.

"You're just like your father." She looked at the table. "You were always so thoughtful. This is nice." She sat, removed the tea bag, and poured a splash of milk. "Mmm. Perfect."

Jack placed the eggs and muffin on a plate and, with a flourish, presented it to her. "Breakfast is served."

She smiled up at him. "You didn't have to do this."

"I wanted to. I had a great time this weekend. Every time I come home, you always make my favorite dishes."

"Well, I'm your mother. I love you, and I don't get to take care of you enough." Tears welled in her eyes, but she shook her head. "I'm so glad you came home this weekend."

"Me too. Thank you for including Em. She had a great time."

Maggie looked at him, brow raised.

Jack laughed. "Honest. She told me so. She's a really good person, Mom."

Maggie took his hand. "I just want you to be happy."

"I am, Mom. I love her."

Maggie nodded. "This looks delicious."

After she left, Jack cleaned up the dishes and crawled back

into bed with Em. She turned in her sleep and nestled herself into his body. She wouldn't have done that two months ago.

He dozed off and woke up an hour later alone. Damn. He found her in the kitchen chatting with Jimmy. "Hey."

Jimmy stood.

"Don't go," Jack said. "I'm making breakfast."

"Didn't you eat with your dad?" Emily said through a yawn.

"That was hours ago. Pancakes?"

"Hell yeah." Jimmy sat and leaned the chair back to balance on the back legs. "So anyway, that's my plan. I don't know if it'll work out."

"Well, I think that's great."

Jimmy was still in sweats. "I thought you started your internship today?" He'd planned to spend the morning in bed with Emily. Maybe show her around town more. Later. Much later.

"I don't have to be there until noon. They're having a luncheon for the interns, then orientation in the afternoon."

"Oh."

After breakfast, Jimmy went upstairs while Emily washed the dishes. She shooed Jack out of the kitchen, saying he'd done enough for one day.

Just as he was about to knock on Jimmy's door, it opened, and Jimmy plowed into him. He pushed Jimmy back into his room and closed the door behind him.

"What the fuck?"

"Keep it down, will you? Listen, man, I need to be *alone* with Emily. I'll give you a thousand bucks to get out sooner than later."

"Keep your money."

"Come on, Jimmy."

"No, I mean, keep your money. Give me twenty minutes, bro. I'll be out of your hair."

Jack smiled. "Thanks, man, appreciate it."

Jimmy opened the door but stopped. "You're a good brother, Jack."

Luckily a breeze didn't blow or Jack would've fallen over. They'd had a great time this weekend hanging out, drinking, and playing pool. Jack always regretted that his leaving to pursue his dreams had hurt their relationship. He just hadn't known how to fix it.

True to his word, twenty minutes later, Jimmy drove off to pursue his dreams. And he and Em were alone for the first time in three days.

EARLY THE NEXT MORNING, JACK GOT UP TO MAKE breakfast for his dad, but he was already at the table eating a bowl of cereal. Jack sipped coffee as they debated this seasons Yankees' roster.

After Will left, he mixed up the egg batter for French toast.

His mom walked into the kitchen. "You're spoiling me."

"Sit, drink your tea."

"I'm rather ashamed of my behavior toward Emily."

He stacked two pieces of French toast on a plate. "Here."

Maggie sighed. "I worry about you all the time."

"Mom—"

"No, let me finish. It doesn't matter that you've been taking care of yourself for the past ten years. I feel...robbed." Maggie used her napkin to dab the corners of her eyes. "In April when you called and asked if you could bring this girl to dinner, I was worried you were rushing into another relationship." When Jack went to speak, she held up her hand. "I really liked Christie when we met her. She was sweet, and it was obvious how she felt about you, and how you felt about her. But, she changed."

"Yeah." Changed was an understatement.

"You've always fallen headfirst in love." Maggie smiled. "You're just like your father. At first, I thought Emily was cold, too reserved for you. Kind of how Christie ended up, but Emily's nothing like her. I know she's been hurt, but you're my son, and I was concerned for you."

"You seemed rather determined not to like her. Em said that first day you didn't like her. I told her she was crazy, but she was right." Jack laughed.

"Why is that funny?" Maggie asked.

"Because she was right that you were looking out for me."

"Always. No matter how old you get. I want all my children to be happy and find wonderful spouses."

"Love you, Mom."

"I think that Trish and Brad are getting engaged soon." Maggie smiled. "I worry about you the most. You were always such a thoughtful, sensitive child, I was afraid the world would chew you up and spit you out. But you are your father's son, so much like him, so much stronger than I gave you credit for."

"Mom..."

She took his hand. "Maybe I'd hoped you'd come running home, finish school, become a teacher, and settle here. I'm so proud of the man you've become. I guess I'd just hoped to be a little more responsible for it."

Jack hugged her. "You are. You guys always supported and encouraged me, I couldn't have done it without you."

EMILY HEARD THE BEDROOM DOOR OPEN AND CLOSE. The sound of Jack undressing had her heart beating faster. He climbed into bed and snuggled up behind her.

"That feels good," she moaned.

"What does?" Jack asked, nestling his erection against her butt.

"You being back in bed."

Jack thrust his hips.

"That too."

Kissing the back of her neck, he whispered, "Turn around then."

He protected them and lay over her, kissing his way up to her torso. When he kissed her lips, he thrust inside her.

"Feels so good," she moaned.

He thrust again, kissing the top of her breast before taking her nipple into his mouth. His lips caressed every inch within reach.

Her heart thudded in her chest as heat rushed between her thighs. Warmth spread throughout her body, and she found it hard to breathe. If ever she was in danger of combusting, it was now.

Returning to kiss her lips, Jack wiped a tear off her cheek. "Hey, am I hurting you?"

"No...it's just..." Emily looked away.

"Tell me."

"Last Wednesday, it seemed like we had so much time together before you had to leave again. I had such a good time with you this week, but it's going so fast."

"I know." He kissed her gently, propping up on one elbow. His eyes filled with sadness.

"I don't want you to feel bad about this."

"What do you want me to do?" Jack asked.

Emily smiled weakly. "Nothing, it just took me by surprise. A lot of things about being with you have."

Jack brushed the pad of his thumb over her lips before kissing them. "You can talk to me about anything."

Emily swallowed back the emotions that rose in her chest. He was leaving for over a month. "That first week we spent together was crazy. I mean, how it all came about was crazy for me. I know that's probably standard operating procedure in rock star."

Jack smiled. "It was crazy for me, too, nothing standard about it."

Emily closed her eyes but forced herself to continue. "It didn't help that Nicki left with you. I miss her. But she's happy living on the road with Curt. And we have to get used to this. You're gonna be on tour for eighteen months."

Jack's smile dipped.

"I don't want you to feel bad about that. You wanted me to tell you how I'm feeling."

"It's important that we're totally honest with each other."

She nodded. "You love it, and you're amazing at it, and the fans love being able to see you. I just have to suck it up. This week has been full of normal stuff, and it's been even more amazing than I thought it'd be. But the other times...it's been two days here and there. And just when I feel like we're reconnecting, you have to leave." Tears streamed down her cheeks. "I'm sorry."

"I need you to talk to me about this stuff."

"Well, right now, I'm feeling like a pretty crappy girlfriend for making you feel bad for doing what you love, what you were meant to do." She touched his cheek, grazing her fingers over his stubble.

He handed her a tissue, and she wiped her eyes. "You're the best girlfriend ever."

Emily doubted that.

"I love you. You're perfect the way you are."

Emily scoffed. "I know you love me, and I know it's stupid, but some days, I imagine that you'll call me and say you met someone new."

Jack's chuckle turned into deep laughter.

Emily swatted his arm. "Hey, stop laughing at me. This isn't funny."

"That's not what I'm laughing at, baby. I worry about the same thing. I'm so afraid that when I'm on the road some guy is going to come in and sweep you off your feet. And you'll realize that you could have everything you want and none of the baggage that I come with."

"I wouldn't call being a musician baggage."

"No, but being famous is, isn't it? It's a hard life. It's a life on the road. There are weeks and months at home, writing a new album, and if we're lucky, recording close to home. But once touring starts, it's a grind. I love it, but it isn't easy."

Emily kissed him. "Do you really think I'm waiting for someone better to come along?"

He grinned. "I didn't say be better, just available."

She chuckled. "I'm definitely not available. I thought I'd have all this time to write since you weren't around to distract me."

His hand trailed down her belly and between her thighs. "Like this?"

Her hips lifted off the bed as his fingers toyed with her. "Yeah, like that." She swallowed a moan. "Half the time I end up staring at the screen, the blinking cursor mocking me. I'm wondering what you're doing. How did your interview go? How was your workout with Buzz? I hope Buzz is doing okay. How did your epic miniature golf battle for supremacy turn out?"

He laughed as he continued to finger her, sending jolts of pleasure throughout her body. "Know what I'm doing? I'm wondering what you're doing and wondering if you're thinking about me. I'm afraid that you're going to conclude that the time together isn't enough to offset the time apart."

Jack leaned down and kissed her as the first wave of her orgasm washed over her.

When she settled back on the bed, Jack said, "I know you like me, and I know I'm chapters ahead."

A short laugh escaped her lips. "Chapters? You're on book three, and I'm on the second act of book one. But my life is better for having you in it."

Jack pulled her on top of his chest and kissed her. "I'm glad we had this talk."

Emily laughed. "I did all the talking."

"Exactly. I'm always telling you how I feel, trying to be open and honest with you, and I feel you holding back, and I understand why, but I don't like it. I love you, and that's not going to change. You're it for me."

"I—"

Whatever she'd been about to say got swallowed up by Jack's kiss. He nibbled his way to her neck, alternating between nips and licks. Her body tingled, from the top of her head to the tips of her toes. His hands cupped her butt, kneading her flesh gently with his strong hands. She managed to get her hands between them, wrapping her fingers around his cock. "We never did finish what we started."

He released his hold on her, and Emily sat up and lowered herself, taking him all the way into her body. She flattened her palms on his chest. He cupped her breasts. She leaned down and kissed him, their tongues tangling. His eyes glittered with love as she slowly tortured him.

"Baby, you're killing me."

"You'd do things differently?"

"Nope." Jack's hands wandered down her sides and around her hips.

Too late, she realized what he was doing. "Stop."

"No."

"No?" Emily stopped moving. "Can't you ever just let anything go?"

"Correct me if I'm wrong, but your ex tried that, and it

didn't work out for him." He sat up, his cock pushing deeper inside her. "I want to touch every inch of you, especially while we're making love. Nothing should be off-limits." He kissed her lips gently then nuzzled her ear. "Please?"

Emily shut her eyes and nodded. She knew he was right, and she didn't want to make the same mistakes. He pulled the pillows out from behind him and sat back, resting his back up against the headboard. Sun spilled through the open curtains. She wished the room was dark.

His hands slid down her thighs and over her knees. He lingered there, tracing the thick, raised skin of the scar over her right knee. She scrunched her eyes closed.

"Does this hurt?"

"No," she said, barely a whisper.

"How does it feel?"

Emily didn't want to tell him.

"Talk to me."

"I feel nauseated."

His hands moved to her back, and he pulled her to him. "I'm sorry, baby."

Her eyes were so tightly closed she had no idea how the tears managed to escape. They burned down her cheeks, but Jack wiped them away with his thumbs as he kissed her. "Do you want to stop?"

Jack was trying to help her, make her less self-conscious. Emily didn't think that would ever happen, but she didn't want them to stop now. "Make love to me."

He helped her off and came up on his knees. Jack kissed her as he urged her onto her back. He kissed his way down her body, avoiding her right leg. His tongue dipped between her thighs, and her back arched off the bed.

He kissed her belly, breasts, neck, and finally her lips. He slid inside her, rocking her gently, whispering words of love.

Someday soon, she'd say them back.

Chapter Thirty-Four

At noon, they drove into Manhattan to meet Barbara Callow. Emily had been quiet since they'd made love. Jack hoped he hadn't pushed her too far.

One of the apartments had sold, and the two they'd looked at were too small. He'd gotten used to the space of a house, and he had an idea he needed to run past Em and his parents.

As they sat in traffic on the way back to her place, he decided now was as good a time as any. "I was thinking of getting a three-bedroom apartment."

"Why not tell Barbara that before we looked at two bedrooms?"

"I know it's too soon for you to move in, but I wanted to know what you thought."

"About what?"

"I was thinking maybe Jimmy could move in. I won't be living there until the tour ends, that way he could stay in the city while he does his internship at Cone and O'Neill, and next year, he'll start his master's at Parsons. It'd be a lot less traveling."

Emily didn't answer; instead, she looked out the passenger

window. Why was he so nervous?

When she finally turned to look at him, she was smiling. "I think that's a great idea."

"You do?"

"Yeah, you guys seem to be getting along better. This'll give you a chance to move forward."

"That's a great point I'll be sure to make to my folks when I talk to them about it."

"We were there for four days. Why didn't you?"

Jack rubbed the back of his neck. "I only just thought of it, and I wanted to talk to you first. If we don't kill each other, he'll probably still be living there when you're ready to move in." He'd felt more confident about that in his head.

"I see." She resumed viewing the outside world through the side window.

He was ready now. Several minutes passed, and he changed the channels on the radio five or six times. Or fifty or sixty. Now that they'd cleared the Lincoln Tunnel, traffic vanished, so he floored it.

He couldn't stand the silence. "Em, I know you're not ready, and it's too soon to even bring it up, but we talked about this. If you didn't want to come today, you should've said so." What the hell had he just said? He was losing his mind.

"You wanted my help and approval. You have both. And I'd be fine with Jimmy living with us."

Jack quickly maneuvered the SUV to the shoulder and threw it in park. He undid her seat belt, pulled her onto his lap, and kissed her. Forced to break the kiss because he needed air, he leaned his head back against the seat. He took gulps of air, but it wasn't enough.

"What was that for?"

Her eyes were glazed over and her lips swollen. "You said 'living with us.'"

She smiled and extricated herself from his lap. "Let's go home, rock star."

Home.

Emily stopped at her neighbors and picked up her mail, which included a small box.

Home. The word rang over and over in his head. He loved the sound of that. He'd be leaving Friday morning for over a month without her, but right now, he didn't care. She'd called their time together normal, agreed to live with him someday, and called her place home. It was her home; maybe that was what she'd meant.

"Give me a minute." Em walked into her office and closed the door. Jack paced and waited. She had a funny smile when she saw the package. He hadn't gotten a look at the sender's address; he hoped it wasn't from the fucker.

He went to the kitchen, pulled out some cans of tomatoes, and started a red sauce for dinner. He chopped the garlic and onions and threw them in a sauté pan. He was so busy trying not to cut off a finger that when she touched his arm he jumped.

"Sorry, didn't mean to startle you." She smiled. "Come into the living room. I have a present for you."

He washed and dried his hands. A small box, wrapped in purple paper sat on the coffee table. She patted the seat next to her. "Come on sit, I won't bite. Yet," she said with a suggestive waggle of her brows.

Jack sat and the only thing that kept his heart in his chest was the fact that she smiled at him. "It's not my birthday. You didn't have to get me anything."

She leaned in and touched her lips to his. "Do you want to set the standard that gifts can only be given on birthdays?" Her fingers traced the heart he'd given her.

A smile crept along his lips. "No."

She sat back and tucked her legs under her. "Go on,

open it."

He picked up the package and shook it. It made a slight jingling sound. He tore the paper off, and a plain white box revealed itself. He lifted the lid, and a wide grin broke across his face. Nestled on a bed of cotton was a jack-in-the-box keychain with a single key. Blood rushed through his veins. Em smiled wickedly. "This is to ho—here."

"Yeah, I figured that way you don't have come to my office to pick up a key."

She doesn't want me at her office?

She touched his thigh. "We can still have lunch. I just thought since you'd be staying with me when you're home, it'd be easier."

He held the key chain from two fingers. "Is this what you got in the mail?"

She smiled shyly. "I ordered it two weeks ago, but it took forever to get here. I'd hoped to give it to you last week."

She almost looked embarrassed. He leaned in and kissed her. "Best present ever. Thank you."

"There's more."

The box was small, but he doubted it contained anything else. He lifted the cotton.

"Not in the box." She stood and took his hand, entwining her fingers with his. She led him to the spot where the fucker's recliner had been. "I thought this would be a good spot for a guitar, and maybe a small amp, but you'd have to keep it down."

He felt like he was inside a dream. A wonderful, comforting dream. He never wanted to leave her. Before he could form words, she led him down the hallway to the bedroom. She tugged her hand free and opened two of the dresser drawers nearest him. They were empty. Then walked to the closet and slid open the left side.

"I figured it might be easier if you wanted to leave some

stuff here. I don't know if you need any closet space, but it's here if you want to use it."

He was still in the dream and hadn't responded. He closed the space between them and lifted her into his arms, kissing her. "I'd love that." He swallowed the lump that rose. "Are you sure?"

Her only answer was to cock a brow at him, which made him laugh.

"I mean, you don't need the space for yourself?" *What the fuck's wrong with me?* He hadn't even dreamt of her offering him space.

She smiled, her eyes alight. "Well, I'm a girl, so if you don't want the space—"

He kissed her. "I want it." He tumbled them onto the bed. "I want you."

Em undid the button on his jeans, sliding the zipper down slowly. He reciprocated, and then lifting her shirt, he kissed her belly as he cupped her warmth. "Shit." Removing his hand, he licked his fingers. "I left a pot of sauce simmering on the stove." That lovely flush that started below the neckline of her shirt turned him on.

He shut off the stove and returned to her, removing his T-shirt as he strode into the bedroom. She lay on the bed wearing the satin and lace emerald bra and panties he'd bought her. His heart fluttered in his chest. For the fifth time in as many days, he fell deeper in love with her.

EMILY WOKE JACK EARLY FOR SLEEPY MORNING SEX. When she finally dragged herself out of bed, she forced herself to do yoga. She usually looked forward to it, but since their time was winding down, she'd rather have stayed in bed with him. He made breakfast while she showered.

She was slammed with catching up when she got to work, and before she knew it, Jack texted her that he was there for their lunch date. She met him outside, and they went to the same Italian restaurant.

Jack stared at her.

"Do I have something on my face?" she asked, trying to hide her smile.

His throat worked as he swallowed. "Is that the blouse?" He seemed to have trouble forming words.

"Blouse?"

Swallowing hard, he leaned in. "The one you said I could rip off you?"

She looked down, inspecting the blouse. "Why, yes, it is." She sucked her lips in to avoid smiling.

Jack groaned and shifted in his seat.

Her smile wouldn't be held back, so she picked up her water and took a sip.

"What do you have on under that?"

"It's new."

Another more pained groan escaped his lips. This time, his hand disappeared under the table as he shifted.

Emily shook her head. "Lewd thoughts in public have consequences, Jack."

His eyes finally met hers. "Tell me about it." They glittered with lust. "What time will you be home tonight?"

Home. The very idea of a home with Jack warmed her. Not the heated sensations when panic gripped or that trapped feeling where it was hard to breathe. This warmth came with a sense of contentment she'd never before experienced.

EVEN THOUGH SHE HAD A TON OF WORK TO CATCH up on, her bosses insisted she leave at five. She'd protested, but they'd done everything to convince her to leave but wink and smile at her.

By the time she put the key in the door, she was so turned on she hoped Jack was ready. She'd teased him earlier in the restaurant, but she'd teased herself as well.

As soon as she was inside, she yelled, "I'm home."

Silence.

She'd parked next to Jack's SUV, so she knew he was home. Unless he'd gone out for a run. Her heart plummeted to her feet. "Hello?"

A lump formed in her throat. The apartment was too quiet. She swallowed hard as she trudged up the stairs, the soles of her flats echoing in the silence.

She exhaled when she reached the top of the stairs and saw Jack's open guitar case next to the couch. Relief washed over her, and her breathing returned to normal.

He'd told her how he'd sensed she was gone the day she'd snuck out of his hotel room. Her wedding day. If she hadn't been in so much pain at the time, she would've laughed. It no longer hurt; it was a lifetime ago.

Emily hung her purse on the railing, and as she rounded the corner to go to the bedroom, she stopped short. Jack stood naked, except for his guitar, at the threshold of their bedroom. He strummed a few chords and sang.

Welcome home, so glad you're here
Take my hand, the time draws near
I'll hold you close and love you 'til dawn
Time flies and I'll be gone
but I'll be back soon and
I can't wait 'til you take my hand and welcome me home.

Jack lifted the guitar over his head and leaned it inside the bedroom. His eyes glittered with love as he strode toward her.

With every breath she took, her body pulsed with need. Desire pooled low in her belly, and her clothes felt heavy and oppressive.

When he reached her, Jack pulled her into his arms and kissed her. Heat exploded inside her as their tongues danced. Her hands roamed over the muscles in his back and down to his butt. She pinched him.

Jack pulled back and raised a brow. "So that's how it's gonna be?" A satisfied grin settled over his lips. He backed her up against the wall and palmed her breasts, and his thumb and forefinger plucked her painfully hard nipples. He took her mouth in a primal kiss, and then his lips trailed to her ear, nipping along the way. "I want to rip this blouse off you."

Emily's body went liquid, but she didn't fall. Jack had her. He'd never let her fall.

She nodded and twined her arms around his neck, pulling him in for a hot, wet kiss. His hands roamed around her sides, pulling her blouse out of the waist of her pants. She nipped his tongue and bottom lip; his erection pressed against her belly.

When he pulled back, his eyes were deep blue and sparkled with lust. His hands stroked up her sides. He undid two more buttons on her blouse and cupped her breasts in his hands, gently kneading them. His pupils dilated when her nipples knotted. He leaned in for a kiss and then quickly pulled back and grabbed the plackets of her blouse and tore it open.

Buttons flew and dropped with a light clicking sound as they hit the hardwood floor.

Jack moaned as he stared at her black lace push-up bra. "Oh fuck, Em..." His Adam's apple bobbed wildly as he swallowed, and the muscles in his jaw twitched. "Say it."

"Jack..." His gaze met hers. She'd planned on dragging it out, but she just couldn't wait any longer to feel him inside her. "Please fuck me now."

He yanked the blouse off her, and she undid the button

and zipper on her pants. Jack tugged them down, taking her panties with them. As she stepped out of them, Jack grabbed a condom off the dining room table, rolled it on, and crushed her against the wall as he assaulted her lips with his.

Jack lifted her, and she wrapped her legs around his waist. His cock slid into her slowly as he kissed her tenderly. The calm before the storm. He pulled out and thrust back in. The sensations spread out from where their bodies were joined to the top of her head and the tips of her toes. She felt weightless in his arms. Over and over, Jack fucked her hard. And she loved it.

Her body gripped him as she came, taking him with her. Jack growled, "I fucking love you." He turned them and sank to the floor, still inside her.

Emily had never felt more connected to another person in her entire life; she felt as if they were one. She couldn't clearly see where she ended and he began. And it had nothing to do with sex.

For the first time, she couldn't imagine her life without him.

THE NEXT DAY FLEW BY. JACK MET HER FOR LUNCH again and had dinner waiting when she got home. They made love, and she fell asleep in his arms. She hadn't had a nightmare since Saturday.

He'd wasted no time filling the empty space with acoustic and electric guitars and a small amp. He'd also filled the dresser drawers, and a pair of tan slacks and a blue button-down shirt hung in the closet.

They'd made plans with Eddie and Sheryl to have dinner on August sixth. She'd vowed to tell them who Jack was before that. She wanted to be with him and realized that when they were together none of the rock star stuff mattered. He loved her. And she was falling in love with him.

Jeff was going to pick Jack up at seven fifteen for their nine forty-five a.m. flight to Cleveland. He had an interview at a local rock station, and he'd make it just in time as long as the flight wasn't delayed.

Emily woke Friday morning at five. Jack sat on the edge of the bed, his head dipped low. "You okay?" She stroked his back.

He flipped on the bedside lamp. She lay on her side, and he stretched out next to her, their heads sharing a pillow. "Em..."

The sadness in his eyes caused a fluttering in her belly. "What?"

"I'm trying not to put more pressure on you. I know I promised to be patient, but I haven't lived up to that, and I'm sorry."

She kissed his lips. "You've been patient, for you. But nothing worked out how we thought it would. I'd expected to spend months torturing myself, going over what went wrong with Sully." Emily caressed his chest. "I just know that if I do something you don't like you'll let me know. If I'd devoted myself to what went wrong, like I'd planned on doing, I'd have driven myself crazy. This is better." A sudden tear slid out and dropped on the pillow. "I'm going to miss you."

"This is going to fucking suck." Tears formed in Jack's eyes. "Em..."

His voice was pained. Her heart leaped to her throat. She was barely able to croak out, "What?"

"Promise me, if you ever want to end things..." Jack closed his eyes, and tears ran down his cheeks. He turned onto his back. "You'll do it in person, not over the phone."

"Baby," Emily cupped his face in her hand and kissed him softly on the lips. "I'm not going to break up with you." How could he still think that? Hadn't she proved to him she was all in?

Jack heaved a sigh. "It's happened before."

Emily nodded. She took his hand and placed it over her heart. "I promise to never break up with you over the phone, in a text, email"—she looked away and then back—"or a letter."

"Hey, we agreed that was my fault." He smiled at her, but she looked away. "What?

She swallowed hard, and her eyes stung with tears. "Did you know it takes four days to get to California by train?" A sad laugh escaped her lips. "I thought about maybe meeting you there since you're going to be in California for five days. But it would take me eight days just to get there and back..."

"Em, it's okay."

She sat up. "No, it isn't. If I could fly, then at least we'd be able to see each other on weekends. And what about when you go to Europe for six weeks?"

"Em, it won't be easy, baby, but we'll get through it."

"If I wasn't such a wuss, we wouldn't have to get through it."

"Hey, you were on a plane that could've crashed. That would screw with anyone." He stroked her arm. "You've been through enough."

She nodded. Jack understood, but she still felt guilty.

Jack kissed her deeply. "We still have a little time left."

Emily straddled his hips. She handed him a condom, and when he was ready, Emily took him in her body. Leaning forward, she gently scraped her teeth over his nipple. Jack's groan sent shivers down to her toes. She loved touching him, and he never rushed her, no matter how uncomfortable he got. She kissed up his neck, finally melding their lips. He tasted savory and warm, like home.

When he broke the kiss and urged her onto her back, she

didn't resist. How could she? She was helpless to resist him. He'd been shocked she'd given him a key to her place. Finally, she caught him off guard; he'd been doing that to her since the day they met.

He settled between her thighs and, smiling down at her, slid deep. He slowly withdrew and took her again. He kissed her deeply, his tongue gently exploring her mouth. She tingled from head to toe. The first waves of pleasure lapped at her. Tensing around him, she panted for air. The slow build drove her crazy, and her hips lifted to meet his thrusts. He nibbled her earlobe, sending jolts of pleasure down her neck. This time, the tension broke, and Jack swallowed her cries of pleasure, adding his own.

Time slipped past them until they could no longer put off leaving the warm pleasure of their bed. They showered together, and Emily hoped the spray of water washed away the tears she couldn't stop. The last thing she wanted was to make Jack feel bad about leaving. *How the fuck had Siobhan done it all these years?*

At ten after seven, Jeff called. Traffic was heavy, and he'd be at least fifteen minutes late. Emily hadn't been this grateful for fifteen minutes since she was a kid.

Jack shoved his phone in his pocket. "What's that smile for?"

"Whenever my dad would come home from a deployment and it was time for bed, Riley and I would beg him for five more minutes, and we'd all cuddle. After five minutes, we'd beg again. He always gave us three five more minutes. When I was really little, it felt like an eternity." Melancholy stole her breath. "We're running out of five more minutes."

"Come here." Jack's arms closed around her and the sense of contentment returned. She rested her head on his shoulder, loving the scent of him. Inhaling deeply, she wanted to stock up for their month apart.

A single knock told her their time was up. She forced a smile and stepped back. Jack grabbed his bag, and they held hands as they went down the stairs. Jack opened the door.

Jeff stood at the ready.

Emily wished traffic had been worse.

Jack dropped the bag and hauled her up close. "I love you." His lips crushed hers.

"We're already running late."

Emily tore her lips away from Jack's. Turning her head to Jeff, she said, "Five more minutes?"

A warm smile broke across his serious face. "Three." He took Jack's bag and walked to the SUV.

Three minutes later, she watched Jack trudge down the walkway. As he reached the SUV, he turned and waved. She wanted to run to him but didn't. He disappeared behind the truck, and a few seconds later, the truck rolled to the end of the driveway, and Jeff turned left on Plum Avenue. Emily waved as the truck passed, but Jack didn't see her because his head was down.

They'd gotten off to a rocky start, ironically, not because Jack was a rock star but because of her past. She wouldn't let the past dictate her future anymore.

No more yesterdays. Only tomorrows.

*****

Want more? Need more? Sign up to my VIP reader group, and you'll receive access to exclusive cut and extended scenes only available to my subscribers.

Jack and Emily's epic story concludes in book 3 of the *Rocked in Love* series. Keep reading for an excerpt from *All Your Tomorrows.*

All Your Tomorrows
Excerpt

Chapter One

Now that Jack's week with that whore is over, they'll be apart for over a month. Whoever said absence makes the heart grow fonder was a fool. I'll be seeing Jack in Chicago, and he won't know what hit him. He'll see me in a new light and forget all about her.

Chapter Two

As Jeff drove past Em's door, Jack forced himself not to look at her. Her beautiful hazel eyes had been clouded by sadness, and it was his fault. He had to leave her because he had a tour to finish. He would always have a tour, an album to record, or a press junket that would keep them apart.

Jack barely noticed the miles as they passed except to note they were putting space between them. Now that he understood why a normal life was so important, he wanted more than ever to be able to give it to her. Even if that meant giving up the career he loved. He could go back to school and get a degree in teaching. His parents never would've imposed their wishes for his future on him, but he knew his mom had thought he'd make a great teacher.

He also loved working with his hands, and he'd spent many summers working with his dad. His dad never said so, but Jack got the impression that he would've loved to add "and son" to his business.

Their nine days together had been amazing. He thought about all she'd done for him: working extra hours to get another day off, engaging with his family, genuinely wanting him to have a good time, and doing whatever she could to ensure it. She hadn't told him yet that she loved him, but his dad had been right. Actions spoke louder than words. He knew in his heart that she loved him, but she was reticent to say it, and he even understood why, but he really needed to hear it.

In the past, it had never been hard to return his focus to a tour. But since the first time they were apart, he hadn't been able to give it his full attention. They had a tight schedule on this run, and during the only two-day break, they'd be shooting the video for their fourth single.

His fingers traced the lines of the jack-in-the-box keychain she'd given him. His girl had a sick sense of humor, and he fucking loved it. He loved that she made jokes while they were having sex. *Shit, don't think about the sex.*

"You okay?" Jeff's voice cut into his thoughts.

"Yeah."

Jeff cleared his throat. "Look, man, I know it's none of my business, but..."

It wasn't like Jeff to hesitate. If he had something to say, he said it. "What?"

"You're not just having fun here, are you?"

"You mean with Emily?"

"Yes."

"I want to marry her."

Jeff nodded slowly. "All right then."

Jack smiled. "What if I was just having fun?"

"It wouldn't end well for you."

Jack felt the threat in Jeff's voice. "I love her." Now that he'd be gone for over a month, he needed to be sure she was safe. "As soon as it can be arranged, I want you back here and watching her."

"No."

"What the fuck do you mean no?"

Jeff kept his eyes on the road. "Any more letters from the stalker?"

"No. Hopefully, that's over now." Jack knew that wishing it wouldn't make it so, and even though her apartment was more secure, he wasn't going to take any chances with Emily. "Look, I trust you—"

Jeff nodded curtly. "I know a guy."

"I want you to do it. Have this guy take over for you."

"No."

"Why not?"

"Because this guy won't get caught."

Jack scoffed. "Why, is he a fucking ninja?"

"No. Emily knows him."

"Who is it?"

"Ron Gilles. We served together."

The name rang a bell. "The Marine who punched out the reporter?"

A slow smile crossed Jeff's face. "The very one. That reporter was lucky. If it'd been me, he wouldn't have walked away." He cleared his throat. "When his name came up in the background check on Emily, I reached out to him."

Jack's body tensed, and his heart pounded. "You did a background check on my girlfriend?"

Jeff's deep laugh filled the SUV. "Of course. Settle down, Jack, you're in good shape, but you can't take me."

"Wanna bet?" Jack fisted his hands. "Why?"

"One, it's my job to know who's around you. And two, I was curious."

Jack rested back against the seat. He wasn't really pissed, and it was part of Jeff's job. "You're devious." Jack had always thought Jeff operated aboveboard. "Anything else I should know about?"

Jeff smiled. "Two words, Jack. Plausible deniability."

Now, it was Jack's turn to laugh. "You really think that'll save me when Em finds out?"

"No, I'm pretty sure she'll rain hell down on both of us. So, we'd better make sure she doesn't find out." Jeff parked and shut off the engine. "Listen, I know this stalker shit is wearing on you, but whoever it is will make a mistake and get caught. Gilles will keep an eye on Emily."

Jack had done a good job of not thinking about it while he'd been with Em and his family, but Jeff was right; it was wearing him down. He needed this person caught and arrested. Now. "Isn't there anything else we can do?" He knew that if there was, Jeff would be doing it. But a man could hope.

"Unfortunately, we just have to wait for them to make a mistake." Jeff hauled his bag over his shoulder.

Jack grabbed his bag, and they walked toward the terminal. "Whatever it takes to get Gilles to help us, I'll pay."

"I figured as much, so it's already been arranged. He's going to do a few days of recon, and then he'll make contact. Captain Prescott was well-respected by everyone, but Gilles owes him." Jeff stopped before entering the terminal. "Prescott saved his life in Kosovo."

Jack felt the respect that Jeff had for Em's dad. He couldn't even imagine what it was like to serve in the military. He'd never thought much about Jeff's service, but he respected him, now more than ever. Em had downplayed it, but he had a new respect for the families of those who served. They sacrificed, too. While Jack had grown up in the suburbs of New York, Emily had lived on military bases, never knowing if she'd see her dad again. Her mom must've been strong too, taking on that life, basically raising two kids on her own for much of the time. A lump formed in Jack's throat. He would've loved to have met them.

Jack knew in that instant he wouldn't do that to Em. He'd

had a great childhood, and he wanted to be there for his kids like his dad had always been for him. And for Emily. She'd never have the normal life she wanted, the normal life she deserved, if he didn't make some changes. Jack needed to talk to the guys. When this tour was over—

"Hey, we're gonna miss our flight." Jeff elbowed him. "Come on, you'll have plenty of time for thinking on the plane. Just don't make any rash decisions."

Jack swallowed hard. "Was it that obvious?"

They got their luggage tags at the check-in kiosk. "It's not an easy life, but most of the families I've known have no regrets. They're proud of their soldier. And proud to do their part. The divorce rate is high, but the families that survive, well, none are stronger."

Jack realized for the first time that he had no idea about Jeff's personal life. Now he felt like a dick. "What about you? Married?"

Jeff's eyes saddened for a second before his face returned to its neutral mask. "Divorced."

They dropped their bags at the luggage check-in and headed toward security.

Jack nodded. "Sorry to hear that."

Their flight to Cleveland was delayed, and Jack was pissed that he could've spent more time with Emily. Walking away this morning had been the hardest thing he'd ever done. How the fuck was he going to do this for the next two years? Or for the rest of his life?

By the time their flight finally landed in Cleveland, Jack knew something in his life would have to change. He loved music, and being in the band was the best, but if he couldn't have both, his choice was clear.

Traffic from the airport was a bitch, but Jack made it to the interview just in time. They played a few acoustic songs.

"This is Terri Caron, your afternoon DJ, and we are proud

to have Stone Highway in the studio with us today. Wow, that was great. You've been together for ten years. That's a long time in this business. I've never heard a bad thing about you guys. Are you really as close as you seem?"

Jack smiled and relaxed. Ever since that interview in New York, he'd been a little leery. "We've been friends longer than that, and sure, there are some days that we piss each other off, but we don't let it get so bad that we can't stand each other."

"Buzz, how are you doing?"

"I've been sober for nine months and one week today, so I'm doing great."

Applause and whistles sounded from the control booth.

Terri clapped along. "That's great. So good to hear. So many times, these things end in tragedy. Is it harder being on tour now that you're sober?"

"Not really. My brothers and our crew have been there and supported me every step of the way. I'm so grateful to all of them. And my family have been great, too. Our fans are so supportive. Every gig, they have signs encouraging me. I've been very lucky."

"That's awesome," Terri said.

"I'd like to add that Buzz has worked really hard, and I'm so frickin' proud of him," Curt said.

"We all are," Elliot added.

"I've interviewed dozens of bands over the years, but I gotta say that you guys really seem like family. And I really think that comes across in your music."

"Thank you, Terri. We are a family, and we consider our crew and the fans as part of that family," Curt said.

"I understand that, as a thank you for your fans, you guys have a special song that you close out your shows with. Can we hear that?" Her pale blue eyes sparkled at Jack.

He knew that look, so he didn't smile in return. He had

no interest in being *that* friendly. "Sorry, it's for the fans that come out to our gigs."

Her full glossy lips pouted. "Okay, understood. Can you at least tell us the title?"

Jack shifted in his seat. "It's called 'With You.'"

Terri's brow lifted. "Sounds like a love song. Was it inspired by anyone special?"

They'd done a good job of keeping their relationship private so far, and Jack had no intention of blowing it now, so Jack's only reply was to shrug.

Elliot cleared his throat. "Actually, it was inspired by someone *very* special."

Terri's face lit up at the prospect of getting a scoop. "Do tell."

Jack had no idea where Elliot was going with this, but the guys knew that Emily was fame shy.

Elliot leaned in closer and winked at Terri. "Siobhan and I are back together."

"Congratulations, that's great."

While both those statements were true, they were unrelated, but Elliot played it perfectly. Devious fuck that he was, he loved nothing more than telling a lie with the truth. But as a consequence of his announcement, he and Siobhan wouldn't have the privacy they usually enjoyed. Jack hoped that Elliot knew what he was doing.

"This is Terri Caron, your afternoon DJ, with Stone Highway in the studio today. All you lucky fans that have tickets for the concert at the Jacobs Pavilion will have beautiful weather tonight. Thanks for coming in."

"Thanks for having us, Terri," Curt said.

Jack stood and shook hands with Terri. After a couple of pictures, Jeff and Brick escorted them out of the radio station. A couple dozen fans waited outside, so they took some pictures and signed some autographs. One girl wanted him to sign her bare breasts, but Jack politely refused.

Once they were in the SUV, Jack turned to Elliot. "Thanks for that, man."

"No problem, brother." Elliot smiled. "You've covered my ass all these years."

They were already running late for soundcheck, so Polson and Miller went to the hotel to bring Nicki and Siobhan to the Pavilion.

He'd only left Emily this morning, but he missed her like crazy. Jack knew he was being a selfish prick for wanting Emily with him, but he couldn't help it. But he'd also never ask her to give up her career—or the stability it came with—for his. She'd worked too hard to rebuild her life after her family died, so that narrowed his options down to one. He'd have to be the one to give up his career.

E mily was having a hard time concentrating during the meeting with their client Coffee Nirvana. She felt like something was missing. Not something but someone. Jack. They'd only been apart for seven hours, and already, she was in sorry shape.

They wouldn't be seeing each other for over a month. During their first week, when they'd planned out when they'd be together, she hadn't thought twice about being apart from Jack for that long, but as their relationship progressed, each time she'd seen him, it had gotten harder to watch him leave which had surprised her.

"Emily, do you have anything else to add?" Lonny Tremaine, CEO of Coffee Nirvana asked. They were a small family-owned company, and he was hands-on in every aspect. Lonny was also single, and every time he came in for a meeting, he reminded her of that. At first, it'd seemed like harmless flirting. He'd even commented on her engagement ring. But since her relationship with Sully had blown up, it seemed a little less harmless.

Shit. Not that she'd ever get involved with a client, but she was very much taken. Emily smiled. "No."

From across the conference table, Ben smirked and Jerry smiled. The gruesome twosome had been smiling at her all day and making little comments about how she glowed.

"Lonny," Ben said. "I really think this change of direction is needed to stay ahead of the competition."

Lonny nodded. "Well, you've never steered me wrong, so let's do it."

Ben and Jerry stood and shook hands with Lonny. Emily escaped to her office as they walked him out.

But not for long. "Emily, may we have a word?" Jerry stood in the open doorway to her office.

Inwardly, she groaned, but she said, "Sure." She followed Jerry into their office. This time, the groan escaped when he shut the door behind them. She'd been distracted during the meeting, and now, she was going to hear about it. She needed to focus when she was in the office, and if this was how she was on day one apart from Jack, she was in serious trouble.

"Have a seat." Ben sat on the corner of Jerry's desk.

"Can't you plant your ass on your own desk?" Jerry said, as he sat in his leather chair. He scowled at Ben as he ran his hand down his whiskers. Even though it was June, he still hadn't shaved off his winter beard.

"Tell me, Jerry, are you planning on auditioning for a spot in a Grateful Dead cover band?" Ben asked.

Emily chuckled.

Jerry gave Ben the finger.

They never behaved this way in front of the rest of the office. Emily enjoyed their sibling rivalry. Which made her think of Jack and Jimmy; she was sure they'd made progress in their relationship this past week. Jack had even suggested that Jimmy could live in his apartment in the city once he got one.

Jimmy was a good kid, and she understood how he felt about Jack since she'd lived in Riley's shadow.

"What's so funny, young lady?" Jerry asked with fake indignation.

"I was thinking you were going to audition for ZZ Top."

Ben roared with laughter. "Seriously, Jerry, it's time for that thing to go before birds start nesting in it."

"I'll have you know Marjorie likes it. She says it makes me look distinguished."

"If you wore a flannel shirt, you could get a job as a lumberjack." Ben walked around his desk and sat in the leather chair.

Jerry flipped his brother off again. His smiled warmed as he turned toward her. "I take it you enjoyed your time off?"

Crap, here it comes. "Very much." She took a deep breath and exhaled slowly. "I'm sorry. I know I've been distracted since I got back, but I'll pull it together."

Ben smiled at her. "Emily, we're just glad to see you so happy." He turned to his brother. "I don't think I've ever seen her so happy. Have you?"

"Nope."

Emily's brow furrowed. Since she'd been engaged for over a year until April, Emily was confused. Her relationship with Sully hadn't been perfect, but she'd been in love with him. She'd had their whole life planned out. A sinking feeling in her chest had her swallowing hard. She couldn't do that with Jack. His life was unpredictable. But before she allowed the fear to take over, Emily reminded herself that Jack was a good man. He would never cheat on her, and he supported her writing, and she supported him.

The problems in her relationship with Sully now seemed so obvious, but they hadn't been at the time. She wouldn't make the same mistakes again. Ever since the confrontation with Sully outside her apartment, Emily had realized that Sully wasn't the man she'd thought he was. She'd had no idea he'd been so jealous. She'd thought they'd been open and honest with each other but now realized that she'd been just as guilty of not being honest as he'd been. She'd kept parts of herself locked away. The parts from the accident and losing her family, and that had been wrong. She hadn't wanted to burden him with her fears, but she should have.

She knew she'd have to be more open with Jack.

"We lost her again," Ben said.

Emily snapped out of her head. "I'm so sorry, I don't know what's wrong with me lately."

Jerry's expression softened. "You're in love, my dear."

Emily swallowed hard. She'd been in love with Sully, too, but it hadn't been like this. He'd made her happy, and she'd always felt comfortable when they were together. They both loved black-and-white movies, and... Had she just boiled their relationship down to a love of black-and-white movies? Surely, they'd had more in common than that? Sully liked country music, but she preferred rock. He read financial reports, and she read romance novels. And only now, she realized they were both broken.

But with Jack, for the first time in ten years, she felt whole again. They complemented each other in a way she hadn't seen since her parents. He was spontaneous and adventurous, and he helped bring out those long-dormant qualities in her. He could be pushy and aggressive, but he'd definitely toned down.

"But I was in love before." She'd been about to marry Sully, but now, when she thought of him, she felt gratitude. If they'd gotten married, with all their false ideas about each other, they'd have most likely divorced. The more she thought about what he'd said that day he'd picked up his stuff, the more she realized she hadn't been fulfilling his need for total devotion, which her love hadn't even begun to satisfy.

Maybe there was a woman out there like that for Sully, but

it wasn't her. It wouldn't ever have been her. And she wouldn't have wanted or expected that from him. Maybe that was why he'd been compelled to cheat; he somehow knew they weren't meant to be together. Of course, he should've just talked to her.

"When will you be seeing Jack again? His tour schedule looks pretty packed," Jerry said.

"He won't be able to fly home until the end of July." Home. To her. She hated this. She hated that she was such a coward that she couldn't get on a plane. They'd still be apart, but she could've taken a few days off around a weekend and flown to him. This was their reality, and Jack was willing to deal with it, so she needed to as well.

Jack had left her many times before, but for some reason, today felt worse. She needed to get back to work; she needed the distraction.

"How's the new book coming?" Ben asked.

Emily smiled. "Good. I think I'm more than half done." Her smile faded. "I'll have plenty of time over the next month." A humorless laugh escaped her lips.

Ben nodded. "But then you'll have a month together."

Emily blinked slowly. "Yeah. But then he leaves for six weeks in Europe. They have a couple two-day breaks, but those flights..." Emily wished she had no doubts that she could handle Jack's lifestyle, but she did. When they were together, she never thought about how much time they'd be apart. There was only them together. She wasn't prepared for this. Even if she could fly to see him in Europe, she only had so much time off work. And after this year, she'd have even less.

Jerry looked at Ben, and when he turned back to her, he smiled. "I'm sure it will all work out."

He sounded so sure Emily wanted to ask how he could know. But she didn't. She'd received the check from the Sullivans, but she hadn't decided what to do with that money yet. She loved her job and her family at B & R, and she loved writing, and until now, she'd always had both. Now, if she could only figure out a way to have Jack at the same time.

WHEN EMILY GOT HOME FROM WORK, HER apartment was so empty. She missed coming home to Jack. Missed his smile and him asking about her day. His guitars and small amp were still there, but without him, the place felt barren. She'd been so excited to get home from work the past two days, excited to see Jack. Even though it was Friday, she felt sad. It wasn't as if she didn't have plenty to do: writing, of course, but her apartment could use a good cleaning, and Nicki had given Emily her latest manuscript to read.

She dropped her purse over the railing and looked around. She remembered how last week Jack had made dinner and drawn her a bath. He'd even scrubbed her tub. Even though this relationship had moved at warp speed, she'd loved having him here last week. It had felt so normal to see him there when she got home, and for five out of their nine days together, she'd had him all to herself, and she'd loved it. Jack had said a few odd things this past week. He wasn't happy that they wouldn't be together, like Curt and Nicki were and now Elliot and Siobhan were, too.

Jack was doing what he was meant to do. The band's music spoke to people, helped people, and Emily couldn't be so selfish as to keep Jack to herself. She needed to find a way to support him in his career so he could continue to do what he loved, what the band loved, and give their fans the music they needed.

The answer was so obvious she had to sit down. "I need to take my own advice. Pack 'em up and bring 'em along, I said." At the time, she'd been trying to help Elliot see that a nontraditional life for his kids wasn't necessarily a bad thing. It was up to her to find a way to make this okay for Jack.

After dinner, she called him.

"Hey, baby. I miss you." The noises of backstage receded.

Emily checked the time. "Did I interrupt soundcheck?"

"No. We got here late, then there were some technical issues, so we just finished."

Emily relaxed back on the sofa. "Looks like the weather will be good for your gig tonight. No rain."

"Yeah. That's always an issue with outdoor gigs, but we've been lucky so far. Got any plans for the weekend?"

Emily's throat tightened. She wished he were here. "Vince is in town tomorrow, and Eddie and I are going to see him."

Jack sighed. "Sheryl won't be going?"

"No, she's got a shift at the hospital tomorrow, and Teddy and Michael have a cub scout hiking trip."

"What about Nicholas?"

Emily liked that Jack remembered her nephews' names. "He's only three, so he can't join until he's five. But they'll get plenty of Uncle Vince when he stays with them in August for two weeks. He spends a couple of weeks every summer so he can bond with his nephews."

"I wish I could be there."

"Me, too." Emily swallowed the emotions that were overwhelming her. "But since Vince will be here in August, I'll introduce you then. And I'm gonna tell Eddie who exactly he'll be meeting when we have dinner." Emily smiled.

"I'd love that, baby."

The noise on Jack's end increased, and Emily heard kissing sounds. "Tell Emily we miss her," Elliot said loudly enough so she could hear.

"I miss them, too. I'll let you go."

"I have a few minutes still."

"Okay."

"How was work today?"

"Good." Her heart ached at how distant this conversation felt. She knew he was holding back out of respect for her wishes, and she was still trying to catch up to him. Sometimes, she wondered if she ever would.

Get your copy of *All Your Tomorrows.*

*****

Exclusive Offer

Building relationships with readers is the best part of sharing my writing. I send a newsletter about twice a month with details on new releases, special offers, and other fun bits.

I love my subscribers, and to thank you for joining my reader group, you'll have access to exclusive bonus content: epilogues, cut or extended scenes, cover reveals, and insider updates.

Sign up: jessicamarloweauthor.com

Enjoyed this book?

YOU CAN MAKE A BIG DIFFERENCE.

Reviews are one of the most important things readers can do to help authors. Especially indie authors. It's a tough business, and getting readers to take a chance isn't easy.

If you enjoyed this book, please consider leaving an honest review—no spoilers, please. Reviews on Goodreads and BookBub are also helpful. I would be grateful if you could spare five minutes to do that. Long or short, it would really help me out.

Thank you very much.

Jessica

About the Author

Jessica Marlowe has always loved reading. Inspired by a story that wouldn't let her go, she has written her first three books. She loves music (especially hard rock), animals (all kinds), autumn trees and jacket-weather walks, naps (after all that walking), and wine (certainly unrelated to napping).

As a side hustle, Jessica writes instruction manuals for glamping equipment. Just kidding.

Jessica is the author of the wildly popular Rocked in Love rock star romance series. (What? It could happen 😉)

You can connect with Jessica at jessicamarloweauthor.com or by email at jessica@jessicamarloweauthor.com.

Novels By Jessica Marlowe

Rocked in Love – **Rock Star Romance Series** – **Must be read in order**

With You (Jack and Emily - Book 1)

Rock star and all-around nice guy Jack McBride is single but not for long. Emily Prescott is newly single and not interested in a relationship, especially with a rock star. But the attraction demands satisfaction, so she offers him one night. Jack agrees but has no intention of letting Emily get away.

No More Yesterdays (Jack and Emily - Book 2)

Emily has agreed to this relationship, but she has no idea how hard it will be. Jack drops in whenever he has a two-day break from touring, but things never seem to go as planned. Emily's nightmares are getting worse as the truth pushes its way to the surface. Jack has never struggled so much with being apart from a girl. His stalker is still out there, and Jack's not taking any chances. He'll do anything to protect Emily even if that means going behind her back to keep her safe.

All Your Tomorrows (Jack and Emily - Book 3)

Jack can't imagine his life without Emily by his side every day and in his bed every night. And with the six-week European leg of their tour looming, Jack has a hard choice to make. Emily makes a decision about her future, but will it be the biggest mistake she's ever made, or will it allow her to fulfill all her dreams?

Printed in Great Britain
by Amazon